P9-CFT-093

Praise for

GOOD LUCK WITH THAT

"A searing, heartrending examination of self-love and self-loathing. . . . [A] story of learning to love oneself and living a life that leads with that love, in all its joy, sorrow, failure and triumph."
—*Entertainment Weekly*

"Kristan Higgins is known for novels that wring every emotion from you—you'll find yourself laughing one moment, then dabbing tears later. Her latest, *Good Luck with That*, shows she hasn't lost her knack for spanning the emotional gamut."
—*The Philadelphia Inquirer*

"Don't miss this emotional read about love, friendship and self-acceptance."
—HelloGiggles

"Higgins (*Now That You Mention It*) writes with uncommon grace and empathy about a fraught topic for many people: weight. . . . This novel is a winner."
—*Publishers Weekly* (starred review)

"[A] heartbreakingly gorgeous story of female friendship and what it takes to feel comfortable in one's own skin."
—*Booklist*

"Higgins's astute, perceptive eye to the best and worst of human nature enhances the poignancy of a sensitive topic, which she navigates with humor and grace."
—*Kirkus Reviews*

"Wholly original and heartfelt, written with grace and sensitivity, *Good Luck with That* is an irresistible tale of love, friendship and self-acceptance—and the way body image can sabotage all three."
—Lori Nelson Spielman, *New York Times* bestselling author of *The Life List*

Praise for the novels of Kristan Higgins

"The path to love is bumpy and strewn with land mines in this surprisingly deep charmer from rom-com queen Higgins.... Emotional resonance balances zany antics in a powerful story that feels completely real."
—*Publishers Weekly* (starred review)

"A special writer at the top of her game." —NPR

"[Higgins] only gets better with each book."
—*The New York Times Book Review*

"The kind of book I enjoy the most—sparkling characters, fast-moving plot and laugh-out-loud dialogue. A winner!"
—#1 *New York Times* bestselling author
Susan Elizabeth Phillips

"Both gut-wrenchingly emotional and hysterically funny at the same time.... Kristan Higgins writes the books you don't want to end."
—#1 *New York Times* bestselling author Robyn Carr

"Tender, sexy and hilarious as only Higgins can write it. A story to savor." —*Library Journal* (starred review)

"Higgins's complex, witty characters will seem like close friends, and readers will savor each and every page as they find that love comes in many different flavors and forms. Demand will be high for the latest from this women's-fiction star." —*Booklist*

"Higgins's latest tour de force is a captivating read about two sisters dealing with love, loss and new beginnings."
—RT Book Reviews (5 stars)

GOOD LUCK WITH *THAT*

KRISTAN
HIGGINS

BERKLEY
New York

BERKLEY
An imprint of Penguin Random House LLC
1745 Broadway, New York, NY 10019

ISBN: 9780451489401

Berkley trade paperback edition / August 2018
Berkley mass-market edition / April 2019

Printed in the United States of America
1 3 5 7 9 10 8 6 4 2

Cover photograph by Laura Berdasco Sanchez
Cover design by Emily Osborne
Book design by Laura K. Corless

This one is for all of us
who've cried when looking in the mirror.
Here's to never doing that again.

ACKNOWLEDGMENTS

At Berkley: There are so many people to thank, but none more than Claire Zion, my brilliant editor, and Craig Burke, head of publicity. Thanks to you and the entire Berkley team for gracing this book with enthusiasm, talent and heart.

At Maria Carvainis Agency: Boundless gratitude to Madame herself for her faith in me, and to Martha Guzman for her constant care and attention to detail.

At Author Rx: Thanks to Mel Jolly for taking care of all the things I never would've thought of on my own.

Additional, huge heartfelt thanks to:

Coaches Dave Bellemare, Mike Ford and Jack McShane, who always judge children on the content of their character rather than on the speed of their feet—thank you for helping make my son an even better person than he already was.

Christian Alberico, a role model in kindness, leadership and hard work, and to his parents, for raising a truly great person.

Diana Phung and Natalie Alamo, for their insight into the duties of a preschool teacher and some really fun stories as well.

Silvi Martin, for her Spanish translations, constant good cheer and friendship.

Alison Harrisberger Warford, who shared with me the spirit of Admiral, the quiet and noble friend we all should be so lucky to have.

Joss Dey, Jennifer Iszkiewicz, Anne Renwick, Stacia Bjarnason and Huntley Fitzpatrick, my beloved friends and fellow writers, for the laughter, the catchphrases, the wonderful weekends, the honesty and the friendship.

Terence, Flannery and Declan, thank you for being exactly who you are. I can never seem to find the words to say how much I love you, but love you I do, and with all my heart.

To write a book about a subject as emotionally charged as body acceptance, weight and health was an undertaking. I built on my personal experiences with the issues the characters tackle in *Good Luck with That* and sought out a variety of other sources and experiences as well. If you're interested, you can find a list of those sources at kristanhiggins.com /good-luck-with-that-research. Specifically, however, I would like to thank the following medical and mental health specialists: Jeff Pinco, MD; Stacia Bjarnason, PhD; Margaret O'Hagan-Lynch, LPC; Samantha Heller, MS, RD, CDN; Nadeem Hussain, MD; and Julia Kristan, RN.

Most especially, however, thank you to the dozens of honest, brave, funny, intelligent people who shared their personal stories online, anonymously and through face-to-face conversations with me.

And to you, readers, who have chosen to spend a few hours with this book. Thank you from the bottom of my heart.

PROLOGUE

For once, no one was thinking of food.

From above, they were just three teenage girls, bobbing in the middle of the clear blue lake, a rowboat drifting lazily nearby as they splashed and laughed. A blonde and two brunettes, one with black hair, one with brown. Their voices rose and fell. Occasionally, one of them would slip underwater, then pop up a few yards away. Hair would be slicked back, and the swimmer might flip on her back and look up at the sky, so pure and deep that day, the thick white clouds floating slowly past on the lazy breeze.

Just the three of them out in the lake, an unauthorized swim time, rebels all, at least for the moment, free from the constraints and prescribed activities of Camp Copperbrook, where girls ages eleven to eighteen were sent to lose weight. For now, the three weren't fat girls . . . they were just normal, and they were enjoying that elusive state of simply *being* as they goofed around in the lake. Emerson floating, ever dreamy; Georgia sidestroking efficiently; Marley twisting and wriggling like an otter.

They'd lost the oars to the rowboat, so one by one, they'd

jumped in the water to fetch them. The lake was so silky and cool against their skin that no one wanted to get back out. They were weightless, and graceful. They were practically mermaids. After a while, they just floated on their backs, swishing their hands once in a while, kicking lackadaisically.

The sun was bright but behind the mountain; birds dipped and wheeled above the lake. From the pine-ringed beach came the far-off sound of the occasional whistle from one of the counselors, some laughter from other campers, a snatch of music.

Tomorrow, everyone would be going home.

"I love it here," Emerson said, a wistful note in her soft voice. "This is my happy place. Right here, right now. I can't believe we won't be back next year."

"Me too," Georgia said. "It sucks to age out."

"This has been the best summer," Marley said.

Georgia lifted her head, checking to see how far away the boat was, then settled back into the water like it was a mattress.

None of them felt their weight in the clear stillness of the lake. There was no chafing, no sweating, no lumbering. No aching joints, no straining muscles and, at this moment, no labored breathing.

True peace was rare when you were fat. When you were fat, you wore armor to protect and deflect. You were either sharp and bitter, inspiring fear in potential bullies, or you were extra cheerful to show nothing mattered at all, not the snubs or the insults or the degradation. When you were fat, you worked so hard to be invisible. You lived in fear of being noticed, singled out, of having someone point out what you already knew.

You're fat.

And these three girls were all fat.

But at this moment, they just *were*.

A black-and-white loon popped up right next to Marley's head. She shrieked and flapped her hands, and the bird dove, disappearing into the depths.

"It tried to peck me!" Marley sputtered.

"You scared it to death," Georgia said, snorting with laughter. "Relax. It's just a bird."

"I thought it was a shark," she said.

"I'm pretty sure we're safe from shark attacks," Emerson said.

"Unless it's a lake shark," Marley said, and they all laughed again, the sounds floating up into the endless sky to join the creamy clouds.

Then a long whistle blast came from the camp, and a voice magnified by a bullhorn. "Marley, Georgia, Emerson! Get back to shore now!" It was their bitchy head counselor.

The three girls groaned in unison.

"She's so mean," Emerson said.

"She's skinny," Georgia added. "She shouldn't be here. It's bad for morale." They laughed again at the truth of her words.

Georgia was the first to obey, flipping over and swimming neatly to the boat, gathering the errant oars on the way. Getting in wasn't so pretty. "Party's over, girls," she said as she settled herself in the seat. Marley was next, able to raise herself over the side with ease, the most athletic one of the three.

Emerson . . . Emerson needed help from both of them, and even then, it was hard. Whatever grace the three girls had in the lake was shed like drops of water as the reality of their bodies returned to the gravity of the water-free world.

"When I'm skinny, I'm going to swim every day," Emerson said, panting from the exertion.

"When I'm skinny, I'm going to rock a bathing suit," Marley said, pulling her sturdy one-piece away from her body. "This thing is worse than a corset. I can't wait to take it off."

Georgia didn't say anything, just picked up the oars and fitted them in the locks.

"Let's make a list when we get back," Emerson said. "All the things we'll do when we're not fat anymore. Things we can't even dream of now."

"We can dream," Georgia said, pulling on the oars. The boat slid forward, and Marley trailed a hand in the water. "Nothing wrong with dreams."

"A list sounds like fun," Marley said. "It'll motivate us to lose weight. We can call each other when we cross stuff off."

Little waves slapped against the bow as they got closer to shore. Georgia's strokes slowed, and she docked the oars for a moment as all three of them looked back at the purple and pink clouds burnished by the setting sun, the pine trees turning black in silhouette.

Sitting there for one last moment, they all knew the magical afternoon was over, yet no one could quite let it go. After all, how many days like this do you get in life? How often can you really be free, alive . . . weightless?

That's the problem with perfect moments. They end.

Though no one would say it, all three girls knew things would never be quite the same again.

CHAPTER 1

FOUR YEARS AGO

Dear Diary,

I love starting a new journal. It feels so clean! Like, who knows what I can fill up these pages with? Maybe you'll be the diary where I write about my first love, my trip to Rome, my engagement ring, my babies! Okay, that's probably getting ahead of myself, but you never know. I was watching <u>Ellen</u> the other day and this woman was talking about how fast life changed when she lost weight. So maybe mine will, too.

Emerson Lydia Duval.

Emerson Lydia Duval.

I love my name. I still can fill pages of a notebook writing it over and over. Lydia was my mother's great-aunt; she died in the Holocaust. She'd been a ballet dancer, apparently. I love carrying her name, though I try not to imagine what she'd think of my outer self.

Emerson Lydia Duval. Someone with that name is definitely elegant and beautiful, hip without being trendy. She clearly went to Smith College, don't you think? She's tall, beautiful, <u>slim</u>. (God, I love that word!) But she can eat anything she wants, of course. Sometimes, though, she's so busy she forgets to eat, because unless it's a really special meal, food is an afterthought, not 98 percent of what she thinks about. She played on the volleyball team in college. Or no, she played field hockey, the ultimate rich-girl sport. (Georgia played, now that I think of it.)

Yes, Emerson Lydia Duval played field hockey at prep school and college, because she loves being outside. She founded her college's hiking club. Still an avid outdoorswoman, she adores animals, but her heavy travel schedule doesn't let her have a pet. Her clothes are loose fitting and effortless, but so stylish, and when she does put on a black cocktail dress and her Christian Louboutins, you can hear men's jaws hitting the pavement all over the city.

This other Emerson Duval lives in New York. No, San Francisco, in a sleek high-rise building. She flies first class but uses the time and extra space to work tirelessly for the nonprofit she founded while in graduate school at Stanford. She doesn't need the money; Other Emerson has a trust fund. (Not that I'm knocking the plain old inheritance I have.) But Other Emerson barely touches it. Her one indulgence is that apartment. Gotta have a nice place to live, and occasionally, to entertain as part of her job. It's her haven, tastefully furnished with a view of the Bay Bridge, and when the fog rolls in . . . perfection!

Emerson's parents have a small (huge!) place in Paris, and she visits when she can. Her mother, a professor at La Sorbonne, takes Emerson shopping for chic clothing, and her dad asks for her input on the latest building he's designing. Emerson's bilingual, of course. Tri-, really, but she doesn't feel her Mandarin is up to snuff. (She's modest. It's flawless.) She's just as comfortable discussing the economics of sub-Saharan countries as she is dressing up for the Met Gala.

She has a boyfriend, bien sûr. He's funny and devoted and looks like a young Idris Elba. He's a surgeon, probably, or a tech genius. He loves her desperately and is waiting for the day when her life will allow her to say yes. He bought the ring after their first date.

Yeah.

I'm not saying I'll ever become that Emerson. I mean, I know I won't. I just like thinking about her. She keeps me company.

In my imagination, Other Emerson could be friends with someone like me — someone who gets stared at every time she leaves the house. Someone who's judged and found disgusting every single day. Someone who weighs three times what she should. She would see the real me, not just the fat. She wouldn't see the fat at all. She'd see the funny, kind, sweet person I know I am but who no one else tries to see. My mom did, of course, but she's gone now. Georgia and Marley, they do, too.

I wish they lived closer. I guess I could move, but I love this house. Mama's house. Except for college, I've never lived anywhere else.

Ah, well. Hang with me, Other Emerson. Who knows what life will be like by the time this diary is filled up?

CHAPTER 2

Marley

It's those deathbed promises that bite you in the ass.

Granted, I did *not* start the day aware that I'd be driving through four states to stand by a hospital bed, trying not to sob. I'd started it by thinking about what I'd make for breakfast, then lunch, then dinner. I'm a chef, and a fat girl. Food is everything.

But right now, my face was frozen into what I hoped was a comforting smile. The left side of my mouth was twitching, and my eyes felt weird and hot. It was hard to remember how to breathe, and when I figured it out, the hospital air tasted stale and flat.

Outside the room, there was bustle and clatter, voices and squeaking shoes. In here, though . . . silence except for the wheeze of Emerson's breathing and the beeping of the monitors. Yes, yes, the monitors. Look at that. HR 133, O2 87%, BP 183/99.

I'm not a doctor, but I knew those numbers weren't good. Even if they were, the evidence was in the patient.

I wasn't even sure it was Emerson. That was her face—sort of. Hard to recognize amid the tubes and wires and the second chin so big it rested on her chest . . . and God, the mountains, the *acres* of flesh. When . . . how had she become so huge? I didn't understand how it could have happened in such a short time. But it wasn't short, was it? We'd gone away for the weekend maybe seven years ago, and we saw each other again at Georgia's wedding almost six years ago, and yes, she'd always been the biggest one of us, but this . . . I never expected this.

Thank God that's not me, I thought, and guilt made my fake smile stretch even more. *Do something, idiot!* my brain commanded, so I ran a hand through my hair, snaring my pinkie. I glanced at Georgia, who was blinking rapidly. No fake smile for her, just her brows knit together as she tried to take in what we were seeing.

Why hadn't we known Emerson was this far gone? Why hadn't I reached out more? My heart was galloping in my chest, and tears burned in my eyes.

Emerson appeared to be sleeping, her eyes closed. Apparently, she was exhausted from greeting us, and from . . . existing.

"Promise," wheezed Emerson.

I jumped. Okay, she was awake, then. Her eyes were swollen into slits, but I could see her look at me first, then Georgia. In her hand she clutched an envelope, but clearly she was too weak to lift her arm to hand it to us. Or her arm was too heavy. Or both.

"Promise you'll . . . do it," she whispered.

"Uh . . . yeah," I answered, still too stunned to know what I was really agreeing to. "You bet. Of course we will. We'll do it with you. When you get better. Emerson, you know you'll get better. You will. You're in the hospital, they're taking great care of you, you're not going to . . . you know! Right? Right, Georgia?"

Cutting a glance at Georgia, I saw she was still frozen. A quick elbow to her side solved that.

I heard her force a swallow. Then she said in a near whisper, "Yes. Exactly. I was just thinking the same thing. You . . . you'll be fine." She paused, and I heard her take a deep breath. "I'm quite, quite sure."

For a former lawyer, Georgia's lying ability sucked.

I took a step closer to the bed and patted where I thought Emerson's foot would be under the covers, hoping it didn't hurt. The blanket and sheet had pulled to the side, as if they weren't big enough to cover her, revealing her knee, the elephantine thigh, the hugely muscled calf—muscled from carrying her body. Her skin was red and stretched so tight it looked like it might burst with the slightest touch, like an overfilled balloon.

Jesus.

My heart twisted. Every time we'd seen each other— every single time since we met—the three of us had talked about how this was a new chance to do what we'd all sworn we'd do before.

Lose weight.

Because all three of us had been fat/heavy/overweight/ metabolically challenged/curvy/big all our lives.

And here we were. Still not skinny. But my God, the stakes were life and death now.

I was fat—let's just call it what it is—forever relegated to Lane Bryant and the plus-sized corners of department stores. Georgia, while currently on the smaller side of things, had yo-yoed so often that the two of us fantasized about the village we could've populated based on our cumulatively lost body mass alone.

But Georgia and I had never been like *this*.

The three of us had met at fat camp—pardon me, at Camp Copperbrook, an Intensive Residential Nutrition and Exercise Program for Girls. All of us had been eighteen, all heading for college, hoping *this* summer would be the one when we could Lose That Weight for Good and Really Start Living. Emerson and Georgia had been camp regulars; I only got to go that one time after begging, whining and guilt-tripping my parents.

In six weeks, I lost fourteen pounds and gained two friends. Georgia and I stayed close—we were both from New York, had gone to colleges an hour apart and visited each other at least a couple times a semester. When she went to Yale Law, I'd go to Connecticut to see her, and she'd come down to spend the odd weekend with me at my parents' house.

But Emerson was from Delaware. She was super close to her mom and didn't like to travel. I think Georgia and I had seen her five times in the sixteen years since camp.

But I *had* tried with Emerson. Just last year, I'd tried to organize a girls' weekend for the three of us. Emerson was the one who canceled at the last minute.

Maybe it was because of this. Her size.

Aside from Facebook occasionally alerting me to the fact that Emerson had posted a picture of flowers or kittens to her page, it was fair to say that the adult version—*this* version—of Emerson Duval was a stranger to me. It was shocking to see what had happened these past few years. She'd always had the most weight to lose, but still . . .

Please, God, I prayed. *Please, Frankie. Don't let this be the end.*

Then again, Frankie had left me, too.

Emerson seemed to have fallen asleep.

From the hallway, we could hear someone giving a tour. "This is one of our bariatric rooms, specially designed to fit the super-morbidly-obese patient. Our walls are reinforced with steel plates to support the grab bars for patients up to a thousand pounds"—a *thousand* pounds—"and our toilets allow extra room for aides to assist the patients. The doorway is bigger, as you can see, and—".

Georgia flew over to the door. "Do you mind?" she hissed. "There's a human being in here." She closed the door, and dashed a hand across her eyes.

"Thank you," wheezed Emerson, her eyes still closed.

My mouth started to quiver. She didn't sound good. Not at all. That squeak in her lungs, her labored breathing . . .

Emerson lifted her hand again, her arm flopping back to the bed. Right, right. The envelope.

"You're going to be fine," Georgia said, her voice steadying me. "You're where you need to be right now. But sure, if it makes you feel better, we'll take it." She stepped closer to the bed, took the envelope out of Emerson's hand, glanced at it, swallowed, and held it up for me to see.

To be opened after my funeral had been written across the front.

A sob popped out of me. "You're not . . . dying, Emerson," I managed to say. "You're just . . . you just need help."

"You're going to get better," Georgia said, her voice firmer now that she seemed to have gotten over her initial shock. "You have to, Emerson. You're wonderful and funny and kind, and we love you."

Tears were streaming down my face. I reached for Emerson's hand, which was cold and clammy, and gave it a squeeze. "We do," I managed. "You hang in there, Emerson. You can get better."

Emerson smiled a little, eyes still closed.

Just then, the door burst open again. "Bath time!" announced a nurse, one who was carrying a good sixty-five extra pounds herself. (Estimating weight is one of the superpowers of the fat.) "Ladies, if you don't mind." She gave Emerson the once-over and sighed. "Why do they expect me to do this alone?" She stuck her head out in the hall. "I'm gonna need an assist in here!"

"Lovely," Georgia muttered. She went over to Emerson's head and patted her shoulder. "Don't give up, okay? We love you."

Emerson opened her eyes. "I love you both," she whispered.

Georgia's face scrunched.

I wiped my eyes and kissed Emerson on the forehead. Her cheeks were bright red—high blood pressure. "Bye," I whispered, my throat clenched tight. "See you soon." *Please, God. Please, Frankie.* "Love you," I added, in case my deities weren't going to come through.

The nurse bared her teeth at us in what was clearly not a sincere smile.

As we were walking to the elevators, a doctor called out. "Excuse me? Are you Ms. Duval's friends?"

We stopped. "Yes," Georgia said.

"I'm glad I caught you. I'm Dr. Hughes." He was a tall, lean man with a kind face, not much older than we were. "Emerson gave me permission to update you. I was hoping I could talk to you for a minute, if you don't mind."

"Of course," I said.

"I'm sure you can tell your friend isn't doing well."

"We can see that," Georgia said.

Tears welled in my eyes once more. I wiped them away, noticing that my hands were shaking.

"You may want to stay close," he said. "She's had a blood clot travel from her legs to her lung, which is why she's having trouble breathing. She's hypertensive, has fluid around her heart, lymphedema . . . that's what causes the swelling. Her organs are shutting down."

Oh, sweet Jesus.

"Is she dying?" Georgia asked.

He looked at her, his expression sad. "My best professional guess is yes."

"Isn't there anything you can do?" I asked, hearing the terror in my voice.

"I think at this point, Emerson has exhausted her options," he said.

"Well, what options do *you* have?" I asked. "Obviously, she's very sick. You're the doctor. Help her."

"We're doing everything we can," he said. "But . . . well, when a person has been this overweight for this long, the damage has been done, and we can't always reverse it."

Georgia and I looked at each other. My throat was so tight I couldn't speak.

She turned back to the doctor. "How long do you think she has?"

"A day or two. I'm sorry. She wanted you to be prepared." He gave us a sad, almost apologetic look, then turned to leave. We watched him until he got to the end of the hall and disappeared around a corner.

Georgia was silent in the elevator, silent as we walked to the car.

Me, I was bawling.

. . . .

We've all seen the shows—thank you, TLC—and let's be honest. We watch them to make ourselves feel better. Sure, I was fat, but not six-hundred-pounds fat! I wasn't having KFC fed to me through my bedroom window, was I? I didn't need the firefighters to chainsaw around the front door so I could fit through, didn't need a team of eight to drag me out of the house on a sheet. And I *always* ate healthy food while watching that show. No ice cream during that one, no sir. Ice cream was for *The Walking Dead* (another show that made me feel good about my appearance).

But seeing it—seeing *Emerson*—in person was different. There was no feeling good now.

"You okay to drive?" Georgia asked as we sat in my car.

I blew my nose for the tenth time and nodded. Took a few deep breaths. Started the car and left the parking lot.

"Okay," Georgia said, tapping her phone as I merged onto the highway. "I just booked us a room at the Marriott and e-mailed work to let them know I'll be here a few days. You want to call your mom?"

I did, and asked my mother to cover my clients for the next couple of days. After all, I'd learned to cook at her side. "Of course I'll do it," Mom said, always glad to be needed. "How's your friend? Getting better?" There was the familiar edge of worry in her voice.

"I hope so," I lied. Mom didn't handle bad news well. "Anyway, the list of meals is on my computer. Dante can help. He owes me." Until my little brother had gotten married six months ago, I'd fed him at least three times a week for free. "And be super careful with the Fosters, okay? The father has a shellfish allergy."

I was a personal chef, the kind who delivered meals to people too busy to cook, or people who didn't like cooking. Living in the wealthy little Westchester County burg of Cambry-on-Hudson was a godsend; so many people there worked in Manhattan and appreciated having a delicious meal waiting for them. A lot of stay-at-home moms used me, too, for those nights when they needed a little break.

I wondered how Emerson had managed to get her food. From someone like me? God! The image of her mountainous body . . . I couldn't get it out of my head.

Georgia kept tapping her phone. "How does she—never mind."

"What are you doing?" I asked.

"Looking up some of the stuff the doctor said. God.

Listen to this. The cardiovascular and pulmonary systems aren't equipped to support all that weight. Edema . . . that's swelling, no wonder her skin is so tight. Her skin is literally an open wound, leaking out all that fluid."

I bit my lip, trying not to cry, since I was driving.

Georgia continued reading from her phone. "Acute shortness of breath . . . yep, she's got that. Diabetes. Kidney failure. Cardiopulmonary failure." She shoved her phone back into her bag and looked out the window. "We need to lose weight."

"Okay, for one, Georgia, I don't think *you* need to lose anything. You look almost thin."

"I think I might have an ulcer."

Lucky, I almost said before her words really sank in. "Shit! Are you kidding? I thought you were just eating better! You'd better see a doctor." My voice shook. "I mean, sure, you and I have our food issues, but we're not like Emerson. Why didn't she—" My voice broke. "I wish I'd known."

"Don't cry. You're driving. You want me to?"

"I'm good."

We were quiet for a minute, then Georgia said, "I've never wanted chocolate cake more in my entire life," and then we were sputtering with horrified laughter.

It was our story, after all, the story of so many fat people. *Eat those emotions.*

"What's in the envelope?" I asked.

"We're not looking at it right now," Georgia said. "I hope we never do. Ever."

"Me too."

"If she pulls through, we can just give it back to her. Not 'if.' When. *When* she gets better."

"She has plenty of money, right? From her parents? She can afford the best treatment there is." I swallowed. "And we'll be there for her. We'll do better." I was awash in guilt, the curse of the Catholics. "We know what she's going through."

"No, we don't, Marley. We're just . . . normal fat."

"Have you looked in a mirror lately? You look like you could shop at J.Crew." I hoped I didn't sound jealous.

"Please. Their extra-large is really a small."

"Banana Republic, then."

"Maybe." Georgia turned to look out her window as we pulled up to the hotel she'd found for us. "Emerson will get better," she said, almost to herself.

          . . . .

Emerson did not get better.

She took a turn for the worse the next day, slipped out of consciousness. Georgia and I wept at her side, begging her to hang in there.

At 3:07 p.m., Emerson Duval died, leaving us with our envelope. One slim envelope, to be opened after her funeral.

CHAPTER 3

Georgia

Here's something you don't think about every day: It's hard to bury someone as big as Emerson.

We had to get a special casket. A truck was needed to get her from the hospital to the funeral home, and from the funeral home to the cemetery, because a regular hearse couldn't accommodate her. We had to arrange for a crane to lower her into the grave, next to her beloved mother. We also had to book eight firefighters who would get the casket from the truck to the graveside. I wondered if some of them were the same ones who'd had to drag Emerson out of the house on a blanket to get her into the specially outfitted ambulance when she went to the hospital last week.

How did she get like this? Why hadn't she asked us for help? In the two days that followed Emerson's death, every time we learned some new, tragically sad fact about Emerson's life, it was all I could do not to sob. Marley's eyes leaked constantly. My stomach ached like a hot poker was sticking into it. On the upside, I wasn't hungry.

The day of her funeral started with the wake Marley and I had organized. When we arrived at the funeral home,

Emerson's hatchet-faced caretaker, her cousin Ruth, was already there. The first thing she said to us, in lieu of any kind of greeting, was, "I see the boyfriend didn't show." She then shook her head disapprovingly. "That Mica, *he* was the one who kept bringing her food." Ruth glanced back at the enormous casket, the one the funeral director had diplomatically called the Goliath. Ruth seemed to be getting a lot of malicious satisfaction out of Emerson's death. "Not that she had to eat it, mind you. Look at me. I've never weighed more than a hundred and twenty pounds. Never had trouble with moderation. I don't drink, I don't smoke, I don't like sweets. My cousin, she was weak. It was disgusting, watching how much she'd put away. Mica just sat on her bed, watching her. It was perverted."

"But you kept cashing her checks, I'm guessing," I said. Ruth hadn't been Emerson's caretaker out of the goodness of her heart.

"Someone had to look after her," she said, oblivious to the tone of my comment. "You know how hard it is to bathe a giant like that? How you have to lift up her stomach to dry underneath? That's not easy, you know. All she did was eat and eat and eat. She had no self-control. None."

"Why don't you shut up?" I said.

Ruth looked confused.

"Stop being a bitch, in other words," Marley clarified.

"You could lose a little weight yourself," Ruth said to her.

"I'm going to punch you in the throat if you don't knock it off," Marley said just as the second guest arrived. Marley turned to her in relief. So few people were here, we were glad to see anyone. "Hi. Thanks for coming. I'm Marley DeFelice, one of Emerson's oldest friends, and this is Georgia Sloane, another old friend. You are . . . ?"

"Bethany. We worked together a while ago. She was

really nice." The speaker was a beautiful girl, slim as a gazelle, maybe twenty-six years old.

"She was," I said.

Guilt razored through me, but I thanked God to see that Emerson had at least one person in her life who had appreciated her. Emerson had told Marley and me about her job a few years ago . . . a call center. Customer service. She hadn't mentioned leaving it. She really hadn't been in touch much this past year.

In the end, eleven people came to her wake. A few former coworkers, the nice doctor from the hospital, a nurse, one neighbor and her three daughters, and Emerson's accountant. Marley and I greeted each of them in turn, watching their eyes widen at the size of the casket. The boyfriend, indeed, never did show up.

At the cemetery, it was just Marley, Ruth and me, the firefighters and the funeral director. The crane was parked in full view. Even in death, it seemed that Emerson would be deprived of dignity.

"Would anyone like to say a few words?" the funeral director asked.

Marley was crying too hard to do it. "Emerson was a good, kind person," I said, my voice strained with the emotion I didn't want to release. Not here. "We had a lot of fun together. We'll miss her so much." Not the best speech, but I couldn't think of what else to say.

Ruth sighed, checked her phone and asked if we could go now.

"Whenever you're ready," the funeral guy said.

Without a word, she walked to her car.

Marley put her hand on the casket, wiped her eyes and pressed her lips together.

My own eyes were hot and dry. I took a white rose from the arrangement on the top of the casket—Marley and I had

bought a huge, beautiful display. *I'm so sorry,* I thought.
I'm just so sorry.

When we got back to Emerson's house, Ruth was waiting for us, as was a woman holding a casserole dish in her
hands. She'd been at the wake with her daughters.

"Hi," Marley said.

"Hello, I'm Natasha. A neighbor," she said. "I'm so sorry
for your loss." She handed me the dish, which was still
warm.

"Did you know her well?" I asked.

"No, not really. Hardly at all. She, um . . . well, she
stopped in front of my house once, and we talked a bit.
But she didn't get out much. Anyway. My daughters and I
were very sorry to hear she'd died. She seemed like a sweet
person."

"Thank you," Marley said, her voice rough. "You're
very kind."

She walked down the street, and Marley and I stood
there, looking at the house for a minute. We'd visited her
here once, about a year after her mother died. She'd lost a
lot of weight and was full of energy . . . and I couldn't remember when that changed.

At least the house and neighborhood were nice. She'd
taken a lot of pride in this sweet little place.

I tried not to wince at the sight of the destroyed front
door as we followed Ruth inside.

"Can we see her room?" I asked.

"Fine. She had to move to the den when she couldn't
haul herself up the stairs anymore." She led us down the
hall and opened a door. A bigger-than-usual door. Marley
and I went in, and Ruth followed.

"Maybe you could give us a minute," I said.

"Don't take anything."

My jaw locked. "Ruth. Give us a minute."

She pursed her lips and stepped out, but stood just outside the door, in case Marley and I decided we were in desperate need of one of the cat statues that Emerson appeared to have collected.

Marley looked at me, her brown eyes wet, a hand over her mouth. My head ached.

The king-sized bed was a mess of tangled blankets and a mountain of pillows. The detritus of the first responders was scattered about—gauze, paper, plastic, a latex glove. In the corner was the CPAP machine. Clothes that seemed to be the size of sheets littered the floor.

And then there was the damning evidence . . . a pizza box on the desk, a couple of empty cereal boxes, a package of Double Stuf Oreos, a red and white bucket from Kentucky Fried Chicken.

I could hear my brother's ugly voice in my head letting loose a tirade of disgust. He hated fat people. Especially his only sibling.

On the bureau, which was reassuringly free from food, was a picture. Emerson, Marley and me, taken on our last day at Camp Copperbrook.

We looked so happy. Fat, and happy. Marley looked much the same, though she no longer wore purple eye shadow. I was laughing; funny, I never pictured my face in a smile. I'd lost thirty-three pounds in twelve weeks at camp that summer and could have passed for chubby, but I'd gone on to gain twenty pounds my freshman year at Princeton.

Emerson was the biggest, even back then.

I showed the picture to Marley. "Damn it," she whispered, wiping her eyes.

I looked out the bedroom window. Emerson had been stuck in here, in this room, in that body, for the past year. Our friend had been a prisoner. All she saw of the outside world was through these windows. The leaves on the trees of that one maple, the bricks of the neighbor's house, a glimpse of the sky.

I felt the familiar pinch of pain in my stomach.

Why hadn't she told us?

I knew the answer: shame.

"Let's get out of here," Marley said.

"We'd like to have this," I told Ruth, holding up the picture.

"Fine." She put her hands on her skinny hips. "You know, you two might think you're high and mighty and I'm a bitch, but where've you been these last two years?"

Her words struck a nerve. There was nothing left for us to do, so without another word, we left.

The envelope was in my bag, waiting for us.

It was a long drive home.

....

Four years ago, I left my job at a Manhattan law firm and became a nursery school teacher. The change in career also prompted me to move back to my hometown of Cambry-on-Hudson, New York, a pretty little city about an hour north of Manhattan, overlooking the mighty river. I wanted to be closer to my nephew. Oh, and I'd also gotten divorced.

I'd rented an apartment at first, but as far back as Camp Copperbrook, Marley and I (and Emerson) had talked about living together. Two years ago, when a place came on the market—a town house with a caterer's kitchen in the rental garden apartment—it felt like the universe was telling me something. I called Marley, who lived with her parents, and described the state-of-the-art kitchen. "Want to be my tenant?" I asked.

"Hell's yes, I do," she said. By the end of the day, it was official.

Most of the homes on Magnolia Avenue were like

mine—brick or brownstone town houses built at the turn of
the twentieth century, many having been divided into apart-
ments. The Romeros had an in-law apartment in their
ground-floor unit; the Clancys used theirs as a furnished
Airbnb rental; Leo the piano teacher taught out of a garden
apartment and lived upstairs with his girlfriend, Jenny. And,
in number 23, Marley and me, just like the book.

Now, as we crossed the Tappan Zee Bridge on our drive
back from Delaware, I asked, "Didn't Emerson talk about
moving to New York a couple years ago?" What if Emerson
had moved up here? Would that have saved her? Had she
hated hearing that Marley and I were living together?

"I think that was just talk." Marley paused. "That was
around Christmas a year and a half ago, so she still would've
been kind of . . ."

Huge.

"Yeah."

My stomach puckered and burned, as if I'd swallowed a
hot rock rubbed with jalapeños.

We got off Route 9 and headed into Cambry-on-Hudson,
past the pretty downtown—the Blessed Bean, the coffee
place where I stopped every morning for a double-tall extra-
strong skinny vanilla latte; Bliss, the bridal shop owned by
Jenny from down the street; Cottage Confection, that den of
sin and sugar; and Hudson's, the newest farm-to-table restaurant, where Marley and I went sometimes, her brother
and his husband often joining us.

When we pulled onto our street, I said, "Why don't you
come up and we can read whatever it was she left us, okay?"

"Sure," said Marley. "I'll bring dinner."

"You don't have to." After the past few days, the last
thing I wanted to do was eat.

"Oh, please. It's what I do. I haven't cooked for five days, and it's driving me crazy." She paused. "You could use some food, besides."

I pulled up to the curb. "Okay. I'll make the martinis."

We went into our separate doors—mine up the stairs, hers through the garden gate.

I was greeted by Admiral, my rescued greyhound, age three.

"Hello, handsome," I said, kneeling down for a snuzzle. He pushed his wet nose against my neck and wagged, and I ran my hands over his lean ribs and spine.

Admiral was an elegant gray, a former racing dog. My fourteen-year-old nephew, Mason, had been taking care of him while I was gone, and had sent me pictures of Admiral in various stages of repose. (Ad was basically a couch potato . . . a cat in dog's clothing.) Mason adored him, and welcomed the chance to dog-sit. More than welcomed.

Speaking of my nephew, I had six e-mails from him. These were in addition to the eight texts and two phone calls since I'd been in Delaware. All of them sounded painfully upbeat, all variations on, "Hey, I know you're away, just wanted you to know I was thinking of you, can't wait till you get back, hope you're not too sad, love you."

Mason had a heart as big as the planet.

Somehow, my dickhead of a brother had gotten the world's greatest kid. Father and son could not be more different, and Hunter's brittle, obvious disappointment in his son kept me up at night, especially since his mother, my wonderful sister-in-law, Leah, had died when Mason was only eight. But my general constant worry for my nephew had exploded into all-out terror after what Mason had done last April.

An overdose. Accidental, he said. I wasn't so sure.

One of the worst things about my divorce had been that

Mason lost my husband, too. Rafe had been one of the only supportive male role models Mason had in his life, and I always thought there had been a special bond between them. But now Mason had Marley, who was like an inappropriate aunt and all the more fun because of it. He had Admiral. My dog, whom I'd only owned a year, had done more for Mason's self-esteem than my brother ever had. And he had me.

I called Mason now, and he answered on the first ring. "Hey, honey, how's it going?"

"Hey, G! Are you back?"

"Yeah. It was really sad."

"I'm so sorry."

Just those three words made my heart ache. My brother wouldn't have been able to say them with a gun to the back of his head. I couldn't bear to imagine what Hunter would have said if he'd seen Emerson.

"Thanks, honey," I said, clearing my throat. "And thanks for taking care of Admiral. He said you were an excellent companion, and he wants you to come over this weekend."

Mason laughed. "He did, huh? He was also a great companion." There was a pause; it was possible my brother was in the room, and Hunter resented the fact that his son loved me. I was an embarrassment to my brother. Fat was unforgivable in his eyes, even though the honest truth was, I was probably in the normal zone these days. Not that he had noticed. Nor that it mattered in his eyes.

I'd *been* fat.

"I'll come by on Sunday," Mason said.

"Can't wait. Love you, honey."

If only I could adopt Mason. But that was a thought I'd had a million times, and I still couldn't see a way to do it. My stomach pain flared again.

Definitely time for martinis, ulcer or no ulcer. I didn't

cook, but I made a killer cocktail. One did not attend the fine learning institutions I had—Princeton undergraduate, Yale Law, University of North Carolina graduate school, thank you very much—without learning to be a skilled mixologist.

Marley knocked a few minutes later, bringing a wilted spinach salad, braised chicken with a red pepper sauce and quinoa with almonds and peas. My brain did the mental calorie count . . . probably 350, 400 calories a serving. Even though I knew Marley's kitchen was stocked with good food, I was amazed at how quickly she had once again put together such a beautiful meal. "Delicious, nutritious, fast and low cal," she announced, knowing I still obsessed over every mouthful.

When we moved in under the same roof, Marley and I had made a pact. No food judgment. We'd be living on top of each other, literally, and the last thing we needed to feel was watched at home. If one of us had gained weight or lost it, was overeating or purging, the worst thing we could do was question the other. The rest of the world took care of that just fine.

I poured her a martini. "To Emerson," I said, and Marley's big brown eyes welled up with tears. I clinked my glass with hers and took a healthy swig. The vodka burned in my stomach, but tonight, it was important to have a buzz on.

"To Emerson," she echoed, the tears sliding down her cheeks.

Under the best of circumstances, enjoying food was hard for me. Eating with Marley, with her good example of healthy eating and appetite, was easier. Had been, anyway, until Mason ended up in the hospital.

Eating with Rafael Esteban Jesús Santiago had been pretty great, too . . . at least at first. My ex-husband and my best friend were both chefs. Probably not a coincidence.

But tonight I could only manage a few mouthfuls (though the vodka went down easily). A predictable thought flashed: *Hooray, I'm too sad to eat! Maybe I'll lose some weight!* I rolled my eyes at myself and stood up to clear our plates. "Sorry I couldn't eat more," I said. "It was really good."

"You bet. And you know me. I can always eat. That doesn't mean I'm not still heartbroken."

"I know, hon."

We cleared the dishes and tidied my kitchen. "Is this new?" Marley asked as we went into the living room. She pointed to a print of a rabbit that I'd bought just before we got the call about Emerson.

"It is. I got it for Admiral. He looks at it all day long, don't you, boy?" My dog wagged his tail politely.

"HomeGoods?"

"Marshalls. Same thing. Hey, I was thinking of going to Crate and Barrel this weekend, if you want to come."

"I *always* want to come."

We just sat for a minute, avoiding reading whatever Emerson had given us. As some women could talk about clothes, Marley and I could talk about home decorating, and we shared a love of the same stores.

To be honest, the town house probably deserved better taste than I had, with my propensity for bright colors and made-in-China décor. But the home I grew up in was chilly in both atmosphere and temperature. Every room was eggshell or fog or sand colored, all the furniture muted neutrals. The thermostat was set at sixty-three "for the sake of the artwork," Mother liked to say. Every rug, every sofa, every candlestick and painting had significance—a vase wasn't just a vase, it was a signed Carder Steuben. The rug was an antique Heriz, the painting an Erik Magnussen, the sofa a genuine Fritz Hansen (which meant it was ugly *and* uncomfortable).

As a result, I was a whore for Crate & Barrel, Pier 1 Imports, HomeGoods and yes, Ikea—all those cheerful throw pillows and funky, happy chairs. My mother claimed my house gave her a headache, but my furniture was comfortable, at least, and the colors made me happy.

But not tonight.

I poured Marley and myself half a martini more and took Emerson's envelope out of my purse.

To be opened after my funeral.

"What do you think is in there?" Marley asked. "Her will?"

"No, a will is a huge document." I'd kept my law license and still did some pro bono work. Legal documents were nothing if not long.

"Well, we promised Emerson we'd do whatever it says."

I had a feeling it wouldn't be easy, whatever it was. Admiral leaped up next to me and curled into his little doggy ball. His sixth sense for when I needed moral support was perfectly attuned. I stroked his silky ears, then took a deep breath.

"Okay," I said. "Here goes nothing."

I opened the envelope carefully. Inside was one piece of paper, the handwriting girlish and round, just as we had been.

It was our list.

Our list from Camp Copperbrook.

I scanned it, my throat tight, that hot poker digging into the wall of my stomach.

Oh, Emerson.

I handed the piece of paper to Marley, the memories of that summer surging.

I'd been friendly with Emerson from our other summers at Copperbrook, but it was Marley who made us the Terrible Trio. That summer was the first time I'd felt normal, away from my family, with real friends, breaking the occasional rule, staying up late, laughing till the bunk beds shook. And on that last day, we'd made a list, each of us contributing something or, in the case of the last item, mutually agreeing.

"She kept this," Marley said. "Oh, God, she kept it all these years." She put it on the coffee table and drained the rest of her drink.

Things We'll Do When We're Skinny

- Hold hands with a cute guy in public.
- Go running in tight clothes and a sports bra.
- Get a piggyback ride from a guy.
- Be in a photo shoot.
- Eat dessert in public.
- Tuck in a shirt.
- Shop at a store for regular people.
- Have a cute stranger buy you a drink at a bar.
- Go home to meet his parents.
- Tell off the people who judged us when we were fat.

Promise me, Emerson had said there in the hospital.

"She wants us to do all this? Now?" Marley asked.

"I guess so."

"Why? That was so long ago. I mean . . . these aren't exactly meaningful life achievements for a card-carrying adult." She was nervous, fidgeting with the fringe on the pillow. "Get a piggyback ride?"

"Have you ever had a piggyback ride?"

She gave me the stink-eye. "Any guy who gave me a piggyback ride would collapse or pop a hernia."

"His eyes would explode out of his head," I said. "Gray matter would leak from his ears, and his vertebrae would collapse into powder. Blood everywhere."

"Bite me," she said, tossing the throw pillow at me.

I'd never had a piggyback ride, either. It was such a little thing, and yet so . . . romantic. So normal, the idea that you'd be smaller than your honey, and he'd be playful and manly, and you'd be adorable and spontaneous.

Marley cleared her throat. "Let's go through this list, and see if any of these things matter anymore. We were just kids when we wrote it." She glanced at the notepaper. "Go running in a sports bra? Who wrote that one? It sure wasn't me."

"I did. All those cross-country meets when Hunter was in high school. My mother dragged me to every one." I still remembered those girls, so impossibly perfect, so oblivious to the blessings of good health and beauty. I couldn't take my eyes off them, even though they ignored me.

Even at age seven, I'd known I'd never look like that.

"The point of putting it on the list," I said slowly, "was the idea that someday, I wouldn't want to . . . you know. Hide."

"Fat acceptance?" Marley said.

"More like the idea that we could be skinny."

"Well, shit," said Marley. "Shit on rye."

"Don't make me want carbs," I said, and we snorted in unexpected laughter, which in Marley's case quickly became tears again.

I picked up the list. "The privileges of thin people," I murmured.

Because that's what it had been. These were the things thin girls got to do, things that were out of reach for us fatties. The list was stark and innocent, slashing like an unseen razor with its yearning . . . and honesty.

When Rafe took me home to meet his parents, I remember thinking, *I should've lost more weight for this.*

"Can I see it again?" Marley asked. She studied the paper. I remembered the notebook—a pink cover with purple peace signs. Emerson had always been writing in it; she was one of the few people I knew who kept a diary.

"Actually," Marley said, "I *have* had a cute guy buy me a drink. Gays count, right?"

"I think we were picturing straight guys. Benjamin Bratt, remember?" We'd all had that *Law & Order* addiction.

"Oh, God, I *loved* him. So Benjamin Bratt has to buy me a drink? All right. The sacrifices I make." But I could hear the pain under her words. She'd had a crush on a guy for the past five years—one of her brother Dante's FDNY coworkers— but it had yet to progress to anything. He was an idiot, in my opinion. Marley was the best person on earth. So instinctively kind, so funny, so generous . . . and yes, sure, overweight, but she carried it well—she'd always had a waist and great boobs. She could get away with zaftig or Rubenesque.

Not me. I'd always been fat-fat, like a troll, like an egg. There was no romantic word for how I was shaped.

"'Tuck in a shirt,'" Marley read. Back at Copperbrook, we had talked about the ultimate skinny girl's outfit: a pair of jeans and a white T-shirt, tucked in. She looked at me now. "You could totally work that, just sayin'."

"With Spanx and a waist trainer and liposuction and black magic, sure."

"I'm serious. You look great."

I shrugged. Whenever I looked in the mirror, which I did only when necessary, I still didn't see what I wanted to.

"'Eat dessert in public.' I already do that, so rest easy, Emerson," Marley said, moving on.

I didn't. I hadn't had dessert in . . . well, since my wedding cake, probably. I was more of the junk-food type. My first love was salt.

But since Mason's overdose, accidental or not, food and I had become even more hateful enemies.

"'Hold hands with a cute guy in public,'" Marley continued. "That won't be a problem. I can run up to a hot guy, grab his hand and drag him a few yards. Check."

My ex-husband and I had held hands all the time. And he'd been extremely hot. I couldn't count the number of times people had looked surprised to see us as a couple.

"'Tell off the people who judged us when we were fat,'" Marley read. "Great. We'd have to line them up in a stadium. Can we start with your asshole brother? 'Tell off,' that means stab in the eye, right?"

"We don't have to do this," I said, setting my drink down on the coffee table. "This is what three teenagers thought would be the ultimate . . . whatever. It's not really for adults. We're thirty-four. Almost thirty-five."

Marley lay back and gazed up at the ceiling. "But we promised Emerson we would. She'll never get to do these things, G." Her voice thickened. "And she kept this list all these years."

I swallowed, and Admiral put his head on my leg. "I don't know. It seems . . . empty, really. And my plate is pretty full these days. Work and Mason. The FFE." I did some pro bono legal work for the Foundation for Female Entrepreneurship, which gave out business and legal advice and sometimes money for disadvantaged women looking to start their own businesses. Couldn't let the Yale law degree go completely to waste.

I didn't see what purpose the list would serve, frankly.

Marley rubbed her eyes. "Yeah. I understand." We sat in silence for a few minutes until she spoke again. "I'm zonked. Time for bed."

"Okay. I'll see you tomorrow."

She left, and my apartment felt oddly empty. Like something was missing from the moment. Unfinished business. I had to shake myself to close the door after her.

A half hour later, I was soaking in my big, beautiful tub, Admiral curled on the floor next to me. I loved baths. I'd invested in a gorgeous tub for myself, big enough so I could feel small and delicate, and tonight, I needed to do something to make myself feel good. The sadness of Emerson's funeral had caught up to me.

The list brought up a lot, too. All the misery of being a fat teenager in America, trying so hard to be invisible, quiet, not to draw attention to myself.

Still, I'd done stuff. I traveled a little bit, five days here, a week there. I'd been to Paris and Rome, albeit when I was in college. I had a great job, all my students hugging me, smiling, offering me their instant, innocent love. Granted, I made a lot less than when I was a lawyer, but I could pay my bills, thanks to the inheritance from my grandmother, and I had a nice investment portfolio curated by my dad, who managed a big mutual fund. I had a house, a dog, a nephew. A longtime best friend. I'd even been in love once. I didn't need to do the things on that list.

Except I'd said I would.

CHAPTER 4

Marley

Be in a photo shoot. *(Sort of.)*

"Please wait while I get my checkbook."

I closed my eyes and tried not to sigh.

This particular client was a special type of ass pain. Granted, I was grateful for ass-pain clients, because I charged them more.

But I loved most of my clients. Some saw cooking as too much of a chore, which was hard for me to understand, since I grouped sex and cooking in the same category of sensual delight. Others had food allergies and issues that made food prep difficult. Some were genuinely too busy. Some just hated it; Georgia admitted to dry-heaving if she had to touch raw chicken.

Here in the wealthy, charming little town of Cambry-on-Hudson, a lot liked the status of having a personal chef. Cambry was just twenty minutes from Yonkers, where I'd grown up, but a world apart. Here, there were things like equestrian clubs and preschools with tuitions equaling those of many colleges. So being able to say you had a personal chef . . . well, people liked that.

And so . . . Salt & Pepper, my little company, founded

by me, staffed by me and occasionally assisted by my mom and Dante. Dinners (and lunches, but mostly dinners) prepared just for you, according to everything you love and any health considerations you might have.

My skills went beyond cooking. I was an organizational wizard. Got celiac disease? Don't worry; I would never show you a menu with a speck of gluten on it. Peanut allergy? There's a counter I used just for your food. Your kids hate bananas? No worries! I'll make sure they get their potassium another way. Dairy nauseates you? Good old Marley will take care of you.

I loved it. I loved my clients, even the snooty yoga moms who pretended they cooked my dinners themselves or treated me like a serving wench when I did the occasional dinner party. I loved them because they needed me.

And then there was Will Harding.

I had already put his food on the counter, as I did five nights a week. Today, he'd chosen grilled salmon, crispy roasted baby potatoes and a tomato-and-avocado salad. For some reason, he felt the need to check under the lids, as if I'd topped the salmon with ground glass instead of kale-almond pesto.

I reminded myself that Will had been one of Salt & Pepper's first clients. He used me five times a week; most of my clients were the one- or three-times-a-week types. Some used me only for special occasions.

But Will never told me he liked the food, never gave me any feedback at all. In fact, he barely spoke to me.

I wished Frankie were here. I wished she were my business partner, my roomie, my best friend. I wished she were standing next to me, rolling her eyes as Will wrote out his check.

My twin sister had been dead for thirty years, and still, I had these feelings every day—the yearning for her company, even though I barely remembered her. The ache of feeling half of a pair instead of a whole person.

I sighed and tried to pull out some of my Keep on the Sunny Side attitude from the vault in my heart. Sometimes that good cheer came naturally, and sometimes it was like walking through tar. It had been harder going than usual since Emerson's funeral.

How long did it take to write a check for the same amount every single day?

Wastes my time. I'd started a mental list of Will Harding's flaws months ago. And number one on that list was *prejudiced against fat people.*

Oh, yes, I noticed the way he scanned me, his face carefully blank. What? I wore my chef whites with the cute little logo over my heart—a set of salt and pepper shakers dancing, little smiley faces alight with joy. Mason, Georgia's nephew, had made it for me on his computer, the clever lad.

But Will gave me that look that we overweight women know so well . . . the look that said, *No, thanks,* and also, *You're fat . . .* fat being as egregious a sin as being a serial killer of puppies. The look that said fat was worse than hateful or dishonest or cruel.

Will returned from the back room—I was only allowed in the kitchen—and gave me the look now. I forced my face into a smile, waiting for him to hand over the check.

"That cold sore you had is gone," he said.

I blinked. An entire sentence! And such a sweet thing to say, no less. "Yes."

"Good." He handed me the check, and I took it, careful not to let our fingers touch. Once that had happened, and he had jumped back.

Not for the first time, I thought about dropping him. It was a little creepy, our routine. His whole house was always dark, shades drawn, only the counter island lights on in the kitchen. Every day, I was let in almost the second I knocked, because he waited for me. Then came the setting down of the bags. The verification of their contents. The writing of the check. The dismissal.

"Thank you," he said now, as he did every night. "Good-bye."

"Enjoy the salmon!" I said with fat-girl jollity. "See you tomorrow!"

"Thank you," he repeated. "Good-bye."

It was always a relief to get out of there. Oh, the house was fine. Whether or not Will Harding had bodies stashed in his freezer was another question.

When I got into my car, I took a second to text Camden—Mr. November in the FDNY calendar. (My darling baby brother was Mr. April.) Camden worked with Dante and, occasionally, slept with me.

I loved him, of course.

Just left the serial killer's house, I wrote. Am still alive.

Dante—"the gay firefighter," Mom always said, as if she had more than one firefighter son—had done me one huge favor in his life, and that was joining FDNY. Sure, sure, saving lives and protecting property, that was great. More importantly (for me, anyway) was nearly unlimited access to New York's Bravest. Dropping by his firehouse with a pan of eggplant Parmesan or four dozen cannolis to endear myself to my brother's coworkers was one of my favorite activities. Yes, it was exactly as you might imagine. I'd go into Battalion 11 on the Upper West Side, hear a chorus of manly voices saying, "Yo, Dante, your sistah's here! Heya, Marley, whatcha bring us, hon?"

I really was only there for Camden Fortuno. He was everything—gorgeous, brave, strong, funny, friendly, gorgeous, a firefighter, did I mention that? Okay, sure, his name was a little dopey—there are those Italians who have a penchant for picking out the WASPiest name possible to pair with their Old Country last name. My mom didn't fall prey to that trap—we were Eva, my older sister; Dante; Marlena (yours truly); and my twin, Francesca, aka Frankie, may she rest in peace.

Camden, on the other hand, had a sister named Huntley and a brother named Wickham.

At any rate, Camden was . . . well. See above. Plus, he was *nice*.

The three pulsing dots on my phone's screen told me he was typing a reply to my text. A second later, it popped up.

Thank God. What are you doing tonight?

My heart leaped. "Be cool, be cool," I said to myself.

Camden and I had never been on a date. Once in a while, I'd go out with my brother; his husband, Louis; and some of the gang from Battalion 11. That was about as close as a public date as I'd had with Cam. But in the past five years, we'd nevertheless ended up back at his place six times, where sexy time had indeed ensued.

Maybe he was asking me out now.

Not much, I typed back. Almost done with my deliveries. What are you up to?

Working, he wrote back. Have a great night!

Well, shit.

You too! I typed. Considered adding a smiley face, wisely decided against it, clicked off my phone and sighed.

Each time Camden and I had slept together had been after a party. Each time, Camden had been a little drunk; each time, he'd asked me not to tell my brother.

Each time made me love him all the more. Don't judge me.

But being a twin without a twin is like having a hole in your heart. Even though Frankie and I had been only four when she died, I was meant to be half of a pair. Small wonder that I latched onto friends the way I did, leaped at the chance to be Georgia's tenant, visited my brother twice a week, called my older sister to check in (not that she ever called me first). And yes, ever since passing puberty, I'd been on the prowl for a husband.

Camden would fit the bill quite nicely. I just had to get him to that point.

Well. I had three more deliveries. Two were Manhattan commuters who wouldn't be home when I dropped off their stuff. I made short work of those, programming the ovens to start preheating in an hour, stashing the food in the fridge, instructions taped to the boxes.

Rachel Carver was last on my list, and one of the few people who really deserved having a meal dropped off once a week, though she was a pretty great cook herself. You could tell by the ingredients in her fridge, and the fact that her kids ate things like fish and spinach and curry.

But her daughters were four-year-old triplets, and she was divorced, so who better to use Salt & Pepper? Rachel and I had become friends in the past six months since she'd started using me, and sometimes I stayed for a glass of wine if she was my last client. Her girls all went to St. Luke's preschool, and all were in Georgia's class, which meant I was a rock star by association.

"Marley, Marley, what did you bring, it smells good, look at my picture, play with me, Marley!" the girls chorused as I came in.

Their beautiful little faces made my heart hurt. I was so jealous of them, and I adored them, and they were that age, that age . . . and if I wasn't careful, I'd start crying. *Please turn five,* I mentally ordered them.

"Hi, Marley," Rachel said, wading through her daughters

to relieve me of the food. "What did we order tonight? I forgot."

"Panfried chicken, sugar snap peas, and mashed sweet potatoes with cranberries," I said. "Extra deliciousness for you, princesses!"

The little girls hugged my legs and grabbed my hands, jockeying for position. I hoped they'd live to be a hundred and all die at the same exact instant, holding hands, surrounded by their progeny. I loved these girls. I did. Even if they made me feel like I'd swallowed a shard of glass.

"Can you stay for a glass of wine?" Rachel asked.

"Sure," I said. "How are you?" One of the girls held up a necklace for me to inspect. "Oh, Rose, that's lovely. Is that macaroni? It's so sparkly."

"I made one, too," said Charlotte. "But I threw it away, because I hated it."

"I love macaroni," said Grace from around her thumb. "I ate mine."

"Girls, why don't you go upstairs and tidy up your room so Marley and I can have some grown-up time?" Rachel suggested, stroking Grace's head. She had that blissful look of maternal love on her face.

My poor mom. I couldn't remember a time when she had that expression; the loss of Frankie had carved heartache into her face in a hundred little lines.

If I ever became a mother, Rachel would be my role model. More likely, though, I'd be the type with a messy house and a mega-sized box of pinot grigio in the fridge, who'd shoo the kids out of the room so I could look at pictures of Channing Tatum online.

The girls obeyed—Rachel didn't even have to yell. As they swarmed up the stairs, the jealousy flared again. They were so lucky, those triplets.

"How was the funeral?" Rachel asked, pouring me a glass of wine (from a bottle, not a box).

"Ugh," I said. "Horrible." I hadn't told her the cause of death, nor about Emerson's size. Fat-girl loyalty. Rachel was one of those willowy beauties, and even though she was incredibly nice, I couldn't betray Emerson by talking about her weight.

"I'm so sorry," Rachel said. She put her hand over mine and squeezed it, then blushed. She was very shy, and I got the impression that I was one of her first post-divorce friends. Her sister lived down the street from me—Jenny, who owned the bridal boutique and regularly featured plus-sized gowns in her window displays, which I appreciated.

"How did you know her?" Rachel asked, tucking her smooth blond hair behind her ears. "She was Georgia's friend, too, right?"

"We go all the way back to summer camp," I said.

"So sad, losing an old friend."

Guilt and grief made my throat tighten. "Here's a question for you," I said. "When we were in camp, we made this list of things we wanted to do as . . . um, adults. Emerson kept it all these years, and when she was . . ." *dying* ". . . sick, she asked us to do the things on it."

"That's lovely," Rachel said simply.

"It is?"

"Oh. Isn't it?" She leaned back in the chair. Her stomach was flat. How could that be, when she'd had the three-for-one special packed in there?

Maybe someday I'd get hypnotized to see if I could remember being in the womb with Frankie.

"Sorry," I said, snapping out of it. "Um, I guess it is. It's just that they're things that a kid would think an adult should do. Like have a good-looking stranger buy you a drink. Which isn't really that cool in this day of Rohypnol and stuff. Be in a photo shoot. Stuff like that."

Rachel smiled. "Well, Rohypnol aside, it's sweet. She must have wanted to make sure you fulfilled those dreams."

"So you think we should do it? The things on the list? They're kind of . . . I don't know. Awkward."

"Well, a lot of things in life are awkward at first. Dating. Making a new friend." She shrugged, her beautiful collarbones shifting elegantly under her skin. Collarbones fascinated me, since I had never really seen my own. Rachel dropped her gaze to the table, her cheeks growing pinker. "Sometimes it's worth the effort."

"True enough. I'm glad *we're* friends." She smiled, looking relieved, and I felt a surge of love for her. *Be my friend, Rachel! Be my best friend!* I couldn't have enough of those.

"Mommy!" one of the girls bellowed from the top of the stairs. "I have to poop!"

"That's Rose. She needs moral support," Rachel said. "Guess I should go up there and cheer her on."

"Thanks for the wine."

"It was great seeing you." She smiled and went up to watch her child defecate.

I drove home, melancholy keeping me company, and went into my now-dark apartment. Maybe I should get a dog, like Georgia. Then again, I practically had joint custody of the speedy beast. Most weekends, I'd go with Georgia to the Little League field, which was fenced in, so we could let Ad race around like the fine athlete he was. I had a key to Georgia's place and sometimes let him out in our little fenced-in garden if she was stuck somewhere.

I checked my phone. No further communication from Camden. Not exactly a surprise.

However, my baby brother had sent me a picture of himself in turnout gear holding a puppy.

More fame! said his text. Tomorrow's Daily News cover shot!!!

You're a camera whore, I wrote back. Mom still loves me best.

Last year, Dante had saved a little girl from a house fire. New York 7 Eyewitness News had been on the scene, so every visit to our parents' house now included footage of Dante running out of an inferno with a child in his arms, tossing off his helmet and laying her on the ground so Camden could give her oxygen. I didn't mind watching that video one bit. Obviously, the little girl lived. Dante had a charmed life. He never knew Frankie, so unlike Eva and me, he lacked that hole in his heart.

Ha, came his answer. I'm the baby AND the gay son. You don't stand a chance.

But you're so ugly, I texted. At least you married well.

I had a soft spot for Louis, who appreciated a large woman and thought I was stunningly beautiful, as any good gay brother-in-law should.

We're all going to Hudson's on Friday, Dante typed, naming a cute little restaurant in my town. Dante and Louis lived in Tarrytown, just south of Cambry-on-Hudson, but they liked the posher restaurants and shops here. Lots of people will be there.

Lots of people might include Camden.

Okay. Can't wait to see you, stupid.

You're stupid, he wrote back.

No, you are.

Such was our way of showing love.

Yes, I'd go. For one, it'd be fun, hanging out with the platoon. And even more than that, I'd have the chance to see Camden, and hope that he'd need a ride home, and maybe would invite me up. The last time that happened was at the Christmas party eight months ago.

Don't tell your brother.

Code for *don't tell anyone.*

Curse of the fat chick. I was pretty enough—the classic Sicilian look, big brown eyes, curly black hair, rather fabulous cleavage, thank you very much. I was also kind of a workout freak and always had been—I took kickboxing, Zumba and yoga, and ran (wearing a sports bra that looked like armor, mind you, but I could run). My blood pressure was normal, my cholesterol "exemplary," according to my doctor. I ate healthfully (except when at my mom's). I was a loyal friend; I was cheerful and optimistic. Not one person who ever ran into me had a worse day because of it. I was even nice to Will, my weird-as-a-serial-killer client.

But thinking about the list Emerson gave us on her literal deathbed, or trying *not* to think about it, made me realize that I wasn't as happy or well adjusted as I pretended.

Because I would like it if Camden Fortuno let me tell a few people.

Because I wanted to hold his hand. In public.

Because I wanted him to give me a piggyback ride, the way Louis had done for my brother last summer during an FDNY picnic.

And I wanted Camden to bring me home to meet his parents.

From upstairs, it was quiet, which meant Georgia was probably doing legal things for the girl-power foundation she volunteered with. In other words, I had no distractions. The list called to me like the ring called to Sauron.

For most of my life, ever since I became aware that I was fat, a mantra had pulsed through my head. *When I'm skinny. When I'm skinny. When I'm skinny. As soon as I lose weight. As soon as I lose weight. As soon as I lose weight.*

That's when life would really begin. When I'd be seen as a stunning beauty (cough). When my doctor would stop explaining portion size at each annual physical. When men would start viewing me as wife material. When I could stop thinking about weight and clothes all the time. When I got skinny, my real life would start.

Maybe it was seeing Emerson's death . . . or maybe, worse, that glimpse of her life we'd gotten at her house. She'd been trapped in her body, waiting for something to change, until it finally did. The job . . . then Mica . . . then dying.

I was never going to be a size 6. Not with my genes, not with my love of food (and wine). I'd been on so many diets, had long ago grown tired of weighing and measuring and calculating everything I put in my mouth. It was sacrilege, an offense to my people. Hadn't I been weaned on ricotta cheese? Wasn't our family motto "nobody leaves the table till someone's dead"? And how could I not eat, when Frankie *really* hadn't been able to eat, had had no appetite no matter what my mother fed her? I was the twin who lived. I *had* to eat.

I'd been chubby from birth, and with Frankie being so tiny and frail, my chubbiness had been celebrated, had been a relief to my perpetually terrified parents. I graduated to fat before I was eight years old.

All those diets later, and here I was, still fat. Not hugely obese, but yeah, packing plenty of extra weight. Can't-shop-in-the-regular-stores fat.

Eva was probably fifty pounds heavier than I was. Mom and Dad were no role models for eating, and someday, my very blessed brother was going to have to reckon with his heritage. I *did* exercise. I did eat a mostly plant-based diet (except at Mom's). I didn't want to be one of those people who couldn't enjoy food because she was obsessed with being thin.

So I guess that meant . . .

The thought was slow but solid in coming, like a tank making its way through the rubble of a war-torn country.

I guess that meant this was as good as it was going to be. That *I* was as good as I was going to be.

I sat there on the couch for a minute, the silence pressing down on me.

"You're never going to be skinny, Marley," I said out loud. The words echoed around me.

I'd read all the books, all the articles. I knew that losing weight and keeping it off was statistically harder than climbing Mount Everest. I knew that basic biology would fight to keep my fat cells alive and kicking.

But now, sitting here alone—more than alone, the twin-less twin—the thought seemed to seep into my bones.

I would never be thin.

I went into my bedroom. The walls were painted dark blue, my comforter was white, and I had a mountain of pale blue and white pillows. The windowsills held a dozen photos of my family, and most recently added, the picture of Georgia, Emerson and me at Camp Copperbrook. And there on the dresser was the last photo taken of Frankie and me. Looking at it now, I felt . . . guilty.

I took off my clothes, every piece, and stood naked in front of the full-length mirror on the back of the door.

Yes, I had a belly. My breasts were large, but proportionate, more or less. My ass was impressive, my thighs fat—there was no other word for it. I would never have a flat stomach, and my arms were plump, no matter how often I lifted weights at the gym.

This was my body, and it worked.

I could waste time wishing to be small. I could get surgery. I could starve myself and never eat the foods I loved again.

That wasn't what I called living . . . and I was the twin

who lived. I couldn't just wait for everything to happen someday. I owed it to Frankie, I owed it to Emerson, and I owed it to myself. The list, written half a lifetime ago, was still telling me what I was missing.

I heard Georgia's footsteps over my head and dialed her before I thought more about it, still in front of the mirror, still buck naked.

"Hey," she said.

"I'm doing the list," I said, staring at the picture of my sister and me. "But I'm not losing weight. I'll do it the way I am." I paused then, but she didn't say anything. "You in?"

"I'm in," she said.

"Great." I hung up.

Right now, without waiting or talking myself out of it, I would tackle something on the list, though perhaps not while naked. Ah. I knew what to do. I pulled on clean Salt & Pepper chef whites, went into my bathroom and tamed my hair as best I could. Put on some mascara and blush and lip gloss. Got out the good camera, went into my always-immaculate kitchen.

Salt & Pepper's website had plenty of pictures of my food. It had none of me. I was afraid that people wouldn't trust an overweight chef (though most of us did seem to pack on the extra pounds, and no mystery as to why). But for the people who were looking for healthier alternatives . . . maybe they wouldn't want to see my chubby cheeks and figure.

But one of the items on the list was *Be in a photo shoot*.

Since *Glamour* wouldn't be calling anytime soon, this would have to do. I set the camera up in various places, set the timer, smiled and posed. I held a whisk in one hand, stood in front of the stove, leaned over a bowl of fruit. When I had about two dozen, I clicked through to see which one was best.

I didn't love any of them. *You're alive,* I reminded myself. Alive and mostly healthy other than the extra pounds. *You're a good, kind person.*

I uploaded the photo I disliked the least and added it to the "About Marley" section.

Score one for me.

On Friday, I'd make it a point to see Camden.

Then the games would really begin.

CHAPTER 5

Georgia

Eat dessert in public. (Failed.)

"Good morning, Miss Georgia!" said Khaleesi as she bounced into the classroom.

"Hello, angel," I said, mentally thinking, *Hello, mother of dragons, breaker of chains.* The names. Honestly. "How are you today?"

"I'm fine! Guess what? Mommy and Daddy take showers together. They say it's to save water."

"Isn't that nice," I said, biting down on a laugh. Kids really did say the darndest things. It was only the second week of school, and, as was the pattern, the kids were info-dumping on me.

"Does your mommy and daddy take showers together?" she asked, biting on the end of her hair.

I pushed her hair back and slid off her tiny backpack. *No, darling, they haven't spoken to each other in more than twenty years.* "I don't know. I don't live with them anymore, because I'm a grown-up."

Khaleesi's lower lip pushed out. "I'm gonna live with my mommy forever," she said.

"That sounds lovely," I answered. "Go sit in circle time, okay, honey?"

"Miss Georgia, I missed you!" said Grace Carver, one of the triplets in my class.

"I missed you, too, sweetheart."

Grace hugged my legs, and then her sister Rose came up and did the same thing. "I love you, Miss Georgia," she said fervently.

And people asked me why I left the law. For hugs, I said. For the sheer joy of going to work each day and being with four-year-olds.

The myth of teaching nursery school was that we just played with and/or ignored the children all day. At St. Luke's, at least, that wasn't the case. We developed spatial relationships and vocabulary, improved muscle tone, built social skills, taught the kids how to be part of a group, how to interact, how to be kind.

Four and a half years ago when I started here, I'd also gotten a pre-K teaching certification from the state. St. Luke's took pride in the education and dedication of their teachers. I came from Princeton and Yale, and since being hired here, I'd gotten an online master's in early childhood education from the University of North Carolina.

In other words, I was a full-fledged teacher, much to my mother's chagrin ("Why do you want to take care of other people's children, like some third-world nanny?") and my brother's disgust ("It figures you couldn't make it in the real world"). My father, stepmother and their two daughters, on the other hand, loved what I did.

"Crisscross, applesauce, hands on your lap!" I sang, and my fifteen little charges sat obediently, their faces looking up at me with delight and anticipation.

Just then, there was a knock at the door, and it opened to

reveal Mr. Trombley, the director of the preschool. "Miss, ah . . . Miss Slum? If you have a moment?"

Although he had hired me, the man had yet to learn my name. Miss Slum was definitely on the winner's list of misnomers, which included Miss Short, Miss Sly and Miss Stallion.

"Sure thing. Lissie, can you take over?" I asked, and my assistant, a lovely girl just out of college, stepped in to start our morning songs, which were all about being helpful and kind.

I followed the big boss down the hall. Mr. Trombley, though not a great lover of children, had nonetheless foreseen the booming need for preschools forty years ago. He had started St. Luke's Preschool for Exceptional Children way back then, tapping into Cambry-on-Hudson's love of status.

"We have a new student starting today." He lowered his voice. "A student of *color.*" A good third of the kids at St. Luke's weren't white, something Mr. Trombley still found shocking. "Acidoso? Avocado? I'm not clear on the name. The child will be in your class."

"Wonderful," I said. My class was small this year, only fifteen kids. Sixteen meant every kid would have a partner when we paired off.

He opened the door to his office and ushered me in. I jerked to a stop.

"Clara," I breathed. "Hi."

Her eyes widened. "Oh, my God! Georgia! Hello! How are you?"

My former sister-in-law got up to hug me.

Clara Santiago could not have a four-year-old. Could she? And my God, she was pregnant!

The poker burned into my stomach.

"You know each other?" Mr. Trombley said.

"Um . . . yes. We . . . we go way back," Clara said. "This is my little one, Silvi."

Remembering my job, I knelt down. Silvi was beautiful, with the same dark eyes as her mother.

And her uncle, Rafael.

"Hi, Silvi. I'm Miss Georgia, one of the teachers here. What's your favorite color?"

"Yellow," she said.

"Mine too!" I said, and she smiled. It worked every time. But my heart was thudding, and there was a buzzing noise that I was pretty sure was coming from my brain.

My ex-husband's niece was going to be my student. I hadn't seen him—or his family, obviously—in almost five years.

"We just moved up here," Clara said. She was six years younger than Rafe, which made her twenty-eight. "My husband took a transfer. He's a computer geek with TechRoots. We were in New Jersey, down near Vineland, but we wanted to be closer to Mom and Dad, and . . . well. Cambry is so pretty. Great schools."

So she was nervous, too.

"Mr. Trombley," I asked, "can we have a minute?"

He scowled—it was almost his naptime—but left. "Silvi, do you know how to write your name?" I handed her a piece of paper and a pen from Mr. Trombley's desk.

"Of course I do! I've been doing that since I was two!" She sparkled up at me, and I felt a rush of love. She was delightful.

"Would you mind writing it for me? As neatly as you can, okay?"

"Do you want my middle names, too? Because I can do everything."

"I do. That would be wonderful."

As she bent over the paper, I looked at Clara. "Will this

be okay?" I whispered. Did she want to check with Rafe? Did he hate me? Did the whole family? What had he told them? Had they always suspected we wouldn't last?

"Of course it's okay," Clara said, smiling. "I'm sure you're an amazing teacher."

The Santiago warmth and kindness was not limited to Rafael, of course. There was that poker again.

"Thank you," I said. "I'm really happy to see you. How's the family?"

"Everyone's great," she said. She patted her stomach. "Due in four months. Another girl. My parents are thrilled."

The thought of the elder Santiagos stabbed me. They'd always been so nice.

"I'm going to be a big sister," Silvi told me. "I want to name the baby Dandelion."

"That's a very pretty name," I said, and Clara smiled. "Your little sister will be so lucky to have you as her friend."

"I know," she said, smiling. You had to love the confidence of some kids.

"Silvi, are you four years old?"

"Mm-hm." She held up four fingers to confirm her answer.

"Excellent! I know a lot of people who are four," I said. "Do you want to meet some of them?"

"Can I come, too?" Clara asked.

"What do you think, Silvi?" I asked.

"Sure, Mommy!" she said, taking her mother's hand. She took mine in the other, and we left the office. Mr. Trombley was leaning against the wall, eyes closed. He jerked to attention.

"St. Luke's offers the very best preschool education available," he recited. "Please let me know if I can do anything at all to make your child's experience a rich and joyful time of learning." He was reciting from our mission statement. I knew, since I'd written it.

"I will, and thank you," Clara said. "It better be a joyful time of learning," she added in a low voice, "for what we're paying."

"It's not cheap," I agreed, and she grinned at me, little Silvi skipping between us.

I remembered Clara laughing on my wedding day. She'd caught the bouquet, which had made her boyfriend—God, now husband, that's right, Marco Acevedo—so happy.

Clara didn't mention Rafe now. Neither did I.

"Silvi, you're going to make lots of new friends here," I said as we came to my cheerful red door, which was covered in leaves with the kids' names on them.

"Let's hope that's true!" she said.

I couldn't help but laugh—she clearly had an excellent grasp of language. I opened the door, and fifteen little heads swiveled toward me. "Class," I said, "we have a new friend."

"Yay!" the kids cheered. In most cases, four was an age untouched by bullying or spoiling or misery. There were exceptions, of course, but four was rather golden. Rumor had it that even my brother was pretty cute at age four. Unfortunately, I hadn't been alive to witness it.

I introduced Silvi to everyone and asked Charlotte and Bertie to be her SuperFriends for the Day, crushing the hearts of all the other kids who loved that duty. The job consisted of paying special attention to a classmate who might be new or having a tough time for whatever reason. Everyone would get to be Silvi's SuperFriend by the end of next week. My class was a socialist nation, more or less.

Clara bent down and hugged her daughter. "I'll see you in a little while, honey," she said.

"Bye, Mama!" Silvi said as Bertie towed her away.

I stepped out with Clara, whose eyes were starting to get shiny. "She'll be fine," I said.

"Oh, I know. It's me I'm worried about."

I patted her arm. "You'll be fine, too."

"It's just . . . it's a big step."

If I were the hugging type, now would be the time. I patted her arm again. She brushed her tears away and took a deep breath. "Well. Thank you." She paused. "Rafael is doing fine, by the way."

The sound of his name hit me hard. I swallowed. "I didn't want to ask, in case . . . well, in case you wanted to keep things separate."

"Don't be silly. You were my sister-in-law," she said. "And Rafe loves Silvi. I imagine he'll come to see her here at least once."

"I'm sure he's a wonderful uncle."

"He is." Clara looked through the door window. "Well. I should go before I start sobbing for real."

"Save that for the car." This time, I did hug her, though it felt stiff and weird. "See you at two."

She nodded, tears slipping down her face. But she smiled and went off.

I sucked in a long breath. Let it out slowly.

Silvi would've been my *niece*. The thought was like a punch in the stomach. That sweet little girl, calling me Auntie, or G, the way Mason did.

And I'd be seeing my ex-husband again. *I should lose weight*, came the automatic response to anything important that loomed on the horizon.

The poker in my stomach twisted.

I opened the door and went back in to the kids.

....

One of the perks of teaching preschool—aside from the infinite love for and from the kiddies—was that it ended at two p.m. Most days, I met Mason around two fifteen, when high school let out, the time when he was least likely to be hounded by my brother.

Hunter and I had gone to prep schools. Hunter went to Trinity-Pawling, which was regrettably close to home, an all-boys school he had loved, the place where he'd become a savage athlete. I'd gone to Concord Academy, farther away in Massachusetts, and by then Hunter had been in college, so our paths didn't cross so much. Happy times.

At any rate, I'd hoped that Mason would thrive at boarding school the way many kids did. His elementary school had been private, the same one Hunter and I had gone to, and just about every single one of his classmates went off to prep school. The plan had been for Mason to go to Trinity-Pawling, too.

Then, at the end of April, Mason took eleven Tylenol PM tablets at once and . . . well. He didn't go to Trinity-Pawling. He did go to the ER. No liver damage.

He swore it was an accident, said he'd just had a very bad headache and wanted to get some sleep. Accident or not, Hunter had been scared enough to keep him home and even got him a counselor, though Hunter had resisted that at first. Counseling was for the weak, Hunter thought. The hospital wouldn't discharge his son without one, though, so Mason had a therapist, thank God. He was allowed to finish eighth grade from home, me tutoring him, to my brother's chagrin.

Now Mason was attending the very excellent public school, which irked Hunter, who'd wanted him at his alma mater. Even though I checked in with my nephew every day, I sometimes jolted awake at night, remembering the sight of him in the hospital bed, a tube up his nose, tears in his eyes. That's when the pain in my stomach started to get really bad and when I reverted, once again, to eating almost nothing.

Every fat girl starves herself at one point or another. It had never made me actually thin, not like those poor girls who look like skeletons and stop getting their periods. But at different times of my life, I had enacted their habits . . . just never long enough for any real drama. The point was control . . . and grief . . . and self-loathing; when they all got bundled up together, sometimes it was denying myself food rather than drowning myself in it that worked. And after April, after Mason's overdose, well, that was one of those times. Because on top of all the old wounds, I'd completely missed the fact that Mason was desperately unhappy.

Since that event, Mason remained relentlessly cheerful around me. But his nails were chewed to the quick, his posture meek, his clothes oversized. He'd always been a small, slight kid, but now it looked like he was trying to disappear, and God help me, I understood wanting to be invisible. He hadn't gone to public school before; he didn't know the kids in his class.

Like I had been, he was on the outside.

Hence, a list.

The truth was, I'd decided to do Emerson's list even before Marley said she was in. I'd promised Emerson I would, and I owed her that much. Also, maybe, just maybe, there was something valuable about revisiting those teenage dreams.

Mason was a teenager, and like I'd been back then, he wasn't exactly thriving, no matter how hard he smiled. A Google search told me 5.8 million articles said writing down goals was a step in the right direction.

Most days, my nephew and I met at my house after school so we could take Admiral for a walk. Today, Mason was already there, Admiral looking regal at his side. It was early September, and Cambry-on-Hudson was clinging to summer with shimmering blue skies and low humidity.

"Hi, honey!" I said, unable to stop the endearment.

But Mason wasn't a typical fourteen-year-old boy, and his face lit up at the sight of me. Admiral put his paws on my skirt and allowed me to pet his elegant face. I smooched Mason, and we started walking down the block toward the park.

"Greetings, good people of Cambry," said Leo, the piano teacher, as we passed his courtyard. He sat in a battered chair, a puppy at his side. I'd noticed Leo when I first moved in—he was ridiculously good-looking, so it was hard not to. But relationships were not my thing. Been there, done that, had those divorce papers.

"Hey, Leo. Hi, Thor," I said, letting Admiral stop to sniff Leo's adorable little puppy, who tried to bite Admiral's ear. My dog put a paw on Thor's head, gently ending that bit of mischief. "How are you?"

"Just fine. How you doing, Mason?"

"Great!" Mason said, picking at a shredded cuticle but beaming nonetheless, a smile that tried too hard. The boy could be standing in a puddle of his own blood, and his answer would always be the same.

"Taking your aunt out for some air, doing your Christian duty, I see," Leo said with a wink.

Mason's shoulders dropped an inch, and his smile grew more genuine. "I guess. Hey, Leo, am I . . . am I too old to take piano lessons?"

Mason's mother had played the piano. My throat tightened.

"Of course not," Leo said. "Give me a call. For Georgia's nephew, anything." He grinned at me.

"Okay. Maybe I will. Thanks!"

"You're very welcome."

Mason and I continued down the street.

"I didn't know you wanted to take piano lessons," I said.

"Well . . . maybe. Kind of. I don't think Dad would let me." He bit an already bloody cuticle, saw me looking and shoved his hands into his pockets.

"Maybe we can work something out," I said. Unfortunately, Mason was one of those overscheduled kids—therapy, tutoring in math and science (I'd been let go once Mason passed eighth grade), swimming at the Cambry-on-Hudson Lawn Club pool, CrossFit twice a week with Hunter. It would be tough to sneak in even an hour a week for a lesson, let alone practice time. Besides, Hunter didn't have a piano.

But I did.

There was an ice-cream truck parked on the street. "I'm starving," Mason said.

"Then let me buy you a cone."

Eat dessert in public.

I could have one, too. Mason went up to the window and ordered a SpongeBob-shaped ice-cream cone. "You want something, G?" he asked.

"Um . . . ah . . ." I looked at the side of the truck, where all sorts of hideous frozen dyed offerings were painted. I could get some soft serve. Just vanilla.

I glanced behind me. A fortysomething mother stood behind me with two kids, about eight and ten. She was slim and tall, her hair perfectly highlighted, wearing designer yoga gear, a heavy diamond band weighing down her slender hand. Everything I wasn't—skinny, married, a mother, secure.

"G? You want anything?"

"No, thanks, honey," I said.

Fail Number One.

Mason got his treat and ate it in about three bites as we

walked to the end of the field, and I tried not to think about ice cream, or how tiny that woman's ass was, or how she managed to keep so fit. Surgery? Lipo? Anorexia?

At the far end of the park was the baseball field, and we brought Admiral in so he could do what he was bred to do—run. He started off, sleek and low, a blur of gray fur and canine muscle, impossibly fast as he ran around and around and around. A few people stopped to look at him, asking questions about his breed. I let Mason answer; he was so good with adults.

Kids his own age, not so much. When Ad was finished and came over to us, panting, I clipped the leash on his collar.

"How was school today?" I asked as we walked. I knew from experience it was easier to talk if you didn't have to make eye contact.

"It was okay."

I waited.

"I wanted to sit with some other kids at lunch, but . . . they all know each other." He shrugged.

"So you ate alone again?"

"Yeah, but it was cool. I read." No wonder he'd been hungry. He probably hadn't eaten anything.

I glanced at his sweet face, still so boyish. His lips jerked in a smile meant to assure me, but instead it revealed the misery underneath. We reached a bench, and I sat down. Admiral jumped up as well, curling into his impossibly limber yoga position, almost a perfect circle, like a cinnamon roll. Mason sat down on my dog's other side, petting his head.

"Honey," I said, weighing my words carefully, "you know my friend who just died?"

"Emerson. Yeah." Of course he remembered. He was kind and thoughtful.

I cleared my throat. "Emerson left this list for Marley

and me," I said. "Sort of a . . . challenge list. Doing things that we want to do, but don't because they're, uh, outside the comfort zone."

"What kind of things?" he asked. He looked so much like his mom it hurt my heart. What she'd ever seen in Hunter . . .

"Well, it was a list we wrote when we first met at camp. When we were teenagers. Things like . . . well, little things. Tuck in a shirt, which is hard if you're fat."

"You're not fat."

"And you're very sweet."

"Seriously, G."

"Anyway. It's sort of like a"—I didn't want to say *bucket*—"list of things we wanted to accomplish or experience. Have a cute guy give you a piggyback ride, flirt with you. Stuff that felt impossible back then."

"Yeah. I could never flirt with a girl, that's for sure."

"Well, the thing is, maybe we could do the list together. Except your list could be stuff just for you, since obviously you don't want a stranger to flirt with you, because that would be creepy."

This earned a snort. "I'm fourteen, Georgia."

"Exactly. That's why your list would be different than mine."

He said nothing, but I could feel his mood sink. Admiral put his head on Mason's leg in sympathy.

"It would be easier to do if I had a partner in crime, so to speak," I said. "I mean, Marley's doing it, too, but she's super confident, you know? It's harder for me." Mason didn't look at me. "I know you're having a tough year, sweetheart," I added quietly. "And I've been exactly where you are. Sometimes you have to push yourself to make things better."

Mason just continued to sit silently, staring at the ground.

"Just little things," I said, covering his hand with mine. Ours were about the same size these days.

"What things would be on my list?" he finally asked.

"I don't know. What do you think?"

He shrugged.

"How about taking piano lessons?" I suggested.

"Like my father would ever let me. It was a dumb idea."

"But that's exactly the challenge. To stand up for yourself and do something that's a little bit hard." He said nothing. "I wish you saw yourself the way I see you, Mason."

"Right back at you, G."

"Touché."

Mason bit his ragged nail. "I don't know. I mean, Dad always talks about setting goals and stuff, too. Just not the kind of goals I want."

"Yes, that's the idea. These would be *your* goals, not his." I knew it was a tall order, to ask someone like Mason (and me) what would make them happy. When you spent so much time disappointing people, it wasn't a question you thought about much. "If you need help making your list, maybe we could do it together."

He looked at me, then down at the ground. "Maybe. Yeah."

"Want me to come for dinner one night this week?"

"That'd be great." Neither of us said it, but we both knew—Hunter was easier to take when allies were present. "Yeah, I could see the benefits of having some . . . whatever. Goals. Benchmarks. And not the kind Dad wants, which is basically world domination."

I glanced around, saw that none of his peers were around, and gave him a quick hug.

"I gotta go," he said. "Math tutor's coming."

"Okay," I said, standing up. "Think about some things. They don't have to be huge. Just . . . stepping-stones. Okay?"

"Okay," he said, and sure enough, there was a smile there. A real one.

"I love you," I said.

"You're gross." But he was still smiling when he handed me my dog's leash and walked across the park to Hunter's house.

I had lesson plans to work on, and some paperwork to file for one of the clients at FFE—a woman from the Bronx who wanted to start a farm-to-table nursery here in Cambry. Once she'd been a heroin addict; now she was an organic farmer. I loved the foundation, loved helping these women get a start at a new career, but at the moment, I still felt a little unsettled.

On impulse, I decided to visit my father. He was always good for the soul. I could do the paperwork on the train, and ask my dad to pony up some money for the foundation— he was excellent at writing checks—plus visit my half sisters and see my stepmom, all in one fell swoop.

Twenty minutes later, I was on the train, clacking along the mighty Hudson. I caught a glimpse of myself reflected in the window. I was surprised at how little room I took up.

Even on my wedding day, I'd wished I was thinner. That day when a woman was supposed to feel most beautiful, I felt a little ashamed. Guilty. I could've lost more weight.

Rafael's face flashed in my memory, the smile that took over his whole face, his bottomless eyes that could say a thousand words with one look. He'd been so happy that day.

Me, not so much.

Okay. I couldn't go there right now. If Rafael Santiago was going to pop back up in my life via Silvi, then he would, and I'd handle it and be polite and cordial and pleasant. All those things.

When the train pulled into Grand Central, I filed out with all the other people, like a school of fish, dividing to go out the respective exits. I passed Zabar's bakery, forbidding myself to look. They had the best pastries.

Not for me, though. Too many calories, too much butter, too much regret later on. Once upon a time, I hadn't been above sticking my finger down my throat. I didn't want to start down that path again, so the best thing would be to avoid a bakery at all costs.

My dad's place was only twenty or so blocks from Grand Central. I walked; I could use more exercise. And you know what else? I *was* going to lose the last bit of weight. I could do it. Emerson would want me to do it. The memory of her, helpless in that bed, wheezing, every part of her in some kind of distress . . .

I was so close to being thin. The possible ulcer, the stress over Mason's overdose . . . the reflection of myself in the train window, smaller than I'd been maybe ever . . . I pulled out my phone and called my mother.

"Hi, Mom," I said.

"Oh, Georgia, it's you," she answered, never a master of caller ID.

"Um . . . Mom, remember that spa you go to upstate? Hakuna Matata or something?"

"Sagrada Vida?"

Exactly what I said. "Sure. That one. I was thinking about . . ." I took a breath. "About going for a weekend."

"Really!" The joy in her voice was usually reserved for Bergdorf Goodman's annual shoe sale. "Really, Georgia? You're going to lose some weight? I'm absolutely *thrilled* for you."

Princeton. Yale. Law review. Another advanced degree. New career nurturing children. Helping women start businesses. But nothing excited my mother as much as the idea of me getting thinner. Despite having lost weight a hundred times in my life, it had never been enough for the super-thin Kathryn Ellerington Sloane, also known as (for unfathomable reasons) Big Kitty.

"I'll go, too!" she said. "I could use a little cold lipo. Maybe a teensy bit of Juvéderm."

Shit. "Um, okay. Marley will be coming, too. It's, uh, an early birthday present for her." Of course, Marley knew nothing about this, but I wasn't about to be alone at a weight-loss spa with my mother.

"I'll make the reservations. I'm a VIP member, and it's hard to get in, but they love me there. Georgia, you *have* to get the hydrovisconic. You think you have good bowel habits, but when you see—"

"I have to go. Thanks, Mother. Talk soon."

There it was, that moment when you sign away your soul to the devil. But I was almost there, and I'd been hoping to be *there* my entire life. As much as I fought it, I was just as obsessed with my weight as my mother was. So. I'd eat Marley's healthy dinners, and I could cut back a little at breakfast and lunch. It wasn't like I was hungry these days, anyway. Even less so since seeing Emerson die.

I put my phone in my purse and picked up my pace, matching the New Yorkers, burning a few more calories.

My father and stepmother lived in a large, funky apartment in Chelsea, right near the High Line. As I walked through into the sleek, sophisticated foyer, the doorman picked up the house phone. "It's the lovely Georgia to see you, Mr. Sloane," he said, and over the receiver, I could hear my father's happy yelp.

Two minutes later, I was being hugged by Dear Old Dad, swarmed by my half sisters, and offered a glass of wine by my stepmother.

Dad's new family was everything ours hadn't been, and his guilt over that made him a better father to me. I'd take it. After all, I'd pretty much forgiven him for ditching me when he left my mother.

My parents had divorced when I was eleven. For a long time, my father was Sad Dad, idling outside our house on Tuesday nights and every other Friday, waiting for me. Hunter was already away at school, so the remaining three years before I went to Concord Academy featured just me and Mom, the dreaded visits from Hunter, and our cold, sterile house.

Back then, I hated my father for leaving me with Mom and Hunter, loved him fiercely because he never mentioned that I was fat, resented him because he didn't have the power to make me skinny. But with a mother who was obsessed with my weight, and a brother who didn't miss a single chance to tell me I was fat, it was a relief to be with someone who never talked about it. And he did send me to Camp Copperbrook every summer. What else was he going to do? Give me a gastric bypass for my twelfth birthday?

Once, I asked my father why I couldn't live with him. He teared up and mumbled something about how he wanted that, too, but yada yada whatever. I stayed with Mom of the jutting hip bones and skeletal sternum, the critical eye and the disappointed sigh.

When I was twenty-two, Dad married Cherish, an exotic dancer, then twenty-five. Another skinny woman, something Marley and I discussed at length. Dad, who loved his fat daughter, had married two extremely beautiful, extremely lean women.

But Cherish was fantastic. I mean, it was weird having a stepmother who was as lithe as mine was, not to mention so frickin' young. Still, I got it. She was warm and funny and open. She adored my dad; they laughed all the time, she flirted with him, held his hand and didn't go crazy spending his money (though, yes, her engagement ring was a sight to behold—three carats, Cartier, so big it looked fake).

They had two daughters, my half sisters: Paris and Milan (Dad had a thing about geographical names, apparently), ages nine and five. I was their godmother in addition to their sister.

Obviously, Dad was my favorite parent.

"Read me a book!" Paris demanded now, twining her arm around my leg. "Junie B. Jones. She's funny!"

"You look so pretty," Milan said. "Mama, can I get hair like Georgia? I hate curly hair!"

"And I love curly hair!" I said. "We should trade."

"Play with me, play with me," Milan chanted.

"Girls, let Georgia sit down for a minute," Cherish said. "She's been working hard all day. Sweetheart, you're going to stay for dinner, of course, aren't you? Spend the night! There are clean sheets on your bed." I had a room here, wooden letters spelling my name over the door, just like Paris and Milan had, and a soft little giraffe on the queen-sized bed.

"Stay! Sleep over!" my sisters demanded.

"I'll stay for dinner," I said. "I should've texted. I'm sorry."

"You don't need to text," Dad said. "This is your home, too."

"Well. Thank you."

I braided Milan's hair, read to Paris, told Dad and Cherish funny tales from preschool—Axel burying himself in the stuffed animals, Primrose stating on her "getting to know you" worksheet that her mommy was a doctor and her daddy drank wine for a living.

Sitting at the counter as Cherish cooked and the girls

played with my dad, I was bathed in the warm glow of their happiness. Cherish liberally added hot pepper and jalape-ños, since it was Taco Night. I wouldn't be eating much of that dish, not with Mr. Ulcer waiting. Good. Another few calories sacrificed to the skinny gods.

"Guess who I saw the other day?" she said, smiling as she chopped onions.

"Tom Hiddleston? And you told him about me, and he wants to marry me and father my children?"

She wiped away her onion-induced tears with the back of her hand and took a sip of wine. "Not quite, but the guy I saw was still pretty cute." She glanced around to make sure my father and the girls were occupied. "A certain ex-husband of yours. Rafael Santiago." She let the syllables roll off her tongue with the appropriate accent. "Me and my friend Willow? We went to his place."

"Where is your family loyalty?" I asked, feigning calm (and trying not to correct her grammar).

But seriously. Two mentions of Rafe in one day was too much for my fragile, girlish heart. The lava in my stomach seemed to harden into volcanic rock, heavy and black.

"We had just gone to the natural history museum, you know?"

"Georgia, we saw dinosaurs!" Milan yelled from the living room, where my dad was rolling around with them.

"Really!" I said. "That's so cool!"

"Stegosauruseses," she said.

"Yeah," Cherish continued. "And we came back here, and Joe, your daddy, that is, he'd come home early, and he said he'd watch all four kids, so me and Willow should go out for a nice dinner after chasing the little demons around the museum all day."

I didn't remember my dad *ever* coming home early when

I was little. But I could see why he'd want to with this family. "Go on." My heart was pounding.

"So we went down to Tribeca, and the restaurant, it's called—what's the place where the bulls run?"

"Pamplona."

"Right. God, you're so smart. You should try out for *Jeopardy!*, you would slay. Anyway, I didn't know it was his place till I saw the menu, and at the bottom it says, Rafael Santiago, executive chef and owner. So I say to Willow, 'Hey, my ex-stepson-in-law owns this place! We gotta ditch.'"

New York was a small town of eight million. This kind of thing happened all the time. "Hmm," I said.

"The thing is," Cherish went on, waving the knife in the air to punctuate her words, "we'd already ordered drinks, right? So we're waiting for the server so we can get the check, okay, because really, Georgia, I do have your back, but then the girl brings over these complimentary tapas."

"I love tapas!" Paris said. "Can we have tapas, Mommy?"

"Maybe tomorrow, honeybun." She lowered her voice again. "And then all of a sudden, there he is, handsome as ever, and he remembered me."

He would remember her. He remembered everyone he ever met.

After her waterfall of words, Cherish was quiet a minute, adding the onions to the ground beef. "He looks good," she said. "He told us to come back anytime, and he sent you his regards."

I nodded. Fake-smiled. Took a sip of wine and felt it hit the sore spot in my stomach. I could just about hear the words in his slight accent—*Please send Georgia my regards*. Everything he said sounded beautiful. His father was from Spain, his mother from the Dominican Republic, and they'd moved here when he was fourteen. His younger sisters didn't have the same accent; they sounded like Staten Islanders.

For Rafe, English had been a second language, but he spoke it better than most Americans, his phrases always slightly formal, his words sounding more important, more beautiful because of . . . well. Because he was himself.

"You should stop by," Cherish said, patting my hand. "Say hi to him."

"I won't," I said.

She patted my hand more firmly. "You never know."

We moved to the table, held hands while Dad said grace (something that had never happened when he lived with us), and they ate and I pretended to. The girls chattered like a pair of happy starlings, and Dad's love for his family shone from his eyes. Cherish couldn't pass him without touching him, stroking his neck, a kiss on the head.

"I'm so happy you're here," Dad said, squeezing my hand.

"Me too, me too! So are we!" the girls said, and I felt that familiar happy sorrow I always felt here. Glad for this family, sad to be on its fringes. I was grateful that at least there was a place for me here, even if my stepmother had been a stripper and my father was twice her age. Even if it hadn't happened until I was twenty-three, it felt nice to be part of a family.

After supper and bath time, the girls demanded that I tuck them in, which I did, singing to them in my off-key voice, kissing their foreheads, noses, cheeks. Cherish again invited me to spend the night—she really was the best stepmother. But I said no. "I have an early morning meeting," I said. "By the way, Dad, the FFE could use another check."

"What's that stand for again?" Cherish asked.

"The Foundation for Female Entrepreneurship," I said.

"One of these days, Joe, I'm gonna start a business, too," she said. "I just don't know what yet."

"Whatever you'll do will be fantastic," my dad said.

"Agreed." I smiled.

Dad got out his checkbook. "What's the business this time?"

"Farm-to-table garden."

"Nice." He wrote a check to the foundation, added an extra zero and gave it to me. Guilt money, I suspected, over leaving me with Mom all those years ago. But it was for a good cause. He gave me a long hug. "I'm so glad you came. I always love seeing my little girl."

I hugged him back tightly. "Same here, Daddy. Hey, by the way . . . Mason could use a little time with you."

"I left two messages with Hunter," he said. The Sad Dad expression came over his handsome face.

"Keep trying. Mason gets out at two fifteen if you wanted to just pop up some weekday. He usually comes to my house right after school to walk Admiral."

"I'll do that." He stuck his hands in his pockets. "Want me to call the car service? They could drive you right home."

"No, thanks. The train will be faster."

My father was wealthy. Both my parents were from money, as we Yankees like to say (or not say). Mom had never tried to get a job, despite her degree from Bryn Mawr. "Darling, I don't *need* to work," she'd say. Dad did something on Wall Street in the mysterious world of finance, made a ridiculous salary and obscene bonuses, and my Christmas and birthday presents were always fat checks.

Cherish kissed me good-bye. "Pamplona. Don't forget. You and Marley, you guys could just innocently drop by. I'm just sayin'."

I half smiled, half sighed. "Good night, Cherish. Bye, Dad."

There were hardly any other passengers on the ride back to Cambry-on-Hudson. Rocked by the erratic rhythm of the train, I leaned my head against the window and tried not to think about Rafael Santiago, my ex-husband, the man who thought he knew me, the man who was the love of my life.

The man whose last words to me had been, "Get out."

CHAPTER 6

Dear Other Emerson,

Today is the first day of the rest of my life. I'm really, really excited. One day at a time. One meal at a time. This time will be different! There's good, healthy food out there, and I will eat it and only it, except for the very occasional and small indulgence. And I will enjoy it. I mean, a good salad is absolutely delicious, right?

Immediately, I picture a hot fudge sundae with really dense whipped cream, and salted almonds and dark, dark liquid fudge. The cold, creamy ice cream sliding down my throat. Not just once, but again and again and again. In public, in a cute little ice cream parlor where I fit into the chairs, and where people smile at me and say, "Oh, doesn't that look good! I'll have what she's having."

I have never had dessert in public. The disapproval, the disgust, the hatred over seeing a fat person eating just for fun.

I'm so hungry.

But, not gonna go there! I cleaned out my fridge yesterday, and filled it up with lettuce and kale, veggies and cottage cheese and chicken breasts.

I want a cheeseburger. Hot and rare, pink inside, juices running, the snap of red onion packing just enough bite.

I'm well aware that my food cravings sound like porn.

Two years ago, my mom died of fast-moving colon cancer. She didn't even try chemo. It was too far advanced. The doctor said her weight played a role. Like skinny people didn't get cancer. My dad was skinny. Died of a heart attack at age fifty-two.

I don't want to die before my life really starts. I have to give myself a chance. I'm only twenty-nine years old.

My knees hurt. They should. I weigh 372 pounds. If I lost half my body weight, I'd still be considered obese.

How do you climb Everest? One step at a time, bitches. I give the middle finger to my fridge, guzzle some water, eat three carrots and pull on my sneakers, struggling to reach my feet. That alone makes me breathless, but it's okay. Time to go outside and start my new life.

I bet you run, Other Emerson. I can picture it so clearly—you look awesome in those tight designer workout clothes, your ponytail swings, and your strides are long and loose and easy. I can be like you, Other Emerson. I will be. I'm starting today.

I do this from time to time. Start a new life. Clean out the fridge. Lose weight. Gain it back. But this time, it's going to stick.

I inherited my mother's house and all the money she got from Grampy when she died. Before that, I lived in an apartment nearby. Once, I imagined that Georgia and Marley and I would share a place in Manhattan, like Rachel, Phoebe and Monica on <u>Friends</u>. But I live in Delaware, and they live in New York. Not in the city, but close to it, which is pretty cool. And they aren't as bad as I am. They're normal-fat. Me, I'm about three times what I should be.

Anyway. I love my house. I moved in when Mama's cancer was diagnosed, and I've never left. I redecorated a little after she died, trying to distract myself from that howling, bottomless grief. I took off the wallpaper, painted in fresh springtime colors, trying to make it mine, so I wasn't just another fat person who lived in her parents' house. The living room has pale blue walls, and there are plants in the sunny kitchen. My grandmother's old enamel-topped table is where I sit every day, eating off sturdy Fiestaware. Georgia and Marley visited me just after that, and they thought it was great.

I do, too. I just wish no one knew me. I wish I'd moved here as a stranger. I think that might've been easier. Instead, Mrs. Eckhart, who once told me I didn't need Halloween candy (I was six), always stares at me as I lug in groceries, mentally assessing what I've got in my bags. (I double-bag the Coke and ice cream and anything else I don't want her to see.) Billy Patterson, one of the kids I used to babysit, ignores me. When he was six, he told me I was his best friend. Now, ten years later, he stares through me, afraid that one of his friends might realize he knows the fat freak.

I loved babysitting. I wish I could still do it. Kids liked me because I actually spent time with them and didn't just talk on the phone. Parents loved me, too, because I was so responsible. Sometimes they'd leave me pizza money or brownies. Sometimes carrot and celery sticks. Hint, hint.

Some of the happiest days of my life were babysitting, before the kids realized that fat was something to be disgusted by, to make fun of. Before they learned to be afraid that they'd turn out like me. I mean, maybe I'm projecting, Other Emerson, but I remember the cuddles Billy would give me, how he'd beg me to read another book. Once, he told me he was scared a skeleton lived in the toilet tank, and he was so grateful when I took off the top and showed him there was nothing there.

I miss being loved. I miss my parents so much, especially my mom. We were best friends. Those nights where we'd get in our pajamas and bust out the treats and watch TV . . . those were the best.

I can't think about that stuff, though. It'll make me too sad, and when I'm sad, I eat. Today is a new day. New day. New day. That's my mantra.

Outside, it's beautiful. Springtime in Delaware, cherry and crab apple blossoms so dreamy and soft, birds twittering, a dog barking down the street. I start walking briskly (ish) down the sidewalk. I don't have a sports bra in my current size — most stores don't carry my size, and Amazon was out of stock. You, Other Emerson, can probably shop anywhere. Anyway, I'm bouncing and wobbling, despite the two tight T-shirts I wore. My thighs are slip-sliding past each other because of the nylon shorts. (Don't worry, I'm wearing a superlong T-shirt to hide as much of myself as possible.) My back fat is jiggling, and my arms chafe against my sides.

Sometimes I see girls running in their sports bras and tiny pairs of shorts, their stomachs flat, their breasts high and snug, and it's like they're another species.

Look at this! I'm already down the block! This is kind of great, really, being outside. Walking is fun, aching knees aside. Mr. Duncan is cutting his grass. I wave. He waves back. He doesn't even hate me. There's the eyesore house, as Mama used to call it — it was vacant until recently. The roof needs repairs, the house needs painting, and at least three windows are cracked. But someone put a little pot of flowers on the porch. Maybe it's a nice family. Or a single guy. You never know.

I might garden this year. Last year, I was too depressed, but that would be great exercise, digging and planting and communing with nature and all that. I imagine my new neighbor stopping by — he's fixing up the eyesore, and he'll say what a beautiful garden I have. "Pretty girl, pretty house." I'll hand him some fresh herbs or a flower and flirt right back, and we'll get married a year later. We'll have children, and I'll cuddle them so much. My husband, too. We'll fall asleep entwined together. I won't need the CPAP anymore.

I can smell garlic, and my stomach rumbles. What I wouldn't give for a giant bowl of pasta with butter and garlic and Parmesan cheese! My favorite meal! Well, one of them. I can't be unfair to eggplant Parm. Or fried chicken. Or peanut butter and Fluff, which Mama used to make me when I couldn't sleep. A couple of weeks ago, I made three of those sandwiches as a bedtime snack. On white bread, too, which is basically poison.

Two blocks now. Sweat is streaming down my back, but hey, that's the point. Heart rate up, and I'm still going. I want to be healthy. I want to be normal.

I can do this.

When I get to the third block, I'll turn around and head back. I probably burned a thousand calories. Hefting this weight around is not easy.

"Watch out, piggy." A kid zooms past on a bike. He's maybe ten, already a snot. "You're gross," he calls over his shoulder.

"Your parents regret having you," I yell back.

He laughs. It _was_ kind of funny. And I'm so used to being mocked that it doesn't really matter.

Besides, when I lose weight, I won't have to put up with it anymore.

I can do this. Slow and steady wins the race. I walk another block before turning around, just to show I can. Eight blocks, all in all, four blocks up the street, four blocks back. That is a very respectable workout. My knees are burning with pain, my back feels like someone hit me with a baseball bat, my left foot throbs, and I could probably start a fire from the friction between my thighs. I'm officially drenched in sweat, but it's all good.

I want to be normal. I just want to be normal.

CHAPTER 7

Marley

Eat dessert in public. *(Nailed it yet again.)*

"Thank you for seeing us," Mom said, clenching my hand in a death grip. Hers was shaking. "We're so excited. This is Marley, my daughter, short for Marlena, she's the sister, you see. The twin who didn't die."

Maybe I'll get that phrase on a T-shirt. Kind of like The Boy Who Lived, but slightly more pathetic.

"Hi," I said to the psychic. She was a fake; I had experience in this. Way too much experience. "Nice to meet you."

"I'm Deirdre. You're not a believer. It's fine," she said. "Come in, come in."

Deirdre's living room was decorated all in purple. There was a purple wall hanging depicting a Hindu goddess with four hands, a purple neon crucifix, a statue of a purple Buddha in one corner, and a poster of Prince from *Purple Rain* over the fireplace.

"You come highly recommended," Mom said. "My friend Judy? Her cousin? Their daughter came to you. Ellen. Do you remember her?" Mom clenched my hand even harder, grinding the bones together in her desperate, sad excitement. "Do you know the Long Island Medium? On

TV? She's so talented, isn't she? Such a gift! A blessing to families who . . ." Mom's voice choked off, and I patted her arm.

"Let's set the mood," Deirdre said. She lit some incense, which immediately began to tickle the back of my throat. Mom and I sank into the soft purple couch as if swallowed. "Someone is coming through. A child."

"It's Frankie!" Mom blurted. "My baby!"

"Yes . . . Frankie. A little boy."

"Girl," I corrected.

"Yes, a girl, I see that now." I suppressed a sigh. "A girl. Very pretty."

"She was," Mom said. "She was beautiful. Frankie was short for Francesca."

"Frankie has a special connection to you both," Deirdre said.

"No kidding," I said. My mother had already told this fraud everything she'd need to bilk my parents for a couple hundred bucks. Daughter, twin, dead.

"She wants you to know she didn't suffer," Deirdre said.

That may or may not have been true. I was too young to know. Eva, my older sister, didn't talk about Frankie, and Dante had been born three years after her death.

Mom was weeping into one of Dad's handkerchiefs. I rubbed her back. She glanced at me with wet, grateful eyes.

This was our thing, Mom and me. Our mother/daughter/dead daughter thing. Forgive the black humor. Trying to contact my dead four-year-old twin once a month was wearing. Maybe on Frankie, too. *Sorry to yank you out of heaven, sis,* I thought. *Hope you're okay.*

"She's showing me an 'M,'" Deirdre said. "Whose name starts with an 'M'?"

"Mine does, as I believe you were just told," I said. "Also, 'M' could be for 'Mom.' Just tossing that out there."

Deirdre cut me a look and droned on, giving vague messages about love and not our fault and happiness and watching over. All good, don't get me wrong.

When I thought of my sister, there was nothing *real*, no clear memories. Just the shrine in my parents' living room—three corner shelves made by my father, which held eleven pictures of Frankie, the bracelet she had as a newborn, the bracelet she'd worn during her last trip to the hospital, a lock of her hair tied in a pink ribbon and framed, and Ebbers, the penguin stuffed animal she'd slept with every night. Four white votive candles, one for every year of her life.

I didn't so much remember Frankie as I envisioned my mother's memories of her. Any scrap of memory I had myself had long been drowned by Mom's reminiscing, each retelling of a Frankie story wearing down my own recollections bit by bit, till all I had left was as flat and faded as the photos.

I'd been nine pounds, fourteen ounces at birth. Francesca was four pounds, three ounces. She never really recovered from our time in utero, where it seems my food issues began. Pictures showed a slight, pale child, the only one of us to have the Northern Italian genes from Dad's side. She was blond and blue-eyed; Dante, Eva and I all had curly dark hair and brown eyes. Sometimes I envied Dante. He never knew Frankie. He never lost her.

"She was a sweet, *sweet* child," Deirdre said.

"She was," Mom whispered. I nodded for her sake.

Family lore said that Frankie was my opposite in everything. She never cried; I had tantrums. She was tired all the time; I was affectionately called the Tornado. She had trouble eating—dairy, peanuts, gluten were all life-threatening. Even with my mom's obsessive attention to feeding her, she just didn't like food, something my mother still puzzled over. How could a person not like food? Any food? *Look at Marley. She eats everything not nailed to the floor!* Once, the stories went, I'd even eaten an entire stick of butter.

Apparently, I slept with Frankie from the day I was old enough to crawl out of my crib and into hers. Mom was terrified I'd roll on top of her and smother her. After all, I was the Henry VIII of toddlers, tall for my age, heavy for my size, bursting with energy. Frankie's diagnosis was mysteriously called failure to thrive.

Clearly, she got the shantytown side of the womb. No one ever guessed we were twins.

Then one day, Mom took Frankie to the doctor's office, then to the hospital. Three days later, our parents sat Eva and me down and, barely able to speak the words, told us Frankie was in heaven. Seven-year-old Eva didn't come out of her room for a week.

I got my pillow and started putting it next to me where my sister had been. That was the only real memory I had, carved into my heart when my father understood what I was doing and, sobbing and heartbroken, took the pillow away.

"Can she tell me what heaven's like?" Mom asked, jerking me back into the present.

"She says it's very beautiful. So much light. Like nothing we've ever seen," Deirdre answered in something of a monotone. "You'll all be together again."

"How soon?" Mom asked. "Can she tell me?" Twenty years ago, my mom found a lump in her breast that turned out to be a cyst, but being the good Catholic she was, she had believed it was a sign that her death was imminent. Still did.

"She doesn't say," Deirdre said. "But she says time is different there."

"Okay. I think that covers everything," I said. "Any other platitudes, Deirdre?"

"She's fine, not in any pain," she said. "And she loves you very much."

That broke my mom. She buried her face in her hands, sobbing, and I suppressed the urge to kick Deirdre. "I'm sorry," Mom said. "My husband and I, we've been so blessed. Three healthy children, we know we're lucky. It's just . . ."

"You can cry, Mommy," I said. "It's okay. We understand."

With that, I helped my mom up and guided her out to the car.

Next stop was the cemetery, which we visited at least once a month.

Frankie's gravestone was made of white marble. When she had died, Mom and Dad bought the plots on either side of her, for themselves. The statue of a little girl angel was carved into the headstone. When I was little, I thought it was a fairy, which made me happy. Frankie had been a little fairy child herself, pale skin and big eyes, thin and delicate.

There was a bouquet of apricot-colored roses. "Oh, how nice," Mom said, kneeling to examine them. "These must be from Dante. He's such a good boy."

"Yes, he is," I said. "Perfect in every way."

"All three of you are. Frankie was, too." Her voice was thick with tears. She brushed a few blades of grass off the base of the headstone. "We're here, honey. Praying for you."

I never got that, despite twelve years of Catholic school. I mean, Frankie was in heaven. She didn't need our prayers—she was already enjoying the afterlife. I used to picture heaven as a place where you got to do whatever you wanted . . . a divine amusement park, more or less, where you could fly, swim with dolphins, visit other planets and have soft-serve ice cream with rainbow shots every day.

My mother's hair, black and curly like mine, had more and more gray these days. I put my hand on her shoulder and gave it a squeeze. I envied her the memories she had of my little twin. All I had was the lack of her. The Frankie-shaped space that the pillow hadn't been able to replace.

"You want to have lunch?" I asked.

"Sure. Let's stop by the diner, get a little cheesecake. I could eat."

We could always eat. "Sure, Mommy," I said. We'd sit and eat way too many calories apiece, and Mom would tell me stories of my sister I'd heard a hundred times before. "I'd love to."

CHAPTER 8

Georgia

Tell off the people who judged you when you were fat.
(I don't really see that happening. Ever.)

On Thursday I donned my mental armor and went to my
brother's house for dinner. I'd had to enlist my mother's
help, because if I'd just called Hunter and said, "Hey, can I
come for dinner one night?" the answer would've been no,
didn't I know how busy he was, he was an engineer, not
some dumb nursery school teacher who got to play with
stuffed animals all day long.

But Big Kitty and Evil Brother had an unholy alliance,
the same one that allowed her to look the other way when he
tormented me as a kid. Hunter was her precious firstborn—
the child she wanted, unlike me, the child of perimeno-
pause. He was good-looking, fit and athletic; I was not. She
could take him to the Cambry-on-Hudson Lawn Club and
show him off; once, when we were going to an Easter
brunch there and I was about twelve, I remember her tugging the zipper of the too-small dress she insisted I wear,
saying, "What will people say when they see I have a fat
daughter?"

At any rate, I'd called her, made some noises about how

I was thinking about inviting everyone to dinner—her, Mason, Hunter, Dad, Cherish and the girls—and she played right into my hands.

"Let me talk to Hunter." An hour later, my brother texted me a warm and lovely invitation.

Mom said you want to come for dinner Thursday. Be here at 5 and pick Mom up first. Don't even think about asking Dad and his new family, because I'll slam the door in their fucking faces.

He could always work writing greeting cards if the chemical engineering didn't work out.

Hunter was seven years older than I was. We had never been close. We rarely played together, and if we did, it could turn ugly in an instant. One time, for example, we were at our grandparents' summer place in the Adirondacks—a beautiful old cottage on a lake where we'd spend every July before summer camps were part of our lives. Hunter and I were standing on the dock fishing, and it had been lovely, really; me about five, him twelve. We stood there in the shade of an old maple that overhung the lake, catching nothing, saying little.

Then, to my surprise, he cast his line and handed me the pole. "Turn the reel, nice and slow," he said, and I did, thrilled that my big brother was teaching me something.

Then the line hummed and pulled. "I caught something!" I exclaimed. A fish leaped out of the water, and it was *big*, at least to my five-year-old self.

"Give it to me!" Hunter snapped, grabbing the pole from my hands. He yanked upward, and the line broke. The fish splashed away. Also lost was the shiny lure Hunter had been using.

"You're so stupid!" he said, shoving me so hard I fell in the water.

I climbed back onto the dock, sputtering and upset, and managed to get a huge splinter in my palm. "I fell," I said when the grown-ups asked me what happened. I knew better than to say that Hunter pushed me.

"Hunter, you were supposed to be watching her," Dad said. My mother defended her boy; I don't remember the words, but I remember knowing I'd somehow made everyone unhappy.

My brother didn't speak to me for the rest of that trip. The memory of standing with my brother, having him offer me the pole so I could fish, too . . . that just made his cruelty worse.

As we got older (and I got fatter), he didn't introduce me to his friends. The few pictures we had of the two of us together showed him stiff and unsmiling, looking away from the camera or glaring right at it. I always looked nervous. I learned early on to give him a wide berth and thanked God when he went to boarding school.

It wasn't just me. Life irritated the hell out of my brother. He'd glare at people in the library, yell at our parents or me, slam doors so hard the house shook, break a glass when Dad dared to ground him. God forbid I had to go anywhere with him in the car; he was the epitome of road rage. When Dad moved out three years before I started at Concord Academy, Hunter broke all the windows in his bedroom and punched holes in the walls, which was blamed on my father's desertion, even though Hunter was eighteen at the time.

Our mother excused his behavior every time. "He's a hothead," she'd sigh, almost fondly. "My father was the same way. He has a good heart, though."

I never saw that heart, not until he brought Leah home. I was sixteen. With her, he was a different person—solicitous,

charming, smiling, even a little bit nice to me, or at least not
hostile. It made me feel off-balance. Instead of making fun
of me for being fat, he asked me how I was doing at school,
almost like he was trying to trick me.

Leah had been kind and beautiful (and so slender!).
When they got engaged, she insisted that we go out for
nachos, just us two. "I don't have a sister, either," she said.
"I was so happy when Hunter told me he had one."

"Mm," I said, wondering why she was being nice. After
all, if Hunter had given her his version of me, the fat, lazy,
stupid, boring, useless little sister . . .

"I know you two aren't close," she said, almost reading
my mind. "I hope that will change."

"Well . . . uh, Hunter was . . . tough to have as a brother."

"You mean his temper?" She smiled. "I know. We're
working on that."

His temper, I learned in my Psych 101 class at Princeton, was probably intermittent explosive disorder, which
consisted of rage, irritability, tirades, shouting and sometimes violence. But God forbid that he actually be diagnosed with anything that needed treatment. By then, I
knew better than to bring it up to my mother, but I worried
about Leah. A lot.

To his credit, Hunter seemed like a good husband. And
at first, he seemed like a good father, even. Then, when
Mason was about seven, Leah was diagnosed with stage IV
lung cancer; she who had never smoked and grew up in a
household where no one else smoked, either. For nineteen
agonizing months, she died in inches.

On my last visit to her, the day before she died, I promised her I'd look out for Mason, who was already my brother's opposite in every way.

My nephew was kind, sweet, shy and generous. Like his
mother. After Leah died, he became horribly anxious, all

too aware that his father wanted him to be aggressive, taller, stronger, more athletic, more talkative. Without Leah there to balance Hunter, every comment my brother made went unchallenged, unfiltered. Mason's nails were chewed bloody, which offended my brother, and he had this habit of tugging his hair when he was nervous. It broke my heart to see him fake-smiling almost constantly, an ineffective shield to Hunter's constant orders to *sit up straight, join the conversation, don't just sit there like a lump, man up.*

Big Kitty said it was good that Hunter was "strict." My father . . . well, Hunter had never forgiven him for the divorce. Sometimes I was able to get Mason down to the city to see my dad and Cherish and the girls, but not very often. Leah's parents came out from California twice a year, and they Skyped, but it wasn't enough. April's event had shown us that.

My mom loved Mason, one hoped, but in a more theoretical way. More, perhaps, because Mason was Hunter's son rather than because he was his wonderful self. She wasn't the type to babysit or take him to see a show, but she'd kiss him, tolerate a few minutes of him talking about *Lord of the Rings* or *Guardians of the Galaxy*, then shoo him away so she and Hunter could talk. She rarely saw him alone, only with my brother. Hunter didn't let Mason out of his clutches too often. Especially since the overdose.

So this dinner . . . I was grateful, even if it wouldn't be like eating with Marley's family, where everyone was kissed at least six times. I'd counted.

"Isn't this nice!" Mom said as we walked up the steps to Hunter's impressive house. It was where he and Leah had lived after their marriage, a lovely Victorian on the other side of the park where Mason and I took Admiral almost every day. "My entire family, together for a meal." As always, her eyes dropped to my torso to assess whether or not I deserved food.

"Hi, Ma," Hunter said, kissing her cheek. His eyes cut to me. "George."

His nickname for me, just in case I ever felt pretty and feminine. "Thanks for having us," I said, handing him a bottle of wine. He was a collector. He looked at it, rolled his eyes and set it on the counter. Since I knew nothing I chose would ever be good enough, I took great pleasure in buying the shittiest wine I could find. This particular vintage had cost me $4.99 and was made in Florida. It had taken me forty-five minutes in the very nice wine shop to find a bottle that bad, and I didn't regret a single second.

"Where's Mason?" I asked.

Hunter and Mom were already talking and thus ignored me. There'd been some *idiot* at Hunter's job who'd *dared* to disagree with him, and Mom was clucking and murmuring her sympathy and amazement that her son hadn't already been anointed their king. Since I was here to help Mason with his list, I was glad they were engrossed.

I went into the living room. It always surprised me that Hunter's house was comfortable and welcoming. Then again, Leah had been the one to furnish it back in the happier days, so it made sense. There were leather couches and lovely paintings, dark wood floors and, along the western wall, floor-to-ceiling bookcases, unfortunately filled mostly with tomes on running.

But here was her worn collection of the Old Mother West Wind books, which I'd read as a child myself and loved. *Little Women* and *Anne of Green Gables. The Dark-Thirty* by Patricia McKissack, which Leah had loaned me once and which had scared the bejesus out of me.

There were also about a dozen pictures of her—alone, with Hunter, with Mason, the three of them together.

If Hunter hadn't been such a shit . . . if he wasn't so obsessed with creating Mason in his own image . . . if he hadn't treated Mason's overdose like a weakness instead of a cry for help, maybe I'd have felt sorry for him, widowed at thirty-five, left alone to raise a child.

I stared at a picture of Leah pushing Mason on the swing out back. Both of them were laughing in the photo.

Dear, sweet Leah. I wished it had been Hunter who died instead, but those things never work out, do they?

"Hey," came my nephew's soft voice. "That's a nice one, isn't it?"

"It sure is." He came over, and I put my arm around him. "I remember this one time when she brought you to Yale to see me," I said. "You weren't even one, and we went through Sterling library, and you discovered the echo. You'd yell, then laugh and laugh, and she and I started laughing, too, and some snotty professor gave us the stink-eye. And your mom said, 'Mister, if you have a problem with a baby laughing, your priorities are seriously messed up.'" Except she'd said *fucked-up*, right there in the hallowed Ivy League temple, and the professor had been scandalized. "And guess who was my professor next semester?"

"Oh, man, really?"

"Yep. I didn't care. She was right. You were so stinking cute." I gave him a squeeze. "Still are."

"Gross, G."

"And yet true." I cocked an ear to the kitchen, where from the sounds of it, Hunter was making our mother a martini. "Want to work on the list?" I asked.

"Yeah, okay. I guess." He paused. "Don't tell my dad about this, okay? You know how it is. He'll take over and fill it up with stuff I can't do."

"Sure. Our secret."

We went into the den, which was smaller and where we'd be less likely to be overheard.

"I haven't come up with anything yet," he said. "Maybe

try to gain some weight." He blushed. "I wish I was taller. Some kids in my class, they're totally ripped already."

Body image issues weren't reserved just for women. "Well, that will come. You have years of growing in front of you." I paused. "You eating okay?"

"Yeah. I eat all the time. But Dad wants me to eat like he does."

"Rusty nails and yams?"

He snorted. "Basically. Sorry in advance about dinner. I suggested mac and cheese, but Dad said he hasn't eaten cheese in decades."

If I knew Mason, and I did, he'd joke and pick his cuticles and put off this list as long as possible. I took out my iPad.

"Let's pick an easy thing first. You're a freshman in high school, all the extracurricular stuff is starting. How about join a club?"

"Yeah. Maybe. I guess. They have a gamers thing and, uh, a coding club?"

I understood his hesitancy. Hunter would hate both of those, so if he knew about them, he'd be sure to voice his disdain.

"Great," I said, typing in *Join a club.* "See? Not too hard. Another thing could be . . . I don't know. Eat with some other kids at lunch." My stomach hurt at the thought of him alone, pretending to read. I'd done the same thing at Princeton with their wretchedly snobby eating clubs.

He bit a cuticle. "Does that have to be on there?"

"Well . . . maybe you could just think about it. Get the lay of the land. It's still early in the semester. I'm sure a lot of other kids are looking for people to eat with." Quite possibly untrue, but I typed it in anyway. "What else?"

"Dad wants me to have a social life. Says it's unnatural to be alone so much." He cut me an apologetic glance. "I had friends at my old school, but they all go somewhere else now. And you don't count. You know. To him."

"I do know. Plus, your aunt shouldn't be your only social life, no matter how awesome I am." I typed in *Do something with a friend*.

He was biting his lip now, chewing on it.

"You can do it, honey. Believe me, you're not the only kid who's a little . . . unsure of himself."

He sighed. "I want to believe you."

"Do it. Believe me. By the way, Marley is great for pointers, socially speaking. Especially with the fairer sex."

"What? You mean, like, dating? G, there's no way I could get a girlfriend."

"We'll laugh over this when you have eleven girls ask you to prom. How about for now, just talk to a girl? Trust me. Marley can help."

"Fine," he said, blushing. Aha. So he *did* want to talk to a girl. "How about, um, get As in all my classes?" he suggested.

That sounded like something Hunter would say. But if we put that on the list, and he got a B or C, would he feel like a failure? I paused for a minute. "Maybe something better would be 'Check in with my teachers to make sure I'm clear on the material.'" Mason was so good with adults. I had a feeling getting to know his teachers would make him a lot happier at his school.

"Yeah. That's better. Good idea, G."

And that way, his teachers would get to know him, too.

"I have to do a public speaking thing for school," he said. "That could go on the list, too."

"Sure." I typed it in. "Take piano lessons?" I suggested.

"No. This is probably already too much."

"But you asked Leo that day."

"We don't have a piano."

"And yet your aged aunt does."

He smiled. "You're not *that* old, G."

"Thank you, darling child." I tousled his hair. "Okay. We'll leave that off for now. I think this list is a good start, don't you?"

"Start? Will I have to do more?" He looked stricken.

"No, no," I said soothingly. The last thing I wanted was to create more stress for the poor kid. "This is great. Remember, the idea here is to do things you want to do. Even if they make you uncomfortable, you'll be glad you did them. Right?" He smiled at me. "We can text each other if we cross something off, okay?"

"Okay. Sure. There's no time limit, right?"

"Nope. None at all."

"Good." His shoulders dropped.

"Mason!" Hunter yelled. "Dinnertime."

I raised my fist and gently bumped it against Mason's hand. "We got this," I said. "You and me and Marley. The three musketeers of List-Land."

CHAPTER 9

Marley

Have a cute stranger buy you a drink.
(Preferably not a gay guy or someone over the age of seventy.)

When I got home after my deliveries that night, I went straight to the shower, used the extra-good shower gel, shaved my legs and moisturized every inch of my skin. Tonight was Friday, the outing with Dante and the guys, and yes, Camden would be there. I had confirmation from Dante.

I had told Georgia about my photo shoot, and shown her the results. Tonight would be the first time Georgia and I tried something on the list together.

Emerson had had a boyfriend, the infamous and invisible Mica, who fed her to death. Obviously, she helped by eating, by not getting up, by succumbing to the pain of obesity and the shallow comfort of food. But Emerson had said in more than one e-mail that they genuinely loved each other. She had been over the moon about him.

Clearly, she'd been whitewashing their relationship, if what the evil cousin Ruth had said about his obsession with her size was true. God.

But even so. She'd been in love. She'd gone on dates and held hands in public. I still had the e-mails and messages, and that one cute picture of the two of them.

No nonrelative male had ever said he loved me. Relationships before this had consisted of the occasional shag in college. One semi-regular guy named Charles I met online a few years ago. We met for a drink once, went to his place, messed around and were each other's booty call for the next couple of months. We never appeared in public after that first time, and I wised up and told him we were done. Not sure if he even noticed.

So when I met Camden, who *talked to me in public*, who laughed at my jokes, who said such thrilling things as "You look nice, Marley," and "Man, this eggplant is amazing!" . . . he was different. Not different enough, not yet, but still. We fat girls sometimes take what's offered instead of what we really want.

The truth was, men liked me. Many of them even liked my figure—my fabulous boobage, my generous butt, my wild, tangled curls. And I liked men. I liked talking to them, flirting with them, watching them. I *loved* men. I wanted one of my very own. Yet here I was, almost thirty-five and never once had I been introduced as "my girlfriend."

"This one's for you, Emerson," I said out loud, picking out a low-cut peasant blouse. Next I added a short, swishy skirt and three-inch heels. Did my makeup with an expert hand, thanks to many thousands of hours at Sephora, and then went upstairs and banged on Georgia's door. If I knew her, and I did, she'd pretend she'd forgotten about our plans for the evening. "You promised you'd come!" I reminded her.

"You don't have to yell," she said, opening the door.

"I'm not yelling. I'm Italian. And you're not dressed."

"I kind of forgot about this, and I have a lot of work to—"

"Nice try. Come on, I'll pick you out something cute."

Georgia had no idea how to dress. As a lawyer, she'd worn navy blue suits that made her look as feminine as a Ford pickup truck. As a nursery school teacher, she wore long skirts for floor sitting, flats and tragically shapeless sweaters. Sometimes she sported the same turtlenecks my grandmother bought from Eddie Bauer, which made me want to cry and throw them on a pyre (or give them to Nonny . . . why waste?).

Georgia sighed.

"Admiral," I said to her dog, who was waiting politely to be noticed, "tell your mommy that she's going to have so much fun tonight." I petted his narrow head. "See? He just said it. Even your dog knows."

"Marley, I'm kind of tired."

"I don't care," I said, marching her upstairs to her room. "Oh, I love the new pillows!" They were green and blue and had little mirrors in them. I opened her closet door and surveyed the ocean of navy and gray. "Sad," I said. "So sad. You should try to dress how you decorate."

"So this party . . ." she said.

"It's just people at a bar, and guess what! It's on the list. 'Have a cute stranger buy you a drink at a bar.' Don't you make that face at me. Emerson is watching."

She rolled her eyes but didn't fuss.

Georgia had lost a *lot* of weight. We weren't supposed to discuss it, but the truth was, she needed to buy new clothes. I pulled out the smallest pair of jeans I could find as she made the sound of air being released from a balloon. "Quiet," I ordered.

She really had nothing appropriate for firefighter flirting. "I'll be right back," I said. "Put these on in the meantime." I handed her the jeans and a white button-down shirt (sigh), then trotted downstairs to raid my own closet. A cropped purple cashmere sweater, some dangly earrings. (Georgia was a small-gold-hoops person, the occasional tasteful pearls, totally living the WASP cliché.) I also grabbed a funky wooden necklace and the gray suede booties that I loved more than a human should love an inanimate object.

My phone rang. Will Harding, my serial killer client. I had just been there an hour ago.

"Hello?"

There was a pause. "Who is this?"

"It's Marley, Will. You called me."

"Marley."

Pretends not to know me. The list of his flaws was getting longer.

I rolled my eyes. "Your chef? Who comes to your house with food five times a week?"

"Yes. Right."

There was a pause. "Was there something you needed, Will?" I asked.

"Yes. You included four truffles with tonight's dinner."

I suppressed a sigh. "Well, I made some for another client, and I thought you might like them." Also, I probably would've eaten them if I had them in the house, and I'd done plenty of tasting while making them.

"I don't usually order dessert."

Doesn't usually order dessert. In fact, he *never* ordered dessert, which was further evidence of his serial-killing ways. "I know. But you could live a little. Dessert is fun."

Nothing from the other end of the line.

Ah. "You don't have to pay for them, Will. They were a thank-you for being a good client."

"I see. I thought it was a mistake. That they were meant for someone else."

"Nope. Just for you."

There was a long pause from his end. "Well. Thank you."

"You're very welcome."

"Good-bye."

I clicked off and sighed. A guy like Will should've been

doing something on a Friday night. He was . . . well, he wasn't hideous to look at, and being somewhere in his thirties or early forties, he should have a woman (or man), or some friends. Then again, did Ted Bundy have friends? Didn't matter. *I* had a friend, and she needed to be dressed.

Ten minutes later, Georgia looked less like a British schoolmarm and more like a woman in her thirties. Her hair was the stuff of Italian-girl envy—dark blond, sleek and smooth, in a bob that was never frizzy, never messy, never flat . . . just eternally perfect. I applied blush on her cheeks, ignoring the pleading look she sent her dog, and yes, even lipstick. "Now tuck in your shirt," I ordered.

"No."

"Just on one side. It's very hip."

"It looks like I just got out of the bathroom and forgot what I was doing."

"It's on the list. Tuck in your shirt."

"Marley, look at me. I'm already trying. Don't push it."

"You *never* try. When was the last time you went on a date?" I knew the answer. When she'd been married. So that was *five years* without a man. Five years!

Emerson had done us a favor with that list. She totally had. Kicking our asses from the great beyond, like any true friend.

"Fine. Don't tuck. But get in the car, girlfriend. The time has come."

CHAPTER 10

Georgia

Have a cute stranger buy you a drink.
(Or two cute strangers.)

An hour after Marley had tarted me up, I was settled at
Hudson's, the bar portion of which was packed with New
York's Bravest. Her brother, the beautiful Dante, was fend-
ing off lovestruck women as his husband watched in
amusement. One of the firefighters had handed over a DVD
to the bartender, and Dante's famous rescue of the little girl
was playing over and over, much to the delight of the crowd.

Aside from Dante and Louis, whom I'd met a few times
now and who had greeted me like an old friend, I was
largely invisible, which was how I liked it. Marley was at
the bar, having made her way through the sea of men, and
was now talking to her crush, Camden. His eyes kept flickering away from her, a sign that he was scanning for someone better, the asshole.

I knew she was afraid to admit how much she liked him.
She'd brushed off their occasional hookup, but she had the
curse of having an expressive face, and right now, that face
said she was trying too hard to keep his interest. Every once
in a while, he'd look at her almost like he was just remembering she was there. Then he'd smile, as if thinking, *Oh,*

hey! Marley's here! Cool! when he'd been talking with her all along. Nonetheless, she seemed to see him as the brightest star in the sky.

This was the gift of invisibility: I could observe and eavesdrop, and no one noticed or cared. Just one more thing I didn't have in common with my mother, who went to great lengths to be the center of attention—drenched in perfume, always dressed to kill, flirting with every male who walked past in a way that was painful to watch—her fingers at her bony sternum, the toying with her earring, the laying on of hands whenever possible. It always made me want to fold up into myself.

But for now, I was happy enough. It was wicked fun to watch Dante's rescue—one of the moments proving New York was the greatest country on earth, right up there with Sully landing on the Hudson and Derek Jeter's last home game. My scotch was Dalwhinnie, and in addition to the familiar pain in my stomach, I felt a pleasant warmth spreading in my chest as I sipped it. I had never minded being alone, after all. Should've been a sign. Should've paid attention to it. Should never have gotten married.

Marley glanced at me and gave a terrifyingly bright smile, our code for *snap out of it.* I obeyed. Sat up straighter. Smiled back at her. Pushed my hair behind my ears, the unfamiliar earrings tickling my neck. Tried to project a sense of approachability and warmth. Confidence, which was allegedly the sexiest thing of all, thigh gaps and big boobs be damned. Yes. I was an attractive woman. You betcha.

Nothing changed. My cloak of invisibility didn't fall to the ground. It was only with four-year-olds that I could really rock a room.

I kept trying. Fake it till you make it, right? Except I'd tried that with Rafe, and we all knew how that ended.

You watching, Emerson? I thought. *I'm fighting the good fight down here.*

Emerson had been *beautiful*, obesity be damned. Green eyes and cheekbones even with all that weight, the best smile, the cute dimple in her left cheek.

Dead at thirty-four.

I heard Marley's booming laugh. At least she was having fun. Or trying hard.

Despite the horror stories, maybe I'd try online dating. The chance of meeting in a bar was so 1980s. I mean, sure, one would think that sitting in a room filled with many age-appropriate males, at least some of them single and straight, one would attract some male attention.

Nope. Instead, the firefighters, easily identified by tattoos or shirts bearing a firefighting insignia, only talked to each other. Phrases like "Who cares? You only eat ketchup!" were followed by roars of laughter. Someone was being called "Goat Boy" quite often, the reference lost on everyone who wasn't FDNY. One woman held court; she was the captain of one of the fireboats and much revered by her colleagues.

I should've been a fireboat captain. It would've been nice to get an awed response when you said what you did for a living. "Preschool teacher" didn't pack quite the same punch.

I wondered when Rafe would come to see Silvi. Wondered how he looked these days. If he'd remarried by now.

Probably. He should be married. He was born to be married. I should Google him and see. Or, I should *not* Google him. I should firewall his name somehow to avoid temptation.

A man sat down next to me, startling me so much that I jumped. "Hi," he said. "Didn't mean to scare you. Is this seat taken?"

"Uh . . . no. Hi." Had that smiling/false confidence/hair tuck actually worked?

It seemed it had. "You drinking scotch?" he asked.

"Yep. Dalwhinnie. It's very good." I smiled doggedly, relieved to have something to report to Marley by the end of this hellish night. Whoops. Didn't mean to let a little honesty slip out there. Well, if it was the *Inferno* version of hell, I was only on the third circle. The vile slush circle.

"Are you here with the firefighters?" the guy asked.

"Not exactly. I'm with my friend, whose brother is one of them. Dante? The guy on TV there?"

My companion glanced at the screen and grunted.

"I'm Georgia, by the way." I stuck out my hand. He shook it firmly.

"Beck."

"Nice to meet you, Beck."

"I didn't realize there was a thing here tonight. For them." His tone was slightly resentful, but I understood. No fun to compete with such male perfection. It'd be like accidentally showing up to a Miss Italy pageant when you thought you were going to book club.

Beck wasn't unattractive, though his hair looked kind of greasy. (It may have been product; who knew with these metrosexuals?) His skin color was Gollumesque. Then again, I wasn't exactly Beyoncé.

Have a cute stranger buy you a drink at a bar.

Beck could pass for cute. He was a stranger. And Marley would be happy.

Also, I'd have something to tell Mason, who hadn't answered my last two texts. This concerned me. Hunter had probably taken his phone away for some reason.

I finished my scotch and tapped my ring against my glass, hoping to draw Beck's attention to its emptiness.

He didn't notice. "So," I said. "Where do you live, Beck?"

"In Tarrytown. You?"

"Here in Cambry. It's my hometown."

"Nice."

"Mm."

Okay, so the conversation wasn't exactly razor-sharp, but I *was* talking with a man.

And my last date, in answer to Marley's question, had been with Rafael Santiago.

"You want to go someplace quieter?" Beck asked. "My place isn't far."

God! Did he mean to hook up? Was this how things were done these days? Because there was no way I was going to sleep with a stranger.

"Well, uh, maybe another time?" I said. "I mean, I'm here with my friend. And also, you and I just met."

"Right." He smiled a little, and his attractiveness level kicked up a few notches. I tapped my ring against the glass again.

"What do you do for work?" he asked.

"I teach preschool."

He flinched. Should've gone with fireboat captain. "I guess you like kids," he said.

"No, I hate them. Disgusting little germ sponges." I paused. "Yes, I love children."

He nodded. "And you make bank doing that?"

"I do." A rather personal question. "What do you do, Beck?" I'd used his name at least three times already. Wondered if he remembered mine.

"I slaughter cattle."

I laughed.

His face didn't change.

"Oh," I said.

"Someone has to." He drained his drink and slammed the glass on the table, making me jump. "You eat beef?"

"Sometimes," I said. "Not that often." I suspected I was about to become a vegetarian.

"Well, you probably think meat comes from a store, don't you? It doesn't, okay? Every day, I go in and put a nail in a cow's head, and guess what? That's not all! You think I like working in a place where I'm covered in blood all the time? Oh, and it's not *just* blood, either. You think those cows come in all shiny and clean? They don't! They sleep in their own shit, okay? They're stupid animals and they sleep in their shit, and I get to shoot them in the head and butcher them, and the smell! My God! I have to lather up like five times before I get the stink out."

"Can I get you two anything to eat?" The waitress stood next to our table, pen in hand.

Beck looked up at her. "Yeah, I'll have a cheeseburger," he said calmly. "Extra rare, extra ketchup."

"Got it. And you?" she asked me.

"I'm good," I whispered.

"Another drink?"

"My God, yes. Please. Right away." Shit, the list. "Um, Beck, will you buy me a drink?"

"Sure. Will you go home with me later?"

"No."

He shrugged. "I guess I grossed you out."

"You did."

"Yeah, my grandma says to keep the butchering stuff to myself, but hey. You asked. Fine, I'll buy you a drink."

Ta-da! Too bad I couldn't leave right now. "So, um, are you close with your grandmother?"

"Oh, yeah. We live together. Just until I get out of debt. I've made some poor life choices."

So all those dating horror stories were true, then. Still, I couldn't help asking what those bad life choices were.

He leaned his head on his hand, staring into the middle

distance. "Probably I shouldn't have bought the Komodo dragon. You ever smell their shit? It is *foul*. I mean, I thought cats were bad? No. Lizard shit is king. And when it was dying? Kicked the stink up another notch."

The server came. I closed my mouth, took the drink out of her hand and raised my glass. "To Emerson," I said, and swallowed the scotch.

"What?" Beck said.

"Never mind." I stood up, wobbling on the unfamiliar heels. "Thank you so much for the lesson in butchering. And the drink," I said.

"You women are just out to trick us, aren't you?" he asked.

"Yes. Have a good night."

I walked away unsteadily, nearly twisting my ankle, to let Marley know I was going home. She could catch a ride (or a shag) with Camden, and if that failed, she had her brother here. Also, we only lived five blocks away.

I bumped into someone. "You okay?" he said, grabbing my upper arms.

The second I looked at his face, mine burned with recognition, and my stomach pulled together in a hot squeeze.

I *knew* him.

Evan Kennedy. My law school crush. I'd watched him and lusted after him from afar, with all the yearning of an invisible woman. I used to stare at him in the law library, drinking in his ease, his smile, his shoulders, his perfect beauty, his thick, dark Kennedyesque hair.

Before Rafe, he was the only guy I'd ever pictured sleeping with.

I was staring now. Because he was . . . yeah. He was.

"Hey," I breathed. Evan Flippin' Kennedy.

"Hey, yourself." He grinned, and my heart lit up like a Christmas tree. He remembered me!

"Was that guy crazy, or did it just seem that way?" he asked.

"Well, I did get a valuable lesson in cattle butchering."

Evan laughed. He was still holding my arms, and my arms were just fine with that. "You want to grab a drink?" he asked.

"Um . . . yes! Sure. That . . . that would be great."

He guided me to a booth along the wall, and I slid in, buzzed with scotch and adrenaline. We sat across from each other for a second, and I could feel my heart twisting in a combination of elation and nervousness. "So how are you?" I asked.

"Better than you, I think." That *smile*. Then he offered his hand. "Evan Kennedy."

My mouth fell open. "Yeah. Um . . . yes."

His hand was waiting. I shook it automatically.

He didn't recognize me.

"Do you have a name, pretty lady?"

"Georgia. Georgia Sloane." I smiled, waiting for his synapses to fire.

"Great to meet you. What are you drinking?"

"Um . . . scotch. Dalwhinnie."

"Nice choice." He flagged down the server while my brain flailed around for what to say. *We've already met. We went to law school together. We sat next to each other in Torts.*

Maybe it was the slight buzz from the two drinks I'd already had. Maybe it was a game, seeing how long it would take for the pieces to fall into place.

Whatever the reason, I didn't say anything.

I was heavier back then, but surely not . . . unrecognizable.

Then again, the woman sitting across from Evan Kennedy

was different. Slimmer. She had dangly earrings and makeup and high heels.

This version was having a cute guy buy her a drink in a bar.

Ah. I knew what I'd do. The second he mentioned Yale, I'd pretend I hadn't recognized him, either. Or he'd say he was a lawyer, and I'd say I'd gone to law school but changed careers, and then we'd laugh over it. It would be adorable. A meet-cute, I think they called it.

"So what do you do, Georgia Sloane? Are you from around here?"

"I am," I said. "I live just a few blocks from here. I'm a preschool teacher."

"Really? I love kids. What age do you teach?"

"Four-year-olds."

"My niece is four! She lives in Berlin, so I don't get to see her much, but we FaceTime. Great age, isn't it?"

"It sure is. What do you do, Evan?"

"I'm a consultant for an investment firm. It's really boring, though, unless you have a sick fascination with leveraged finance in the healthcare market. Can we talk about movies instead? I'm kind of a geek. I go to the movies at least once a week. I also have a pretty serious popcorn addiction."

He was charming. I was slightly drunk.

So we talked about movies.

But in the back of my head, a memory played over and over . . . One precious spring night, Evan and I had walked from Crown Street to the law school, and we'd had an actual conversation that had sustained me for *months*. It was nothing special, that conversation, but it had been with him.

I kept waiting for him to say, *Wait a sec, hang on, I knew a Georgia Sloane! Did you go to Yale?*

He didn't. There wasn't one flicker of recognition on his face, not one pause in conversation.

And the longer we talked, the less I wanted him to remember. The shame of my less-than-ideal weight drowned out everything else from that time. I tried to talk myself out of that mind-set and failed.

"Would you like to have dinner with me sometime?" Evan asked. "I work in the city, but I'd be happy to come up here, if that'd be easier."

"I go to the city all the time," I said. "My family lives in Chelsea." The best part of my family, anyway.

"Can I call you, then? I hate to cut the night short, but I have an early flight to DC tomorrow." He smiled, sure of the answer, as one would be when one was a scion of a great American family, follically and dentally blessed.

"That would be great." We exchanged phones, typed in our numbers, and Evan said he'd call me tomorrow. Then he left.

Marley popped over the second he was gone. "Oh, my God, he was *so* cute! Tell me you like him! Tell me!"

I blinked a few times to clear my head. Definitely wouldn't be finishing that third drink. "I like him," I said.

"Then why do you look like Admiral just barfed all over your bed?"

"No," I said. "It's . . . he was nice. He was really nice. The thing is, we went to law school together, and he didn't recognize me."

She sat down. "Oh."

"But that's okay, right?"

"Sure! It'll click the next time he sees you. You only talked for a couple minutes."

More than that, but she had a point.

"The list is working, isn't it?" she said happily. "Camden bought me a drink. First time ever."

"Yeah, I got a drink, too." Two, actually. "We can check that off, I guess." I smiled. After all, I couldn't fault Evan for not recognizing me, right? It had been a long time. Maybe I really did look different.

As I left, one of the FDNY members jumped up to open the door for me. "Have a good night," he said, smiling. He looked like Thor.

"Thank you," I said belatedly. The night air was cool on my hot face, and I was glad to be walking the five blocks home.

I shouldn't be distressed. No. I should be the opposite.

I knew better than to believe that exchanging numbers meant an actual date, but something had happened tonight. Evan Kennedy asked me out. Thor held the door for me. A butcher had sat down and unburdened himself—not quite as fun as the other encounters, but still a new experience.

Three men had noticed me. One may have just been instinctively polite (Thor), but the butcher and Evan . . . they had *seen* me. It could've been argued that Thor would've held the door no matter what my weight, but I had no evidence that was true. Even taking Thor out of the equation, I strongly suspected that Beck the Butcher would not have asked me to come home with him if he'd met me seventy-five pounds ago. And I knew beyond a shadow that Evan would not have asked me out seventy-five pounds ago, because he hadn't.

I wasn't fat anymore. That was a good thing, to quote Martha Stewart.

It just didn't feel so good.

CHAPTER 11

Dear Other Emerson,

I fell off the wagon. I'm sorry.

It wasn't really my fault. I had ten good days. Ten! In a row! That's a record, I think. You saw me, right? I was eating healthy and taking walks. I was thinking about you and all the beautiful clothes you wear, how you stride through the airport, how people look at you and wonder if you're an actor or a really chic senator. No matter what, they know you're important.

I took walks. I kept my food diary. I didn't cheat once. The diet literature said I was guaranteed to lose weight. Guaranteed.

I know weight is just a number (pause for laughter . . . when you weigh more than three hundred pounds, it's a helluva lot more than a number). They say it's how you feel, your energy level, how your clothes fit. But I wear dresses or skirts all the time. Yes, they cost a lot. There's a lot of fabric here. Jeans, please. I haven't worn jeans since fat camp.

That was the best summer. I should give Georgia and Marley a call. I wonder how much they weigh these days. Georgia called a while back and told me how she had to have her picture taken for the school where she's working, and how weird it felt to smile when you HATE having your picture taken because you're fat. I know you don't know what we're talking about, Other Emerson—clearly, you could model. You don't have to worry about it looking as if you don't have a chin—or even worse, like you have three.

I guess I'm putting off what I really need to tell you.

I gained weight on my diet. And I don't look even a tiny bit slimmer. In fact, I've never weighed this much in all my life.

381 pounds. I couldn't believe it. The scale had to be wrong. I reset it, checked again, moved it to another spot on the floor, reset it again.

381 pounds.

Obviously, I cried. I mean, what the _frig_? What's the point of eating egg whites and asparagus and four ounces of grilled chicken with a fricking salad for lunch and quinoa and salmon for dinner and you're drinking only water when your stomach growls constantly and your mouth is crying out for the sizzle and fizz of a Coke? What's the point when you have dreams about eating? When you have to drive home a different route so you won't pass China Buffet because you're so damn hungry?

So I took some diuretics and ended up with diarrhea so bad I was in the bathroom for two hours.

When I was finally done with that, I got on the scale again, and yes, I was down six pounds. Eff off, scale! Water loss, sure, but down six pounds.

My hunger gnawed at me, and so I went to the fridge and saw the aging leftover lettuce and half of a hardening grilled chicken breast, and before I thought more about it, I ordered a pizza. I deserved it. I'd lost _six pounds_.

Don't judge me, Other Emerson. I haven't had anything good to eat in ten days.

This would be my indulgence. A large — no, make that a medium, I had restraint, see? — a medium pie with extra cheese and pepperoni, and the crust with the cheese that they'd been advertising on every channel for two weeks.

When the kid delivered it, I had the box open before he was even off my porch. Sat down in front of the TV, pulled up Netflix and oh, God, the pizza was so perfect, so good, still warm but not burn-the-flesh-off-the-roof-of-your-mouth hot, and before my show had even booted up, I'd finished one slice and was reaching for another, and it was so, so good, the soft, gooey crust, the salty, spicy deliciousness of the pepperoni. The joy of having my mouth full, of taking bite after bite and still having more.

Yes. I ate every single piece of pizza. Ate and loved. It was heaven, and the relief . . . I can't even tell you. The _relief_ of eating again.

I washed it down with water — not Coke, Other Emerson, I am making healthy choices, after all. Also, I didn't have any Coke in the house.

Finally, finally I was full again. Finally.

Except not really.

The books tell you to _enjoy_ your food, really _taste_ it, not to _worry_ about calories (please). They say to be in the moment and _experience_ the feeling of fullness, satiety, whatever.

That pizza had been _so_ good. And it was my day of indulgence, the books say I can have one, after all — and Other Emerson, listen. You aren't _here_. You didn't have the entire weekend stretching out in front of you with nothing to do except scroll through social media and watch TV. _You_ can go to the movies without worrying if you'll fit in a seat. _You_ can ride your bike through San Francisco or take a hike in Muir Woods with Idris Elba. _You_ get free tickets to the symphony, I bet.

My house smelled like pizza. And my God, I loved pizza.

My hand was already on the phone, and I turned off the part of my brain that knew this was wrong. I hit redial, ordered another pizza, same as the first, and my heart pounded in anticipation as I waited. Watched my show, now able to enjoy it because I had eaten and more food was on its way.

When the bell rang, I went to the door and opened it. My next-door neighbors, the Donovans, were standing in their yard, mid-fight. They love to fight outside so we can all enjoy the show, but they stopped at the sight of the pizza guy, on my steps for the second time in ninety minutes.

A note about the Donovans. I have a tidy lawn, thanks to the guys who come every week and take care of it and who like me because I give them iced coffee and cookies. My house is adorable and well maintained. I smile at everyone in the neighborhood. The Donovans, on the other hand, have two cars on blocks in the backyard, overflowing trash cans, a broken railing on their front porch and a dead Christmas wreath on their door, even though it's now June.

And yet they think they're better than I am. They might be white trash, but they aren't _fat_, and they paused in their screeching.

God, I wished I could tell them off! I'd say, "You know, I'm a _person_. I have hopes and dreams and feelings, and I pay my taxes, unlike you two, so stop giving me the stink-eye every time you see me. Drop the damn skinny-supremacy righteousness and take a look in the mirror. Take a look at your _souls_."

I don't say these things, of course. I never do.

"Hey!" I said to the pizza guy, pretending to be surprised. "I . . . I don't understand. I think you got your order screwed up. You were just here an hour ago." Insert fake laugh. "Well, here, I'll pay for it. Are these good frozen, do you know? Like, can I just wrap it up and stick it in the freezer?"

The guy gave me a dead-eyed stare. I wasn't fooling him. I paid, took the pizza, waved to the Donovans and went inside.

I ate half of the pizza, the TV keeping me company.

I should've just ordered a large. One large would've been better than a medium and a half.

I couldn't think about my TV show, even though I ostensibly loved it. The half pizza was too present.

If I wrapped it up, it would be there in the fridge tomorrow, and I'm always hungriest first thing in the morning, Other Emerson. I wouldn't have the willpower to whip up egg whites if there was cold pizza calling my name.

I think we both know where this story is heading, don't we?

I might as well eat it now, I told myself. Get it over with in one big binge, then feel all the more committed tomorrow.

And so I ate it all.

It's okay. Just a blip. Just 4,160 calories in one sitting. (Of course I looked it up, then cried when I saw the facts.) But it was done. I have to shake it off. One step back, two steps forward.

Soon, you and I will merge, Other Emerson. And I will be just like you—the kind of person who loves pizza but eats only one slice before feeling full. One slice. We won't even finish the crust.

My stomach hurts now. I'm sorry, Other Emerson. I really am sorry for being this way. I can't even look in the mirror anymore. I hate myself. I hate my fatness. I hate being so weak.

No one will ever love me. Not like this.

CHAPTER 12

Georgia

Hold hands with a cute guy in public.
(Did that, and yes. It was everything.)

Go home to meet his parents. *(That one was awful.)*

No one expected me to end up with anyone, let alone a Latin chef who was drop-dead gorgeous.

I certainly didn't.

My mother . . . no. Despite the fact that I had found someone (she'd predicted I wouldn't, because I'm, you know . . . fat), she wasn't thrilled. Rafael Esteban Jesús Santiago was a brown-skinned man who worked in a restaurant, and to my mother, that killed it right there. Also, his family was Catholic, a religion that had always puzzled her. "All those statues," she'd muse. "What do they mean?"

My father, too, was stunned, though his surprise was on the joyful side. Rafe had asked him for permission to propose, and Dad had burst into tears and hugged him.

Hunter . . . his take was that Rafe was probably gay, because didn't gays have a thing for fat women?

Rafe said it was love at first sight. It took me fifteen months to believe him, three months to alienate him, and somewhere in between there, we got married.

We met during my third year of law school at Yale, in the cozy little city of New Haven, where, for about a square mile and a half, you were in a place that closely resembled Brooklyn meets Hogwarts. Most of my class came from super-prestigious colleges. Some, like me, had worked between college and law school. I had spent two years with Teach For America in the Bronx and loved it, but for some reason, I'd felt like I had to become a lawyer. Maybe to prove I was smart, so Yale it was.

Yale Law wasn't easy. It wasn't particularly hard, either. Then again, I had a nearly photographic memory, so I had an edge in that area, remembering case law with an X-Men type of ease. The school was a launchpad for greatness. Graduates would become presidents, senators, members of the Supreme Court, work for the Innocence Project, found nonprofit organizations and for-profit corporations. (The fact that I eventually became a nursery school teacher did not make it into the annals of Yale's history, I'm quite sure.)

By the time our third year rolled around, we'd all done at least two summers working for law firms and nonprofits all over the world, and at that point, our futures were about as secure as futures got. I was a little uneasy . . . though I did well in school, I kept waiting to feel like I was a good fit. Those summers interning didn't exactly make me yearn to practice law. Marley kept telling me I was crazy; I'd be POTUS in no time and would hire her as White House chef. There was also the seduction of doing what was expected of me, family-wise. Both my grandfathers had been attorneys; Big Kitty's father had been special counsel to Ronald Reagan. There was the little-girl part of me that still wanted to win my mother's approval and shut Hunter up. So I kept at it.

By my third and final year at Yale, I had a couple of offers to practice environmental law. My five-year plan involved losing weight (of course), sticking around until Mason was happily settled in prep school, then transferring to California and becoming the person I'd always wanted to be—fit, happy, secure, confident and independent.

And then I met Rafael, fell in love and totally screwed up my life.

Let me back up a little bit.

While I didn't love the law, I did love law school. My years at Concord Academy and Princeton had been . . . endurable, even pleasant at times . . . but I never felt like I fit in. I wanted to be liked—who doesn't?—but I was so tired. All my effort went into being more outgoing, funnier and thinner, which would make everything else in the world easier (so I thought). I'd gone endless rounds with every variation of eating disorder that existed. Bingeing, purging, puking, diuretics, starvation, more bingeing, detoxing, manic phases of exercise, no exercise at all. For years, I tried every trick the Internet offered—strapping ice packs to my stomach to try to freeze off the fat, drinking lemon juice and cayenne pepper, vinegar and cabbage juice. All done like a dirty secret, the shame of not being able to lose enough constant and bleak.

Nothing worked enough. When you're surrounded by peers at their peak of beauty, it's impossible to forget your own imperfections. My weight was like a Dementor, always close, always stealing happiness, something I always tried and failed to escape.

It was exhausting.

Only my friendships with Emerson and Marley gave me a break from all that self-loathing of my physical self, and luckily, Marley was close enough when we were in college and when I went to Yale, so we saw each other a lot. Many was the time I'd invited her to a party at Princeton in order to ease my sense of not belonging. When I was teaching in the Bronx, I saw her at least once a week, and the same was true when I went to New Haven, Metro-North trains making it easy for us to visit.

During my stint as a high school teacher in the Bronx, I'd lost weight, thanks to the endless work hours and high stress of teaching in an impoverished public school where the teachers were desperately trying to give the kids even the smallest chance.

By law school, I was somewhere in between my heaviest and lightest, which is to say I was overweight but not as much as I had been.

And once I got to Yale, it seemed we were more focused, more mature (one hoped). Did I eat and breathe SCOTUS cases from fifty years ago? Not really, but I understood them. I could argue them.

The law school class was small, and by the end of three years, everyone knew everyone, more or less. I had friends. Body-wise—because no matter how beautiful a mind you might have, it's almost impossible to dodge body issues—I finally settled down, not gaining, not losing, for nearly two years.

I didn't date. I had never dated, after all. But on that first day of Torts, I sat down next to Evan Kennedy and did a double take, then felt my face flush. He was that attractive. From that moment on, I had a special radar where he was concerned, my skin prickling when he came into a room, my ears always able to catch his laugh, his voice. I always assumed he was, yes, one of those Kennedys . . . he mentioned Hyannis Port once in a while and phrases like *my uncle Ted* slipped out occasionally. Of course I had a huge crush on him. Oh, God, I did. How could I not?

But Evan and I didn't really run in the same circles. It was okay. I didn't have the time, anyway (so I told myself). But it really was fine. I just wanted to get to my true adult life, have a place of my own, get a job and start living.

My classes had shown me I was sensible, had a gift for seeing to the heart of the matter and a habit of waiting till others had finished speaking to make my point, at which time my classmates would start nodding. There was a lot of "What Georgia said" and "I agree with Georgia." After a childhood spent being a disappointment to my mother, a curse to Hunter and overpraised by my dad, I liked myself more than I ever had. Even though I was still thick and graceless and, in my own mind at least, unremarkable to look at, I was doing okay.

One night in the fall, my core group of friends and I went to a new restaurant. New Haven was always spawning new eateries, and this one featured tapas and a great drinks menu. There were seven of us—two couples and three singletons (two men who'd never asked me out, and myself). Monique and Reggie had just announced their engagement, which was hardly a surprise—they'd been together since the first day of Torts. We were toasting them, eating and talking and trying not to be too obnoxious as we discussed the latest case before the Supreme Court. After all, there were other people here, normal people with jobs and families. We ivory-tower people could be nice, too.

Toward the end of our meal, a man in chef whites came over to our table. "I hope everything was to your liking tonight," he said, a faint accent in his voice.

"Oh, it was wonderful! Amazing! Well done!" came the chorus.

The chef smiled, and I felt a warm tightness start in my stomach. His eyes stopped on me, and stayed there.

"Everything was great," I said.

"I am so glad," he said.

His hair was dark and pulled back into a short ponytail, and he had a neat beard and mustache. He was a little shorter than average, and slender, and there was nothing really remarkable about him.

Except his eyes. His eyes were . . . well. They were dark

and turned down at the corners, big brown eyes with thick eyelashes. And his smile, God. He looked so happy. Just because we'd liked his food.

"I hope you'll come again," he said.

"Reggie Elliott," said Reg, offering his hand. "This is my beautiful fiancée, Monique Fontaine."

"Rafael Santiago," he said, and I practically slid off my chair.

Now *that* was a name. And the way he said it . . . my God.

"Hello," murmured Helen, who was sitting next to me.

My friends gave their names and shook his hand, and he made his way around the table, schmoozing like any good chef.

"Where are you from, Rafael?" asked Bennett.

"Barcelona," he said, and I swear, my ovaries doubled in size.

I was the last one at the table. He was talking to Helen now, and my heart was thudding and hot. I was abruptly nervous—what if I forgot my name? What was it again? What if my voice squeaked? What if I went into a fugue state and humped his leg?

He took my hand in both of his. I *definitely* wanted to hump his leg. God! This was not like me! Lust and I collided, and I sucked in my stomach without thinking. His hands were warm and smooth, and he held mine with the faintest bit of pressure. An electric current twined up my arm, hot and tingling.

I was supposed to speak, wasn't I?

"Georgia Sloane," I said. "Dinner was excellent." Did I sound normal? I hoped so. I wished I'd had an exotic name, like Marley, who was Marlena Apollonia DeFelice. My name was boring. Too WASPy. Too . . . forgettable. I didn't even have a middle name.

Get ahold of yourself, a part of my brain hissed. *You met President Obama last year, remember? Calm down!*

"Georgia," Rafael said. "I'm Rafe." He held my hand a minute too long, and his brows came together a little, as if he was surprised. "I hope you'll come again."

"No, yes! We will. Absolutely!" I babbled. "Thank you. Great. It was great." *Smooth, Georgia.*

He let go of my hand, which fell to my side, limp. "Can I get you anything else tonight?"

The group assured him we were all set, and so he went back to the kitchen, and I tried hard not to watch him.

"Friends, I believe Georgia has a crush," Helen said, and I felt my face burn. I smiled and rolled my eyes amid their kind laughter, and I didn't deny a thing.

A minute later, the waitress came over with two bottles of champagne. "To toast the happy couple," she said.

I looked over at the kitchen—it was open, and Rafael Santiago was looking at *me.* Right at me. He gave a very old-world nod, a hint of a smile on his beautiful lips, and then went back to work.

It took me three days of intense planning (and yes, crash dieting) to figure out how to get back to the restaurant while being incredibly casual about it. I asked my professor to lunch, told her a few of us had eaten at this great new restaurant—El Encanto, which I'd later learn was Spanish for *the spell.*

I was already under his. Insert the cheesy music.

When we walked in, Rafael came out of the kitchen almost immediately. "Georgia," he said, and my name sounded round and beautiful and lovely. "I am so happy to see you again." He took my hand in both of his again, and words failed me. Then he turned to my professor. "Hello, I am Rafael Santiago, one of the chefs here."

Lunch was interminable. It may have seemed like my

professor and I were discussing the finer points of *Sierra Club v. Morton*, but I can assure you, my mind was elsewhere.

When we'd paid the bill, I did something unprecedented. I lied. "Shoot," I said, looking at my phone. "I have to return this call. I'll see you tomorrow?"

"Sure thing, Georgia," my professor said.

I called Marley, who was, as ever, my go-to friend in times of awkwardness. She picked up right away.

"Hello," I said. "It's Georgia Sloane returning your call."

"Why, hello, Georgia Sloane," she answered merrily. "Did I butt-dial you? I don't think so. How the hell are you?"

"I'm fine, thanks. How can I help you?"

"You could rub my feet. Why are we talking like this?"

"Absolutely. I'd be happy to."

"Is this one of those weird phone calls where one of us is killing time so we don't look like such dorks?"

"Yes, that's right."

"And why are we killing time today, Ms. Sloane?"

"I could be ready to make that move we discussed last April." When we'd discussed my perpetually singleton state over mojitos, down at the Jersey Shore with Emerson. Hopefully, Marley would remember.

She did. "Oh, my God, is there a *man* there?" she squeaked.

"Not quite yet, no." My face was pulsating, I was blushing so hard.

"But we're pretending to have a deep and meaningful conversation so he'll notice you?"

"Yes, exactly."

"In that case, I'd like to tell you that the president would like to appoint you to the Supreme Court. Can I tell him you said yes?"

"That's extremely flattering. Would it be all right if I think about it?"

"No, lunkhead. It's the Supreme Court! Say yes."

My heart froze, then charged ahead. Rafael Santiago had just come out of the kitchen and was looking at me.

"Thank you so much for the offer. You'll hear from me soon."

"You'd better call me tonight and tell me everything," Marley said.

"Of course. Thank you again." I hung up and stuck the phone in my bag, and the chef approached. Even the soles of my feet broke out in sweat.

"Did you enjoy your lunch?" he asked.

"Yes," I said, and my voice cracked.

He smiled. "Do you have to leave right away?"

"No."

"May I sit down?"

God, his *manners*. "Yes." Me, on the other hand . . . I should try to come up with something other than one-word answers.

It was past two, and the lunch crowd had mostly cleared out. We looked at each other, though I couldn't hold eye contact for more than two seconds.

"Um . . . how long have you worked here, Rafael?" I asked, wondering if that was a stupid question, wondering if he just wanted to ask me if he could cater for Yale, wondering if he was looking for a green-card marriage, wondering why a guy who looked and spoke the way he did would hit on me, if indeed he was hitting on me.

"About a month," he said. "Before this, I worked in Pamplona, where my father grew up." He smiled. "It's a beautiful city. Have you ever been?"

"I'm afraid not."

"Ah. Someday, I hope."

Those were eyes you could get lost in.

"Georgia Sloane, would you have dinner with me?" he

said at the very same moment I said, "Do you use a lot of butter in your cooking?" because it was the only thing I could think of to say.

He laughed, and I fell in love with him right then and there.

We talked for two hours that day—two hours!—until he had to get back to the kitchen.

Of course I went out with him—to a movie, because I'd been terrified that I'd run out of things to talk about.

It was my first date. Ever.

He took my hand in the darkened theater, smiled at me, and didn't say a word during the movie. For the first time, I didn't even want popcorn. His hand was warm and calloused, and he held mine firmly, and to this day, I have no recollection of what movie we saw.

Afterward, we walked home, had a deep discussion about Matt Damon versus Ben Affleck. It was easier for my lawyer's mind to get started on a conversation with a "versus" in it. At my little apartment, as I fumbled for my keys and wondered what normal people did (ask him up? ask him if he wants coffee? a drink? tell him to drive safely?), he took my face in his hands and kissed me.

Just a gentle press of the lips, warm and sweet and perfect. My keys fell out of my hand, and I kissed him back.

I'd never been kissed before.

It didn't matter. That kiss showed me what kissing was all about.

"Can I see you again?" he whispered, his mouth barely leaving mine.

"Yes, please." I felt him smile. One more kiss, oh, yes, I *loved* kissing, my whole body was melting against his, my insides squeezing and pulsing. He pulled back a little, kissed me on the forehead, then rested his forehead against mine. Our bodies were barely touching, but to me, it was like we were wrapped in gold, this man I barely knew and already loved. He cupped my face in his hands and looked at me, and I thought I could stare into his bottomless dark eyes for the rest of my life.

"I will call you tomorrow," he said, then went down the steps. I watched him go, stunned by that golden warmth, by his charm, his kindness, his specialness.

He turned and smiled. "Good night, Georgia Sloane."

I may have waved, still in the sweet shock of first love.

He did call me the next day.

We went on another date, and another. His hours were crappy—he worked six nights a week, but he had Mondays off, and we did ridiculously romantic things, like drive down to the Maritime Aquarium at Norwalk to watch the seals, take walks at East Rock Park, wander through the old cemetery in the middle of New Haven, meander through the Yale Center for British Art, which I hadn't managed to see in three years at school. And, eventually, we even slept together.

That one took months to accomplish.

Oh, we made out a *lot*. He was the best kisser on the face of the earth. Sometimes I could forget my physical being and just melt and surge with the hot wanting, the slide of our mouths, the taste of him, his beautiful skin and silky hair.

I *wanted* to sleep with him. I just didn't exactly want him to sleep with *me*, because then he'd have to see me without clothes, and I wasn't sure I could stand that.

So, until the fateful day, I was the Couch Contortionist, because there were always areas I didn't want Rafe touching. He was physically perfect, at least in my eyes, which was terribly unfair. He could put his hand on my breast, but not on my waist. There was a roll of fat there. What if he felt the Super-Smoothie-Under-Shaper that had cost me

$125 and squished my torso into one firm, sausage-like casing? Even him touching my upper arms bothered me. I told him I was ticklish. That only got me so far.

He thought I was shy, rather than petrified. He asked me, gently, if I had had any bad experiences with men. And yes, I had . . . of the empty-as-a-vacuum kind, because at the age of twenty-seven, I was still a virgin.

Here's another confession. I was putting him off until I could lose more weight.

I loved seeing Rafe's eyes light up as I ate something he'd made. It was almost foreplay, knowing his hands and creativity had gone into making what was now in my mouth, and he wanted me to like it, to love it, to want more. But the calories, the calories. Weren't my thighs big enough? I had to be so careful, more than ever, with everything I ate.

I knew we *would* sleep together, and I knew he'd be good at what he did.

But in the back of my mind echoed every insult, every unkind nickname, every taunt my body had ever elicited. Hunter, loudly exclaiming his disgust at my rolls of fat at the country club pool when I was six and I thought I looked cute in my first two-piece suit. My mother's constant admonition not to eat so much, so often . . . or, conversely, telling me to eat more kale, more lettuce, more appetite suppressants. I remembered going to the mall with my friends to buy the requisite white dresses for graduation from Concord Academy, Kendra Hughes trying—and failing—to zip me into the biggest size they had while our other friends waited outside the dressing room, clutching their teeny, single-digit-sized dresses, feeling sorry for me.

So I put him off until I'd lost fifteen pounds . . . by which time my fear that he'd break up with me for *not* sleeping with him overshadowed my body image woes.

On the fateful night, I made him turn off the lights.

"I think you are very beautiful, Georgia," he said, a little sadness in his eyes.

"Thanks," I said briskly. "But I think it'll be awkward enough, though, don't you?"

"No, I do not," he said, and there went another chunk of my heart.

But he turned off the lamp, and when he kissed me, when we lay down on the bed, free from clothes, it was everything. Even though I was still imperfect. Even though I winced when he ran his hand over my abdomen.

"Your skin is so soft," he whispered, kissing my neck, my shoulder, his hands finding all the places no one had ever touched.

This love was like being sucked into a tornado, a thrilling, terrifying ride, not knowing where I would land, if I'd be broken when I did. It was so foreign. That saying about love making the world new wasn't enough to encompass my feelings. It was more like I was an alien visiting a strange planet. Being loved, feeling safe . . . being first in someone's eyes was not something I understood.

He brought me home to his family in Staten Island— mother, father, three younger sisters, two aunts, three uncles, seven cousins, two grandparents. They were lovely, hugging me, Rafe occasionally translating for an aunt or uncle who didn't speak English, his sisters teasing him about dating someone "ten times smarter than you, Rafe. A hundred times. A million." I smiled and laughed and even ate a little bit.

"They loved you," Rafe said smugly when we left. "As I knew they would."

But they didn't love me, of course. How could they? I'd been completely fake, forcing myself to talk, to spin answers about my family into something happier, to be bright and cheerful and Marley-esque.

The real me was the one who'd gone to the bathroom and pressed my knees together to stop their shaking. The real me had hidden food in her napkin and dumped it in the toilet because I couldn't afford the calories. The real me yearned to be home, alone and safe. The real me yearned for Pringles and a pint of Ben & Jerry's, because I didn't know how to do this relationship thing.

And yet, I *loved* him. I loved him so much it was too much. He had such power over me. The thought of him leaving me made my entire soul shudder in fear.

He wanted to meet my family. Dad and Cherish and the girls, no problem. They adored him. When Rafael held Milan, then a baby, I had to look away, my heart so full I thought it might rip apart. The fear grew and grew the longer we were together.

When I finally took him home to meet my mother, Hunter and Mason, I felt almost a sense of relief. This false image of me would take a hit, and he wouldn't love me so much, and it would be easier. More real. I wouldn't feel that sense of doom that this beautiful, alien world of love wouldn't last, because the longer it did, the more I wanted to stay there.

"Hola," my mother said as we went in. "¿Habla usted inglés?"

"Sí," he said, "pero me alegra tanto que hables español, Señora Sloane."

"I don't . . . I'm sorry, I don't speak your language," Mom said, her voice louder than necessary. "Would . . . you . . . like . . . to—"

"Knock it off, Mom," I said. "His English is better than yours, and he's not deaf."

"Is that how you introduce us?" Mom said with a martyrish sigh. She took a sip of clear liquid, which I'd bet my left arm wasn't water.

"Mother, I'd like you to meet Rafael Esteban Jesús

Santiago," I said, using his full name for maximum effect. "Rafe, my mother, Kathryn Ellerington Sloane. Big Kitty to her friends." The dear man didn't bat an eye.

"A genuine pleasure, Mrs. Sloane." He took her hand and bowed over it, like Mr. Darcy. Mom looked at me, confused, but stood aside so we could go into the chilly white foyer.

Mason, then eight, was waiting eagerly to one side. Hunter's heavy hand gripped his shoulder, lest the child show happiness or enthusiasm. "Hi, guys," I said. "Rafe, this is my brother, Hunter, and his wonderful son, Mason. Hi, sweetie."

I opened my arms for a hug, and my nephew wriggled away and wrapped his skinny arms around me. Then he offered his hand to Rafe. "I'm her nephew. Her favorite person."

Rafe laughed. "I will remember that. It is very nice to meet you, Mason. I have heard many good things about you." He offered his hand to my brother. "Hello, Hunter. A pleasure."

"You're a cook?" Hunter said, shaking Rafe's hand once—hard—then dropping it.

"Yes. A chef, actually."

"Same thing, right?" Before Rafe could answer, Hunter left the foyer. "Can we get this going, Ma?" he asked over his shoulder. "I realize George has never brought anyone home before, but I'm starving."

Dinner was stiff and awkward, Rafael doing his best to charm my mother and brother and failing miserably. Mason, on the other hand, peppered him with questions about Spain, the Dominican Republic, California, Alabama and Texas, all places Rafael had lived.

My mother looked puzzled the entire time, and Hunter didn't make eye contact with anyone except his son, issuing terse orders—*sit up straight, don't play with your fork, why aren't you eating, stop fidgeting.*

"Hunter, I was very sorry to learn that you lost your wife," Rafe said. "And Mason, your mother."

Shit. Leah had been gone for almost a year, but we never spoke about her.

Silence fell over the already quiet table, and Hunter leveled a hate-filled look at me. "My dead wife is none of your fucking business," he said, making Mason flinch. "That's just great. Great. Thanks a lot, *George.* Mason, we're leaving. Now."

Mason's eyes filled with tears. "Bye, G. Bye, Mr. Santiago."

"I'm so sorry to have brought up a painful subject," Rafael said, standing up. "Please forgive me."

Hunter ignored him, grabbed Mason by the arm and towed him out. A few seconds later, the front door slammed, and they were gone.

"It's not you," I said in the ensuing silence. "That's pretty much how my brother leaves every family event."

Big Kitty tutted. "Really, Georgia, did you have to tell your . . . friend about Leah? You know how much your brother loved her."

"Was I supposed to pretend she's still alive, Mom?"

"Again, I am very sorry to have brought up a difficult topic," Rafe said.

"He was just waiting to have a tantrum," I said. "It's what he does, it's who he is."

"He must be very sad."

I rolled my eyes. *Sad* and *asshole* were different things.

"When do you go back to Spain, Ramone?" Mom asked.

"Rafael," I said, sighing.

"I'm sorry. When do you go back to Spain, *Rafael*? There, are you happy now, Georgia?"

"So happy."

"I am an American citizen," Rafe said. "I was born in Huntsville, Alabama, actually. My father is an engineer. He was working on the space shuttle at the time. Most of my childhood was spent in Barcelona, however." He smiled. "I will be staying in New York for the foreseeable future."

"And your parents . . . are they . . . can they . . . stay?"

Rafe looked at me in confusion. I closed my eyes. "They're American citizens, Mom."

"Georgia, please. You act like I'm *racist*." She snorted and poured herself some more wine, sloshing a little on the tablecloth. "Ramone, I am the furthest thing from racist in the entire world."

Later, as I was putting on my coat, my mother whispered, "At least someone wants you."

Yeah.

We left and got into the car. Rafe sat there a minute, hands on the steering wheel. "So, do you think they liked me?" he asked, and we laughed so hard it took us fifteen minutes before we were safe to drive.

But . . . there's always a but, isn't there?

Here's what Rafe didn't notice.

The looks that said, "He's with *her*?" anytime we held hands. One night we went out for dinner, and afterward, Rafe went to get the car. As I waited, the server said to me, "It's so nice to see a brother and sister who get along so well."

Brother and *sister*? Me with my straight blond hair, green eyes and white, white skin, Rafael the complete opposite? He'd kissed me twice, damn it! "He's my boyfriend, bitch," I said, leaving to wait on the sidewalk. When he pulled up to the curb and asked why there were tears in my eyes, I said it was the cold.

He had no idea about my insecurities, and I hated myself

for having them. The girls of Camp Copperbrook used to talk about this, listing our qualities . . . smart, kind, loyal, funny, everything that mattered. I'd been taught to remember the good parts of myself.

But I was also the girl who'd hidden in her room at home to eat marmalade straight from the jar. The girl whose cousin had shown her how to barf when she was ten. The girl who had stopped being invited to sleepovers in seventh grade because Taylor Rhodes told her "we don't want to be seen with you anymore." I was the girl who had won the New England Regional Debate Tournament and found a note taped to the back of my sweater that said *fat-ass.* I was the girl at Princeton who overheard a roommate whispering in the hall that she didn't want to room with me next year because the sight of me getting dressed made her feel sick.

I couldn't tell Rafe about those things. They were just too pathetic, and the last thing I wanted was his pity . . . and for him to start wondering if all those people had a point.

When Marley met him, she was fantastic. "Nice to meet you, Rafael Santiago—oh, and by the way, I'm only ever going to call you by your whole name because it's so stinkin' beautiful."

"My whole name is Rafael Esteban Jesús Santiago," he said, grinning.

"Oh, my *God.* I believe in cloning, just for the record," she said, putting her hand over her heart.

Sitting there, smiling, holding my boyfriend's hand, I had the dark thought that Rafe and Marley would make a better couple. Marley was funny and bright, always the life of the party, making friends wherever she went, just like Rafe. Though she weighed more than I did, her size wasn't as big an issue to her as mine was to me.

But for whatever reason, he loved me. Me.

When he proposed, in bed, during sex—*Marry me,*

Georgia, please say you will—well, how was I supposed to say anything but yes?

It was like looking through a keyhole at the most beautiful garden in the world. If I could get in, I would be so happy there.

So I told my mother, who asked if I was pregnant, and he told his parents, who cried with joy.

I took a job in Manhattan. A week before we'd met, Rafe had agreed to be a partner/executive chef at a place in the city, and he'd said he'd give it two years. We found an apartment, but Rafe said it would make his parents happier if we didn't officially live together before the wedding. I thought that was adorable.

Plus, then I could starve myself and do sit-ups till my abdomen screamed in pain, and I could take diuretics and Rafe wouldn't know.

I was getting *married.* Everyone would be looking at me, Fat Georgia, and I wanted to be as beautiful on our wedding day as I could possibly be. Rafe deserved it.

But who was I kidding? It was all about me. The ultimate challenge, the unreachable star for fat girls everywhere—to be slim on our wedding day. Slim, slender, sylphlike, willowy, lissome, svelte . . . even the words were lovely.

My eating issues bared their sharp teeth. I subsisted. Celery. Cottage cheese. A spoonful of peanut butter. I only ate regular food when I was with Rafe, and then I only took a few bites.

I dieted myself down to the thinnest I had been since eighth grade, thin enough to wear a dress size that they actually had *in stock* at Vera Wang. I was light-headed much of the time, exhausted, but I was going to be thin on my wedding day, goddamnit.

Rafe's parents wanted us to get married in a Catholic church, and because I was vaguely Protestant and couldn't actually remember the last time I'd been to a service, I said yes. Also, because it pissed off my mother.

At my bridal shower, my size was discussed a great deal. How amazing it was, how fantastic I looked, how horny Rafe must be now that I was "tiny," how did I do it, was it hot yoga or gastric bypass or cabbage juice or phentermine? I smiled demurely, seething inside. It was none of their fucking business (and yes to the cabbage juice; that was a fun week, let me tell you).

Marley changed the subject and asked about my job, but it didn't work. No accomplishment of my life measured up to my weight loss, apparently. Princeton, Yale, my shocking salary as an attorney, my apartment on the Upper West Side . . . who even cared? I was thin! Or thinnish.

"Just a few more pounds to go," my mother said. "Fifteen. Twenty at the most." I looked at her sharply, surprised despite a lifetime of experience with her priorities. I wanted to tell her about my nights spent in the bathroom, puking till nothing but bile came up, or taking drugs that gave me diarrhea so bad my ass was raw. I wanted her to say that Rafe was the luckiest man in the world, that he'd better be worthy of me, her precious, brilliant little girl.

Instead, she pinched my waist. "Yes. Fifteen at least."

"Be careful when you get pregnant," one of her friends warned. "If you don't lose the weight, he'll stray." Like he was a dog who'd wander off, tempted by a steak.

Rafe wanted kids. Of course he did. Thinking about dark-eyed babies made my heart hurt with so much love that I nearly cried. Was it normal, I wondered? Was loving someone supposed to be fraught with terror?

Our wedding was huge, Dad sparing no expense for his oldest daughter. The ceremony was held at Santuario de Nuestra Señora de Guadalupe en San Bernardo—that is, the most beautiful, colorful, lively church I'd ever seen, with pictures of overfed little angels and the Virgin Mary with golden beams shining out of her and Jesus bleeding on the cross. I thought my mom and my half of the guest list might faint when they came in. Flowers everywhere, incense, the ceremony in Spanish and English. Rafe's three sisters were my bridesmaids, Marley my maid of honor, Paris our flower girl, Mason our ring bearer. Emerson, who had asked *not* to be in the wedding party, came up from Delaware.

As my father, who was crying like a baby, walked me down the aisle, I had a flash of panic. There were so many people in the church that I couldn't see Rafe. An instant, rock-solid conviction flashed through my head. This was a dream. Of *course* he wasn't there. I would never get a guy like that. And even if I did, it wouldn't last.

Then he *was* there, and riptides of love and fear warred in my heart. As we said our vows, Rafe's beautiful brown eyes were wet.

How could this last? This woman lighting candles in front of a statue of the Virgin Mary wasn't me! I wasn't the type for this wedding, this family, this man. Rafe was going to find out, and he'd leave me.

Our plan was to go on a honeymoon to Spain next year, after we had established ourselves in our jobs. But even as I talked about it at the reception, I knew. I wouldn't be going to Spain. I felt it in my bones. Things like this didn't happen to people like me. But I smiled, and tried not to cry, though I had to press my face into Rafe's shoulder during our first dance as husband and wife. Everyone, including my husband, assumed my tears were tears of joy. Not terror.

My dad gave us three nights in the Central Park Suite at the Mandarin Oriental as a gift, and Rafe carried me over the threshold and everything. Then we moved into the small but lovely apartment on the Upper West Side, and real life began.

Rafe had the restaurant. I was a first-year associate in a huge law firm with nine hundred other lawyers, hustling every day into the Chrysler Building with the other over-worked associates. Rafe came home at two a.m., and I got up at six thirty, sometimes earlier, since there was a com-petition at my firm—as there was at all big, important firms in the city—for who could put in more billable hours.

When we were together, though, it was . . .

Oh, I want to tell you how perfect it was. How loving and kind he was, because he was. How my heart actually sped up when he came home, how he would kiss me so gently if he thought I was asleep, how he'd get up to make me breakfast, even though he'd only been asleep for a few hours.

All those things happened. I just didn't trust them.

I started to get jumpy. The three-day honeymoon had caused me to gain five pounds, my body starved for calo-ries, greedily storing each one away. At work, it was too easy to say yes to Chinese or Thai food, to grab an over-stuffed sandwich or hot dog. I'd tell myself I'd only take a few bites, but as I worked through every lunch, I'd find my meal gone.

And then, I'd come home to an empty apartment filled with luscious food made by my new husband's hands.

The weight started to come back. Of course it did, but that too-familiar feeling of failure did not stop me from eating.

And then, there was this . . . *thing* Rafael did. All the time, and it drove me crazy.

He constantly told me how beautiful I was. I know what you're thinking. *The bastard! How dare he!* He loved look-ing at me. He'd come into the bathroom when I was taking a shower and pull back the curtain to chat and give me the Spanish look of love, and I hated it. I'd spent my entire life covering up, and he wanted to peel away everything, literally and metaphorically.

One night after we fooled around, I got out of bed and pulled on my sturdy cami, panties and pajamas.

"Why are you getting dressed, *corazón*?" he asked. It meant *heart* in Spanish. Even the endearment was too much, too big, too hard to believe, and I hated myself for thinking all those things.

"Because it's bedtime," I said, keeping my voice casual.

"Sleep without clothes."

"I get cold," I lied.

"I'll keep you warm." His eyebrow lifted, and there it was, that surge of disbelief and love and irritation all rolled into one. Sex (still in the dark) was one thing. Letting him see my naked body without prep time, without posing, holding in my stomach, showing my least-worst angle? No, thanks.

He didn't get the hints.

I didn't *want* him to fondle my ass when I was brushing my teeth. I didn't want to be told over and over until it was just white noise that I was beautiful, hot, sexy, whatever. Sometimes I felt like saying, "Can you knock it off for one day? Please?"

You'd think that being told all those nice things would've helped my self-esteem. Instead, it did the opposite. It constantly made me aware of my body, its many flaws and imperfections, my cellulite and stretch marks unearned by pregnancy.

I was much more comfortable when we were talking over dinner, preferably out somewhere, so that he wouldn't immediately turn whatever conversational intimacy we might have into sex. Those times, walking along the High Line or Christmas shopping for his family . . . those were a hundred times happier for me than when Rafe started kissing my neck while I flossed.

One night when Rafe was working (like most nights), I decided I had to start eating healthy again, as I sort of had in law school. I purged the fridge of everything bad—mayonnaise, cheese (we had eleven kinds!), the sickly sweet soda he loved, wine, beer, the super-fat and horribly delicious coconut yogurt, four kinds of ice cream (his weakness, not that it added a single damn pound to him), the cured meats, the orange-almond pudding he made that was as addictive as meth and about as good for you. Rafe took cream *and* sugar in his coffee. Cream. Not even half-and-half.

I got rid of it all.

"What has happened?" he asked when he opened the fridge the next day. "Have we been robbed? Where is our food?"

"I'm not feeling great these days," I said. "I thought we could do some clean eating."

"*Corazón*, where is my . . ." His face showed his disbelief. "Where's the cream? Where's the lamb I bought yesterday? No *wine*? All this food, gone? Wasted?" He turned to me, horrified.

"I brought it to the soup kitchen." What I could, anyway. They wouldn't take anything that was open or homemade.

"Without even asking me? There was at least four hundred dollars' worth of food in there . . . Georgia, you should not have done this."

"Not everyone can eat the way you can, Rafe. Everything is too rich."

"So you throw away a week's worth of food?" He slammed the fridge closed. "I am a chef! I need certain foods here, to practice and experiment."

"Even though you have an entire restaurant at your disposal?"

"This is my home, too. You cannot just throw away food because you don't want to eat certain things."

"Okay. Sorry." I wasn't. He'd made two kinds of cake on Monday, his day off. Two! I "took them to work," by which I meant I ate half of one Tuesday night when he was at the restaurant and threw the rest in the trash before I could eat even more.

He sat on the end of the couch. "I know you have gained a little bit of weight, Georgia." I flinched inside, because this was the first time he'd ever mentioned it. "But that does not matter to me. I hope by now you know I think you're beautiful."

"Oh, okay. So now that I have your approval, I can just let go of everything else." Like him saying that could take away a lifetime of hatred and obsession over my physical self. The *ego* of it. The typical male, thinking that if he loved you, all *must* be right with the world. "Has it ever occurred to you that your opinion is not the only one that matters?"

He blinked. "What do you mean?"

For an instant, a massive wave of rage and helplessness and hurt almost crashed down on us, drowning us in an ocean of blood from every little cut I'd endured since before I could remember. *She could be so pretty. Too bad she doesn't look like you. Just stop eating. Doesn't she care about her weight?*

It was too much, too big, too scary. "Look," I said. "I want to eat a little healthier than you cook. Is that so much to ask? Have I offended you by asking that? If so, I'm very sorry." I wasn't, and he knew it.

"Fine!" He threw up his hands. "We will eat healthier. In case you've been too busy to notice, your husband is a chef. He can cook anything you want."

"Maybe I don't want what you make."

That got him. "Yes. Because I am such a terrible cook and am scheming for you to have heart disease and die young and inherit your millions. You have found me out, Georgia."

"Why are you being such a dick? You know what? Never mind. I have work to do. I'm sorry, but I can't fight about food right now. I'll give you the money and you can buy more cheese."

"Yes. And now you have an excuse not to make love tonight."

That one hit me right in the chest, but I looked down at my laptop. "Work, Rafe. I have work to do. We don't all get to play in kitchens every day."

Thus, our first fight was about food.

He was a chef. He didn't understand that food was my enemy when it was practically his lover.

Mealtimes together, few though they were, became tense. Either I overate, resenting him for cooking something irresistible, or I barely ate, insulting him. I couldn't tell him that eating what he considered to be a normal portion would make me gain weight. That while he ate slowly, savoring the meal, I wanted to shove it all in my mouth at once, have seconds, and thirds, then vomit it all up in the bathroom. I felt like he was watching me all the time, daring me not to eat, or daring me to starve myself, always noticing what I put in my mouth, always measuring it.

It was like living with my mother again. At night, when he was at the restaurant and I was working, always working, I'd order Chinese or Thai food, then take the empty containers down to the trash so he wouldn't see them in the kitchen bin.

I knew I was the problem, but I couldn't help it. I couldn't find the words to talk about *it*—food, weight, size, sorrow, insecurity. Who would love a person with such hang-ups? The woman he'd met and dated had been confident and funny and dry. I loved him too much for him not to love me . . . which was making me hate him.

Food, my eternal foe and best friend, had come back to ruin me.

Our happiness was eroding. Our sex life suffered, because I was too worried about being attractive enough, hot enough, daring enough. I started thinking of ways to avoid sex, then overcompensated when we did do it. Rafe never knew who he was getting—someone who'd have cramps/period/migraine/sore throat, or a voracious sex beast acting out a scene from a porno.

"There is something wrong between us," he said one night in the dark after a round of weird, insincere sex.

The words were a knife.

"I'm sorry," I said. "I'm really stressed at work." And then I launched into a tale of a complicated case I was working on, using every legal term I could, every detail, every coworker involved.

He knew I was lying. He wasn't stupid.

Though he came home late every night, he started coming home later. Was he sleeping with someone else? I couldn't blame him. Was she one of the servers, one of those naturally slender, blessed and beautiful women with great asses, flat stomachs and perky boobs?

The space between us grew deeper, a great murky sinkhole in the middle of that beautiful garden I'd glimpsed.

Meanwhile, ironically, work was going great. I didn't love it, but I told myself no first-year ever loved work. But my briefs and input were getting me the coveted attention of the senior partner in our division, Anthony Dewitt.

He was in his late thirties, divorced, handsome, appreciative of my work and near-perfect memory. Anthony was also just a tiny bit flirty—not in any way that made me uncomfortable, but in a way that made me feel . . . special. When I handed him a brief, he'd glance through it and murmur, "Where have you been all my life?" One Friday night around seven (we had a trial coming up), he leaned in my doorway and said, "Do you have plans for dinner? Oh, wait, of course you do. You're a newlywed. Lucky guy, your husband."

"Actually, he'll be working till one or two tonight," I heard myself say.

"Want to grab something? It's the least I can do, since you're here, slogging away for me."

It wasn't an affair. But it sure as hell let me put more distance between Rafe and me, and I felt safer that way. Safer from Rafe.

Anthony was nice. We were close enough that we could share little bits of our pasts, far enough that we could keep the ugly parts hidden. Rafe, in contrast, was a hunter, tracking me, waiting for me to show myself, his gun always raised.

Anthony wore killer suits, always with a beautiful silk tie and pocket square. Just like my dad. He texted me from time to time, always about work, never anything inappropriate, but he did it more and more often as he grew to rely on me. And always in that super-friendly way. Georgia on my mind, page 4, under 3.1.4.3(d). 10-12% reduction in ozone . . . is that correct? Love, Ray Charles.

Get it? "Georgia on My Mind," the iconic song, the only reason I could find to love my name.

That, and the way it sounded when Rafael said it.

I dropped by the restaurant at least once a week to show my support (and remind any female staffers that Rafe was married). I always made sure to be outgoing and cheerful and affectionate, trying to show Rafe how proud I was of him. Because I *was*. He worked like an ox, his food was magic, and the restaurant was a runaway hit, garnering a great review in the *Times*. He was amazing and wonderful, and he made me nervous every minute we were together.

Except for that first fight, we didn't talk about what was really wrong. A lifetime of arming myself against my family, pretending not to care, had trained me to duck and cover any real emotions.

One rare Sunday afternoon when the weather was nice and my eyes had gotten sticky from reading case law, Rafe and I took a walk, heading for Central Park. We held hands, but it was stiff and strange and awkward, like our hands no longer fit together.

"We need to talk," he said as we crossed Central Park West, the Dakota looming darkly.

"About what?" I was *such* an ass. I knew what. A little kid passed us on a scooter, his nanny following listlessly, eyes on her phone.

"About us. About how you will come to the restaurant, all sweetness and hugs, but pretend to be asleep when I come home. About how you lock the bathroom door when you are taking a shower. About the way you don't look me in the eyes anymore."

I swallowed. Was there anything worse than a man in touch with his feelings?

"I just like some privacy in the bathroom, that's all. I don't need an audience when I shave my legs." My cheeks were hot with shame.

"What is going on, Georgia? You are not happy. You are on that phone of yours all the time."

"Well, I have to be! I'm a first-year associate, Rafe. And I *am* happy. I'm just . . . busy. And yes, marriage is an adjustment." *Tell him, idiot,* begged some distant, well-adjusted part of my brain.

My self-loathing about my body, my lonely childhood,

my brother's endless campaign of hate, Big Kitty's obsession with my size, my father becoming a family man only after he'd left me behind . . . all of those things had tattooed my soul, and the words inked there said *not enough*.

This marriage was built on sand. The woman Rafe fell in love with was fiction.

I didn't have the words to tell him those things.

He stopped walking and looked out over the Sheep Meadow, where couples were lying on blankets, soaking up the sun. Four or five kids were playing tag, and one little girl was spinning in a circle, giddy and laughing.

"Do you want a divorce?" He didn't look at me.

"No!" Did I? Did our marriage already have an infection that couldn't be stopped? "Do you?"

"No." His eyes were so sad. We continued walking, but I couldn't think of a single thing to say.

But the word had been spoken, and the infection turned into gangrene. We all know what the cure for that is. Amputation. To soften the blow, I started to justify to myself why divorce would be for the best.

We'd rushed into this, after all. We'd only known each other a year before getting married. We were from different cultures (his, warm and loving; mine, repressed and cold). Our work hours were ridiculous. We were a case of opposites attract.

All of a sudden, I couldn't remember the last time I'd seen him smile. At me, anyway. He smiled at work all the frigging time. The thought made me angry and guilty and heartbroken all at once. I missed the old me, the one who was confident and quiet. The one who'd been appreciated for being wallpaper, the one who was never expected to . . . well . . . shine.

And then there was Anthony, my boss—steady, constant, easy. Rafe simply wanted more than I could give.

Anthony didn't need anything other than my good cheer. If there was a level of flirtation beneath our work (and there was), it was harmless.

Right.

When our department won our case, Anthony took us all out for dinner—three lawyers, two spouses. "Where's your husband?" Anthony asked me. They'd met once or twice, when Rafe had come to my office to take me to lunch. "I love that guy."

"He had to work, unfortunately." The truth was, I hadn't told Rafe about this dinner.

"We should've gone to his restaurant, then!"

"It wasn't a good night for him," I lied. "A private party." Shame curled around my heart like an ember.

"Well. I was hoping he could be here for this." He handed each of us a small, narrow box. Inside was a Cartier watch, absolutely stunning.

"Kind of a tradition at the firm," he said. He put it on my wrist, his fingers perfectly neutral, and did the same with Nana, the other female lawyer on the team. Did his eyes linger on mine? Did it matter?

For whatever reason, that dinner was the point of no return. Rafe got quieter and quieter, his hours and mine making it so we were almost surprised to see each other.

Rafe brought up counseling. We went to one session, where the therapist opened with, "Most couples who come to counseling are already finished with their marriage." For the next forty-five minutes, we gave stiff answers and received nothing in the way of advice on how to fix our sorry state. We never went back. Rafe stopped trying to talk, to knock down the wall. After all, I'd spent twenty-nine years building that wall. That motherfucker was sturdy.

I continued to do well at work, though a creeping realization was dawning . . . I didn't like being a lawyer. It was like I was cursed with this memory, my ability to formulate those tortuous, endless legal sentences. There was no challenge for me, no thrill, just the dredging up of facts and making connections between case law and our clients' issues.

But there was Anthony with the compliments, the slightest edge of chemistry between us bringing an energy to the workday, the conversations, the many, many texts. We went from talking only about work to something slightly more personal—a text from him at nine p.m.

You have to watch Breaking Bad. I think we should hire Saul Goodman. Why hasn't anyone told me to watch this show?

Me: I'm sorry. I thought you lived in America. Breaking Bad has been over for years. Plot spoiler . . .

Him: Don't you dare. I want Walter to live a long and healthy life as drug lord of the desert, teaching Walter Jr. his craft.

Me: Sounds like a Father's Day Very Special Television Event.

It was harmless. Mostly. And then came the inevitable blurring of lines. A text saying I looked extra nice that day. A second later, another text, saying if that was inappropriate, he was sorry.

I told him it wasn't, and thanks. Also, I liked his purple handkerchief and tie combo. Very dapper.

A month later Rafe and I acknowledged our first anniversary with an awkward dinner and lovemaking afterward. We didn't bring up the misery of this first year.

A few weeks after that, he came home at ten p.m., which was early for him. I had been working and eating out of a quart of pork lo mein, having polished off two egg rolls already. I jolted out of my chair when he came through the door, horrified that he'd caught me bingeing.

He sat down on the couch across from me and just looked at me for a minute. The shame of my meal sat between us—the wrappers, the dirty plate, the half-empty bottle of wine. The history of me was on that coffee table. I hated him for seeing it and sucked in my stomach hard, wishing, wishing, wishing I hadn't gotten fat again.

It was always about weight.

"I read your texts," Rafe said quietly. "While you were asleep last night, I took your phone to see where your attention has been."

There were probably hundreds of texts from Anthony by now. I'd never erased them. All of them bespoke intimacy, friendship, humor. All the things Rafe and I had lost.

I started to defend myself, then stopped. Technically, no, Anthony and I had never crossed a line. But my toes were on that line, and even if I never would've cheated on my husband, I *had* wanted another man to come between us.

The shame burned.

"I think it is time that we consider a separation, Georgia."

I wanted to cry. To beg him to start over with me. To tell him I'd be different.

"So you're pulling the jealous Latin husband, then?" I said instead. "I didn't think you were so insecure."

"You are the one who is insecure, Georgia! Do you think I have missed the fact that you have a problem with eating, with your weight? And yet I love you for more than those things. Why does that not matter as much?"

"So your love should erase every bad thought I've ever had? I'm sorry. It's not that simple."

"You refuse to talk to me about it. That is not love. Instead, you have turned to this other man."

"Why would I ever imagine you can understand? You're a chef. You just don't get it."

"So I have to become obese in order to love my wife? Is that what you are saying?"

"Did you just call me obese? Wow! Wow, Rafe!"

The fight was ugly. We both yelled. And when I said my last words to him, words so horrible that I hated myself like I never had before, he covered his eyes.

My heart broke.

"Get out," he said quietly, not taking his hand away.

I had made him *cry*, and self-hatred punched me hard. "Rafe—" I began.

"Please, Georgia. Get out."

Step by step, I had ruined the most wonderful thing that ever happened to me, ground it into the dirt because losing him was easier than living with the fear of losing him. The *stupidity* of it, the cruelty of my heart, was something I could not bear. To have hurt Rafael, the kindest, most wonderful person I'd ever met . . .

"Okay," I whispered.

That one small word ended our marriage. It was better that way. I was just skipping ahead to the inevitable ending. That's what I told myself, anyway.

CHAPTER 13

Marley

Stop eating when you're sad.
(It's not on the list, but it sure as hell should be.)

"Yes, Mom! I'll be there," I said. "Don't you dare call the police again."

"Honey, it was that one time."

"One time for me, one time for Eva." I tucked the phone against my ear and turned the crank on the pasta maker. Gluten free for the Goldbergs, gluten full for the Levinsons, so I had to make two batches and didn't have time to argue with my mom. And yet, arguing was the song of our people.

"Fine! Sue me! I was worried. I'm your mother, I love you, you were late, and I pictured you dead in a ditch with crows pecking out your eyes."

"That's beautiful."

"You'll understand someday. When you have kids of your own." The familiar threat/plea/prayer.

"If that happy day ever comes," I said patiently, "you can teach me your positive visualizations. Crows pecking, ditches, dying. And just for the record, I told you I wasn't coming *that one time*. I called you, texted you and e-mailed you."

"Honey, it was our family dinner night. You never forget!"

"I *didn't* forget, Ma. I had a hair appointment. The one time in the history of my life I missed a family dinner! Dante misses all the time, and you never harass him."

"Sweetie, this is not harassing. This is love." She paused. "Also, your brother saves lives for a living."

"Mother. You had the police do a safety check on me at the hair salon."

"You didn't answer your phone!"

"I was having highlights done! I didn't hear it ring."

"So? Of course I was worried. I still worry."

The unspoken hung in the air. *I lost one child already. I can't bear the thought of losing you, too.* I softened. "Mom. I *am* coming tonight, so rest easy. I'll see you in just a few hours. I have to go, okay? I'm cooking. Love you."

"I love you, too, baby."

I smiled, tapped end with floury fingers and got back to work.

The kitchen was the best part of my apartment. And listen. This apartment was fantastic.

Unlike my best friend/landlord, I didn't go crazy with colors. It was very tasteful down here, the kitchen and living room walls the color of wet sand, the trim painted white. I had a gorgeous brown leather sofa and a floral-print armchair. Lots of framed photos, lots of plants, including pots of herbs on the kitchen windowsill, more planted in the courtyard garden, which burst with plants—flowers, hydrangeas, a little Japanese maple tree, boxwoods, and a lilac tree whose scent made me drunk in the spring.

All my doing. Georgia had a black thumb; I loved growing things. Loved flowers. Loved bringing them to Georgia, who was always so charmed, and to my mom, who would always snap a shot and put them on her Instagram account, the better to shame Eva, who did things like forget Mother's Day.

Also, I hated having downtime.

Being alone was okay if I was super busy. Being *quiet* and alone . . . I hated that. That's when the not-here of Frankie dragged me down.

People love twins. It's a universal delight, and faces light up all across the world when they hear the magic word. *Twins! You're so lucky! How fun!*

What do you do when you're like me? I hated telling people I'd had a twin who died. It was too huge, too sad. Once, a long time ago, I'd asked Dante not to use the word *twin*, and in a rare moment of pure empathy, he'd hugged me long and close. "I wish you and I were the twins," he'd said, even though he was seven years younger, and I cried so hard I think I scared him.

Anyway. I turned on some Bruno Mars to cheer myself up, as he never failed me. *Sorry thinking about you makes me sad, Frankie.*

I went into the courtyard. I snipped some parsley and pinched off the basil blossoms so the leaves wouldn't get bitter. Pulled a few weeds, picked some zinnias to put in a jar, one bouquet for me, one for Georgia.

Georgia, who was looking so thin these days. Thinner than I'd ever been.

That's the first thing you think of when you see another woman, isn't it? *Is she skinnier than I am?* For a long time, I was the least obese of our little threesome.

Not anymore. When we'd gone out to Hudson's that night, I had to struggle not to envy Georgia's smallness, even knowing how she'd come to it: a possible ulcer and the stress over Mason, combined with the eating disorder she'd fought with for years—skipping meals, purging, manic exercise. She'd never gotten skinny enough to meet the criteria for true anorexia, but she'd had all of the demons.

So Georgia was getting thinner, hopefully not because of an ulcer but because of my excellent meals, though to the best of my knowledge, she still hadn't seen a doctor. Emerson was dead. I was the fat one now, even though I'd done an hour of cardio this morning, followed by an hour of yoga. Still fat. There was no getting around it. And there was no avoiding the fact that I would have loved to be Georgia's weight right now. Size matters, as much as you don't want it to.

But while Georgia struggled with food, thanks to her skeletal mother, I loved it. Food was family. I couldn't divorce food. My mom had taught me to cook, and nothing made me feel as calm and loving as being in the kitchen. I was so glad I'd found a way to make cooking a career. It was Georgia's ex, the wonderful Rafe, who'd really given me the kick I needed, hiring me as a line chef at his restaurant though I had no experience, telling me which classes would help me. I adored Rafe. There's something incredibly appealing about a man who's smitten with his woman. Back then, he couldn't look away from her, and he touched her constantly. His voice was different when he talked to her, and his eyes always grew soft when she walked into a room.

It broke my heart when they split up. But as I didn't talk about Frankie, Georgia didn't talk about Rafe, and I respected that (mostly).

She still loved him. She hadn't been the same since their divorce. Or no, that was wrong. She went back to being the same. For a little while, though, she'd been someone different, back when they were dating. She'd reminded me of an orchid—their leaves dull and unremarkable, the buds clenched tight for months. But when those buds open up, there's no more beautiful flower in the world.

Georgia had been like that with Rafe. He'd been the eastern sun, and she opened in the warmth of his love.

Le sigh.

These days, she was back to being a tight little ball.

Le poop.

Well, I had work to do. Seeing my pale sheets of dough come out of the pasta maker in thin strips of linguine, breathing in the smell of basil and lemon . . . I just didn't understand people who didn't like to cook. I was grateful to them, since they were my living, but I didn't get it. Georgia had eaten out of cartons (or not eaten at all) until I moved here. She and Will Harding had been my first clients.

And Emerson . . . God knew what she had eaten.

I should've known Emerson was getting worse. I should've sensed it.

I hadn't known Frankie was so sick, either. Granted, we had only been four years old, but you'd think a twin would pick up on these things.

The timer rang, thank God. I turned the heat off under the chicken, laid ten portobello mushrooms on the grill and drizzled them with olive oil, then got out the Bibb lettuce I'd bought at the farmers' market this morning, so sweet and crisp I could've eaten an entire head of it. As it was, I ripped off a few leaves and ate them, the crunch of the lettuce perfect, the smell clean and fresh.

I wished I could've saved Emerson. I wished I could've given some of my fat and strength to Frankie. I wished I didn't have to make up for all that Frankie didn't get to do.

It wasn't always easy, being the twin who didn't die.

Now there was this list, and the challenge of going for it, even weighing what I weighed. I'd already checked off two of them—my (personal) photo shoot, and getting a cute guy to buy me a drink.

And yes, I'd gone home with Camden. Drove him home, because he'd been tipsy. He lived in New Rochelle, mind you. That was forty minutes each way.

I'd offered to let him "crash" at my place, but he said he had something to do the next morning. And so, yep, I did the good-friend thing. He fell asleep on the way there, his head against the passenger seat window, and I put my hand on his knee.

The longing to be part of a pair had wrapped around me hard in that moment. I won't lie. I *needed* another half.

When we got to his apartment, I tucked him in, put the trash can next to his bed in case he barfed, left a glass of water on the night table and then left.

Seems I'd been downgraded from friend with bennies to designated driver.

That being said, I did get a really cute selfie of the two of us at Hudson's, and yes, I posted it on Instagram. *Out with New York's Bravest!* I'd captioned it. Dante saved the picture from being too romantic by photobombing, bless him. Otherwise, it might've seemed like I was trying too hard.

Pause for laughter. I could've probably gotten Mark Watney off Mars with the same amount of energy I'd put into being entertaining without being a comedian/being friendly but not hitting on him or letting him know I liked him/but totally understanding if it wasn't the right time.

All that to drive him home and tuck him in.

I'd been in love for five years, and this was what I got. It was getting old. *I* was getting old. Older, anyway. It wasn't cute anymore.

Next time, I swore, I'd just tell him. *I want to be your girlfriend. I'm enough that you want to sleep with me—now be with me. We can at least try it.*

I could do that. Sure.

....

That evening, I made my rounds, evading the Levinsons' Great Pyrenees dog, who always wanted to molest, drool on and shed on me, making me appreciate Admiral all the more for his extreme politeness, short fur and well-behaved salivary glands. At the Putneys' house, I rearranged the stuff in their fridge and wiped down their counters, since they were slobs and I couldn't bear to picture my excellent food on sticky counters.

At the next stop, I chatted with Nellie Ames, a sweet old lady whose grown children hired me to make sure she didn't subsist on Lucky Charms and Kit Kat bars alone. Though it wasn't in my job description, I tidied her living room and fed the cats, then showed her how to text her great-granddaughter. (Sorry, kid.) Finally, I kissed her soft, wrinkled cheek and said good-bye.

"You're wonderful!" she crowed, texting away with her gnarled forefinger.

The last delivery of the evening was Will Harding. If we had our usual three-word exchange, I'd be on time at Mom's and avoid either a speeding ticket and/or a full-blown Amber Alert.

He was waiting by the door, like . . . well, like a serial killer. As usual, he was dressed in completely unremarkable clothes: khakis and a button-down shirt. He was a plain-looking guy, saved from being completely forgettable by his hair, which stuck up in odd places and gave him a sort of tousled, Jason-Bateman-if-he-played-a-serial-killer vibe.

"Hi!" I said, always exuding more energy with him, the

human black hole. "Homemade linguine with basil, asparagus and chicken. The butter sauce is in this container; if you
keep it in the fridge, it'll solidify, so just toss it in a frying
pan for a couple minutes if it does. I didn't want to pour it on
too soon or the asparagus will get soggy. Tomorrow's lunch
is that Asian noodle salad you like. I included a side of aru-
gula, too. It's good for you. Dark leafy greens, you know?"

Will just stood there.

May kill people in his spare time.

"Okay," I said. "I have to run. Maybe you can pay me
tomorrow?"

"I would like to pay you now."

I glanced at my watch. "Fine."

He went into the next room and took the checkbook out.
Slowly wrote me my check. Slowly came back into the
kitchen. My keys were already in my hand.

He didn't hand me the check.

"I'll just take that, then," I said.

"I have a favor to ask," he said, still not handing over the
check. Instead, he looked steadily at my chin.

"Okay. Go ahead."

"Two weeks from Tuesday, would you make something
that's not on your menu?"

"Sure. Can I call you tomorrow about it?"

"I'd like orange beef teriyaki. The Chinese kind."

I suppressed a sigh. "You bet."

"In the brown sauce. The rice should be sticky."

"I'm sure I can make that. But, Will, I have to leave now.
My family has an event."

"Also, would you . . ." He broke off.

"Would I what?"

"Would you make enough for two?"

"Of course." My portions could always serve two, but I'd
double it. I held out my hand for the check.

"And would you stay and eat with me?"

I couldn't help twitching in surprise. "Oh! Um . . . uh, what day again?"

"Two weeks from Tuesday," he said. "Are you free?"

"I don't know. Um, I really do have to—"

"Would you check? I imagine your calendar updates to your phone."

He was right, of course, but I could practically hear my mother wringing her hands. "I'm old school," I lied. "I'll call you tomorrow."

He looked down. "Fine."

It occurred to me that I had never seen Will Harding smile. I had never seen him have any expression, really, just that same face, a little tense. It was possible that he had Asperger's, maybe, not that I knew about those things.

He had never asked me to make dinner for two.

It occurred to me that he might be a little . . . lonely.

"I'm free," I found myself saying. "I'm almost positive. I'll see you tomorrow. Now, I have to leave, or my mother will call the police."

"Thank you," he said, finally handing me the check. "Good-bye."

Traffic was not great. I clenched the wheel, zipping around slow, non-native New Yorkers, and walked into my parents' house at 6:33, just three minutes late.

"Where have you *been*?" Mom asked. "She's here, everyone! Finally. We were so worried."

"Hi, Ma," I said, kissing her cheek. "Hi, Daddy."

"Hello, muffin," Dad said, giving me a hug. "How's my girl?"

"Just fine," I said. I put my food contribution—a salad—on the counter.

"You said you'd be here at six thirty," Mom said.

I ignored her and made the rounds, hugging Dante and

Louis, who were holding hands on the couch in their newlywed bliss. "So good to see you the other night," Louis said. "Did you have fun?"

"So much fun," I lied. "I'd never seen that video of Dante before. Very exciting."

"Which video of Dante?" Mom asked.

"Something about him rescuing a little girl?" I winked at the boys.

"Of course you've seen it! We had a screening party here! I was going to put it on later so we could watch it again."

"I was being sarcastic, Ma. I have it memorized. It's burned on my soul."

"Well, it should be. Not everyone gets to save a baby like that." Her voice got choked up as she gazed with puppy eyes at her son.

"Hey, Eva," I said, patting my sister on the shoulder. She wasn't the hugging type, which made her a freak in our family.

"You're late," my sister said, looking up from her phone. "A hundred and eighty seconds."

"Sinner."

"I hope dinner's not too cold," Mom said. "I was hoping to eat at six thirty, and now it's six thirty-seven."

"Can I at least change out of my work clothes?" I asked.

"No. Here's your wine." She pushed a glass into my hand. "Come on, everyone."

The boys got off the couch, and Dad came into the living room so we could toast Frankie.

Her pictures were fading. Maybe Eva, who did something complicated and brilliant in the computer world, could scan them and pop the color up a little.

I hated this ritual. Hated it and participated in it every time I was here, which was really far too often.

Even in pictures, you could tell Frankie was failing to

thrive. Too small, too delicate, too pale. I looked at Ebbers the Penguin, his flat black eyes filled with judgment.

For a second, I almost remembered the feeling of Ebbers between us on the nights when I slipped into Frankie's bed. Or maybe that was just my wistful hope—to have a memory of Frankie that was more than a story I'd been told.

"To our beautiful Francesca," Mom said, her voice quivering. "We miss you, angel. We love you."

"We miss you, Frankie," we all echoed, even Dante and Louis, who'd never met her. Eva was stone-faced. We had never talked about Frankie, she and I. Not once.

In an Italian family, you talked about everything except what really mattered.

I chugged my wine, and we trooped into the dining room. Mom wiped her eyes, and Dad gave her a hug and kissed her temple. My parents held hands wherever they went. In some ways, Frankie's loss made them into just one person, like two trees that had grown into each other over the years, wrapping around and protecting each other.

I tried to picture Camden here, as my other half. He'd fit in nicely. I knew he was close to his younger sister. This past summer, he'd gone to the Adirondacks with his whole family. He liked to eat. He was even Italian, which would make Mom and Dad happy.

We took our usual seats—Mom closest to the kitchen, Dad at the other end, Dante and me facing the living room, Eva and Louis across from us.

The table was barely visible under the food Mom had made, and as ever, the sight and smells of food cheered me. Eggplant Parm, my favorite! Meatballs, Dante's fave, made with ground veal, beef and turkey. Chicken oregano, Eva's favorite and a close runner-up for me. Sausage and broccoli rabe, Louis's favorite. Garlic bread, everyone's favorite. The

green salad I'd brought—the one hint of healthy eating. Ca-
ponata with pignoli nuts, ziti with sauce, fresh mozzarella
cheese.

"We gonna say grace?" Dante asked around the meatball already bulging in his cheek. Eva was tearing into the
bread, dunking it in salted olive oil, and Dad was shoveling
a slab of eggplant Parm onto his plate.

"Dear Lord, thank you for our beautiful children and my
amazing wife," Dad said cheerfully.

"Aw! You two!" I said.

"I hope Dante and I are half as lucky as you two, Tony,"
Louis said, getting a smile from my father.

"Do you mind? I'm eating," Eva said, getting the middle
finger from Dante.

"When are you boys gonna have a baby?" I asked. "I
want to be an auntie."

"Since you mention it in that subtle way of yours," Dante
said, "we're thinking next year, maybe we'll start looking
at adoption. Right, babe?"

"That's right," Louis said. They exchanged a look of mutual adoration.

"There's no pasta e fagioli?" Dad asked mournfully, since
we only had enough food to feed Europe.

"I *told* you, Anthony, I'll make it tomorrow!" Mom said,
wounded. "You said you wanted fresh moots"—our way of
saying mozzarella—"so I found it, and let me tell you, it
wasn't easy, mister, I had to go to four grocery stores and
paid eleven dollars for it at Whole Foods, honestly, who can
shop there, don't they have children to put through college?"

"Speaking of kids, Eva, do you ever think about adopt-
ing?" Louis, bless his heart, asked.

"No, I hate children," she said. "People, too, now that I
think of it."

"Don't say that!" Mom said. "Shame on you, Eva."

"She does," I confirmed. "You're new to the family, Louis. You'll learn."

"I hate people except for those sitting at this table," Eva amended. "I'll love your kids, Louis. Just don't ever ask me to babysit. Ma, pass the eggplant. Please."

My sister was an odd duck. A wonderful duck, but strange. She'd recoil when our cousins offered their offspring for her to hold, skipping every baby shower and most weddings. I knew she belonged to a science fiction book club. Otherwise, what she did in her time off was a mystery.

Like me, she was heavy. No. She was *really* heavy, a lot heavier than me. But she didn't seem to mind a bit, whereas I was already cutting myself off from the bounty of my mother's table and would run five miles tomorrow to cancel out the calories I did pack away. Eva had never had a boyfriend (or girlfriend) that I knew of, never mentioned wanting one. Freakishly, our mother didn't give her a hard time about it, whereas I was reminded of my tragic, childless, single state at least once a day through a variety of media.

"Well, I hope you do adopt," Dad said to the boys. "I'd like a grandson."

"I'd like a niece," I said.

"I'd like the ziti," Eva said. "Ma, this food is amazing."

Mom beamed. "Well. I did work all day and my feet are killing me, and I'm so hungry because I did want to eat at six thirty but Marley was late, and now my food is cold, but I'm glad you like it."

"Marles," Dante said, "you coming to the fun run in Central Park?"

"What fun run?"

"You said you'd come. Remember?"

"This is the first I'm hearing of it." Another family trait, not mentioning events where one was expected to show up.

"It's the New York City Fights Hunger thing. Oh, Ma, these meatballs."

"New York should just come here," Eva said. "No hunger at this table, right, Ma?"

"That's right, baby." She smiled and patted Eva's hand.

"You should come, too, Evie," Dante said.

Eva gave him a look. "To run?"

"It's good for you."

"Have we met?" Eva said.

"You could lose a little—" His comment was cut off by Eva's hearty smack to his head. "Fine," he said. "At least my nice sister will be there."

Go running in tight clothes and a sports bra. Oh, dear God. It was on the list.

"I'll be there," I said. Georgia could come, too.

We talked and ate some more (thank God I brought salad). Otherwise, it was a nonstop orgy of artery-hardening deliciousness. I always laughed when someone used the phrase *Mediterranean diet* in terms of health. Clearly not my ancestors' part of the Mediterranean.

"So, kids," Dad said after we'd all had thirds and were starting to slow down. "Your mommy and I, we have something to tell you."

"Is it cancer?" Dante asked. "Who? Which one? Ma, is it you? Daddy?"

"It's not cancer!" Mom said, crossing herself. "Where do you get these ideas?"

"Oh, thank you, Jesus," Dante said, crossing himself, which made me cross myself. Louis did the same, then Dad. Eva abstained, but she did knock on the wooden table. You could take the Catholic out of the girl, but not the superstition.

"No one's sick," Dad said, which resulted in another round of the signing of the cross, more knocks on the table.

"But Mommy and me, we've been thinking. We're not so young anymore."

"You're sixty-two, Dad," Eva said. "You probably have forty years left."

"From your lips to God's ears." Another round of crosses and knocks. A strand of hair got tangled in my necklace, and I tried to separate the two. Stupid hair, always going where it didn't belong. I'd cut it, but I'd tried that once and ended up looking like a poodle.

"Anyway," Dad continued, "we're hoping to be around for a long time, but we've been thinking it's time to sell the house."

I stopped trying to free my hair. Dante froze, a whole meatball impaled on the end of his fork. Louis's big brown eyes swiveled toward him. Eva's mouth dropped open.

Mom wasn't making eye contact, just staring at her plate.

My eyes went to Frankie's shrine.

"Well, that's exciting," Louis said. "Where will you go?"

"We were thinking somewhere warmer. The winters, you know."

"How much warmer?" Eva asked. "New Jersey warmer, or Florida warmer?"

"Oh, Florida," Mom said, waving her hand. "Who wants to go there? The bugs. The alligators."

"We've been thinking Maryland," Dad said. "We like the Chesapeake Bay. Very pretty. Lots of ducks."

"Have you even *been* to Maryland?" Eva asked. "Not that I disapprove, but maybe visiting the state first would be a good plan."

"We made an offer on a house," Mom said.

"What?" Dante screeched.

There was something wrong with my chest. I couldn't look away from the pictures of Frankie. This had been her house, too. For that exact reason, I never, ever would've suspected my parents would sell it.

"We won't go if you don't want us to," Mom said.

"No, no, it's totally up to you," Eva answered. "Right, guys?"

"We'd visit all the time. Eva, we could stay with you. You have that second bedroom," Dad said. "A month or two in Maryland, a month with you."

"Sure," Eva said. "You can stay as long as you want."

Dante and I exchanged baffled looks at her equanimity.

"You're a good girl," Mom said.

"So you'd still be here a lot," Dante said. "For birthdays and stuff. Grandchildren."

"Of course!" Mom said, affronted. "You think we won't be good grandparents? Get us a baby and you'll see. It's just . . . winters. We hate winter now. We're old."

I jumped as a sharp pain lanced my shin. Eva, kicking me. "Um . . . yeah! Sure! That sounds really exciting, Mom. Dad. That's great. Maryland's so pretty."

"Want to see?" Dad asked. "It's real nice. Plus, two extra bedrooms for when you kids come to visit. It's the Dogwood model. Awfully pretty. Almost as big as this place, but one-floor living, you know? I have pictures on the computer."

We left the decimated table and trooped into the den, where Dad pulled up pictures of what looked like a very posh park surrounded by lovely, newly built cottages on wooded lots.

My mother still wasn't making eye contact.

"Can you afford this?" Dante asked.

"This house here is worth a lot," Eva said. "Close to the city, good school district. They'll get close to a million for it."

My parents were always the most solid of the middle class. Dad had his own plumbing business, which had always been a good living, putting food on the table and a roof over our heads. They'd loaned me ten grand when I started Salt & Pepper, and Dante and Louis's wedding had been gorgeous. Mom had been a stay-at-home mama and then, when Dante graduated high school, she'd gotten a part-time job shelving books at the library.

But what Eva said was probably true. A nice enough house in a decent neighborhood within spitting distance of the city . . .

Well, shit.

"See the kitchen?" Mom said now. "Isn't that nice? And the closet space! You wouldn't think there'd be so much in a little house, but there is."

"Beautiful," I said. My voice sounded a little strange.

"Who wants dessert?" Mom announced when she felt we'd seen enough. "I made a cake. Two, actually, because Louis, honey, I know you love chocolate."

"You're good to me, Patty," he said, putting a brawny arm around her shoulder. "You'll come back and bake me a cake every now and again, won't you?"

"Of course! You kids come visit, we come up here . . ."

"Eva, you have no problem with the parents living with you?" Dante asked once Louis was in the other room with our parents.

"No. Why would I?"

I told you she was odd.

They wandered back into the dining room. I followed, but didn't dare look over at Frankie's shrine. As always, my tiny twin was the elephant in the room. How could they leave the place where her short life had taken place? It felt wrong. It felt *horrible*.

But I didn't say anything. I just sat back down with the family and ate a slab of orange polenta cake.

CHAPTER 14

Dear Other Emerson,

I'm going to let you in on some Fatty Top Secrets.

1. Sometimes, I go through the fast-food drive-through and I pretend to be talking on the phone when I order so the cashier will think I'm buying food for an entire family, not just myself. I always laugh and say, "I just wanted a coffee! This is turning into a huge deal! Fine, you can get a Big Mac. What does Daddy want?" Then I drive to the window. "Kids," I tell the pimply teenager. "They're like locusts."

2. The clothes made for people my size are craptastic. Try finding a decently made pair of pants in a size 34, Other Emerson. I dare you. Guess what? Designers want nothing to do with us. You can buy a dress by Isaac Mizrahi or Armani or Donna Karan, OE. Not me! Most clothes are basically polyester sacks with holes cut for arms. Burkas or tents, usually in black or ugly-ass floral prints my grandmother wouldn't have been caught dead wearing. Plastic buttons and tacky sparkles so no one will

notice you're three hundred pounds overweight. Yo, Fat Acceptance People! Get on this!

3. I smile at everyone because I'm afraid they hate me on sight, so I try to be extra sweet. Though I don't do it on purpose, I even talk in a softer, higher-pitched voice than I use when I'm talking to myself, or with Marley or Georgia. (I need to call them, by the way. It's been a while. I just worry that they're doing better than I am, that they'll leave me behind. I'm embarrassed at where I am in life. I mean, Georgia graduated from Yale Law, for the love of God. Marley has that family and always sounds so happy. Anyway. I'll call them soon. If I lose some weight, maybe I'll invite them down.)

4. People assume I'm stupid because I'm so fat. Like I'm clueless as to how I became this way, so I must have a super-low IQ. People often talk slowly to me, assuming I can't keep up.

5. I do my grocery shopping at the lowliest stores, and I shop late at night. Can you imagine me at Whole Foods? Please. I wouldn't fit down their skinny little aisles. I think it was designed to keep people like me out.

6. I spend way too much time fantasizing about the Skinny Life. Where men will give me piggyback rides and buy me drinks and call me for no reason and ask if I want to have dinner with their parents, because yes, our relationship is that serious. I can kill HOURS with this kind of thinking, OE. Hours.

7. This is a hard one to admit, even to you, Other Emerson, but here goes. These days, I try not to make friends with fat people. It was one thing at Camp Copperbrook. Marley and Georgia are pure gold as friends. But a couple weeks ago, there was a woman at the library who tried to start a conversation about

books. I gave her one-word answers. Why? Because she was fat. Not as fat as I am, but I could already imagine the looks we'd get if we dared to go out for coffee. Two obese women, having fun? It's not allowed! We might be bullied or mocked more than we are individually, and I don't have Marley's guts or Georgia's slashing comebacks (slashing, but she always blushes just the same, because it still hurts).

8. Sometimes kindness is worse than cruelty. The other day, I was trying to get back into the swing of things, back to a healthy lifestyle like they talked about at Camp Copperbrook. So I took a walk. It was harder and slower than the last time I wrote about walking, because I'm heavier now. Always heavier. So I figured I'd push it, do more than I thought I could, and all of a sudden, I fell. I tripped on a tree root that had worked its way through the sidewalk, and then I was down, on my stomach, my arms and legs scraped, my chin against the concrete.

I couldn't get up.

I'm too fat to get myself up off the ground, Other Emerson. Billy Patterson, the boy I babysat who once loved me, was across the street with his friends, and he laughed in this loud, fake way, and I wondered, tears falling onto the sidewalk, how anyone could be so cruel. Mrs. Eckhart, who was driving past, did a double take, but didn't stop. I got to my knees, but my foot slipped, and I was back down again. My chin was bleeding.

Then this lady, Natasha, came out and yelled at Billy & Co. to shut up. Natasha and her kids moved into the eyesore house in our neighborhood, the one with the patchy yard and rotting roof. She helped me up (grunting, it was so embarrassing) and asked me if I wanted to come in for a glass of water or a Band-Aid. But I just couldn't. I was too embarrassed. I thanked her and tried to hurry home, bruised and bleeding, my back killing me, my knees burning, but it was Natasha's niceness that, for whatever reason, hurt the most.

9. I don't look in the mirror anymore. I just can't stand the sight of myself. It makes me too sad, and what do I do when I'm sad, Other Emerson?

I eat.

CHAPTER 15

Georgia

Stop constantly wishing we'd lost more weight.
(That should've been on the list.)

"Tickle."

"Tag."

"Tank."

"Tatiana!" said Tatiana, and I smiled at her.

We were doing letter and sound recognition, a component of the language and literacy part of nursery school.

Right now, we were trying to get every kid to name a word that started with *T* without any other chatter, which would reinforce their focusing skills as well as their literacy. So far, our record was five words in a row, which was pretty good, given that everyone here was only four and had the attention span of a gnat.

"Theater," said Silvi.

Lissie, my assistant teacher, shot me a glance. Silvi was advanced, already reading. I felt a flash of pride for Clara, followed by the increasingly familiar buzz of nerves whenever anything related to Rafael entered my consciousness. For nearly five years, I'd done a damn good job of keeping him out of my head.

"Turd," said Geronimo, and the kids dissolved into giggles.

"He said 'turd'! He said 'turd'! Turd!" they shrieked. Axel got up and ran in a circle, a victory lap of sorts. Khaleesi started to cry, since she hated all things bowel-related, and Lissie comforted her.

"We got up to six 'T' words! That's a new record, so good work," I said. "And, Geronimo, you're very funny, but let's keep bathroom talk for bathrooms and when you have to go, okay, sweetheart?" I glanced at the clock. "Great job, everyone. And look at the clock! It's time to clean up."

"Clean up, clean up, everybody clean up," the kids sang. We had a song for everything.

I directed the kids—Khaleesi and Cash could put the stuffed animals away, Silvi and Wren could bring the paintbrushes to the sink, Dash and Roland could put pink reminder slips in everyone's cubby about bringing in special cuddle friends on Friday. Nash and Primrose reshelved books. I helped kids find their lunch boxes, gave out hugs, checked to see if paintings were dry enough to be taken home.

Then, at 2:00 on the dot, Lissie opened the door to let the parents in to get their kids. Donna, the teacher in room 2, let her kids out early every day . . . she was one year away from retirement and really over teaching. The hallway was mobbed with kids and parents, and for a second, I didn't see him.

Then Silvi shouted, "Uncle Rafe!" and he knelt down, opening his arms as she ran to him.

My body reacted before my brain—knees softened, my left leg wobbling, the instant heat in my stomach rising through my chest and neck into my face, my hands buzzing with adrenaline.

He was here.

Clara had put him on the authorized-pickup list. I'd

known this day was coming, but now that it was upon me, I couldn't seem to . . . to . . . what was the question again?

Rafe picked up his niece, kissed her on the cheek. "Hello, sweet girl," he said, smiling.

Then he looked at me, and his eyes . . . I couldn't believe I'd gone so long without seeing those eyes, so dark and beautiful, either the happiest or the saddest eyes in the entire world, depending on his mood.

They were happy right now. Because of Silvi, of course.

He was clean-shaven, and it made him look younger. My heart felt weak and thin.

"Georgia," he said, and my stomach squeezed. His accent always made my name sound lush and delicious.

"Hello, Rafe," I managed. "It's good to see you."

He was more beautiful than ever. Every one of his features was just a little big—nose, mouth, eyes. Generous. His hair was shorter. No more ponytail, and he looked . . . perfect. But for some reason, his short hair and lack of a beard made me want to cry a little, because . . . well, because I hadn't known.

"Miss Georgia, Miss Georgia, I can't find my sock!" said Geronimo, who liked to strip down naked in the bathroom. And thank God, because it gave me an excuse to stop staring at my ex. I took Geronimo by the hand and led him to the bathroom, my heart banging. Never in my life had I been so glad to close a door.

I took in a breath, then picked up the errant sock, which was lying under the sink. "Here you go, honey. Remember what we said about keeping your clothes on in here? Just pull down your pants next time, okay?"

"Okay. I love you," he said, throwing his arms around my neck.

Maybe if I'd been a preschool teacher when Rafe and I were married, we would've made it.

Don't start, my brain said. *You blew it. He asked for a divorce and you couldn't say yes fast enough.*

I put on Geronimo's sock, tied his shoes and had him wash his hands. "That's my boy," I said, ruffling his hair.

"We're best friends," he told me.

"It's nice to have so many best friends, isn't it?" I asked. Couldn't have him thinking he was my favorite, even if he was in my top five.

When I came out, Geronimo's dad was waiting. "How was my boy today?"

"He was excellent, as usual," I said. "And very creative."

"I said 'turd,' Daddy! It starts with 'T'!"

The dad laughed. "I guess it does. Thanks, Georgia. See you tomorrow."

"Bye, gentlemen. Have a great afternoon."

Silvi was giving her uncle the tour. "This is where we paint. This is where we read books. I have this book at home. I have this one, too. Read me this one, Uncle Rafe."

"Silvi, let me talk to Miss Georgia a moment, sweetheart. We are old friends, did you know that?"

My heart rate tripled.

"You are?" Silvi asked. "That's a pleasant surprise!"

I couldn't help but smile. Silvi's vocabulary was rock 'n' roll.

"We are." His hand rested on her head. "Can you look at a book by yourself for a moment, sweet one?"

"Silvi loves books, don't you, honey?" Which he probably knew, being her uncle and all that.

"Yes, I do," she said. "I can read some by myself."

My hands were shaking, so I stuck them in the pockets of my denim jumper (which was just as sexy as it sounded).

Rafe came over and stood in front of me, and my heart wasn't just pounding now, but thrumming. The poker in my stomach twisted again and again.

"Small world," I said, my voice quiet.

"Yes. How have you been, Georgia?"

"Great. Fine. I'm a preschool teacher now."

"So I heard." A dark eyebrow lifted.

"I heard you have a new restaurant. Um . . . Cherish told me. My stepmother? Remember her?"

"Of course I remember her."

"Sure. Why wouldn't you? I mean, how many people are named Cherish, right? Let alone exotic dancer stepmoms, right? Anyway, she said that . . . that she went to your restaurant. And it was good."

Rafe didn't answer for a minute. Why would he? I was babbling like an idiot. I tried to look at him and failed.

"Silvi says she loves school," he said finally. "Thank you for that. The move, it was a little difficult for her."

"She's doing great here." I drew in a shaky breath. "How are you, Rafael?" Forced myself to look at him.

His expression was neutral. I had no idea what mine was. "I'm doing very well, thank you," he said. "I hope it will not be too awkward, us seeing each other from time to time."

Awkward? Not at all. *Agonizing*, that was a better word.

"No. It's fine. Don't worry about me! I'm . . . I'm great. With this, I mean. It's lovely to see you again. Lovely to have Silvi. That's what I meant."

He just kept looking at me.

"Are you seeing anyone?" I asked, then jerked back a little because I hadn't meant to ask.

"Yes," he said. "I am."

Of course he was. "And is she . . . is she nice?" *Is she beautiful? Is she kind? Is she thin? Do you love her?*

My ex-husband didn't answer immediately. The silence swelled. Then he said, "I would rather not discuss her. But yes. She is nice."

I nodded, my face burning. "Well. Congratulations on the new restaurant."

"Thank you."

"Uncle *Rafe*?"

This time, the voice was deeper. We both turned, and there was Mason.

"No," Rafe said, his eyes widening in surprise. "It cannot be. Mason? Oh, *madre de Dios*, Mason! Where is the boy? You are a young man now! Come! Give me a hug!"

There it was, that magical ease and warmth he had with people. Mason obeyed happily, and I swallowed against the wedge in my throat.

Mason had been our ring bearer.

The two of them were chatting away like long-lost friends, which I guessed they were.

That was the shitty thing about divorce. You lost that whole other family, that whole world. Rafe had been so good for Mason, his gentle brand of masculinity a much better role model than Hunter's seething, omnipresent hostility.

Maybe if Rafe had been in the picture, Mason wouldn't have done what he did this past April.

"Mason, please, come meet my niece, Silvi. She is a student here."

"Cool. Hey, little kid. I'm Mason."

"I'm not little. I'm almost a big sister," Silvi said.

"Oh, gotcha. Sorry." Mason grinned at us.

"I forgive you," she said sweetly.

"Silvi, we should go," Rafe said. "I have to work tonight, and I want to take you to the park and perhaps for some ice cream, what do you say?"

"I say yes!" Silvi got up, hugged my legs, then grabbed her uncle's hand. "Bye, Miss Georgia," she sang out.

"It was good to see you," Rafe said. Probably a lie.

Then they were gone.

"Man, that was awesome!" Mason said. "I loved that guy! I mean, except for the divorce and all." He paused, his smile dropping. "Should I have punched him or something?"

"No, no. He's wonderful. We just . . . we weren't right for each other."

My nephew flopped on the beanbag chair. "Good. I've never punched anyone. Dad says getting in a fistfight is part of being a man. I'm gonna try to skip that one."

Ah, Hunter and his Hemingwayesque benchmarks of manhood. And look what happened to Hemingway.

"So what brings you here?" I said. "Were we meeting today?"

"Nope! But I did text you. Guess you didn't check your phone. G, I did something on the list!"

"You did? Hooray! What did you do?"

"I signed up for cross-country, like, yesterday at the last possible second, and today classes let out early, so we just finished our first practice."

"That's great!" I said. I was honestly stunned. We'd had *join a club* on the list, but a sport? I hoped Mason wasn't just trying to please my brother instead of himself, but he seemed so happy I pushed the thought aside.

"Yeah, it's supposedly a good bunch of kids. You know. Not like football or soccer, where everyone hates you if you suck." Mason had been forced to play both of those sports in middle school. Broke his leg getting tackled, as the kid who'd taken him down was a giant. Hunter had been furious, but not with the boy who'd crushed his son. With his son for getting crushed.

"So, tell me about it," I said. "Want to go home and we'll take Admiral out?"

"I can barely stand. I'm, like, close to death here. But if you feed me, I'll come to your place. Or I should say, if Marley will feed me. You never have food."

"I do so have food," I said. "Most of it made by Marley."

On the short drive home, Mason told me with great relish about the horrors of running. "Everything is hurting. My shins, my knees, my, I don't know, my pelvis? My pelvis. My head, my shoulders, my neck. Even my teeth hurt, G."

"It sounds great." I smiled.

"It is! In a freakish way, it's kind of fun. Minus the agonizing pain. I even added something to my list. Finish the course without stopping, which seems crazy impossible right now."

"You'll get there, honey. Good for you."

We pulled up to my house, and he stiff-legged it up the stairs to the door and unlocked it with his key. I was slower, grabbing my bag from the backseat. I had two grants to fill out for my pro bono clients. One of them, Gwen, was opening a textile company. The first time I'd met her, she'd had two black eyes, because her husband had violated the restraining order and come after her.

There was that poker in the stomach again. Why couldn't all women have a man like Rafe?

Hi, my brain said. *I'm with stupid. The one who divorced the world's kindest man.*

Gwen's husband was in jail now. The judge, a friend of mine, had given him a sentence of thirty-five years without parole for attempted murder, the beating had been so bad.

"I have cookies!" Marley said, appearing in the courtyard with a plate. "Can I come up and say hi to Mason?"

"You are always welcome with cookies," I said. Maybe a cookie would ease my stomach. I hadn't been able to eat lunch today because I'd ordered salad with a vinaigrette dressing that had given me heartburn after the first bite.

I should get to the doctor one of these days. The not-insane part of me knew something was going on that needed a doctor's attention. But the other part of me couldn't resist how the weight was still falling off. For a woman who supposedly was so smart, I really seemed to enjoy being deliberately obtuse where my weight was concerned.

Admiral was waiting patiently for his dose of adoration. "Hello, handsome," I said, kneeling down to pet him. "Were you a good dog today? How's that novel coming? Hm?" He wagged, pushing his head against me.

Mason was in the kitchen, chugging a glass of water. "Hi, gorgeous," Marley said, hugging him tight. "Should I not hug you?" She didn't release him. "Are you too old for that now?" She grinned and stepped back.

"Nah. Still good for hugs." He took a cookie and put the whole thing in his mouth.

"Marley," I said, "ask Mason why he's sweaty."

"Why are you gross and sweaty, hon?"

"I joined the cross-country team," he said.

"Holy shit! Good for you, Mase. Tell me everything."

"It's horrible," he said proudly. "I was whipped before we even started." He bent stiffly to pet Admiral, who was waiting. "I mean, I thought the warm-up was the whole workout, and I was like, okay, I'm still alive, at least there's that, right? And then the captain, this kid named Christian? He says, 'Okay, let's go,' and we're supposed to *run* for three miles! The whole way! I had to walk most of it. But not one person made fun of me!"

His words—his disbelief—made my heart ache. "That's fantastic, honey," I said, my voice husky.

"Everyone is so nice," he continued. "It's all about your own time, Christian says. And he's the fastest kid—I mean, he's so fast, G. He said I'll get better every week, and I actually have a lot of potential, and by the time the season really starts, I'll be able to run three miles without even stopping!" He beamed and took another cookie.

Whoever Christian was, I blessed him. I loved him. I wanted to thank his mother and father for raising him right. Instead, I said, "That's amazing. I'm so excited to come to a meet." I hesitated. "What does your dad think?"

His smile faltered. "Uh, well, he gave me a list of his times when he was my age. Also, I'm not supposed to be eating sugar or refined flour. Microbiotics, you know?"

Marley and I exchanged looks. A new generation worried about food.

"Well," I murmured, "like Christian said, it's about your own times."

"Dad ran varsity when he was a freshman," Mason said, his voice considerably less enthusiastic than a minute ago. "He said he'd train me."

I well remembered my brother's meets. If Hunter didn't come in first, he'd be furious. And even though he'd been very good, he *didn't* always come in first. Prep schools tended to breed cross-country runners, and the competition was tough.

Thus, I got to witness a lot of my brother's tantrums— Hunter punching a tree and breaking two fingers, Hunter kicking a window of our car and cracking the glass, Hunter shaking off the congratulations of his teammates, Hunter cutting hateful looks at the parents who dared to tell him how well he'd done.

I was a little scared of how he'd react to his son not being able to finish the course.

"Oh, guess what?" Mason said, eating another cookie. His fourth, I thought, which was good, because it seemed to me like he hadn't been eating too well since April. "Georgia's ex was at nursery school today."

Marley's eyes widened. "A tale perhaps best told over a bottle of wine tonight?" she suggested to me.

"Nothing to tell," I said. "He looks great. His hair is short now."

She waited for more. I raised an eyebrow, indicating that yes, probably best told over wine.

She got the hint. "Speaking of running, Georgia, I'm going to cross something else off our list a week from Saturday. And I'm dragging you with me. Mason, you should come, too."

"I have math tutoring on Saturdays. And my dad takes me to CrossFit."

"Those people are freaks," Marley said.

"I know. I wish I could go with you guys." His face, so happy a minute ago, looked crestfallen now. "What's the thing?"

"Well," Marley said, "this is a very civilized fun run in Central Park. My brother and his husband will be there, and half of FDNY, so in addition to running, we could totally get someone to give us a piggyback ride."

The stupidest thing on the list. "I don't see that happening. I'm very busy." Also, I hated running. All of mankind hated running until they brainwashed themselves otherwise. But I especially hated it, because it was Hunter's religion.

"Still, you're coming," Marley said. "Not only can you get a guy to give you a piggyback ride, you can also run in the appropriate clothing from our list."

"I think I'm having a very serious surgery that weekend," I said. "Or performing one. Either way, I can't make it."

Mason's face fell.

Sigh. "Fine," I said. "Let me talk to your dad, Mason, and see if we can spring you. If you can go, I'll go, too."

"Really?" Mason said, taking another cookie.

"If," I cautioned.

"Super!" Marley said. "We can go shopping for workout clothes. Emerson will be watching from heaven, judging you if you don't."

"Love seeing that Catholic guilt-tripping in action," I said.

"I learned from the best," she said happily. "Let's hit the mall tonight. I'll take you to Ikea as a reward."

"I can't. I have lawyerly things to do."

"Afterward, then."

"Maybe."

"So it's a yes."

I looked at my nephew. "Try to make friends with people who aren't so bossy," I said.

"I would love a friend like Marley," he said, blushing.

"Oh, baby! You *are* my friend! Want another hug?"

"No, I'm good."

"Oh, come on. At least let me pat you on the head."

He laughed, and the sound made my heart swell with love. I went into the kitchen for some water and picked up my phone. Took a deep breath and texted Hunter.

Hey, Hunter, I was hoping I could steal Mason for a few hours next weekend. Charity fun run in the city next Saturday.

I always had to be cool yet cheerful yet not too cheerful in my texts with my brother, lest I irritate him. Still had to walk on eggshells if I wanted any Mason time. The three dots began to wave almost immediately. Oh, God, what if *he* wanted to come? Granted, he avoided doing things with me, but the chance to show off in front of other runners . . .

Marley will be there, I typed quickly. He'd never liked Marley. We're on her brother's team. FDNY.

Just in case my brother's competitive spirit was a little insecure.

The answer came.

He has other plans.

No niceties, no *Thanks, anyway* or *Sorry*. Of course not.

Any chance he could get out of them? I texted. Might be good for him to be around other runners, get some tips.

As soon as I hit send, I knew it was a mistake.

He IS around another runner. His FATHER. I can teach him ANYTHING he needs to know a lot better than some muscle-head firemen living off the taxpayer tit.

Such a charmer. Too bad I couldn't fix him up with, oh, Stalin.

I know, I typed hastily. Just thought it might be good for him. I hesitated, then lied. I think some of the other kids from the team are going, too.

Mason being popular was important to my brother. There was no response for a minute. Admiral nudged my hand with his cold nose, and I sat in the chair and gazed into his eyes. My dog could be rented out for meditational purposes, I swore. He had such a calming effect.

The phone chirped. One word.

Fine.

Success! "You're in, Mason!" I said. "New York City, here we come!"

"Yes!" he crowed from the living room.

And we could see my father and Cherish, who both adored Mason, and Mason could see Paris and Milan (freakishly, his aunts).

It would be the best day ever.

I even forgot it meant I would be running, too.

CHAPTER 16

Dear Other Emerson,

Today, I had lunch in the employee cafeteria, because ... I got a job, bitch! That's right! A real job with coworkers and everything. The last time I had that was right out of college, before Mama died. Since then, I've picked up a freelance job here and there from Craigslist, writing marketing content or proofreading. But those were more to fill the time than anything.

Anyway, last month I decided that I needed a job that would get me out of the house, let me meet people and not be at home eating all the time. And boom! Three weeks later, I was hired.

I'm totally stoked, obviously. I even like the work—I'm a representative at a call center. My job is to soothe disgruntled cable customers. Hey, I get it. TV is my life. Also, they can't see me; it's all phone, all the time.

I showed up fifteen minutes earlier than the fifteen minutes early suggested. That's because I knew the walk from the parking lot to the office would require some rest first. I took it slow and easy, but my knee burned, and my thighs and stomach were wobbling like Jell-O. When I got to the building, I _so_ wanted to sit down on the steps and rest, but I made myself stand. Standing burns calories. Besides, what if I had trouble getting up? So, anyway, I waited for the sweat on my face to dry, though I'd have to stop in the ladies' room to mop certain places and apply the baby powder I always carry. Then I took a deep breath and went inside. Missy, my supervisor, isn't real friendly, but I can't tell if she's just that way, or if it's me being fat. She could lose a few pounds herself, Other E. Not that I'm judging.

The call center is basically a huge room filled with rows of workstations—the typical gray fabric cubicles. People of every size, shape and color were there, which reassured me. And guess what, Other Emerson? Three people said hi as Missy walked me to my desk. One of those was a MAN, and he didn't even say it in the disgusted way. Sure, this happens to you all the time, Other Emerson, but please! This is on par with me being courted for a cover shoot by _Glamour_, okay?

I was out of breath by the time I got to my desk, but I tried not to let it show. Luckily, the AC was freezing, so my sweat dried; at work, you can't just hike up your shirt and mop under your boobs and stomach like you can when you're at home, Other Emerson. You're welcome for the insider intel on being fat. And thank God, the chair was big enough. I counted eight other fat people; I'm not the only one who needs a sturdy chair.

Funny thing about Fat People—we discriminate. Hell's yes, we do. Our first thought upon seeing a fellow fatty is, _Thank God I'm not the only one._ Second thought in my case is, _Crap. I'm fatter than she is._ And then we think—at least, I think— _Are you going to be nice to me, or are you going to compete with me, and if you compete with me, are you going to win? Can I lose more weight than you? Can I be the skinnier one?_

Because the Fat Life is all about weight, always, forever. That's something Marley and Georgia understand, Georgia more so than Marley. Marley wanted to be thinner, but she didn't seem as obsessed as Georgia and I were. She has that great family . . . her mom used to send contraband food, and Marley was so funny when the counselors took it! Anyway, she's always been heavy, but in a nicer way than Georgia and me. And even Georgia isn't in my world of the super obese.

I try not to hold it against them.

Anyway. Three of the fat people (all skinnier, of course) made eye contact, which gives me hope. The other five did not. God forbid we seem like a club or something.

I dressed carefully this morning in a dark blue shirt (to hide sweat stains) and a long skirt and the extra-wide shoes I just bought. Flat-ironed my hair, did a full makeup job, making sure I looked as good as I can.

I'm one of those "you have such a pretty face" fat girls. In fact, Other Emerson, the reason I know you're beautiful is because you look exactly like me, minus 175 pounds (fine, fine, 200, fine, 250). Both of us have green eyes, amazing cheekbones.

Two years ago, I was pretty close to beautiful. I weighed only 269 pounds. Good old speed will do that for you. Whoops! I mean phentermine. I had to go to four doctors before I could get a prescription, and I had to lie about my father's heart attack to get it.

But there was a reason those other three doctors didn't want me to have it. My family history caught up with me, and after an utterly terrifying night in the hospital where I thought I would die alone in a too-small johnny coat all by myself, the phentermine was taken away. Obviously, I miss being thin (ish). Miss not being hungry. Miss having such a clean house. Don't miss the feeling of my chest being crushed, unable to breathe. Don't miss the uncontrollable shaking, constant nausea and paranoia that went hand in hand with cold turkey.

Still, I'd go back on it if I could.

Anyway, back to the job.

The chair held me—score one. Score two, I already knew how to work the phone system, because it's a phone system and not Aramaic. I have an IQ of 138. Two points short of genius, Other Emerson. No doubt, when you took the IQ test, the computer saw your beautiful face, and you got boosted the extra points, so there's no doubt of you being in Mensa territory.

Yes, I'm underemployed. I don't care. This job gives me a place to go every day.

Other Emerson, I'm positive I'll lose weight now for sure, now that I'm not home with all that food calling my name.

Dawn of a new day. I'm thirty years old, Other Emerson. Time for my real life to start. I think you'll be proud of me.

Hi again, OE. It's been a couple of months since I wrote to you. Sorry about that. I've been kind of blue. By that, I mean I've been hating myself a little more than usual. Eating more. Sometimes I think I shouldn't have taken this job.

There are parts of my job that I love. For example, clients can't see me; I'm just a pleasant voice at the end of the phone. My customer ratings are the best of anyone, even though I've only worked here two and a half months.

But there are parts of my job that I hate.

There are a lot of skinny women here in the Chat Room, as we call it, these rows and rows of gray cubicles. Some of the skinnies are perfectly nice, even if they do scan me up and down, their eyes just a little too wide with fascination. "My waist is smaller than her arm! Will she eat me? I hope not!"

"Hi, Emerson!" they might say. Most of them are younger than I am, since this is entry-level work. "Wanna get drinks with us after work?"

"Oh, thanks, that's so nice, but I have plans," I lie, because A) it's no fun to be the enormous fatty in a group of delicate fawns; (3) I think they're just fascinated by my size, and even if they weren't, we can't forget; C) the good chance the restaurant chairs will have arms, in which case I might not fit. Even if they don't have arms, who knows if they'll be sturdy enough to hold me? Also, will the tables be too close together for me to even get to a seat? Will the waiters stink-eye me because they have to move furniture for me?

You never have to think about that, do you, Other Emerson?

In addition to the Delicate Fawns (four of them, a little band of wide-eyed does on spindly legs), there are the not-so-nice women. Megan, Isobel and Tina. Let's be honest. They're bitches. All of them are overweight themselves, enough to see that yes, if they don't Do Something for Real This Time, they're going to end up like me, currently tipping the scales at 386 pounds.

No one has noticed that I'm down almost thirty pounds since last year at this time, since I didn't work here last year at this time. Even so. Once you cross the 350-pound mark, you're a freak.

My supervisor, Missy, is one of these obese-but-not-morbidly-obese people, and she doesn't like that I'm doing so well at my job. She nitpicks on tiny things — "You didn't say, 'Have a nice day.' You know that's protocol." When I tell Missy that I said, "Have a <u>lovely</u> day," instead, she tells me that's proof of my bad attitude, so I apologize, hating her and myself as I do.

She ignores the fact that the Delicate Fawns are incapable of getting to work by eight thirty. Ever. Or that I can handle a third more calls than they do. Or that their customer rankings aren't nearly as good as mine. Last month, Delicate Fawn Katrine got a promotion to assistant associate manager. It's only a title, but please. It should've gone to me. Katrine and I started the same day.

Fat discrimination is a thing, Other Emerson. I'm glad you don't have to endure it.

Another thing that happens at work is that I get a lot of weight-loss information. "My friend?" one of the fawns will say. "She did this diet where you only eat kale? And she lost twelve pounds!" As if twelve pounds would help me. Or, "This friend?" — they always talk with question marks, Other E — "This friend? She had gastric bypass? And she's down, like, a hundred and fifty pounds or something."

"Wow," I'm forced to answer. "Good for her." I don't want to eat kale. Been there, done that. It's not that I don't <u>know</u> what's healthy, for God's sake. No one knows more about nutrition than a fat American female. It's willpower that's the issue. All those fat-haters talk about how weak we are, us super-fatties. They leave out the fact that we might also be lonely, scared, isolated, poor, in pain, sexually abused as kids or any number of things. To much of the world, we're just weak.

Anyway, about gastric bypass... well, I did want that. Right until I went to the horribly honest doctor.

First of all, I've always been scared of getting anesthesia, since my grandmother died that way. In for a lumpectomy, out on a slab. No wonder my mom was so sad. No wonder we had all those special nights cuddled together, EATING CRAP AND HAVING FUN AND GETTING HUGE. Gram left us a bunch of money, then Grampy left even more, so Mom didn't have to work, which in hindsight was a problem, since she was so isolated after the divorce. I'm glad <u>your</u> mom is so happy, Other Emerson.

Unhappy childhoods are a leading cause of obesity. In my case, you betcha. A mother with chronic depression, a dad I didn't see very often. Oh, and we can't forget dear old Grampy, who liked to have "tickle fights." Yes, I was molested.

Anyway. That was a long time ago. I don't want to talk about it now.

Weight-loss surgery. Once, I thought it would be my savior, but nothing comes cheap, does it? I mean, sure, I'd lose weight, but would I really be healthier?

Here's what they don't tell you on that show where they dole out gastric bypasses like Chiclets. You'll have the most hideous gas the world has ever known. You'll feel sick after eating. Your breath will be foul. You'll throw up sometimes, and you'll poop yourself often. You'll be more likely to get ulcers and be malnourished, believe it or not. Insert ironic chuckle.

If that's okay with you, you may still gain the weight back. Even if you don't, even if you hit your goal weight (which is improbable), you'll never look like a thin person. You'll have folds of skin hanging off you—from your arms, like bat wings. Your thigh skin will drape and dangle between your legs, chafing until it's raw. Your boobs will deflate and hang empty. The skin on your stomach will hang down past your crotch, and you can pull it out in front of you like uncooked pizza dough. Let's not even talk about your ass except to say that Google has scarred me forever.

If you get that skin removed (not covered by insurance), well, it's a high-risk surgery with lots of bleeding, hundreds and hundreds of stitches, tubes coming out of you for weeks and a high risk for infection, not to mention nerve damage. Doesn't that sound fun? It's also hideously painful, the doctor told me. The scarring makes it look like you were cut in half, and scars are forever.

Oh, and apparently you're more likely to commit suicide after gastric bypass. Just putting that out there. BUT AT LEAST YOU'RE NOT FAT ANYMORE!!! Excuse me. Not as fat.

I guess I have some anger issues, Other Emerson. Sorry. I'm calming down now.

Another part of work I don't like is the birthdays. There are sixty-two of us at this call center. That means that more than once a week, it's someone's birthday, and birthdays mean cake. Every dang time.

I don't eat the cake. Or worse, I have a sliver, as in "Gosh I'm just a little mouse, can't eat anything after that hundred-calorie salad I just had!" If I had a normal-sized piece of cake, that would mean I had the hubris to view myself as a regular person, and Megan, Isobel and Tina stand there like Macbeth's witches, proudly not eating anything, looking at me with eyes full of judgment.

It's not men who hate fat women. Or, I should say, men don't hate fat women as much as other women hate fat women. When Georgia met Rafe, she was chubby, and he didn't mind. She told me, a note of wonder in her voice, that he never even mentioned her weight.

I can't imagine that.

But . . . here comes the fun stuff, OE.

Today at lunch, I headed for the cafeteria. I only eat salad, obviously, because fat people aren't allowed to eat anything else in public, even if the woman behind the counter gives me a look that says I'm not fooling her. The salads here are pointless— iceberg lettuce, tasteless, anemic tomato wedge, one green pepper slice that makes me burp for the rest of the day. Diet Italian dressing in a little plastic pack.

Don't worry, I told my hunger. I have Oreos. A six-pack. Six Oreos, only 252 calories. That's nothing. I definitely could stick to a healthy diet even with those. I glanced left and right to make sure no one saw, then popped one into my mouth, whole.

Oh, beautiful Oreo! Like a giant black Communion wafer, the flavor so intense, so perfect that I wanted to French-kiss whoever invented these. I chewed slowly, savoring the taste— Enjoy when you DO indulge!

The salad was frigid, which took away its nominal flavor. I'd only had two eggs and two pieces of toast for breakfast, so no wonder I was starving. I ate the tasteless, chilled food slowly, but even so, I was done in under five minutes.

There were five Oreos left in my snack pack. I could finish them in the bathroom. My mouth watered at the thought of that black, crunchy deliciousness, made even better by its secret existence. Without another thought, I slid another whole cookie into my mouth.

"Hi," someone said, and I jumped.

Other Emerson, prepare yourself. It was a man.

A man.

A man!

A not-bad-looking man, carrying a plate with about ten french fries and a wadded-up napkin on it. (He left ten fries. I don't understand how people do that.)

"I'm Mica," he said, and a blush prickled my chest. I waved, pointed to my mouth and smile-grimaced. I'd have to suck off the Oreo silt before I could talk. "I'm new here," he added.

I swallowed, then covered my mouth with my hand so he wouldn't see any black gunk stuck on my teeth. "Hi," I said. "Emerson."

"Beautiful name."

The blush was burning my jowls now, working its way to my cheeks. "Thanks."

"You're in the Chat Room, right?" he asked, smiling, and that was some smile, Other Emerson. His teeth were very white and slightly crooked.

"Yes." I remembered to answer. "Are you?"

"Yep. I started yesterday."

"Welcome," I said, hand still in front of my mouth.

"Thanks! Maybe we can have lunch sometime."

"Sure." My heart pounded like crazy. I'd said maybe six words so far, but I thought . . . it might be that . . . it seemed like he was . . . he might be asking me . . . on a date? Could that be?

He set his tray down on my table and leaned in a little closer. "Maybe we can go somewhere other than here. Not that I have anything against cafeterias. It's just that there's an Applebee's down the street. Or the Italian place downtown? Anyway. Wherever you want. I'm probably being pushy."

I finally felt confident that I'd sucked all the silt off my teeth, so I dropped my hand. "No, not at all. Um . . . yeah. I like both those places."

"So that's a yes?"

What would you say, Other Emerson? How would you deal with a cute guy—a cute, <u>regular-sized guy</u>—flirting with you? I decided that, for once in my life, I'd go for it. Maybe it was because he'd mentioned normal restaurants and didn't seem to think there should be a law against me going to one.

"It's a yes. Name the day."

"Tomorrow?"

WHAT? ARE YOU LISTENING, OTHER EMERSON?

"Okay," I said.

"Thanks." His dark eyes crinkled as he smiled again. "I'll see you around. I'm in row six, by the way. And you're in four."

Oh, my God. He'd scoped me out. He'd made a note of where I sat.

"Mm-hm," I managed.

"See you later."

"Have a great afternoon."

"It's already great," he said, and there was something in his voice that made an unknown part of me squeeze and glow.

He left, and I watched him go, wondering if I'd just made that whole thing up.

Other Emerson, that has <u>never</u> happened to me before. I mean, I know you have Idris Elba and many other men who would cut out their grandmothers' hearts to date you, but me . . .

This is a first.

Maybe I didn't even want those other four Oreos after all.

CHAPTER 17

Georgia

Shop at a store for regular people. *(Sigh.)*

I spent an hour at Gwen's textile studio going over her business plan, tweaking it. "If you hire at-risk kids, you're eligible for this grant," I told her, pulling it up on my laptop.

"That's what I love about you, Georgia," she said. "You're always a step ahead."

I smiled. I liked Gwen, and her work. Her prints were tasteful and subtle and would probably go over big in Cambry-on-Hudson and the other posh towns of Westchester County. Maybe I could convince Big Kitty to hold a home décor event to give Gwen some PR. Had to use those blue-blood roots of mine for something.

"Oh!" Gwen said. "The baby just moved. Want to feel?"

Without waiting for a response, she pressed my hand against her belly.

There it was, the mysterious roll and shift. I felt something hard—an elbow, maybe, or a heel, and unexpectedly, my throat tightened. Two years ago, she'd almost been killed by her husband. Now, she was percolating a life.

"Amazing," I murmured.

"Yeah, who'd have thought, right? I mean, I never

imagined I'd want another man, but here I am. Married and in love and pregnant. Do you have kids, Georgia?"

"I don't," I said, "but I have a nephew I adore."

"Nice," she said.

"Send me this when you're done," I said, getting back to business, "and I'll sign off on it for the bank."

"You're the best, Georgia. Here. Take these." She handed me a stack of classy dish towels—ivory with tiny fern leaves, way too subtle for my bright red kitchen.

I'd keep them, anyway. I thanked her with a hug, and left.

As I drove back to town, I tried to imagine what it must've been like, being afraid of your husband. Even though I grew up surrounded by Hunter's outbursts of fury, the notion that my husband might hit me had never once crossed my mind.

Then again, I'd married the nicest man on the planet.

There was that poker again.

Well. I had shopping to do. Workout clothes. Such a waste of money. I turned off the highway and headed for the mall, that most despised place.

Marley was waiting in front of the Apple Store, chatting up a hipster Genius who was staring at her boobs as he spoke. She didn't seem to mind. When she saw me, she said, "Thanks for the tips, Rune. I will do all those things. Gotta run!"

"Was seducing an Apple youth on our list?" I asked.

"His name is Rune. I guess his parents hated him. Oh, this is fun, Georgia! Shopping in a regular person's store. We should walk in with champagne. Too bad the Genius Bar doesn't actually serve booze."

However, our steps slowed, and we approached the store warily.

Pomegranate & Plum.

Oh, God. Every insecurity I'd ever had stared back at me. "Not here," I said. "Let's go to Marshalls."

"Calm yourself," Marley muttered, grabbing my arm as I tried to bolt. "You're getting workout gear."

"I *have* workout gear," I whispered.

"I've seen those yoga pants," she whispered back. "It's time to burn them. Besides, we'll be running. Those yoga pants would fall off you. Think of Emerson and how proud she'd be of you, shopping in this horrible place."

Pomegranate & Plum was the new must-have brand in Cambry-on-Hudson. I knew this because I saw their logo on roughly 80 percent of the mothers who dropped off their kids each day, the two *P*s mirroring each other. Apparently, alliteration was a thing if you were a merchandiser seducing people into buying things they didn't need.

More proof was in the welcoming sign: *Pomegranate & Plum—Smile. Sweat. Slay.* In other words, wear these clothes to your hot yoga classes as a status symbol to showcase your perfect, often surgically altered body, and rub it in to everyone bigger than a size 6. Or don't go to hot yoga, or Vinyasa yoga, or whatever yoga was hip this year. Just wear the clothes, because really, it was all about the logo.

P&P didn't carry sizes bigger than medium, because God forbid the fatties wanted to work out to, you know, lose weight or anything. *They* could do it in clothes from a less holy place than Pomegranate & Plum, which was a shrine to female physical perfection (and Photoshop, I hoped).

Marley, for all her bravado, appeared to be frozen as well. We stood at the front of the store, clutching each other's arms as we stared. There was exposed brick on one side, which was ridiculous, because we were in the mall, not an old mill building. Hardwood maple floorboards, and none of that laminate, thankyouverymuch.

And oh, the obnoxious signs. *J'aime yoga*, the French

making the statement that much less believable. *Money doesn't matter without love*, which was ironic, because a person couldn't shop at P&P without a good deal of money. *Because I'm worth it*, said another, contradicting the other sign.

Worst, though, were the pictures of the women clad in Pomegranate & Plum clothing (which didn't look a lot different from the stuff I saw at Target and Marshalls, just saying). Giant silk-screened photos hung throughout the store, showing impossibly-slender-yet-muscular women (all white, I noted) doing things that weren't usually seen outside of a gulag.

One showed a beautiful, poreless brunette with skin that looked like it had been oiled, her perfect, gleaming teeth gritted. She was dressed, of course, in P&P's muted colors, a harness on her shoulders so she could pull a pickup truck. As one does. The caption at the bottom read: *Opera singer Elise Kierkegard keeps her vocal cords* and *her body in top shape while wearing Pomegranate & Plum's Excelsior Low-Rise Workout Trousers.*

"Trousers," I whispered. "Because pants are so bourgeois." Marley snorted.

Another showed a blond woman with a long, satiny ponytail and hypnotically sculpted thighs leaping across a mountain peak. *When she's not advising the secretary general of the United Nations, Merrin Hastings loves free-climbing in the Andes wearing Pomegranate & Plum's Penultimate Fleece Hoodie.*

"I went to Princeton with her," I whispered.

"Just think what yours can say," Marley whispered back. Whispering felt appropriate in this Church of the One Percent. "'When she's not wiping little bottoms in her preschool for extremely advanced children, Georgia Sloane enjoys lying on the couch in her Pomegranate & Plum SuperDuper Yoga Jodhpurs, watching *Naked and Afraid*.'"

"Why are we here again? I'm scared, Marley."

She squeezed my arm. "It's like hazing for skinny people. You might puke now, but you'll look back on this day fondly."

"The day I overpaid for workout clothes at a ridiculous store."

"Happy times. That being said, let us not forget the immortal words. 'Shop at a store for regular people.' It's on the list, and I can't do it, so you have to."

"You can shop at regular stores."

"Only in the plus-sized sections, and you know that's not what we were talking about way back when."

She was right. The idea of being able to go into a "normal" store—those where the sizes stopped at 12 or 14—had been an elusive dream back then. I could still remember the three of us talking about it, how we'd go into the dressing rooms, *not* getting the side-eye from the clerks or other shoppers, trying on pants that were too big and having to go down a size. To single digits, even.

Now here I was, possibly about to fit into a medium, and it was weirdly terrifying. Marley took a shirt off the rack and held it up to her ample chest. The shirt looked as if it would fit one of my students. "Think I can get even one boob into this thing?" she asked, and I snickered.

"Can I help you find something?" a voice said, and we both jumped.

A *beautiful* woman, no more than twenty-five, smiled at me, revealing shockingly white teeth. Her skin was dewy, her hair shiny, her eyebrows magically perfect. She was tall and slim, her thigh gap visible, calves perfectly muscled.

"You should be a model," I blurted.

"Oh, aren't you sweet," she said in a flat voice that said she heard it every day, and please, if she could've been a model, did I really think she'd be working here? "What can I help you with today?"

She stared at me, almost daring me to slink back out. Her gaze never flickered once to Marley.

"My friend and I are doing an Ironman," I said, though me doing an Ironman and giving birth to Bruno Mars's child had about the same odds. "I need some clothes."

"Wonderful," she said, still not blinking. "Right this way. My name is Aspen."

"How about that?" I said. "I have sisters named Paris and Milan. And my name is Georgia. We love geography in my family."

Aspen did not respond. Perhaps she was unaware that Aspen, Paris, Milan and Georgia were all places. Perhaps she felt she should be the sole bearer of her name, Colorado and trees be damned.

She led us through the store, past more silk screens of extraordinary people doing extraordinary things in extraordinarily expensive clothes.

"I think she may be a robot," Marley murmured, still fondling the shirt she'd grabbed. "I have to say, this material is very nice. Very slippery. The sweat, should you be so crass as to sweat, will be whisked away."

"I'm supposed to sweat. And slay," I said, feeling the giggles coming on.

Aspen grabbed a few things off racks—gray, navy, black, white. Color was so passé.

"Let me know if you need other sizes," she said, ushering me into a dressing room. She bared her teeth and left, checking herself out in the mirror on her way.

"I'll be right here," Marley said. "Go on. You can do this. I believe in you."

The moment of truth.

I went into the dressing room and closed the door.

Obviously, shopping and I had never gotten along. Mirrors and I had never gotten along, either. My soul was scraped and battered from all the times my mom had taken me shopping as a kid, an adolescent, a teenager. She'd stuff me into a dress two sizes too small, wrestle with the zipper, her toothpick arms straining. "You've got to lose weight, Georgia. This can't go on. You look horrid."

As I got older (and bigger, then smaller, then bigger, etc.), I'd go on my own. The goal was always to hide my size, try to find things that didn't have waistbands, that were loose and flowing. It never did the trick. What looked good on the hanger or the gaunt model on the website just made me look dumpy.

Marley had flair. She could pull off anything. She'd add a scarf to an outfit, put on a denim jacket and some bracelets, a cool pair of shoes, and she'd look great.

I lacked that talent. My outfit today was more of the same—a shapeless gray dress that had looked considerably more cheerful with the red sweater and plastic daisy necklace I'd worn to school. This was one of the many perks of working in a preschool; the kids didn't care what you wore. Sure beat the law firm, where we associates were given an expense account at Saks and very conservative and simple guidelines to follow: suits, navy blue or dark gray.

"Get moving," Marley said from the dressing room couch, where she was clicking away on her phone.

"Are you texting Camden?" I asked, opening the door to peek at her.

"None of your business."

"So yes. I thought you gave up on him after Hudson's that night."

"I did no such thing. I'm just planning on telling him that I want to be a real girlfriend."

"And have you?"

She cut me a look. "No. I want to do it in person. Now stop stalling and get dressed."

I closed the door, pulled off the dress, took off my tights and looked at my nearly naked self in the mirror.

I saw colorless skin. My utterly unremarkable beige bra and panties. In a strange way, it was hard to see myself, almost like I was becoming invisible.

The stone in my stomach burned.

The door opened, and I jumped, covering myself with my arms. It was Marley, thank God, and not the Tree Woman, Aspen.

"Are you freaking out?" she whispered.

"Yes."

"Okay." She gave me the once-over. "You've lost a lot of weight. Take a look."

I lowered my arms, hating this. Marley had seen me much fatter, though. She knew everything already. Even so, my heart was pounding.

With her standing behind me, it was easier to see myself.

"Look. You have a waist. See? You actually curve in here. Turn. Look at your stomach. It's almost flat. I mean, all you have to do is some sit-ups, hon. Fifty squats every day, twenty-five push-ups, twenty-five sit-ups."

"You're so cruel."

"It's not that you're fat. You're just out of shape."

I swallowed. She was right. I wasn't fat.

I was not fat.

That sentence needed to sit for a minute.

"Your face is frickin' beautiful, Georgia. Look at your perfect skin. You have green eyes. You know how lucky you are to have green eyes?"

"Emerson had green eyes, too. And the best cheek-bones." The familiar lump came to my throat at the thought of our friend. I wanted to expunge the memory of her in that hospital bed. I wanted to remember the Emerson from Camp Copperbrook, who still had hope.

"Try on the clothes," Marley said, her voice gentle.

"Is there a problem in there?" Aspen's voice was hard.

"We're making love. Leave us alone," Marley said.

"One person at a time in there. Store policy."

"Well, am I really even a person, if Pomegranate and Plum doesn't make clothes in my size?" Marley said, opening the door to talk to her. "Your bitchy attitude doesn't change the fact that you're a clerk, does it? So go clerk. Go. Off with you." She left the dressing room to stand guard.

I pulled on the shorts. They had a wide waistband that held in my non-ripped stomach. Regular bra off, muted green sports bra on, snugging up the girls quite nicely. Then a cropped shirt. Emerson might've died, but that didn't mean I was going to run with only a bra on, no matter that it was reinforced with steel or whatever magical fiber Pomegranate & Plum had used.

I looked in the mirror again.

My reflection didn't quite look like me.

Marley opened the door. "Wow! You look amazing!"

The hot stone in my gut flared again. "Tell me the truth, Marley. Will people think I look ridiculous?"

"For one, who cares what people think? And for two, only if you poop yourself crawling over the finish line. You look great. And the run's only three miles."

"Only three miles. You're funny."

"Buy these. Wear that snotty little insignia with pride. Let's get out of here before I eat Aspen. I'm starving." She left the dressing room.

I changed back into my gray dress, relieved at being able to cover up again.

The image of Emerson at the end, those weird protuberances, fat upon fat, the massiveness of her, the pain . . . Suddenly, my eyes were wet. I didn't want looks to matter. I didn't want size to matter. But they did. Size had killed

Emerson. Size had me in this store, not quite recognizing myself.

My phone buzzed, startling me. I'd never be that person who could defuse a bomb, that was for sure. I wiped my eyes, pulled my phone out of my purse and did a double take when I saw the name.

Evan Kennedy. We'd entered our names into each other's phones.

And he was calling. Calling, like a human and everything, though not the next day, as he'd said.

"Hello?" My voice was odd.

"Georgia? It's Evan, the guy you met in the bar last week. Not the butcher. The other one."

I smiled before remembering that we'd actually met years before at Yale. "Oh, yes, the not-butcher. Right."

"I'll get right to it. You want to have dinner with me next Saturday? I'm out of state at the moment."

My mouth opened, then closed, then opened again. Marley and I were going to Hakuna Matata this weekend, though I hadn't actually told her anything other than it was a spa. Next Saturday was a week and a half away, which meant I could lose more weight, curse the thought. "Um . . . I have a thing that day. A fun run in Central Park to raise money for the city's food pantry. So maybe Friday?"

"I love running!" Great. Another freak like my brother. "Can I come?"

God, no. "Well . . . the truth is, I'm a terrible runner and I don't want to ruin any good impressions I might've made."

This not-fat woman in the mirror was a pretty accomplished flirt.

"Okay," he said, and I could hear the grin in his voice. "Dinner after the race, then? In the city, or up your way?"

"In the city is fine." I could shower and change at my father's.

"Great! I'll make a reservation somewhere nice. Any neighborhood better than another?"

"How's Chelsea?"

"Chelsea works. I'll text you the details."

"Sounds good. Thanks, guy who is not a butcher."

"You're welcome, terrible runner."

I ended the call.

A date with Evan Kennedy.

At some point, Yale was going to come up, and I'd have to admit to being that fat, quiet girl who made honors in every class, who'd worshipped him from afar for nearly three years.

But for now, it was disturbingly nice to be the pretty girl from the bar.

CHAPTER 18

Marley

Let a stranger touch your naked butt.
(No, of course it's not on the list,
but somehow it was part of my birthday present.)

"Welcome to Sagrada Vida," said the woman at the front desk.

"Thanks!" I said, giving her my best smile. "It's so pretty here!"

"Please lower your voice. We have a quietude policy." Indeed, her name tag said *Whisper*, which I now realized was maybe an order and not a name.

Georgia was glancing around furtively. Her mother was here this weekend, too. But what a nice surprise this was! A spa weekend with my best friend, her treat, here in the beautiful Catskills. This was the kind of thing that the *Sex and the City* gals would definitely do.

Emerson would heartily approve. And I could use a break. My parents' house had sold in ten minutes, more or less, and all of a sudden, their move was looming on the horizon like a tornado. Relaxing with Georgia, getting a little pampering, drinking a few martinis would be good for the soul.

The man who'd brought in our bags now unzipped them.

"Um, excuse me?" I said. "What are you doing?"

He didn't answer, just held up one of my Salt & Pepper boxes.

"Contraband," the man said to Whisper.

"What?" I said. "It's not drugs. It's food. Dark chocolate truffles with toasted macadamia nuts. They're fantastic. Would you like one? I'm a chef."

"We don't allow food from the outside," Whisper, uh, whispered. Like the bellhop, she was dressed in gray. All the staffers were, apparently. The lobby was painted white, the floor was white, and I suddenly felt like I was in a futuristic alien movie in which Georgia and I would soon be spattered all over the wall.

"Oh," I said, shooting Georgia a look. She wasn't making eye contact. "Well, I'm not here to lose weight, not really. Just for the seaweed wrap and facials and manicures." I gave another big smile.

"Sorry," Whisper said, barely audible. "This type of food is distracting for the other clients, and obviously violates our policy." She took another Salt & Pepper box out, giving a little hum of disappointment.

"But those are Mexican wedding cookies," I said. "Everyone loves those."

"White flour isn't allowed here," Whisper said. "Or butter. Or animal products. Or nonorganic produce from more than twenty miles away."

I glared at Georgia. "What have you done to me, Georgia Sloane?"

"I signed us up for the weekend package," Georgia explained. "The Inner Glow. It's your early birthday present."

"Oh!" I said, cheering considerably. "That sounds fun!"

"Please lower your voice," Whisper said. "Also, it's time for your first treatment, Miss DeFelice."

"Goody," I whispered. "So what's first?"

"Let's get you comfortable. Come to our relaxation room, please."

"I *like* relaxing," I whispered, and Georgia and I both started giggling like kids in church. With that, two gray-clad people took my arms and led me away, as if I were headed for the dementia ward.

"Have a good time," Georgia whispered.

"Bye," I whispered back, still giggling. Uh-oh. There was her mother. Ah, well. Not my problem. I was about to glow.

My keepers led me to the relaxation room, which was so dark I bumped into a chair. They told me to change into a robe and sip some herbal tea. I obeyed. The robe was luxuriously silky, but the tea tasted like grass. Blick. Coffee was definitely more my thing, dark and delicious.

"We're ready for you, Miss DeFelice," whispered Lupita Nyong'o or a damn fine look-alike.

"Thanks," I said. "I love facials."

"Me too," she said. Her name tag said Harmony. Whisper. Harmony. I wondered if funky names were a requirement for working here. "Please take off your robe and lie on your side." She held up the sheet for privacy.

"Oh. Okay." Didn't a person usually lie faceup for a facial? I'd only had one or two, but I remember liking it . . . and dozing off. All that steam and flute music.

I positioned myself according to the directions. It was comfy. The table was warm. I might get that nap after all.

Then I felt Harmony's hand on my ass.

"Hey!" I said. "What are you doing?"

"Your first time?"

"Um . . . for what?"

"For the hydrovisconic?"

"Is that a kind of facial?"

She laughed gently, quietly, harmoniously. "Not exactly.

But it's relaxing and wonderful just the same. May I proceed?"

She was so pretty, and her hands were warm. I wanted her to like me. "Sure."

I would live to regret that word. Oh, yes. I would regret it so much.

CHAPTER 19

Georgia

Finally have an honest conversation about weight.
(Not on the list, but a long time coming.)

"Darling," my mother said, taking a slurp of her martini. It was one thirty in the afternoon, and while white flour and chocolate may have been verboten, vodka clearly wasn't. If my mother was any indication, the clientele of Hakuna Matata would mount an armed rebellion if the spa banned alcohol. "So proud of you for doing this."

"Thanks," I said, rolling my eyes.

"I come here once a month."

"Why, Mom? You're already so thin."

"Can't be too rich or too thin, Georgia," she said. Her eyes wandered over me. "Maybe someday you'll see. Besides, it's good for the soul."

"I didn't think you had one."

"Is that your sense of humor, darling? I didn't think you had one."

Touché.

We stood there, looking at each other.

All through my youth, Big Kitty had been stunning in that sharp, ice-cold way. Picture Michelle Pfeiffer as an evil queen. Mom never had an extra pound on her. I never saw her eat dessert, not even once. Never saw her clean her plate. I didn't understand that kind of discipline, that ability to view food as something that would simply keep you alive rather than something that was to be enjoyed, or used as punishment or comfort. When I was young, heads would turn to look at her . . . and her lumpy daughter.

But then came the plastic surgery addiction—the swollen, unnatural lips and subsequent lisp, the completely unnecessary nose job, the fillers that made her look hard and artificial. She changed haircuts week to week, trying, I imagined, to fill her empty hours. Right now, blond extensions curled down her back. The last time I saw her, she'd been sporting a tousled pixie cut. The change was disconcerting.

"You're almost there," she said.

"Where?"

She gave a nod at my midsection. "Your weight."

"Do you know how much I weigh, Mom?"

"You look good, that's all I'm saying. I'm proud of you."

"I think I have an ulcer. Or stomach cancer." That one had just occurred to me last night, when chomping on antacids hadn't done the trick.

She rolled her eyes. "Always such a drama queen. Really, Georgia."

"I have a burning sensation in my stomach almost constantly. It's hard to eat."

"Good! It will remind you not to be such a little pig." She took another slurp of her martini. "Oh, stop looking so wounded. If your stomach hurts, it's probably because you binge so much." My childhood in a nutshell, ladies and gents. "Now. What are you scheduled for? You're still a little chunky for cold lipo, but—"

"I'm going to unpack. I'll see you later." Not to be left

out, I swung by the bar first. "Vodka, straight up," I ordered. The buzz would dull my mother's words, and a little stomach pain would be worth it. I took a hearty slug, and for once, my stomach didn't punish me for it. Good. I deserved nice things with a mother like mine.

I'd booked Marley and me a suite, and it was beautiful, the windows overlooking the rolling hills of the Catskill Mountains. Autumn color was just seeping into the trees. I unpacked, read the pamphlet on the night table. In addition to the expected hyperbole about mind and spirit and fat-suctioning, it urged me to dress in the "custom-made white jersey pyjamas made in Switzerland just for you, our precious guest." This would help me achieve a sense of oneness.

"You had me at 'pyjamas' with a 'Y,'" I said. "Very classy. Not as fun as the sock monkey pajamas I got at Target, but hey. Yours are nice, too."

The vodka had gone right to my head.

There were several pairs of *pyjamas*. I took a pair of the large, pulled them on, knotted the drawstring.

The pants fell right off.

Well, well, well.

I tried the medium. They were roomy, but they stayed on.

I took my drink out onto the balcony and sat on the chaise longue. My treatment package didn't start till tomorrow; I'd let Marley go first, since she was my guest, poor innocent lamb. I took another sip of vodka, and closed my eyes.

One of the regulars at Camp Copperbrook was this girl from Alabama named Faye. She'd been a big girl; all of us were, but Faye had been at least a hundred and fifty pounds overweight. Not as big as Emerson, but almost. It was one of my worst summers, weight-wise; my brother had been home for six weeks before I went to camp, and he'd been even meaner than usual. There was a new hole in my bedroom wall, courtesy of his fist, because I'd told him Dad had called.

The result was that I was at my heaviest from misery-eating and trying to stay away from the house as much as possible, which inevitably turned into a reason to eat—Starbucks or LuLu's Pancake Hut or the movies, where I'd get a large popcorn with free refills.

Anyway, Faye and Emerson were definitely the biggest girls there, and I was in the top quarter. Faye and Emerson had gotten really close, and I was something of a third wheel. I liked Emerson more; Faye was harder for me to read, full of half compliments and constant body scanning. *Are you fatter than I am? Are you losing more weight? Am I prettier than you?*

The next summer, Emerson and I both returned. I'd lost some weight but not enough, never enough; Emerson had gained more. I saw that as we greeted each other on the first day, and my heart ached for her, sweet, shy Emerson. And then one of the counselors pounced on us, hugging us tight.

"Hey-ay," she said. "How y'all doin'? It's me! Faye! OMG, y'all didn't recognize me!"

Because Faye had lost all the weight. All of it. She was tiny. Petite. Her hip bones jutted out above her cutoff jeans, and her thighs were tanned and toned, and Emerson and I stood there, our mouths open as she pranced around us.

"I know! Isn't it amazing? I look fantastic, right?" She turned, stuck her butt out and looked over her shoulder at us. "I might even do some modeling!"

She'd come back to camp to "make sure I don't slide back," she said. But really, I suspected she was back to lord her tiny body over us.

"How did she do it?" Emerson whispered the second we were alone. "She's right. I didn't recognize her."

Faye stayed mum on her amazing weight loss, saying only, "Hard work, y'all!"

Her accent, which we'd found so endearing last year, grated now.

For two weeks, she stuck to Emerson like a burr, the differences vast . . . Faye five foot eight or so, Emerson five inches shorter and two hundred pounds heavier. Faye wore skimpy shorts and little shirts with spaghetti straps; Emerson wore tent-sized baggy T-shirts and shorts that hiked up between her thighs. There was no saggy skin to be seen (and Faye showed a lot of it, stripping into her pj's or bikini right in front of us). Youth? Extra elasticity in her DNA? Breast implants?

She even ate. Tiny portions, to be sure, but she didn't seem bulimic. Didn't seem post-bypass. (Believe me, we could tell. We were experts, even at that young age.)

When you've been fat, your body has devious ways to keep the weight on. Emerson and I did the math—three pounds a week, maybe more. We envisioned the diet, the exercising, the iron self-control it would take. Faye's refusal to let us in on her methods added to our state of jealous wonder. I just wished it had happened to a nicer person.

The biggest question Emerson and I had, whispered between us at night: Why is she here?

You don't come to fat camp when you're a size 2. You come to prove you aren't one of us anymore. And sure enough, after two weeks of mincing around in her tiny clothes, Faye went back to Alabama. Once she'd made us all feel worse about our physical selves, her work was done.

Now I, too, was entering the world of the skinny. In tiny little ways, my life was changing.

I took another long sip of my drink, grateful that my stomach wasn't acting up today, and glad for the buzz the vodka was giving me, loosening my thoughts. Evan

Kennedy would never have asked Fat Georgia out for dinner. Should I care about that as much as I did? Everyone judged people on their looks. It was human nature. Couldn't I just be glad he was interested?

I sighed and closed my eyes.

Apparently, I fell asleep, because I jolted awake sometime later as the door to our suite burst open. Marley stood there in her white bathrobe, hair wild, face red.

"What happened?" I asked, bolting out of my chair. "Are you okay?"

"No! Would you like to know what just came out of me?" she demanded. "Would you like to hear what was flushed out of me and sucked into a tube which led to God knows where, Georgia? Because I just had my colon irrigated, and I want to kill myself! I thought I was getting a facial!"

"Oh, my God," I said, the wheezing laughter starting. "I'm so sorry. What did they do?"

She sat on the bed and winced. "We can never talk about this again. You tell anyone I have been violated in this way, I will kill you. Hydro-something, my ass. Literally, Georgia. My *ass*. I didn't think the Inner Glow package meant small intestines. That technician boldly went where no one has gone before."

I was laughing too hard to answer.

It felt just like camp, when Marley could make everyone happy.

"You're drunk, aren't you?" she said, looking at the martini glass. "You didn't even get one for me. You're a crap friend. Dang, I better avoid using any poop words until I'm hypnotized to forget the past hour and a half. My only joy in life is knowing you have one tomorrow." She grinned. "Fudge has been ruined for me," she added, which set me off into another gale of laughter.

When I'd calmed down (and Marley found the minibar

and poured herself a glass of wine), we went back out onto the balcony and watched the sun set. "I ran into Big Kitty," Marley said. "She's looking very tight these days. Face, not sphincter, though maybe both."

"Did she recognize you?"

"No. I'm batting a thousand in that department."

"I'm sorry."

"Oh, I don't mind. I hugged her and freaked her out real good." She grinned and took a sip of wine. "So, Georgia. We need to talk."

"Don't break up with me."

"I never will." She put her feet up on the railing, her toenails painted light blue. "Why are we here? It's not the kind of spa I thought it was."

I took a slow, deep breath. "I'm sorry. I tricked you. I just didn't want to come alone. And there *are* facials, somewhere."

"We're here to lose weight?"

"I am," I admitted. A prickle of shame crept up from my chest. "I'm not implying you should. I know you're happy with where you are."

"I wouldn't call it happy. I've accepted it. I try to appreciate the fact that my body works, and I'm healthy. But it's a daily battle, G."

"I know. And I just can't win it. All I need is just a few more pounds, a couple more inches, and I might be . . . I might be there."

She nodded at the horizon, the sun sinking into the tree line. She knew. Every fat girl in the world knew that dream. Tucking in that shirt. Shopping at the regular store. Using clothes to show off your body rather than hide it.

We hadn't talked like this since she'd moved to Cambry. We'd agreed we'd talk about everything *but* weight, gain or loss. But if I couldn't talk to Marley about this, and she to me, who else was left?

"The other day," I said, clearing my throat, "I was at the car wash, and the guy came out and asked me what I wanted. I just asked for the regular wash, you know? The eight-dollar one? He took my money and said, 'I'm throwing in the undercarriage treatment for free.' And he winked."

"So romantic," Marley said, smiling a little.

"I know. But that's never happened to me. And at the Blessed Bean the other day, Lucinda, you know her?"

"Yep. She always screws up my order."

"She remembered my name."

"You go there every day. She should know your name."

"But she never has, Marley. For almost five years, I've gone in almost every day, and she has *never* remembered my name. That night, at the bar with FDNY, two men asked me out. Two! You know how many men have asked me out in my entire life?'

"Three."

"Yes. Three. And those guys at the bar . . . they didn't ask me out because I have a sparkling personality and I'm good with kids." I paused, my eyes stinging. "It's because I've lost weight. My whole life, I've tried to lose weight, and I'm so close. So I came here, and I dragged you along." I shrugged, Mason-like, embarrassed and a little ashamed. "The list brought things up, you know? If seaweed wraps and a high colonic take off a few more pounds . . . I had to try."

Marley squeezed my hand. "I understand, hon, I do. But I'm worried, too. You've lost a lot of weight, and sure, you've been eating better since I moved in. But still. You said you might have an ulcer. You can't just let that go. Look what happened to Emerson. She didn't take care of herself, and she ended up dead, Georgia! Just because you're getting thin doesn't mean you can ignore things."

"I know. I do. The stomach pain started after Mason was

in the hospital. It's probably just stress. But some of the weight loss is good. I've been eating better than ever, thanks to you, and I'm happier teaching nursery school, happier without Rafe—"

"Do *not* try to sell that here, sister." She arched an eyebrow.

I took a deep breath, let it out slowly. "Well, okay, but I'm . . . more relaxed without Rafe. We did love each other, but we didn't have a great marriage." The memories of those tense months, the omnipresent sense of failure made my chest feel heavy, but what I said was true. There was a big hole in my life where Rafe used to be, but when he had been there, he was just too big. Too much. He wanted what I couldn't give. Even more, he wanted to give me something I didn't know how to handle.

Love. Romantic love, sexual love, committed love.

Marley set her glass down and tightened the belt of her robe. "Okay, well, getting back to the topic at hand . . . what do you think will happen? When you lose a few more pounds, life is going to be great?"

"In some ways, it's already getting better," I said. "I have a date with Evan next Saturday. I got an undercarriage rinse."

She gave me a long look. "I want you to make an appointment with your doctor when we get back."

"You're right, as usual. I've been meaning to, anyway."

We sat in silence a few more minutes, watching as the pink faded from the sky, the horizon turning purple, then blue. "How's it going with Camden?" I asked.

"Not good," she said. "We text a little here and there, but I can't move out of the friend zone." She looked over at me. "And you're right. It's because of weight. If I was a size six, he'd want me. We'd be married by now."

"So why are you putting so much effort into someone like that? You should find someone like . . . well, like Rafe."

She gave me the stink-eye. "Listen to yourself."

"I know, I know. But does Camden deserve you? That's all I'm asking."

"Maybe? I don't know." She waved her hand in the air. "I want to be with someone. I want to be part of a couple. I want kids. He's a good person, Georgia. All I have to do is—what's that saying?—make the scales fall from his eyes, and I think he could love me."

"He should love you right now," I said.

"I know it. Honest to God, I don't want to have to lose weight. It would have to become my life's work, all that measuring and weighing and passing on all the good stuff."

"You trade one side of the addiction for the other."

"Yes! Besides, I've put so much goddamn effort into forcing myself to believe I'm fine the way I am that if a fairy godmother came down and said, 'Hey, want to be Beyoncé?' I'd have to say, 'Fuck you, Fairy Godmother, where were you when I was sixteen?'"

I laughed. "Only you would tell a fairy godmother to fuck off."

She snorted, running a hand through her gorgeous hair. "I'm unique."

"You're the best friend anyone could ever have. You're like my sister." There was a pause, and I cringed a little. I should've known not to bring up sisters.

"Vodka makes you sentimental," Marley said, her voice husky. A second later, I felt her hand holding mine. "I love you, too. Now let's go to dinner, because I can swear on the pope's personal copy of the Bible that there is absolutely *nothing* in my digestive tract."

CHAPTER 20

Marley

Hold hands with a cute guy in public. *(Or not.)*

Three remarkable things happened the week after my colon was violated.

Eva called me.

Camden asked me out. *He* called *me*.

Will Harding and I had a conversation, and then, shockingly, a fight.

Let's start with number one. A little history is required. Until that day, Eva had never called me. Hand to God, she never once called first, or texted, or e-mailed. She always responded, never initiated.

Georgia and I had decided to soothe our "inner glows" with a trip to the huge HomeGoods in White Plains. I was fondling throw pillows, certain that I needed at least two more. Georgia was exclaiming over the fake orchids and how *real* they looked. (Sometimes she sounded just like my nonny in Boca.) My phone rang. *Eva.*

Since such a thing had never happened before, my completely justified greeting was, "Is it Mom or Dad?"

My eyes filled with tears as I prepared to hear about the death of a parent, or both, probably during a run to

Walgreens in Tarrytown because Folgers was on sale. I reached out for Georgia, who dropped the fake plant and grabbed my hand.

"Hello?" Eva said. "Marley? Is that you?"

"Who's dead?" I asked.

"Um . . . no one." I heard two *thunks* as she undoubtedly knocked on some wood.

"Are they in the hospital?"

"Who?"

"Mom and Dad!"

"No! Not that I know of." *Thunk thunk.*

I let go of Georgia and crossed myself. "You better be right." I paused. "Do you have cancer?"

"No. I don't think so." Knock, knock, another sign of the cross. Georgia looked at me, eyebrows raised, and I adjusted the phone. "Everyone's fine," I whispered, crossing myself again.

"You sure?" she asked.

"Positive," I said. Crossed myself again to be sure.

"Are you talking to me?" my sister asked. "Jesus, Marley, if this isn't a good time, say so."

"I'm here! I'm just surprised, since you've never ever called me first, even once." Now that I knew no one was dead or dying, I resumed gazing at the shelves. Ooh. Pretty iridescent globe thingies on copper sticks. Might be a nice accent in the garden between the basil plants. "To what do I owe this honor?"

Eva heaved the big-sister sigh of tolerance. "Ma wants us to go to the house and tell her what we want so she can make a list."

"What do you mean?"

"Furniture, pictures, the little crappy knickknacks made in China."

I winced and put down the globe-on-a-stick. Definitely made in China. "Why is she giving us her stuff?"

"Because, stupid. They're getting all new stuff for Maryland."

What? The last time my parents had bought a new *anything* had been before I was born. Their once-white towels were gray and frayed, the sheets so thin they were translucent. Now they were getting all new stuff? It sounded very much like someone had a brain tumor. I crossed myself again.

"Eva, before we start divvying up the china, are you . . . have you talked to them about this? Because it seems like this move came completely out of the blue."

"So? They're adults, they're not senile, not yet, anyway, and they want a change. What's the big deal?"

My mouth opened and shut. *Frankie*, I wanted to say, and my whole soul seemed to pull at her name. But Eva and I never talked about Frankie.

"Also, do you really want to open up your apartment to our parents every other month and have Mom rearranging your bathroom drawers?"

"Why wouldn't I? My drawers are a wreck."

"It's weird. You're thirty-eight. You shouldn't be living with your parents."

"Bite me. They'd be living with *me*. But that's beside the point. You and Dante need to come to the house. Can you come on Sunday?"

No. I wasn't ready for this. "I'm very busy this weekend," I said. Not completely untrue; we had the fun run on Saturday.

"Well, get unbusy," Eva said. "Mom said I was in charge."

"You should be in charge. You live to be in charge."

"You're right. Speaking of, I have to go, because I'm in charge of this whole department."

"Hacking the White House, are you?" Her work was classified. Yes, she was that cool.

"That's so two years ago." She paused. "Everything good with you?"

Again, she surprised me. I could not recall her ever before asking how I was. "Everything's fine. You?"

"Fine. Okay. Bye." She clicked off.

I stared at the phone for another moment, wishing Eva and I were the type of sisters who talked. I mean, we talked. Just never about anything meaningful. Frankie, parents, when Dante came out, being fat, being in love, if she was an android. Nope. All those topics bounced right off of Eva's sturdy heart.

Oh, crap, was that the time? I always spent more time in this store than I meant to.

"Georgia," I said, "I have to run, okay? Time to make deliveries."

She emerged from an aisle, staggering under a faux-antique birdcage, dog-head bookends and a red and yellow vase. "I'm gonna fill this birdcage with pink glass balls and Christmas lights," she said proudly. "I saw it on Pinterest."

"Ooh! It'll be beautiful. Here, take the cart and buy me that pillow, okay? Sorry I have to go."

"No worries." She smiled, awash in the bliss of retail therapy. "See you later."

As I drove home, I thought about trying to ask Mom and Dad about the move. On the one hand, yes, good for them. What if I asked them about Frankie and they changed their minds and then Dad died shoveling snow next winter? Huh? That could happen! "In the name of the Father, the Son and the Holy Spirit," I muttered, making the sign of the cross as fast and tight as I could.

On the other hand, I should be allowed to ask, right? I mean . . . I was the twin who didn't die. Everything—

everything—related to Frankie was tied up in that house. Would they take the shrine? Would I have to drive down to Maryland to see Ebbers the Penguin?

I called my mother. We *would* have this talk like a normal family.

"What's the matter?" she said by way of answering. Like mother, like daughter. "Are you sick, baby? Do you have a fever? Tummy ache?"

Whenever I'd been sick as a kid, my mother would bring me cinnamon toast cut into triangles and give me weak tea to drink. It must've been terrifying for her to have us suffer even the smallest virus, but she hid it well . . . at least, back then she did. As I'd gotten older, I picked up on her fear and tried to keep any health issues to myself. Not that I'd had anything worse than a bad cold in all those years.

Sorry for having the world's best immune system, Frankie.

"Marley? Sweetheart, are you there?"

"I'm here, Mom. I . . . I just wanted to say hi," I said. "And I love you."

"Oh, sweetheart. I love you, too."

I couldn't tell them not to go. They deserved a new house near the water. Maybe—just maybe—they *wanted* to get away from Frankie and all the sad memories.

My throat tightened anyway.

"You sure you're not sick?" Mom asked.

"Nope. Just thinking of you."

There was a slightly suspicious pause. "Do you have cancer?" she asked.

I couldn't help but laugh (and cross myself). "Nope. Strong as an ox."

"Good. I have to go, sweetie. I have a hair appointment."

"Enjoy. Tell Silvana I said hi." Mom had had her hair done by the same woman for thirty years. "Talk to you soon."

Then I crossed myself again. You know. Just in case.

When I got home, I packed up the evening's meals. Tuesday was my lightest day, just Mrs. Ames and Will Harding.

Next Tuesday, however, I'd be eating with Will, the Mongolian beef dinner he wanted. Maybe that would be the day he added me to the bodies in his freezer.

As I was loading my delivery box, my phone rang again. *Camden*.

Will's meal—steak with a balsamic reduction, cooked medium rare, along with beet and goat cheese spinach salad—almost dropped to the floor, as my hands were suddenly numb. Like my sister, Camden never initiated a phone call. Once or twice, he'd texted first, though. (Once. It was once.)

Like a well-trained singleton, I waited four rings before answering, pounding heart or not. "Hello?"

"Hey, Marley! How's it going?"

"Good! How are you, Cam?"

"Excellent. I was wondering if you might want to grab a drink tonight."

Oh, my sweet, *sweet* baby Jesus. With great care, I set Will's meal safely on the counter. It was all I could do not to shout *Yes!* into the phone right then and there.

"Um, let's see. What time? I have a thing this evening, but it shouldn't last too long." See? Well-trained singleton.

"How about around six?"

I glanced at the clock (from Target, red, cream and blue, super adorable). My pulse was racing. "I think I can make it," I said, hoping I sounded casual. "Where did you have in mind?"

"At the place in Tarrytown? Down near the bridge?"

A really nice place. My breath caught. "Okay. I might be a little bit late, but I'll see you there."

"Awesome!"

I hung up the phone, double-checked to make sure it was

truly off, then let out a screech of joy so loud that Admiral barked from upstairs.

And Admiral never barked.

"I'm going on a date, Ad!" I called to the ceiling. I imagined he was very happy for me in his dignified way.

That list was *working*. Putting Camden to bed the other night had *not* been a wasted, pathetic way to spend my time. And tonight, I'd tell him I wanted to be a regular girlfriend. No more of this "don't tell your brother" thing. We'd hold hands. Oh, Lordy, we'd hold hands in public tonight!

I had to get moving, change, emotionally prepare for this date, hell's to the yes! Couldn't show up in my chef uniform. I zipped into the bedroom.

"Frankie, I have a date with the man of my dreams, wish me luck, pull some strings, do your thing, okay?" I said to her picture, then glanced in the mirror, pulling the elastic out of my hair and running my fingers through the frizzy, curly mess.

Should I put it up, or down? Did I have any miracle mist left? I did! "Thank you, Frankie!"

I squirted some on and scrunched it through my hair. Now, makeup. I'd do a smoky eye, because you did eyes or lips, but not both, and I didn't want to smear a wineglass with red lipstick. Not a cat eye . . . let's see, just a little dark purple, a little gray, that champagne color, lots of mascara. Some blush, a little clear lip gloss, perfume in my cleavage, boom!

On to clothes. Something low cut, obviously. Camden was a breast man. Heels, extra slutty, with skinny jeans to make me look taller. Sure, my ass was, er, significant, but in all the right ways.

"See that, Emerson? Me appreciating my body for what it is." I probably should stop talking to dead people, but hey. Better than talking to myself.

I changed, tugging up the jeans, then put on the red and white blouse—it wasn't too tight, since the jeans were, thank you, Tim Gunn. Adjusted the girls so they looked their best. Added a necklace that stopped just short of my cleavage to attract the eye there, added some gold hoop earrings for that gypsy look. Brushed my eyebrows into place, since they'd take over a small country if I let them.

Then I grabbed the boxes of food. Stopped at Mrs. Ames's house first; she was sleeping in her chair, God bless her, so I fed the cats and left her dinner with a note written in big letters, adding a smiley face.

On to Will's.

I was running late—it was 5:35, not the usual 5:15, thanks to my date prep. As I went into his house, I noticed his grass needed cutting. Wondered reflexively what Will looked like without his shirt. Then pictured Camden's rippling abs. Now *that* was male perfection.

There was Will, watching from the window like Norman Bates.

I went up the stairs and started to knock, but he opened the door first. "You're twenty-one minutes late," he said.

"Yes, and I'm really sorry."

"Why are you dressed like that?"

"Nice to see you, too, Will." He just stood there. "Can I come in with your dinner?"

"Is it sanitary to cook with all that hair everywhere?" he asked, though he did move aside. "What if you shed?"

I cut him a look. "When I'm cooking, it's always up, okay? No need to worry. Have you ever found one of my hairs in your food? No."

"There's always a first time." He followed me into the kitchen.

"Well, today is not that day, to quote the mighty Aragorn.

My hair was up when I was cooking. I changed because I have plans."

"Yes. I gathered that." There was a pause. "It's nice to see you dressed like a woman, even though you're fat." He looked me up and down, then glanced away.

Oh. Oh, boy. He was in trouble now. Fury coiled in my stomach like a rattlesnake.

"What did you just say, Will?"

"It's nice to see you dressed like a woman."

I dropped the packages of food on the counter, jammed my fists onto my hips and turned to face him. "Even though I'm fat."

"Yes. You look . . ." He gestured at my torso. "Nice."

"You don't go around calling a woman fat, Will Harding. Are you really that stupid?"

He frowned. "But you *are* fat."

"I *know* that."

"Then why are you screeching?"

"I dress like a professional chef, because I am one. Chef whites are not reserved just for men."

"I guess that's true."

"You don't have to guess. It just is. Back to your rude comment, Will."

"What was rude?"

"The word *fat*! It's a rude word! Where do you live? Under a rock? You basically said I look like a fat man. In the world of human females, that's extremely rude."

"You dress in androgynous clothing. I've never seen you in anything else. Your hair is always up, and today it's down. I'm simply making an observation."

"So this has nothing to do with you wanting to tell me I'm fat."

He frowned. "No."

"Yeah, right."

"But obviously I know that you are," he added.

"Jesus! What's wrong with you?"

He folded his arms. "I don't understand why you're mad."

"You think I haven't seen you looking at me, judging my weight all these months, Will Harding?"

"I—I'm—I didn't mean to—"

"You know what?" I snapped. "You're part of the problem with girls and women everywhere hating their bodies. People come in every shape, in case you haven't noticed. We're not all meant to be a size two, and even the size twos have body-image issues, so thanks a lot."

"What does your boyfriend look like?"

"Do you mean, is he a grotesque fatty like me?"

"Is he?"

I pulled out my phone, jabbed at the photos button and scrolled over to the picture I'd taken of Camden and me. "There. Is he fat? No. Is he ugly? No. He's kind of perfect, actually. Are you as tall as he is, Will? Are your biceps as gorgeous as his? Are your eyes as blue? Why not? Why haven't you fixed that, huh? What about your abs? I can tell you that Camden's are quite ripply and magnificent. And yes, he does find me attractive."

I took a breath, my cheeks hot.

"Even so, you are showing quite a lot there," he said, nodding at my chest like a puritanical minister.

"If it bothers you so much, stop looking." He didn't. I snapped my fingers, and his head jerked up. "You know what? I quit."

"What? Why? You look different. You look nice. I noticed. This is very confusing."

"Fine. Be confused. I have a date." I grabbed my purse and left. Slammed the door behind me, too.

How dare Will Harding, who was no cover model

himself, criticize what I was wearing, how I was shaped, how I wore my hair (though yes, sure, I could see his concern about my hair in his food, which is why I did always braid it tightly back when I cooked).

Did he think it was easy, keeping a positive self-image in a world obsessed with thigh gap? Did he think I didn't know how I looked? How much I weighed? I got into my car and slammed the door in case Will was watching, and drove away.

It didn't matter. I was going out with Camden. That was the thing I should focus on. But my cheeks throbbed with anger.

Had Camden asked me out for dinner, or just a drink? I couldn't remember. It hardly mattered. I took a deep breath. Camden had never said anything negative about my weight, my looks, my clothes. Camden liked me. Slept with me. Obviously found me attractive.

By the time I got to the restaurant, I was calm. After all, I knew Will Harding lacked social graces. I shouldn't have been surprised.

I checked my reflection, smiled at myself, took another breath.

I pictured Frankie sitting next to me, the two of us about to go in and have a double date.

What would she have been like as an adult? Would we have been best friends? I thought so. I bet, unlike Eva, Frankie would've called me first half of the time, and I would've called her first the other half in a mutual lovefest of twinship.

For a second, I saw that ocean of loneliness in my eyes.

No. None of this. I was on a date with Camden Fortuno.

The restaurant was crowded and noisy. I glanced at my watch—6:11. Perfect. Punctual enough to be polite, late enough to show this night was no big deal.

There he was, leaning against the bar, talking to a woman who had legs up to her neck, a micromini skirt just barely clearing her ass. Blond hair with that weird under-coating of brown swirling past her shoulders in effortless waves, as if she'd spent the day on the beach.

It didn't matter. Camden attracted women like a rotting corpse attracted flies. He couldn't help it. But *I* was the one he had asked out.

"Hey," I said, going up to him. Should I kiss him on the cheek? Yes? Or no.

"Hey!" he said, bending down. A kiss? Cheek or lips? I turned to kiss him, but shit, it was a hug, and my lips slid across his outer jaw, leaving a glossy slick.

"Sorry," I said, wiping his cheek with my fingers.

"No problem! Great to see you! Amber, this is Marley. Marley, meet Amber."

"Hi," I said, smiling. Poor thing had a stripper's name. I mentally apologized to Georgia's stepmother for that dig at her former profession, but come on. Amber?

"Hello." She sipped her drink through her straw, smiling around it. Was she wondering why a guy like Camden would date a woman like me? If so, soak it up, bitch. (And if not, sorry, you're very pretty.)

"What do you want to drink, Mar?"

Mar. Ugh. "I'll have a glass of pinot grigio. Thanks."

He ordered and waited. "How do you know Camden?" Amber asked.

"He works with my brother," I said.

"Cool."

"Marley and I have known each other forever," Camden said over his shoulder. "We're old pals."

Amber and I looked at each other for a minute. Okay. She'd just seen us kiss (awkward though it was). So why was she still here?

"Uh, what do you do for work, Amber?" I asked.

"I'm a social worker for the state. Mostly kids in trouble."

Not a stripper, then. "That must be intense."

"It is, but it can be super rewarding, too. What about you?"

"I'm a personal chef."

"Awesome," she said.

Camden turned and handed me my drink. "Let's get a table, ladies," he said.

"Sounds great," Amber said.

With a strange feeling in my stomach, I watched as Camden put his hand on the small of Amber's back and guided her through the crowd.

I followed like a good dog, my cheeks burning.

He asked you out for a drink, my brain said. *He's just being nice to her, that's all.*

Sure. That could possibly be true.

The table was a high top, which meant I had to wriggle onto the stool. Being short was another thing about my body that sucked, though it usually got overshadowed by the suckiness of being fat. Amber slid onto her stool as if it had been proportioned just for her.

My eyes felt hot. I took a sip of wine and fake-smiled.

"What's new, Mar?" Camden asked. He put his hand over Amber's.

They were dating. They were *dating*, and Camden had asked me here for no reason other than to show me that.

"Not much," I heard myself say. "The usual stuff. My serial killer client is weirder than ever."

"Awesome," Camden said, smiling. "I love those stories you tell about him. Such a whack-job, right?"

"Seriously?" Amber asked. "A serial killer?"

"No, not seriously." Come on, Amber. Would I willingly

cook for a serial killer? I bit the bullet and asked the question that had to be asked. "So how long have you guys been seeing each other?"

"About a month?" he said. "Sound right, babe?"

"A little longer. Six weeks, maybe." Amber gave me a slight, apologetic smile. So she knew. She knew I was in love with her boyfriend.

Her boyfriend. For five years, I'd loved him, and for five years, he hadn't once considered dating me.

He smiled at me, then at Amber, not a flicker of anything other than happiness in his ridiculously beautiful blue eyes.

"How'd you meet?" I asked.

Sitting there on the uncomfortable stool, my feet dangling as if I were an enormous toddler, saying, "How sweet," I had never felt less like a person in my life. I drank my wine, smoothed my hair back as it tried to coil around my face, grinned like the village idiot and watched Camden fall more in love by the second. Horribly, Amber seemed really nice.

I nodded till I was dizzy. Drank that wine pretty fast.

"We're gonna have dinner, Mar," Camden finally said. "You wanna join us?"

"Oh, thanks, but I have plans," I lied.

"Another time, maybe?"

"Absolutely."

I hopped off the stool, but my heel twisted, and a sharp pain lanced up my left ankle. I grabbed myself before I fell.

"You okay?" Camden said.

"Yup! Just fine!" I said. I took a steadying breath, trying not to let the pain show. Tears, not just from the ankle, were dying to fall. I had to get out of there. Now. "Amber, great to meet you."

"You too, Marley." She smiled kindly.

It took every ounce of pride to not limp out of there. The pain was awful, but I was not going to hobble.

I got to my car, collapsed in the front seat and took off my shoe. My ankle was already swollen.

My breath hitched in and out in mortifying sobs. Maybe the worst thing of all was that Camden had no idea. None. He was just introducing his old buddy to his girl, that was all. He wanted us to meet. His IQ had to be in the single digits. Hot, angry tears sliced down my face. Of course he hadn't asked me on a date. We weren't *ever* going to date.

I pictured Emerson watching from heaven, Frankie on her lap, as they shook their heads sadly. *Poor thing, she never knew. What was she thinking?*

I needed ice for my ankle. Just then, my stomach growled. Yes, God forbid I didn't feed myself. Ice, and food, and probably more alcohol.

I rolled down the windows as I drove so the wind would dry my tears. I should go to Mom and Dad's, as they loved nothing more than taking care of one of their kids. But my tears would freak them out, and God forbid I sob out my love for Camden. Dad would go after him with an ax (a pleasing image), and Mom would be devastated for me.

I could go to Dante's. He and Louis were home, having a baking night with two other couples, according to an earlier text. I'd gorge myself if I went there, and then they'd be obliged to hate Camden, which wouldn't be fair, since they worked together. Besides, I didn't want to be the odd number. Rachel Carver, maybe? No. Too soon in our friendship. Plus, she had the triplets, and it was probably close to their bedtime.

If I went home, Georgia would take care of me, and she'd be so nice, so understanding, but I just didn't want anyone to see me like this—humiliated, injured, embarrassed, my chest bucking with heartache . . .

Okay, enough.

I knew one person who wouldn't pity me. Two, actually; Eva, but she lived on the Upper East Side, and that was too far away.

The other person was Will Harding.

I was furious with Camden, with myself for being so stupid, *and* furious with Will. He'd called me fat. He didn't believe Camden would date someone like me (and he was right, damn it all), so *he* could deal with me now. He owed me.

Besides, he had some really, *really* good food at his house. The food I'd brought him. Could he possibly have eaten it all yet? I always brought big portions. Of course I did. Look at how I was raised. Food, glorious frickin' food.

Abruptly, I turned onto Elm Street. A few blocks more, and I took a right onto Redwood. Got out, left shoe in one hand, and eased my weight onto my injured foot—yikes, it *hurt*—and hobbled up to the door and knocked, hard.

"Will! Open the damn door!" A second later, he obeyed. "I sprained my ankle, and I'm starving." Without waiting for an invitation, I pushed past him, using the wall to hold myself up.

"What happened to you?"

Choosing not to answer, I dashed away my tears, went into his living room and sat on the couch. Brown, microfiber, two matching brown throw pillows—very boring but super comfortable. I dropped my shoe on the floor next to me and took the other one off as well. "Can you get me some ice? It hurts a lot."

"Those shoes are life-threatening," he said. "You have no one to blame but yourself."

"Ice, Will. Ice."

"Fine."

He went into the kitchen, and I eased my legs up onto the couch. Put the boring throw pillow under my hurt ankle and leaned back, letting out a slow breath. I could hear the ice machine clattering, Will muttering to himself.

I'd never been in the living room, though I'd seen it off the kitchen, the only room where I was allowed. All the shades were pulled. A huge TV sat on a console across from me. There was an end table with a lamp. Otherwise, nothing. No pictures, no magazines, no books, no photos, no prints, no decorations of any kind, as if he'd moved in half an hour ago.

He came in holding a box of tissues, a dishcloth, and a plastic bag filled with ice. Draped the cloth over my ankle and eased the ice bag onto it, then handed me the tissue box.

I wiped my eyes. So much for waterproof mascara.

Will didn't comment on my tears, and I felt oddly grateful.

"Should you get this looked at?" he said.

"I just twisted it. Ice, elevation, Motrin and rest."

He went back into the kitchen and returned with four tablets and a glass of water. Watched as I swallowed the pills.

"Do you have any food left?" I asked.

He sighed but made another trip to the kitchen, returning with a plate of the meal I'd brought him earlier this evening.

I took a bite of the salad—beet and goat cheese and spinach—and sighed. Good old food. *It* never had another girlfriend. The steak was cool, but perfect and tender.

"You gonna eat, too?" I asked.

"That's my dinner," he said, nodding at my plate.

"I provide my clients with very generous portions. It's on the website."

"True." Once again, he left the room, coming back a minute later with a plate for himself. He sat on the couch next to my feet, adjusting the bag of ice when it slipped.

"Have you ever dated a fat woman, Will?" I asked.

"I'm reluctant to talk about this, given your earlier hysteria."

"I wasn't hysterical. Answer the question."

He gave a martyred sigh. "Define fat."

"You're looking at it."

"No, I have never dated someone your size." He looked at me. "Have you ever dated an average-looking guy?"

"Define average."

"You're looking at it."

He *was* kind of average, kind of vanilla. Nothing wrong with his face or body, nothing particularly glorious about it, either. His hair was always adorably bed-heady.

"Yes, I have," I said, taking another bite of food. "Actually, no. I've slept with average-looking men. I've never really dated anyone."

He grunted and kept eating.

"So you wouldn't date a woman because she's fat?"

"I didn't say that. What a gift you have for misinterpreting my words."

"Would you?"

"It would depend on if she was a nice person."

"Bullshit."

He looked up from his plate, stared straight ahead, sighed pointedly, then continued eating.

We ate in silence for the next few moments, me way ahead of him. When I was done, I set the plate on the floor and crossed my arms. Looked at Will's profile.

We'd talked more today than we had in the past year combined.

I could really go for some Ben & Jerry's Peanut Butter Cup right now. "Do you have any ice cream?" I asked.

"No."

"Figures."

"You know," he said, "you're just as prejudiced about looks as anyone."

"Really? Please tell me about my flaws."

"That pretty boy you showed me. Would you have dated him if he was ugly?"

"Yes," I said.

"Right. The fact that he looks like Captain America, you hardly noticed."

"Bite me."

The corner of his mouth twitched. He took another bite of steak.

"How's dinner?" I asked.

"Fine."

"Fine? How about something more descriptive, Will? Succulent, delicious, juicy, flavorful, amazing."

"Yes. All those things."

I couldn't help but smile, and he almost smiled back.

When he was done, he stood up, picked up both our plates and took them into the kitchen. I heard him rattling around in there, tidying up. God forbid anything be out of place.

The remote was on the coffee table. I reached for it and turned on the TV.

My 600-lb Life was on. Of course.

Will came back in and sat back down, careful not to jostle my foot. "Lovely show," he said.

"My friend died a little while ago. She was like this."

"Is that when your mother had to bring me my meals?"

"Yes, Will. So sorry to have inconvenienced you."

"Did I say I was inconvenienced? I did not." There was a pause. On TV, the woman was saying how long it had been since she'd left the house.

"That must be hard," he said. "Feeling stuck."

I swallowed, thinking of Emerson. "I should stop watching this show. They're all the same."

"Are you afraid you'll end up like this?"

"You know, if I didn't have a sprained ankle, I would kick you so hard right now." I shifted a little, and the bag slipped. Will put it back.

"I meant stuck," he said. "You're not worried?"

"Will, this might be hard to believe, but I don't spend twelve hours a day lying at the end of the Krispy Kreme conveyor belt with my mouth open, okay? I eat good, healthy food, I go to the gym five times a week, do yoga, take Zumba—"

"What's Zumba? A drug?"

"An exercise class, dummy. I even like to run sometimes. I'm not afraid of weighing six hundred pounds. Are you? Because I bring you a *lot* of food, and I don't ever see you going for a run or out cutting your grass."

Another silence. We watched as Gloria lied to the doctor about her diet and got a lecture about nutrition.

"I'm sorry about your friend," Will said.

My eyes filled with tears. I grabbed a tissue and blotted my eyes. "Thanks."

We watched Gloria try and fail to get out of bed.

"Even if she has the surgery, will she ever be normal?" Will asked.

"I don't know, Will. I'm not an expert on all the fat people in the world." *No* was the answer, based on the *Where Are They Now* spin-off of this show.

"It was a hypothetical question." He paused. "Did your boyfriend break up with you? Is that why you were crying when you got here?"

"I wasn't crying. I was very dignified."

"Can you give me a straight answer?"

Touché. "Yes. More or less. We weren't dating, but I thought . . . well. He asked me out so I could meet his girlfriend. Who is not me, by the way."

Will looked at his knees. "Well. His loss."

It took me a second to realize he'd actually said something nice. To me. "Thank you."

"Was she pretty, this girlfriend?"

"Yes. And skinny. She's absolutely perfect. She could be a model or an astronaut or queen of Narnia. But instead, she's a social worker for troubled kids."

"That seems unfair."

"Thank you. My thoughts exactly."

We both turned our attention back to the TV. Gloria was now terrified that the surgery would kill her and maybe didn't want it after all. But then she had it, and complained in post-op about the pain. Cried when they made her stand up, saying no one understood.

Oh, Emerson, I thought. *I'm so sorry.* More tears threatened, and I swallowed hard. "I should go," I said. "Thank you for dinner."

"You made it." There was another silence. "Should I call someone to get you?"

"No, I can drive. Or, even better, you could drive me home. We only live six blocks apart, you know. You could walk back."

"I can't."

"Why?"

"I just can't." He didn't elaborate.

"You don't know how to drive?"

"I didn't say that."

I sighed, not bothering to hide my impatience. "Fine. I'm going."

He helped me off the couch. There was a wet splotch on his outer thigh, his pants darker there. "Is that from the ice pack?" I asked. "Or did you have an accident?"

He nearly smiled. "It's from the ice."

"I'm sorry. I didn't know I was soaking you."

"It's all right."

I opted not to put on my shoes and hobbled to the door. My ankle already felt a lot better.

"Marley."

"Yes?" I looked at him, and for some reason, I suddenly felt . . . seen. Even more than that, I felt . . . *appreciated.* The air suddenly pulsed with something warm and lovely.

"Please don't quit."

His eyes were the soft, dark blue of denim, of the sky just before sunrise. I'd never really noticed before. "Okay," I said, then cleared my throat.

"I'm sorry for my . . . social awkwardness."

"That's all right. I'm sorry for my Italian temper."

He smiled a little bit.

I thought he'd walk me to my car, but he just stood there, watching as I made my uneven way to the street. "Thanks for feeding me," I called as I got in the car.

"You did all the work." Then he lifted his hand and closed the door, disappearing back into his cave. A second later, the light in the living room went out, and his house was dark again.

CHAPTER 21

Dear Other Emerson,

I know I haven't written to you for a long time, but that's because—brace yourself... here it comes... prepare yourself... you might want to sit down...

I HAVE A BOYFRIEND!

Mica Jennings is my boyfriend, and guess what, Other Emerson? He loves me! I mean, he could have anyone, and he's with me! I can't even tell you how shocked those mean women at work are. Isobel's mouth fell right open when we walked in the other day, holding hands. I repeat: HOLDING HANDS. Just like on the list Georgia, Marley and I made our last day of Camp Copperbrook.

I just smiled and went to my desk. Isobel was in Missy's office within seconds, glancing out at me. By the end of the day, Missy had given me a warning, saying my average phone call took six seconds longer than it should. When I countered with the fact that I still did twelve more calls per day than average, she told me I was smug.

And I am.

Mica is my first boyfriend. I obviously don't count that asshat from college who just slept with me on a bet. But Mica isn't just my boyfriend... he's my _friend_.

He is incredible. He's smart. (I don't know why he's working here, he could do anything, and he probably will, once he finishes his degree.) He's so funny, and his smile just . . . it just sparkles. I can feel my heart swelling every time he looks at me, which is pretty much all the time. He's SUCH a good kisser, my God.

On our first date, we went out to dinner, and when I ordered grilled chicken and asparagus with no butter, he tilted his head and said, "Oh, come on. This place has great food. You sure you want to waste time on plain old chicken?" He buttered a roll for me. I changed my order to pasta (with vegetables, I'm still trying to be healthy). We split dessert, and guess what he said? Guess? "There's nothing sexier than a woman who can enjoy a good meal."

Other Emerson, I am that woman.

He kissed me good night, right on my front steps, in front of the Donovans, who were slack-jawed with amazement. A real kiss. "Will you go out with me again?" he asked, touching my cheek.

Would I go out with him again?! Was he kidding? Of course I would!

He started coming by the house right away, and he was really nice and old-fashioned about it. He'd leave at ten on the dot, didn't want to be pushy. But it was so easy for him to be with me, he said. Like we could talk all night and not run out of things to say. His words, Other Emerson. One night, we went to IHOP and stayed there till two o'clock in the morning, just talking. And sure, we ate pancakes, too.

I told him about my mom and dad, and when I started to cry about Mama, he wiped my tears away like he was Ryan Gosling or something. I told him about Georgia and Marley, and sure, I made it sound like we see each other more than we do. I DO talk to them. Just not as much as I used to. The last time Georgia called, I didn't call her back. It had been a bad week, and I'd been eating too much.

Anyway, I did message both of them with a picture of Mica and me, and they both wrote back to say how excited they were, and how cute he is. I hope they don't think I'm too fat.

You know what's funny, Other Emerson? I hardly even think about eating anymore, now that I'm with someone who doesn't think it's a big deal. I mean, I'm still eating more than I should be, but it's not the binge-fest it sometimes has been. It's just really good food, and a healthy (or generous) portion of it, and Mica smiles as I eat. For the first time in my life, I feel sexy.

I'm so happy, Other Emerson. I'm know you're happy for me, and thank you for that. Maybe Mica and Idris will be friends. I bet they will.

I have to go now. Mica is coming over, and I have to take a shower, and you know how that can take a while with all the powdering I have to do. Don't want to get another yeast infection under my boobs!

See you later!

CHAPTER 22

Georgia

Go running in tight clothes and a sports bra. *(Kill me now.)*

Get a piggyback ride from a guy. *(This is never going to happen.)*

The day of the fun run was perfection—sixty-five degrees, that pure, blue late-September sky. Mason and I had come in together. (My father had promised to come see us and would take Mason back so I could go out with Evan.) Marley came with her brother and Louis.

As Mason and I walked in from West Ninety-fourth to the appointed gathering spot by the Gothic Bridge, he said, "I'm gonna grab a hot dog. Christian says it's important to fuel up before a race."

"He would know. There's a food truck over there. You need money?"

"I'm flush. Be right back."

I watched him go, a spring in his step. He'd begun at least nine sentences today with *Christian says*, and I couldn't be happier.

There were Marley, Dante and Louis, and about a dozen other firefighters from their firehouse. "Georgia, how are you?" asked Dante. "You look fantastic! Doesn't she, babe?"

"She does," Louis agreed, smiling. "You look great."

"Thanks."

The curse of being told you looked great (meaning thin) was that it was a double-edged compliment. Did that mean I'd looked horrible last year or six months ago? What would Dante and Louis say if they knew the truth? *Thanks! Mason overdosed last spring, so I haven't been eating that much, and I might have an ulcer, and also, I've been technically bulimic much of my life, but I'm so glad you think I look great!*

I fake-smiled instead. I'd finally made an appointment with my doctor, so soon I'd know if I really did have an ulcer or some other health issue. And while Marley knew about Mason's overdose, I knew she hadn't told anyone. I shouldn't be so hard on people. I should just take the compliment for what it was.

It was this body of mine, taking up so much less space than it used to. I still felt like an impostor, a stranger in a strange body. Like an amputee might feel phantom pain, I still carried my phantom fat.

"Great day for running, isn't it?" Marley said. She came over and bounced on the balls of her feet. "I took a yoga class this morning, so I'm already stretched and totally Zen." To demonstrate, she put her palms on the ground without even bending her knees.

"You're like a circus freak," I said. She grinned from her upside-down position. "How's your ankle, by the way? Should you be running?" I'd heard all about Camden the Idiot and his too-nice girlfriend.

"Oh, it's fine. It's had days to heal. It was mostly my pride that was sprained. I, um, I iced it right away, and it was fine by the next morning."

"And is the jackass here?" I asked. "I brought a shank."

"You brought a shank? Georgia! That's so sweet."

"I didn't really. But in my heart, I did."

"This is why you're my bestie. No. Haven't seen him yet."

"Marley! Come here for a sec," Dante called. "You gotta see this text from Mom."

She went off to answer her brother's call, and I stood there for a second, alone and exposed in my regular-sized running clothes. I took a deep breath and tried to be Zen, like Marley. Around me were the sounds of laughter and the chatter of the group, the song of the city with its sirens and horns, the roar and breath of it. There were thousands of people here, many dressed in costume for the event . . . some like ostriches, like leprechauns, like fairies. One group was clad in Star Trek officer costumes; another dressed like Star Wars stormtroopers, and they were engaged in a mock (or real) fight. One group all held saplings for no explicable reason. Music played, and the smell of hot dogs and popcorn filled the air.

Marley laughed at something her brother said, and he slung an arm around her shoulder and hugged her. God, I envied her that family! I envied Marley. She'd always been overweight in that luscious, fertile, Rubenesque way, and there wasn't a guy here who didn't look at her in her slutty side-lacing running shorts and red running bra with an appreciative gleam in his eyes. If she was dying of mortification, as I was, she hid it well. Emerson would've been in awe.

Me, I needed a little sunshine, a little time in the gym. Intellectually, I recognized that I looked average. Even so, it was hard not to cross my arms and pray for a sweatshirt. Hakuna Matata Retreat House had worked (best not to dwell on how). I was thinner than I'd ever been, even on my wedding day.

Mason reappeared, cheeks bulging. "Don't tell my dad, okay?" he said. "He's got me on a runner's diet, and it doesn't include hot dogs."

"A hot dog is good for the soul."

"You want one? I could get you one. Here, have mine, and I'll get another."

Such a sweet boy, so eager to please. "I'm fine," I said, patting his arm in my auntie way.

He finished the last bite, swallowing like a python. "Hey, Mason!" Dante called. "How you doin', kid?"

"Great! Excellent! Uh, thanks for letting me run with you guys."

"You bet. Glad to have you."

Mason was looking at the firefighters the way I looked at those posters in Pomegranate & Plum—envious of that ridiculous ideal. My nephew was still skinny as a toothpick, still small for his age. But he would grow, and change, and please, God, be happy. Today, at least he was away from Hunter.

"How's the list going?" I asked.

He shrugged. "I don't know."

"What are you working on?"

"Sitting with kids at lunch." He looked away.

"Do any cross-country friends have the same lunch as you?"

"Yeah, but they're all seniors. I don't talk to them out-side of practice. Plus, they're all really fast. We don't have much in common, running-wise."

"You might be surprised, honey. They might love having you." But my heart hurt, because I knew exactly what he was talking about . . . those horrible designations of rank, the certainty you felt when you knew you didn't belong. "How about 'talk to a girl'?"

"Nope. No progress there, either."

"Is there a particular girl you're hoping to talk to?" I asked, watching one of the firefighters do a handspring.

Another shrug. "Not really." His face flamed. So yes.

"Uh-huh. What's her name?"

"Adele."

"What's she like?"

"She's beautiful and smart and funny, and everyone loves her."

I nodded. Wished I could pick him up and twirl him around, like I used to when he was little, not so many years ago. It had always made him laugh. "I bet she's nice. And I know you are. You don't understand how much a teenage girl appreciates a truly decent boy."

"You're super naive, G, but thanks."

"Hey, handsome!" Marley said, extricating herself from the mob of FDNY. She gave him a hug. "How are you?"

"Great," he said. "And you?"

"I'm kind of shitty," she said, dropping her voice. "The man I love has a girlfriend."

"Ouch," Mason said.

"Tell me about it. Not only is she beautiful, she's a social worker for children at risk."

"Oh, man! I hate them both," he said. "Are they here? I can maybe maim them or something."

"Your aunt said the same thing." She messed up his hair fondly. "I wish you were twenty years older, Mason, because I'd marry you in a heartbeat. You are the real deal. And no, they're not here—not yet, at least—which is good, because I'd probably take you up on that."

Marley. Always able to make people feel better.

"So today's the day, Georgia," she said, turning to me. "We're in running gear, and it's completely possible that we're going to get a piggyback ride, surrendering all dignity. Mason, can you believe that's on our list? A piggyback ride, for God's sake."

"I'll give you one," Mason said.

"Oh, you innocent little lamb! How sweet you are! I'd

crush you or get arrested for molesting a child. Hey, look after your rapidly aging aunt today, okay? She's not a runner."

"It's true. I'm not," I said. "You might have to drag me across the finish line."

"She'll have to drag *me*," he said. "I still can't finish the course at school."

"Georgia, honeybun!" came a familiar voice. "We found you! Hey, Mason!"

"Grandpa!" Mason said, leaping over to give my father a hug. "Hey, Cherish! Hi, Auntie Paris, Auntie Milan!"

The girls practically tackled him, giggling madly at their titles.

"You look amazing," Cherish said to me, giving me a hug. "Hi, Marley, and wow, sweetie! I love your outfit!"

"Thanks, Cherish," Marley said, spinning around to model.

"Pick me *up*, Georgia!" Milan demanded, turning from Mason to me.

I obeyed. She was getting so big. "How's my special girl?" I asked.

"I got a purple sticker in school," she said. "Because of my goodness."

"Then you should get a hundred stickers," I said, kissing her adorable nose. "Hi, Paris, honey."

"Hi, Georgia!" she said. She had already climbed onto Mason's back. "You're my horse, Mason! Giddyup!" He whinnied obligingly. How many fourteen-year-old boys would do that—in public, no less?

My father gave me a hug. "Hello, sweetheart. God, what a great day. My three girls, my handsome grandson, my beautiful wife. Marley, will you take a picture, honey?"

Marley took at least ten, ordering us around, rearranging us.

A long time ago, I'd forgiven my dad for not fighting for me when he and my mother divorced. Even so, it was hard at times like this not to imagine a different life if he'd gotten custody. What kind of a person would I have been? A little easier on myself? A little less of an outsider? Would I have lost weight if I'd been happier?

We'd never know. I'd been left in a sterile house where the air was always thick with maternal disapproval and vodka fumes, Hunter's rage simmering in the background.

"We're gonna go to the finish line, okay?" Cherish said, taking Paris from me. "We'll be cheering for you both!" She kissed Mason on his cheek—his step-grandmother at the age of thirty-eight—and blew me a kiss. The four of them made their way through the crowd.

Then my skin prickled, and a wave of nerves rolled up from my feet and lodged like a buzzing arrow in my stomach.

"Hello, Georgia."

No one said my name the way he did.

Shit.

I turned. Yep. My ex-husband, wearing loose-fitting black shorts, a red and white T-shirt that said *Pamplona*, and tiny horns in his short, dark hair.

"Hey, Uncle Rafe!" Mason said. "How's it going?"

"Mason, my friend! How are you? Marley, how very good to see you again."

"Rafael Esteban Jesús Santiago! How are you?" she said. She gave him a hug—he'd hired her, once upon a time—and gave me a wide-eyed *holy crap* look over his shoulder.

Their hug ended, and Rafe looked at me.

My blush burned its way from my stupid crop top (why wasn't I wearing a sweatshirt? Why?) to my throat, into my jaw and cheeks. "Hello," I said. I could practically hear the chambers of my heart clacking open and shut.

"So cute," someone said. "The horns. Pamplona. Running of the bulls. I get it. Funny." The voice sounded like mine. Ah, shit, it was.

"It is a small world, as they say. My restaurant supports this charity, so all the staff is running." He paused. "You are with the fire department, I see."

It was hard to look directly at him. So I didn't. I just stood there like a stump, looking at his knee. It was a good knee.

"Yeah," Marley said after an awkward pause. "My brother is FDNY, remember? His husband, too. And Mason here is on the cross-country team at school, aren't you, sweetie?"

"Well, I just started," my nephew said. "I'm not really good."

"But you will improve, my friend," Rafe said. He smiled, and my legs turned to water.

Did he have to look so *fantastic*? So adorable in those horns? How did they stay on, anyway? Glue? String? I loved his haircut. I hated his haircut. I missed his calves; I'd forgotten how perfect they were. His beautiful hands. There was a cut at the base of his thumb. I couldn't look away.

Marley gestured behind his back, getting my attention. *Talk,* she mouthed, pointing to her mouth and feigning speech.

"Those hot dogs sure smell good," I said. *Well done, Georgia.* I forced a smile that felt more like a death rictus. The left side of my mouth twitched.

And then a woman emerged from the crowd, also wearing horns, also wearing a Pamplona T-shirt, which was knotted just under her boobs, showing her perfectly toned stomach (pierced belly button, very sexy). Tiny shorts that showed long, muscled legs.

"There you are," she said, sliding an arm around Rafael's waist.

She could've been a model for Pomegranate & Plum.

An ocean of acid sloshed around in my stomach. Where was that handy hole in the ground to swallow me up? I was fairly sure my face was turning eggplant purple. Even Mason winced.

"Heather, let me introduce you," Rafe said. "This is my ex-wife, Georgia; her nephew, Mason; and her friend, Marley, who used to work as a line chef for me. Everyone, this is Heather."

"Nice to meet you, everyone," she said.

Silence fell.

"Yes," I said belatedly. "Nice to meet you, too. You look like a natural runner, don't you? Do you love running?"

Marley covered her eyes.

"I do," she said, proving that she wasn't a real human. She tipped her head against Rafe's shoulder, her claim effortlessly clear.

My mouth twitched, still in its approximation of a smile.

Just then, Camden the firefighter walked past. "Hey, guys," he said innocently, pausing, as we were all frozen in our awkward tableau.

"Camden!" Marley barked, unfreezing. "Give me a piggyback ride!"

She leaped on his back like . . . like Spiderman or something.

And he crumpled beneath her, his chin planting in the grass.

"Marley! You okay?" Mason offered his hand.

"Jeez, Marley, give me some warning next time," Camden said.

She rolled off him and took Mason's hand, letting him pull her to her feet. "I'm sorry, old pal! Guess I thought you were stronger." She looked at me and rolled her eyes, grinning.

I had the best friend in the universe.

Dante, Louis and another firefighter came over. "Marley, try me next time," the other guy said. "Built outta iron, made in the USA." He pounded his chest with his fist. "Nothing brings me to my knees, you know what I'm sayin'? Not like Camden here."

"Yeah, Camden," Dante said. "Don't be such a pussy next time."

"Marley, you want a piggyback ride, you talk to me," Louis said.

The commotion served its purpose. Rafe said, "It was good to see you," and he and Heather melted back into the crowd.

Marley came over to me. "Mission accomplished," she said. "Also, that totally counts as a piggyback ride, you hear that, Emerson?" She brushed grass off her butt. "I have to admit, it felt kind of good to crush him like a bug."

"Thank you," I said. "I owe you. A lot."

....

Running . . . well, it's torture. But torture did at least prevent me from thinking too much about Rafe, as I was busy fighting for my life. Mason and I were equally slow (or he was taking pity on me, unlike Marley, who dashed away at the speed of light). We quickly found ourselves at the back of the pack, being passed by people on crutches, nonagenarians, amputees, and one woman who, judging from the size of her belly, was pregnant with eleven babies.

The first half mile went okay. My lungs sounded awfully loud, though. "Am I . . . dying?" I asked my nephew between wheezing breaths. "Or am I . . . already . . . dead?"

"I know," he said. "It's horrible." He, too, was breathing hard, but he smiled, and my heart lifted.

"I—" (gasp) "—love—" (gasp) "—you."

"Are those your final words?" He might be slow, but he at least could talk.

"I have . . . to stop," I managed.

We did, and I bent over, gasping. My vision grayed. Fainting sounded like so much fun right now.

"Okay, that's good enough," Mason said. "We can do this. It's flat, at least. Besides, you don't want Rafe to see you like this, do you?"

"How sharper . . . than the serpent's . . . tooth . . . is the . . . perceptive . . . teenager." He did have a point. I tried to look a little less ICU, a little more Nike. Was agonizing knee pain just a normal part of running? I bet *Heather* didn't have knee pain.

We started running again. Horrid. It was horrid.

I glanced at Mason, wiping the sweat out of my eyes. Should've worn a baseball cap. God! How many steps in a mile? I'd ask Mason, but I needed to conserve oxygen.

"Hey, we're at the one-mile mark," Mason said. "Doing good, G!"

Two miles to go? I hoped I wouldn't soil myself, but I couldn't make any promises. I trudged/plodded along—pludged—and tried not to hyperventilate. Glanced at my watch. Regretted it.

My face felt like it was on fire—had I sweated off my sunscreen? Probably.

Good God. By the time we hit mile two, there was a sharp pain in my chest, another in my shoulder, and my shins were squealing in pain. We stopped again so I could catch my breath. I liked to think that Mason also needed the break, though he looked great (to my sweat-hazed eyes, anyway).

Off we went again. It was only the idea that Heather the Tall and Slender was nearby, watching and smirking, that kept me staggering in a what I hoped was a forwardly direction. Truth was, it felt like I was running backward. Through tar. With anvils chained to my legs.

"You doing anything tonight? Maybe we can go to a movie," Mason said.

"I . . . have . . . a date." Yes. I'd all but forgotten it, but Evan Kennedy and I were going out for dinner.

If Rafe had moved on, so had I. A little, anyway.

"Really? Cool. Maybe Grandpa would want to see something, then."

Pludge. Pludge. Pludge. God, this was endless. Another glance at my watch said twenty-seven minutes had passed. Most people had finished the race and were milling about, offering encouragement, if not defibrillation and a sweet tank of oxygen, which was what I really wanted. Then again, I was clearly burning calories. I tried to smile, looking for red T-shirts in the crowd. Or horns.

"Go, Georgia! Go, Mason! Go, Georgia! Go, Mason!"

It was Dad, Cherish, the girls, and Marley, who, annoyingly, seemed to have finished already and looked dewy and radiant. If I'd had the energy, I would've waved back, but I simply did not. The end must've been near, and if that meant my death, at least I wouldn't be running.

"I'm gonna sprint the rest of the way, okay?" Mason asked.

"Yes! Go! Good . . . for you!"

In a shocking burst of energy, he took off, inciting his tinier aunts to scream with excitement.

My legs felt rubbery. Was I about to fall? I also had to pee and/or vomit. I couldn't believe I wasn't done yet. This was taking forever. I mean, technically, I was still "running," but I didn't seem to be moving at all. Not measurably, at any rate.

Then suddenly, Rafael, no longer with horns, his hair sweaty and spiked, materialized next to me. Or I was hallucinating. Hopefully, it was the latter.

"Georgia," he said, so crap, he was real. "Are you feeling all right?"

"Doing . . . great," I said. *Please go away.*

"You're sure? Would you like to walk?"

"I'd like to . . . be put in a . . . medically . . . induced . . . coma."

He laughed, and if I hadn't been in such intense pain, I might have laughed, too.

"Well, I cannot help you with that, but can I get you some water?"

"Almost done now," I said. The finish line was a mere (ha!) fifty yards away, the bunting and banner announcing the home stretch.

"Mason looked very strong crossing the finish line," Rafael said. "He has grown so much."

"Yes." I was concentrating on not wetting myself, not having my legs give out, not asking Rafe to carry me or inject me with a strong tranquilizer.

And then there was Mason. "Go, G!" he bellowed, and his face was so dear and sweet that I couldn't help but smile at him, and yes, somehow I sprinted—or at least, ran marginally faster—across the finish line.

With my ex-husband.

"You did it!" Mason said. "You looked great!" He gave me a sweaty hug, handed me a water bottle and beamed. "Wasn't she great, Uncle Rafe?"

"She was. Well done, Georgia." There was a smile in those wonderful, kind brown eyes.

"Thank you . . . gentlemen," I managed, then took the bottle of water, bent over and poured it over my neck.

"I must go. It was good to see you both," said Rafe.

"You too," I said, straightening up. A wave of dizziness made me wobble, and for a second his hand was on my arm, steadying me.

Everything else fell away—the sound of the crowd, Mason, the heat, even my exhaustion—and there was only him, the man who loved me once, who had married me.

I had thrown away so much.

"All right?" he asked.

"Perfect. Yes. Thank you."

He smiled a little, tugging my heart, then went off, and I watched as he was absorbed by the crowd.

Two hours and four Motrin later, I had taken a shower at my father's apartment, in the bathroom attached to my room, which Cherish stocked with lovely-smelling soaps and shampoos and every bathroom item a female might need in a lifetime.

My heels were bloody and blistered from the run, my neck was sunburned. My shins, big toes, knees, calves, Achilles tendons, thighs and ass throbbed with pain. I pulled on a bathrobe and texted Marley to see how she was doing.

Great, she replied instantly. How are you? Sore?

My God, yes, I answered. Is this normal?

It is if you're a lazy-ass preschool teacher. Come to the gym with me once in a while and you won't suffer so much!

You were really great, tackling Camden like that, I wrote.

YOU were really great, coming along so I didn't feel like such a loser. I'm going to the movies with my mom. Gotta run. Also, Admiral sends his love and asks why you don't give him bacon, like Aunt Marley does. xox

Going to the movies with her mom, huh? There was something I just couldn't imagine. I tried to remember if my mother and I had ever done that, and came up empty.

As Mason had hoped, Dad had been free for a movie (of course; he took any chance he could get to be with Mason, since my brother was . . . well, himself). My nephew had texted Hunter, saying simply We're going to catch a movie, not defining who "we" were. I had recommended the wording, knowing my brother would never have said yes if he knew Mason would be with Dad.

I was trying to get my arms over my head to pull on the dress I'd brought—my arms were stiff, and my neck was seizing like a bad engine—when a knock came on the door of my room. "One sec," I said, but Cherish came in anyway.

"Is that what you're wearing?" she asked as I pulled the dress into place.

"Yes." It was a classic dress, I thought—black, loose fitting, three-quarter sleeves. I had cute shoes, which, now that I thought of it, would turn my bloody heels into ground beef.

Cherish made a face. "Hold on," she said, leaving the room. She returned a minute later with three dresses.

"We are not the same size, Cherish," I said.

"Try them on, sweetheart."

I didn't really want her to see me, but . . . well, shit. She wasn't going to be mean. I pulled my dress over my head and stepped into one of hers.

It *did* fit. Maybe not the way it did on her, but it zipped up and everything.

It was a yellow and red floral-print dress, sleeveless, stopping just above my knees. I looked . . . young. Cherish tousled my hair a little bit, floofing it up in back. "There," she said. "You're so beautiful, Georgia. I have some cute wedge sandals that will go perfect with this. Girls! Mommy's gonna do Georgia's makeup! You want to watch?"

And so once again, I was beautified. The little girls oohed and aahed, and put on blush and eye makeup themselves, something I'd never been allowed to do, even for fun, when I was little. "It doesn't help," my mother had said, when at about age ten, I'd tried to copy a classmate's use of eye shadow.

"Ta-da!" Cherish said, misting my face with something. "Take a look!"

I did. There she was again, that same woman I'd been the night Evan Kennedy hadn't remembered me.

She was nice-looking. She looked . . . intelligent. She had pretty eyes, and even though her neck was the color of a boiled lobster, she looked like someone I'd like to know.

"Thank you, Cherish," I said.

"You're welcome, angel. You want me to call a car service for you?"

"No, no. I'll walk there. It's just a couple blocks, but thanks, anyway."

"Bye, Georgia! Bye!" the girls said. Milan had gotten into the red lipstick and looked like a baby vampire, but I kissed her carefully anyway, then Paris, then turned to my stepmother.

"Thanks again. I'll bring the dress back next—"

"Keep it," she said, waving her hand. "It looks better on you, anyway. Have fun, sweetie. Text me tomorrow and let me know how it goes. If you want to sleep over, just let yourself in."

I wouldn't sleep over; I wanted to sleep in my own bed, cuddle my dog and rest my weary bones.

Or, I supposed, I could go home with Evan Kennedy. It wasn't unusual for dates to end in sex; I might've been the queen of celibacy since my divorce, but I did go on the Internet and listen to podcasts. I knew how things were done.

I couldn't imagine sex with Evan, though. Then again, maybe the woman in the flowered dress could.

It hurt to walk. As I hobbled down Tenth Avenue, hoping the walk would loosen me up, I felt a sense of accomplishment. I'd exercised, given Mason a happy day and, biggest of all, had seen Rafael for the second time. It had hurt—a lot—to see him with Heather, but I'd survived it. I couldn't fault him for finding someone else. He deserved everything in life. Especially love. It was my own heart that had proven to be unbreachable.

A man was selling scarves at the corner of Eighteenth and Ninth. "Hey, pretty lady," he said. I looked to my side to see her. There was no one there.

He was talking to *me*.

"Hi," I breathed. "How are you?"

"Better now," he said, smiling broadly.

Holy crap. Yes, yes, feminism, but a random man (or woman) had never ever said anything like that to me. Ever. Not once.

Ah. I had arrived at the restaurant. It was a quiet, upscale place with white tablecloths and a single orchid blossom on each table. Evan was waiting, and he smiled when he saw me. "Hey, Georgia," he said.

"Hi. Good to see you."

I was nervous, I realized. Not just because I was dating the second man in my entire life, but because I really wanted to get the Yale thing over with. My plan was (still) to pretend I didn't remember him, either. Then we could chuckle over small world, yada yada.

And yet, I *didn't* want him to remember me as I'd been at Yale, me ever on the fringe, him ever at the center. But I had to, because we *had* gone to school together, and it was going to come up sooner or later.

"So," I said. "Tell me about yourself, Evan. Where did you go to school?" Cut right to the chase.

"Ah, that stuff's kind of meaningless, don't you think? People throwing around their educational pedigrees like it means anything in the real world."

"Good point." Foiled for now. "Okay. Well. Are you one of *those* Kennedys?" I asked.

"No comment." He grinned. "Want to order a bottle of wine?"

"Sure."

"What do you like?"

"Just about everything."

He studied the wine list like it was a map to the Lost World as my brain generated helpful suggestions of how to kill the elephant in my half of the room.

Georgia: *Hey, I think I went to law school with an Evan Kennedy. You're not . . . wait a sec! You are!*

Georgia: *I'm a preschool teacher now, but I was a lawyer for a year and a half.*

Evan: *Really? I'm a lawyer, too! / I also used to be a lawyer!*

Georgia: *No! What a coincidence! Where'd you go to law school?*

It would be so easy.

But the words didn't come. My old self loomed like a specter, that quiet, fat, sometimes sad girl always hoping and dreading she'd be noticed.

Evan, on the other hand, was completely oblivious as he looked and looked at the wine list. "How about the Henri Boillot Meursault?" he finally said. "It's a French Burgundy." He paused. "A white wine. Chardonnay."

Ah, mansplaining.

"What year?" I asked. "The 2015 was great." Thank you, photographic memory and a father who loved wine.

His eyebrows went up, a little surprised that I passed. "They have a Domaine Roulot, too. Good enough?"

"2012?"

He glanced back down. "Yes."

"Even better, then."

The waiter came over, and Evan ordered.

Let *him* figure it out. Let Evan be the one to smack his forehead, to bring up law school. Let *him* feel like he was forgettable enough that I hadn't put two and two together. I'd just be the woman in the flowered dress who knew her French Burgundies, damn it.

"Tell me about your work, Evan."

"I would, but I like you, so I don't want to bore you to death. I study numbers and healthcare regulations and advise an investment firm on different companies. God, I put myself to sleep just saying that. I mean, I like it, but it's pretty boring to a normal person. Teaching, now, that must be so much fun."

"It is. The school is really progressive, and as you said, four is a fun age."

"Want to see a picture of my niece?"

"Of course I do."

I found myself relaxing. The wine, the candles, the nice-looking woman in the flowered dress sitting across from one of Those Kennedys. We talked about politics, living in New York, the Yankees, how he got to meet Derek Jeter at a fund-raiser.

Yale didn't come up. He didn't ask me what I did before teaching, and I didn't volunteer it. I just sat, my muscles turning into petrified wood, sipping wine and making pleasant conversation.

This would've made Emerson happy, I thought.

When the check came, I was moderately buzzed. The pasta I'd ordered didn't bother my stomach, but then again, the woman in the flowered dress hadn't eaten much of it.

Evan paid the check. "Want to get a drink somewhere else?" he asked.

"Actually, I'm a little tired," I said. "I did that fun run today, and it reminded me that I'm horribly out of shape and really have to get a gym membership."

"You look good from here," he said.

"Right back at you, Mr. Kennedy."

"Can I see you again?"

I said yes. Then, without too much hobbling, I made it out of the restaurant. Evan hailed a taxi. "I had a great time," he said as the cab pulled over to the curb.

"Me too," I said. "Thank you for a lovely dinner."

"You're welcome. Good night, then."

He kissed me, a very pleasant, firm kiss—on the lips and everything—and before I had time to analyze it further, or respond, he stepped back, opened the door for me and smiled down at me. "See you soon."

So this was how it would be, then, I thought as the cab headed for Grand Central. I'd be the pretty woman in the flowered dress.

Fat Georgia wasn't going to be exhumed until she had to be.

CHAPTER 23

Marley

Hold hands with a cute guy in public.
(Still a big fat no. Emphasis on big fat.)

On Monday, after ignoring thirty-two messages and calls
from my mother and Eva about why I couldn't help divide
up the aging blankets and deteriorating pillows of the pa-
rental home, I dropped off Will's dinner and waited for him
to write me my check.

Since my little meltdown on his couch, he'd barely spoken to me this past week. He hadn't asked how my ankle
was. He hadn't asked about Camden. He'd just watched me
unload his dinner on the counter. And while he hadn't exactly been cuddly and warm the night stupid Camden broke
my stupid heart, I did kind of expect a little more.

Instead, he just said the same things as always. "I'll get
your check. Thank you. Good-bye."

Today seemed no different. "Thank you. Good-bye," he
said, looking at my forehead.

"Tomorrow is Tuesday," I said.

"Yes, I know."

"And you still want me to bring the special dinner and
stay?"

"Yes."

"Can I bring anything? Besides the dinner, I mean," I asked.

"No."

"Do you have wine?"

"No."

"Then I'll bring wine."

He nodded, and I left, a little irked, and headed to the other side of town.

Tonight, I was babysitting for Rachel, the mother of the triplets. I wasn't sure how I'd said yes to that, but apparently I had.

"Hi, Marley," Rachel said as she answered the door. "Thank you again for doing this."

"No problem. You look gorgeous." It was true; she looked even prettier than usual, her long blond hair pulled back into a ponytail, a little lip gloss, a little mascara. She was so slim, too, in that completely unselfconscious way that said she'd never had to diet, never had to wonder if she could pull off an outfit.

The girls thundered down the stairs, shouting my name.

"Hello, little girls! Oh, there are so many of you!" I picked up Grace. "Hi."

"Put me down!" she said. "I'm a big girl."

"Got it," I said, obeying.

"Pick *me* up!" Rose said. "I love you. Why is your hair so messy?"

"Rose, honey," Rachel said, "Marley has beautiful hair. So curly and thick!"

"And messy," I whispered, getting a smile from Rose.

Rachel had a beau, and it still hit me . . . not the unfairness, exactly, but the unbalance. Of course she was lovely on many levels, but Rachel had three small children and was already forty, divorced for maybe a year . . . but she had a boyfriend, or at least a suitor. I bet they held hands. I'd been looking for love since I was fifteen and *still* hadn't been on a proper date.

No man had ever held my hand.

"I'll be home before ten," Rachel said. "The girls have eaten already, but I made you dinner. It's in the fridge. There are some cookies, too. Chocolate macadamia."

"Oooh," I said.

"We had some already," Charlotte told me. "But we can have another if you want."

"No more cookies, girls. And don't forget to brush. Be on your best behavior, angels. I love you, and I'll kiss you when I get back." They swarmed her like honeybees around a flower, kissed her and hugged her and told her she smelled good.

"Have fun," I told her. "Don't rush home."

"Thank you so much," she said. "You're the best."

I shut the door after her and turned to my little charges. "Okay, girls. What shall we do?"

"Candy Land, read a story, eat more cookies, ice cream, bubble bath, hide-and-seek!" was their answer.

We read four books, played hide-and-seek. (They were pathetically easy to find, doing things like closing their eyes to hide, or sitting under a couch cushion, legs sticking out.) Then we played Candy Land, which made them hungry—all those sugar references—so I got them each another cookie and put scoops of ice cream on them, so as to cement my role as Everyone's Favorite Adult.

Watching them shovel ice cream into their mouths, I felt a slosh of guilt. Rachel had already given them dessert, and here I was, doing the irresponsible thing and letting them eat whatever they wanted, starting them off on the road to poor eating habits and potential obesity.

Then again, they were only four, and this was one night. Frankie had been four, and so skinny, so frail and tiny.

The triplets were robust little things, with adorable little bellies and sturdy legs. No one was fat, no one was skinny.

"Do you *really* know Miss Georgia?" Charlotte asked me, almost suspicious that I had such a claim to fame.

"I do," I said. "We've been friends since we were teenagers."

"She's our teacher."

"I know."

"I love her," Rose said. "I wish she could live with us."

"Me too," said Grace and Charlotte simultaneously.

I wondered if Frankie and I had ever talked in unison like that.

I herded them upstairs, poured a quarter of a bottle of bubble bath into the tub, and watched as they slid around like seals and bravely put their faces in the water.

When the water cooled, I hauled them out, getting soaked in the process, then got them dressed in their jammies. Each one gave me a good-night hug and wanted a firm commitment for when I'd come back to play again.

"Soon," I said. "Very soon."

They really were angels. Rachel was such a great mom. Georgia often said what good-hearted little girls they were, bright and fearless.

I left the door open a few inches, then went downstairs and tidied up from our games.

Rachel's house was idyllic—clean but not severely so, lovely but livable. There were flowers on the kitchen table, and artwork decorated the fridge. From the outside, it seemed like she had a perfect life. I guess from the outside, mine seemed pretty perfect, too—the fun and creativity of my job; living in a sweet apartment I rented from my best friend; my wonderful, close-knit family.

I knew Rachel's father had died when she was young. But I'd never told Rachel I was a twinless twin. Didn't want to freak her out by mentioning Frankie's age.

Besides, some things were too sad to talk about.

Speaking of the fridge, I opened it up. A dish of rather gorgeous ravioli topped with parsley was wrapped in cellophane with a note on it that said *Thanks, Marley!* with a heart beneath it.

I heated it up in the microwave, then sat at the table, the quiet of the house settling around me.

I didn't like being alone. At home, though I knew it wasn't a great habit, I kept the TV on for company. Georgia was great at solitude, the type who'd set the table for one, pour a glass of wine and eat while reading a book with Mozart playing in the background. Then again, that's how she was raised—very properly, if without a lot of love.

The ravioli were stuffed with porcini mushrooms and crumbled bacon, with just a little Romano cheese. I should get the recipe.

My phone rang. Dante, in an actual phone call, not a text.

"Hey, what are you up to?" he asked. "We're at Hudson's. A whole bunch of us. You should come."

"I'm babysitting my friend's kids," I said.

"Oh. That's nice of you. Well, Mom was pissed you didn't make it yesterday, and I took the quilt from Eva's room. You know, the one Nonny made."

"Eva didn't want it?"

"She's the most unsentimental person I ever met. You should've seen what she was throwing out. That cat and dog creamer and sugar bowl from the 1930s? They're so cute. And the pot holders I made in third grade! The teal and pink ones."

"I can't believe Mom ever thought you were straight."

"It was the fire trucks. They threw her off the scent. Anyway, I put a box aside of stuff you might want."

I did love my baby brother. So much. "Thanks, ugly-face."

"You're welcome, potato-head." I could hear the sounds of laughter in the background, some music.

"You okay about Camden having a girlfriend?" he asked suddenly.

I jerked a little. "Uh, yeah. Why wouldn't I be?"

"I know you liked him."

I considered lying, then decided against it. "Well . . . I did. I'm mostly over it."

"Louis told me to ask. He said you looked sad on Saturday. You know, after you jumped Cam and he fell down."

"He is kind of a weakling, isn't he?" I said.

"He is. He's not here, by the way. If you did want to come by later. Louis and I would love to see you."

"You're a good brother, Dante," I said, my throat suddenly tight. "Even if you are really, really ugly."

"*You're* ugly. Seriously. Come by later."

"Dante, did Mom and Dad do anything with the shrine?"

"What? No. No, not yet." He paused. "You all right?"

"Yeah. Get back to your boo. Tell him I love him and I'm glad you married out of your league."

My brother laughed. "Will do. Bye."

I finished my dinner (I always did), cleaned up and then tiptoed up the stairs to check on the girls.

Charlotte had gotten into bed with Rose, and the two of them were sound asleep, cheeks flushed, Rose snoring the slightest bit.

Oh, Frankie. I'm sorry.

I went down the hall to cry in the bathroom. Most of the

time, I kept the tears down, but seeing the little girls in bed together . . . I missed my twin. Eva was fine, Dante absolutely great. They just weren't my other half. And no matter how untrue it might've been, I always felt responsible for Frankie's death.

CHAPTER 24

Dear Other Emerson,

If Mica and I could live on another planet, we would be so happy.

I mean, we _are_ happy. I love him so much, Other Emerson. And he loves me! He loves taking care of me, loves having sex with me, loves my appetite, my laugh, my smile, my dimples. He tells me how beautiful I am. He says nothing is sexier than seeing me eat, unless it's seeing me eat naked.

When we're alone, it's perfect. We never fight. He rubs my feet, he makes us snacks. (I eat 90 percent of them.) We talk about the past, the future, where we might want to live some-day. He's never left Delaware, and he loves my stories about Camp Copperbrook and the time my father took me to see the Grand Canyon. We love the same TV shows and cuddle up on the couch together like a regular couple.

But I HATE going out in public together. In a way, it's worse than going out alone. I know there are women like me who love their bodies and feel sexy and confident and have snappy answers that put haters in their place.

I'm not one of them. I just smile a lot. My smile tries to say, <u>Please don't say something mean, please don't stare, it's not like I'm unaware of the fact that I'm fat, I'm actually a really nice person and most people like me once they've given me a chance.</u>

It doesn't always work.

I have to tell you something shameful, Other Emerson. I've gained more weight. I shouldn't care—Mica is in love with me, and that's what matters.

But.

But.

But.

I still hate being fat. Still hate myself for my weakness. I'm helpless around food. I love putting food in my mouth, even when I overeat so much that I wake up with knifelike pains in my stomach. Even when my knees burn and my back aches, which is all the time now. Even when I'm breathless just going to the kitchen. The power of food, of tasting and chewing and having more . . . it takes over everything. So I hate myself, but I still eat. All day long, I think about eating, and even when I'm eating, I'm thinking about what I'll eat next. It's like this all the time, OE. All the time.

We went to the company picnic a few weeks ago. My first challenge was getting from the car to the picnic area. I was sweaty already, since it was hot, and by the time we got to the site where everything was set up, I was breathing pretty hard and trying not to show it. At least I had on a big straw hat with a pretty scarf tied around it, so the hat would shade my face, which was no doubt fire-engine red. I used the scarf to blot my face. Thinking ahead, Other Emerson. Thinking ahead. Everyone was already there, and we said hi and put down the potato salad Mica and I had made that morning.

Then came the picnic table challenge.

Other Emerson, I know you have no idea how difficult it is to sit at a picnic table. You just slide right in, ever graceful. For me, there are so many factors to consider. Would I even fit? What if I tipped the table over? What if I got stuck? What if I fell backward because my huge ass couldn't get enough bench?

Thank God, Mica is super thoughtful. He found a sturdy wooden Adirondack chair (no arms) from another site and, while I was cooling down in the shade of a tree, brought it over and put it at the head of the table. "My lady," he said, dropping a kiss on my shoulder, which took away some of the humiliation of not being able to sit like everyone else.

Some of the humiliation, but not all.

When the Delicate Fawns sat with us, it was hard to see Mica next to a woman who was more of his physical match . . . more proportionate. They wore those cute, tiny clothes with itty-bitty straps and flirty skirts that skimmed their thighs. Mica's so _nice_, Other Emerson. Everyone likes him. He's so cute, he could date one of the Delicate Fawns. It's so easy to picture that.

Meanwhile, the other fatties from work shot me dirty looks, because I'd dared to attract the only man at work who was single and at all desirable, because the only other straight, single man, Korbin, A) has a stupid name and B) has serious hygiene issues and wears the same clothes every day. All the other men are married or in relationships.

But the picnic wasn't awful. Three of the Delicate Fawns are downright sweet to me, especially since I've normalized myself with a boyfriend who isn't obese. So the picnic wasn't that horrible, though I would rather have stayed home.

Restaurants . . . restaurants are awful. Mica _likes_ taking me out. "Showing off my lady love," he says, grinning with those adorably crooked teeth, making me a little swoony. But aside from the looks we get, there are the logistics. The strength of the chairs. The weaving through the other tables. The size of the stall in the ladies' room.

But the other night was the worst.

Mica and I went to the movies, to the theater with the big recliner seats and the arms that go up so I can fit comfortably. Mica bought us the giant popcorn and two Kit Kat bars and a root beer to share. There we were, minding our own business, talking, sharing, cuddling . . . but then came the comments.

<u>Oh, yeah, she definitely needs all that food. There are starving children in Syria.</u>

<u>Think that chair is safe?</u>

<u>I didn't think we were here to see Free Willy.</u>

<u>They'll have to call the fire department to get her ass out of that seat.</u>

We pretended not to hear. Or I did, at any rate, whispering to Mica that I loved his haircut, or asking him if he'd seen such-and-such movie or TV show. Kept smiling, kept chatting, keeping my voice low, because God forbid I'm fat AND loud in a public place. I wish I could be like Lindy West or something, smart and fast and cutting and able to change hearts and minds.

But I'm not. I'm shy, and I've been lonely a long time, and I just want to hide from the hate.

Then this girl came over. This really, really pretty girl, dressed like a two-dollar tramp, as my mom used to say. And she leans down to Mica like I don't even exist and says, "I just wanted to say that I think you're really cute and if you want to hook up sometime, here's my number." Then she sticks a scrap of paper into his shirt pocket.

Mica said, "I'm with her. Obviously."

"But you don't have to be," she said.

"Butt out."

She sighed, her perfect boobs rising hypnotically. "Whatever. Keep my number."

And Mica took the slip of paper out and dropped it on the ground, then put his arm around me . . . at least as far as his arm reaches.

See, Other Emerson? He's a white knight. I just don't want to need one. I just want people to leave us alone.

CHAPTER 25

Georgia

Tell off the people who judged us when we were fat. *(Sort of.)*

Grace Carver let out a shriek of fury that made my blood run cold.

"It's *my* turn!" said Hemp Cabriolet, trying to wrestle a paintbrush away from her. "I get the green now!"

"No!" Grace yanked back, nearly pulling Hemp off his feet.

"Mine!" the little boy yelled.

"Okay, okay," I said, intervening. I pried the brush out of their sturdy little fists. "Hemp, did you take this away from Grace?" He had; I'd seen him do it, the little bugger.

"Yes. She's hogging it. She's a selfish hog of green paint, and she won't let me have any and now my day is ruined forever!" He burst into tears. I swore I heard Grace hiss.

The other students paused at their easels to gaze upon the excitement.

Hemp *was* a teeny bit melodramatic. It came from his mother, who had A) named him Hemp and B) told me, with tears in her eyes, that when her husband bought her a blue BMW for her thirtieth, she thought her heart might break into a million little pieces because she *specifically* told him she wanted silver.

I seized on the chance for Another Teachable Moment. "Let's talk about this. Class, can you crisscross applesauce, hands on your lap?"

They collapsed to the floor like rump-shot dogs, as my grandfather would have said, legs crossed, hands clasped.

"Grace, would you please tell me what happened?" I asked.

"I was *painting* and he *took* my brush," she said, her eyebrows nearly touching. She was gifted at the art of scowl, that was for sure.

"I did not! You were a green paint hog! You don't share, Grace! You don't!"

"Hemp, please, honey, wait your turn. Grace, how did it make you feel when Hemp took the brush?"

"Mad!"

"Why, sweetheart?"

"Because I was painting and he made me stop and he didn't even ask!"

"So you were having fun using the green paint," I offered. "And all of a sudden, you couldn't paint anymore, and it was a surprise that Hemp took the brush away."

"Yes. A *very bad* surprise."

I squashed a smile. "Okay. Thank you for telling us about your feelings, Grace." Vocalizing emotions fell under the social development part of our program.

I turned to Hemp and dabbed his tears. "And Hemp, how did you feel when you saw Grace using the green paint? Before you decided to take the brush."

"I felt happy because I liked her painting, and I wanted mine to look like that, too." Imitation, the sincerest form of flattery. His lower lip stuck out adorably.

"Oh, did you hear that, Grace? Your painting made Hemp feel happy! That's a nice thing to say, Hemp. But you did grab her brush and yank it away. Why did you do that, when we all know we should ask for our turn?"

His eyes filled up again, and I gave his hand a little squeeze. "It's okay, honey," I said. "Everyone makes mistakes. It's what we do afterward that matters."

He sucked in a shaky breath. "I was afraid all the green paint would be gone. And I would never ever have a turn."

"Green is your favorite color, isn't it?" I asked.

"Yes. My most, most favorite."

"Can you think of another way to get a turn with green paint?" We had it by the bucket, but I was seeing if he could use some commonsense logic.

The class was rapt.

"No," he said. "Because Grace doesn't share."

"I do, too!"

"Class?" I said. "Do you have any suggestions?"

Silvi's arm shot up, as did Charlotte's, Grace's sister, and the hands of Nash and Cash. "Silvi?"

"He could say, 'Grace, would you please let me borrow the green paint before it's all gone?'"

"Very good, Silvi. Charlotte?"

"He could say, 'Grace, please share with me.'"

"That's a great idea. Don't you think, Hemp? Cash, how about you, honey? What would you say?"

"I would say, 'Grace, I love your painting and will you help me make mine green, too?'" Empathy and conversation reframing, both very advanced skills in conversation. Cash was such a sweetie.

"Excellent, Cash. Nash?"

"That's what I was going to say," Nash said.

"Very good. I like those ideas," I said. "So let's try this

again, Grace and Hemp. Gracie, pretend you're painting, and Hemp, you ask her nicely if she'll share."

"Grace, you make the best paintings and I love green, it's my favorite color and I want a turn to use some green, so can I have a turn? Please?"

"That was very nice, Hemp. Grace, what would you say to that?"

She stared at me stonily for a second, then spoke. "I would say, 'You can have a turn when I'm done.'"

"And would you also say 'thank you,' since Hemp said something so nice about your paintings?"

"I would," she said solemnly. "I would say, "'Thank you, Hemp, it's because I like to paint and I practice painting at home all the time.'"

I smiled. "Very good. And Hemp? What would you say next?"

"I would say, 'Please don't use all the green paint.'"

"And then I would say, 'I won't because I do so know how to share, and also, we have a million green paints and you could just ask Miss Georgia for your own.'" Another scowl, but she'd brought up the logical solution, which was tough for kids this age.

"Of course you know how to share, and you're right, Grace. We do have lots of paint." I sat back on my heels, beyond pleased. "So, class, this is a reminder to use our words, not our hands. And also, when someone understands how we feel, they're more likely to be kind. Good job, Grace and Hemp! You both get happy stickers on your papers for using your words so well. Okay, let's finish up those paintings, because it's almost time for our story."

I went to my computer and pulled up Bach's Cello Suites for a calming influence. Grace handed the green paint to Hemp and even smiled at him.

"Nice way to turn that around," said Lissie, my student teacher.

"Thanks," I said. I added a happy goat sticker to Grace's behavior sheet and wrote, *Used her words very well in expressing her feelings. Improvement on sharing.* Put a smiling sun sticker on Cash's sheet and wrote a comment praising his diplomacy and kindness. For Hemp was a smiling dog sticker. *Good job verbalizing his feelings after grabbing a paintbrush from another student. Able to express admiration for her skill.* A month ago, Hemp had drizzled black paint over one of Grace's masterpieces, so this was a step in the right direction.

I snuck a peek at my phone. This morning—the third morning in a row—I'd reminded Mason he was due to check something off his list, since running (or hobbling) in a sports bra had been checked off mine. No reply just yet.

Am eagerly awaiting a list update, I wrote. You've got this. I believe in you. I stuck in a unicorn emoji for good luck, then went to check on Silvi and Rose, who were playing librarian most adorably.

"Miss Sloane?"

It was Mr. Trombley, the head of the school, leaning in from the hallway. He got my name right! He was staring at the kids, frowning, almost like he wondered why they were here. He deemed children noisy and sticky, which, to his credit, was mostly true. "Can I see you for a moment?"

"Of course. Lissie, I'll be right back."

There was a smear of green paint on my skirt. No worries, since everything I owned could be tossed in the washer and dryer. No cashmere or silk for me. We walked in silence down the hall to his office/nap room.

"Sit down, sit down," Mr. Trombley said, ushering me in. "It's come to my attention that we need a new director of curriculum."

The last director of curriculum was the woman who'd hired me, and she'd been gone a year. In fact, I'd lobbied for the job last spring, since I already did much of the curriculum development. Mr. Trombley had told me they were looking for someone with a different skill set but failed to elaborate on what that was.

"Yes, I know," I said. I hoped he wasn't going to ask me to train the new person.

"Would you like the position?"

I jolted in my chair. "Really? Sure, I would love it!"

"Do you think you're qualified?"

"Um . . . yes. Absolutely." I'd also been qualified last spring. I had the degree in sociology from Princeton, a JD from Yale and a master's in early childhood education from UNC. For the past three summers, I'd taken workshops and day classes, too, quite a few of them on curriculum development.

"Good," he said. "All set, then."

I started to get up, then sat back down.

"Will there be a raise in line with my new duties?" I asked.

"Of course." I got the impression there wouldn't have been if I hadn't asked. "We want to keep you at St. Luke's for as long as possible, Miss Sloane." He smiled, revealing his brownish teeth. "Eight thousand more a year."

Eight? *Eight?* Last year, I'd asked for a $1,500 raise— my first such request at St. Luke's—and been told there wasn't enough money in the budget.

Our budget hadn't changed since then. Guess he'd been lying.

"Twelve," I said.

"Ten."

I almost fell out of my chair. "Done."

"Congratulations, Miss Sloane. My secretary will e-mail

you the necessary documents and deadlines. If you don't mind, write up a press release for the website and parent newsletter."

"I will. Thank you so much, sir."

As I walked down the hallway back to the class, my thoughts were a jumble.

Last spring, I'd been turned down for that very job and a nominal raise.

Last spring, I'd also weighed more. I even remembered what I wore to that meeting, because I'd dressed carefully that day, wearing a navy blue skirt from my lawyer days that cut into my stomach and a jacket that wouldn't have stayed buttoned if I'd taken a deep breath.

Now, I'd just been given a raise, a promotion, and Mr. Trombley had gotten my name right for the first time. Nothing had changed since April . . . except my size.

I turned around and went back into his office. He looked up at me from under his bushy eyebrows. "Yes, Miss Sloane?"

"Does this promotion have anything to do with my weight, sir?"

He didn't answer, but it seemed to get a little chillier all of a sudden. "Are you implying that St. Luke's has engaged in discriminatory practices, Miss Sloane?" His words were clipped.

"No, sir. Of course not." Employment discrimination law flashed through my brain. No one at the school had ever treated me differently than the other teachers. I'd never asked for special accommodations because of my size, and I'd never needed to.

But still.

"I'm just wondering why I was turned down last year for the promotion *and* a raise, and I got both now." My heart beat hard in my chest. Even bringing this up was hard for someone who usually preferred invisibility.

He didn't answer for a moment, just fiddled with the fountain pen he always used. "Perhaps you should just be grateful that present conditions at St. Luke's allow us to, ah, recognize your gifts, Miss Sloane."

I looked him in the eye for a long moment. "Good."

With that, I went back to my classroom, feeling a little bit proud of myself. At least it hadn't been left unsaid. At least he knew it hadn't slipped my notice.

After school let out, I went home, clipped the leash on Admiral and walked over to Cambry-on-Hudson High. The cross-country team practiced every day, the poor lambs, and I wanted to see Mason with his teammates. He'd run in two meets already, finishing dead last but smiling. Thankfully, Hunter hadn't come to those due to work conflicts. Last place for his son was not something I could see him accepting with grace.

There was Mason, still heartbreakingly thin, his skin white as skim milk, like mine. He was talking to another boy, also skinny—most of the team was, however.

When he saw Admiral and me, he said something to the other kid, then trotted over. "Hey, you guys!" He knelt down and petted Ad, who gave his chin one dignified lick.

"How's it going?"

"Great! Christian was just giving me some stretching tips."

"He's the captain, right?"

"Yep. Guess what, G?" He glanced around to ensure no one was in hearing distance. "I talked to her!"

"Adele?"

"Yes! And she's a girl and everything. Not just *a* girl, but *the* girl."

"Oh, my God, that's great! What did you say?"

Another glance. "I said . . ." He grinned, making me wait.

"What? Tell me."

"I said . . . 'Could you pass the ketchup, please?'" His face was filled with utter joy.

"That's brilliant! Did she say anything?"

"She did! She said . . . 'Sure!' Like, in this really happy, nice way, too."

"Oh, honey, that's great."

"And then I said, 'Thanks.' Probably too much, do you think?"

"No! No, it just shows you have nice manners. Mason, I'm so proud of you."

A middle-aged man came over wearing a shirt emblazoned with *COH XC*. "Hi! Are you Mason's mother?" he asked.

"His aunt," I said.

"We're so happy to have him on the team. He gets better every day. Such a nice kid, too. Great attitude."

"Thanks, Coach!" Mason said. "Now, if I could just finish a race without walking . . ."

"Oh, that'll come soon enough," the coach said. "I'm not even worried." He stuck out his hand. "I'm Coach Davis. Nice to meet you. Did I see you at a meet or two?"

"Yes. Georgia Sloane." We shook hands.

He smiled, his kind face worn from hours in the sun. "Okay, Mason, back to practice. Have a great day," he added to me.

They went off. Mason looked over his shoulder and waved.

I waved back, wishing abruptly that I *was* Mason's mother. I loved him more than anything. Leah would've been proud of her boy. I knew that with all my heart.

As I turned to leave, I almost bumped into someone. "Sorry," I said.

It was my brother. "Oh. Hunter. Hey."

He glanced down at Admiral, who lifted his lip just enough to show his teeth. That saying about dogs reading people?

"What are you doing here?" he asked.

"Just taking the dog for a walk. Thought I'd see how Mason's doing."

"He strained his Achilles tendon. Stupid coaches didn't have him warm up enough."

"I think the coaches are pretty great."

"Well, you don't know anything about running, do you?"

He had me there.

"No, but I just chatted with his coach, and he had only nice things to say about Mason."

"Really?" For once, my brother's tone wasn't dripping with condescension.

"Yeah. He mentioned how his times are improving, and what a great attitude he has."

"His times *need* improving." But it wasn't said with as much rancor as most of his sentences were. He looked at the ground for a minute, perhaps pondering what *great attitude* meant.

"He's a great kid, Hunter."

"I *know*, George. Jesus. I don't need a spinster giving me parenting advice."

"Okay. Good to see you," I lied.

"Did you know Mason went out with Dad the other night?" Hunter asked abruptly. "After that race?"

"Yes. I did."

"I *thought* he was going with his friends. Guess he still doesn't have any. It'd be better for him if you'd stop hanging around him. It doesn't look good."

He still could drive me to tears, my shithead brother. I thought of Leah and took a deep breath. "Well, for one, he's making friends. Look at him right now." Mason was laughing with some other kids. "And for two, Dad and I are his family, too, even if you hate us both. We love him. Don't take that away."

"Don't tell me what to do."

As ever, I was held hostage by my love for Mason where Hunter was concerned. "Okay. You have a good day." I gathered Ad's leash and turned to leave.

"You've lost weight, haven't you?" he said, and I jerked to a stop. "It's a start."

I glanced back at him, but he'd already turned away, leaning on the fence, barking orders at Mason.

....

Marley was waiting for me when I got back to the house, holding a manila envelope. "You need to see this," she said. "You got one, too." She handed me mine.

"Hello to you, too."

"Have a seat and open it."

"Okay, okay." I closed the gate and sat at the little iron table in the courtyard. "The garden looks great, by the way," I said.

"Thanks. Read it." She was buzzing with energy, but her eyes were suspiciously red.

I opened the envelope, which was from a lawyer's office in Delaware. My mouth opened as I saw the document.

Last Will & Testament of Emerson Lydia Duval

"Oh, God," I said.

Emerson had left us her house.

And, according to the stock portfolio summary, a total of $3.2 million.

There was a note in her pretty handwriting, too.

Dear Georgia and Marley,

Surprise! You're my heirs. Which, unfortunately, means I'm dead.

I'm sorry I didn't talk to you about this. I guess I thought I'd have more time, but on my last visit to the ER, the doctor told me I was in trouble, so I had to get this done. Don't be sad. Well, don't be too sad. Be just sad enough, and then cheer up, okay? I hate picturing you guys crying over me. It makes me cry, too. If there are splotches on this paper, now you know why.

I think you knew that my mom never had to work because of getting a big inheritance from my shitty grandfather. On top of that, when my dad died, he left half of his life insurance to me, so that explains all this money.

I should've done more with it. I was waiting for life to really start.

You've been such good friends all these years. I'm so sorry I didn't see you more. Even though I knew you'd be so nice about it, I didn't want you to know how big I am.

I want some money to go to good causes, but I'm afraid I don't have a lot of time left, and I don't want Ruth to get wind of any big donations. She checks my laptop when she thinks I'm asleep. You'll pick me out some winners, won't you? Maybe the American Cancer Society, in memory of my mom? Other places, too. It's too hard to think about right now.

I also want you to keep some. That'd make me happy. My present to my two best friends.

My lawyer said I should leave Ruth <u>some</u> money, because she's my cousin and, as a family member, she could contest the will if I didn't. (And she totally would.) So I left her five hundred dollars and the steel commode she made me buy. I'd give a lot to see the look on her face when you tell her. Georgia, you're my executor. (Sorry, Marley, but you're not the lawyer in the group.) I hope Ruth gets so mad her head explodes.

I almost just wrote down, <u>Make sure you record it so I can see.</u> Guess I can look down from heaven and watch.

There's this family in my neighborhood. The Williamses. Single mom, three girls. I don't think they have a lot of money, and their house is in bad shape. Maybe you could give them my house. It would be nice to have a family in here. I think they'd take good care of it.

You're probably wondering why I'm not leaving anything to Mica. He never knew how rich I am, so it's not like he was after my money. I really do think he loved me. Loves me? But I've come to see that he loves me being helpless. I've been killing myself with food, not even trying to be healthy for the two years he and I have been together, and he helped me. Food has been basically poison, and he brought it to me on a tray, smiling the whole time.

That's not the kind of love that should be rewarded, is it?

I'm getting tired now, so I should go. You're probably asking yourself why I don't stop right now. Why I don't quick go to the hospital and check myself in.

Because of food. Because even now, I just can't stop eating. I'm so sorry. I never wanted to be this way, but I'm too tired to fight it anymore.

I want you to know that being your friend was one of the best parts of my whole life. It made me proud. I hope when you think of me, you'll remember how much fun we had at Camp Copperbrook. I think of you all the time.

Please don't be sad. I love you both.

Emerson

Marley handed me a tissue, and I blew my nose. "Damn it all to hell," I whispered.

We should've. We could've. We didn't. No one did.

Marley deadheaded some herb and shredded the leaves.

"First order of business is to kick that horrible cousin out as soon as humanly possible," she said, wiping her eyes. Her chest bucked with a sob. "Jesus, that letter."

"I know." I took a deep breath and looked at the will. It was pretty straightforward. "I bet Emerson would love to be an investor in Salt & Pepper," I said. "Helping people eat well . . . that's a noble cause."

"I don't know. I don't think so," Marley said, chewing on her lip. "That feels too . . . self-involved. I make enough, anyway. Might even expand next year."

"She wanted us to have something from her," I said.

"Then we can, I don't know, go on a trip together or something. Otherwise, let's give it all away."

I looked at the letter again and took a deep breath. "Okay. Come on inside, and I'll pour you a glass of wine. Time to make another list."

CHAPTER 26

Marley

Stop pretending to be happy all the time.
You get to have other feelings, too.
(This list thing is really growing on me.)

I never knew how satisfying it could be, giving money away.

There were legal things Georgia had to do before we could start writing checks, but we'd made a list, all right. The American Cancer Society, St. Jude's Children's Research Hospital, Habitat for Humanity, the Foundation for Female Entrepreneurship (Georgia's pet organization) and a group that gave service dogs to veterans were all going to be very, very grateful.

And Camp Copperbrook was going to have a new endowment for girls who couldn't afford the steep tuition.

The name Emerson Lydia Duval was going to mean something wonderful out there in the world.

And, per our friend's wishes, we set aside a sum for ourselves, enough for a week away. Next summer, Georgia and I would go to Glacier National Park in Montana. A hiking vacation. Georgia had said she'd start coming to the gym with me so she could get in better shape.

We thought a wilderness vacation was something Emerson would've loved to do in another lifetime, another body.

I swallowed. Sometimes it surprised me, how much I

missed Emerson, her sweet voice on the phone or Skype, her unexpected sense of humor in one so shy, the way she listened and remembered, always so invested in whatever I was doing. The first few times I'd told her about Camden, she was so excited for me.

As I'd been about Mica. It was odd. Camden *didn't* date me because of my size, I was almost positive; Mica *only* dated Emerson because of hers. I'd done a little research after Emerson died; Evil Cousin Ruth had said a few things that made me suspicious. *Feeder*, a guy like Mica was called. A person who got off on watching his partner get bigger, providing food, being the one in control.

It was so scary, to realize the only love she'd ever found had actually been a kind of . . . fetish. In a different way, maybe that was how my relationship (for lack of a better word) with Camden was. Screw a fat girl. Or was I just an easy lay? Either way, if I wasn't over him before, I sure was now.

I shuddered.

Well. I had to go to work. Tonight was dinner at Will's, and, I admitted, I was more than a little curious.

I had put some personal effort into this dinner. Oh, yes. One doesn't get called out for being fat and dressing like a man without responding. So first and foremost, I'd made a point to dress like a *woman*. I wore a tight white T-shirt topped by a flower-print cardigan. A stretchy olive pencil skirt that most decidedly did *not* hide my chubby belly and made the most of my generous ass. Sandals of the El Sluttio variety, with a high heel that did wonders for my calves and laces that wrapped around my ankles. A skinny belt to show that, yes, fat girls could have waists. Thin, dangly silver earrings and four silver bracelets. I'd pulled my hair back in a French twist, and, as usual, a few wiry curls had sprung loose.

There, I thought with a final look in the mirror. *Prepare yourself, Will Harding. A woman is coming for dinner.*

I drove to his house, which took all of thirty seconds, and got out of the car, grabbed the bags of food and headed in.

There was a vase of flowers on the bottom step—creamy roses and white hydrangeas, orange ranunculus with dark green ivy and some curly twigs. Utterly gorgeous.

I knocked on the door, and Will answered. "Can you get those flowers?" he asked.

"Hello to you, too. And no. My hands are full. Get them yourself." I went into the kitchen and set the bags on the counter.

He'd set the kitchen table. Very nicely, in fact.

"Those flowers," he repeated. "Would you mind getting them?"

I rolled my eyes. "Yes, Lady Grantham. Of course. For a second, I forgot I was the help. Forgive me."

"Who's Lady Grantham?"

"You are."

I added *Doesn't watch Downton Abbey* to my mental list of his many flaws and went out to fetch the flowers. "Here," I said, presenting them to him. "They're very pretty."

"Yes."

I suppressed a sigh and watched as he put them on the table, exactly in the center, then looked at me. Folded his arms.

"Are you hungry?" I asked.

"Not really."

"Okay." Not for the first time, I wondered why I was here. "Well, I brought wine, because I don't see me getting through this without a buzz on. Why don't you uncork it while I unpack dinner?"

"Sure."

All my dinners came with sides and salads, but Will hadn't specified what he wanted with the Mongolian beef, so I'd just done what I wanted. The whole meal had turned out so well, I was thinking I might have to add it to my regular offerings. It smelled like heaven—thinly sliced beef tenderloin marinated in rice wine, garlic, ginger, candied orange peel and red pepper. For sides, we had long-grained rice with peas, diced carrots, corn and sesame seeds, and sugar snap peas with just a little salt, pepper and garlic, because they were best served simply.

"I'm going to stick these snap peas in the fridge so they don't go limp," I said.

"I'll do it," he said, taking it from me.

"Thank you, kind sir."

He nodded, put the peas away. Then we looked at each other. I raised an eyebrow. He looked at my forehead.

"So this is fun," I said.

"Um . . . would you like to see the backyard?" he asked.

Well, well. I was usually only allowed in the kitchen. From the street, I had seen that his yard was surrounded by a privacy fence ten feet high—you couldn't see anything from the outside, reinforcing the idea that Will Harding didn't like people knowing what he was doing (chopping up bodies, for example). "I'd love to," I said.

I followed him to the back, through the darkened den, the frighteningly tidy mudroom, and out into paradise.

"Good God, Will," I breathed.

In front of me was one of the most beautiful gardens I'd ever seen, lit up by lanterns and fairy lights. The yard was small, and every inch of it was taken up with . . . life. It looked Buddhist to me—a little path made of stones meandered through perfectly manicured shrubs, and an island of moss sat in the middle of a little pond. There was a bank of lush green ferns surrounding a red Japanese maple tree, glowing with color. On the inside of the fence hung at least a dozen planters, overflowing with ivy.

Closer to the house was a tiny slate patio with two chairs and a little table. "Have a seat," he said, wiping his brow with his sleeve.

"This is beautiful," I breathed, ignoring his offer and going into the little wonderland. "Was it like this when you bought the house?"

"No," he said, not leaving the patio. "I made it. There was nothing here when I moved in. Just some patchy grass."

"*You* made this? Get out of here!" There was a pile of stones, balanced on top of each other. "This should be in a magazine, Will Harding! Look at your roses! They're still so beautiful."

"Maybe we should go inside," he said. "The bugs."

There were no bugs that I could see. "I can't get over this."

"Let's go inside," he said. "Please."

"Don't want me to see the secret side of you, huh?"

"Yes. Exactly. I'm Batman, and I shouldn't have shown you the cave."

A joke. He had made a joke. Not a great one, but hey.

I wanted to stay outside, but it was his house, after all. I walked past him, noting that he was rather sweaty. "Having a hot flash?" I asked.

"Very funny."

He told me to sit in the living room and went upstairs. When he came down, he was wearing a different button-down shirt, this one pale blue instead of white.

"Where were we?" I said when he stood there like a lump.

"You wanted wine." He poured me a glass, then one for himself.

"Right. Cheers," I said, clinking my glass against his. "Thanks for inviting me."

He glanced at me, and glugged his entire glass and poured himself a refill.

Alrighty, then. Not the best harbinger for a lovely evening, not if he was trying to drown his sorrows already. Nevertheless, I persisted. "How long did that yard take you?"

"A long time."

"Are you a landscaper or something?" No answer. "A garden gnome? Will?"

"Let's sit here," Will said. "In the living room."

Ah, yes. The plainest and most boring room ever. I suppressed a sigh.

"So what do you do for work, Will?" I asked, sitting in the same place I had when I'd hurt my ankle. He took the chair.

"I think I've told you. I'm a computer programmer."

"Yes. My sister is in cybersecurity. She's kind of a badass." No response. "So what do you program?"

"I write code for children's video games."

"Really? My friend's nephew, Mason? He's kind of like my own nephew, too. He loves computer games." I couldn't help trying to fill the vacuum where conversation was supposed to be. "Children's video games. That sounds like a fun job." Still no answer. "Is it fun, Will?"

"I suppose."

Horrible at making small talk.

"Do you enjoy the work, Will?" I enunciated clearly.

"Yes. I used to. I still do, some days." He looked at his wineglass.

This was going to be a *long* evening. "Do you have any games here? Games that you made?"

He looked back up. "I do. Want to see one?"

"I'd love to." Anything other than trying to carry the whole conversation.

But when he met my gaze before getting up, I noticed again that he had nice eyes. Not really serial killer eyes. Denim blue in color, turning down a little, which made him look a bit sad.

He turned on the TV, clicked a few buttons and a screen appeared. *Yoshi and Spike's Amazing Adventures!—Amazon Rain Forest Edition.*

"It's part of a series," he said. "Kids learn about different ecosystems and everything that lives there. Animals, plants, insects, that kind of thing. Here. You can use the controller to make them move."

"This is so cute!" I said. "My friend Georgia, the one with the nephew . . . she's a preschool teacher. She would *love* this."

Yoshi and Spike were little green aliens with tufts of hair that blew in the wind as they swung from vines onto the tree canopy, somersaulting through the air. "The colors are gorgeous, Will. Oh, a parrot! Did you see that?"

He wasn't exactly smiling, but his face was relaxed. He was on the cusp of smiling, maybe. "I made that."

"Aren't you too cool for school. How do I get points? I want to win."

"You have to match the food with the animal. Nope, parrots don't eat monkeys. Sorry."

I reversed the parrot's direction. "There. Does he like a juicy bug?" The screen chimed, and my score registered five points. "He does!"

"You look nice," Will said. "I meant to tell you that before."

I paused, and my parrot crashed into a tree, but revived on the rain forest floor. "Thanks."

His gaze dropped to my boobage, then back up again. "Anyway. I'll get dinner on the table."

"Want help?"

"No. You keep playing."

"Just throw those snap peas into a hot frying pan for ten seconds." I resisted the urge to do it myself, then turned my attention back to the game. Yoshi and Spike were admiring an anaconda. "Get away from that, you two," I said. "Go see those yellow monkeys."

"Those are golden lion tamarins," Will called from the kitchen.

"They're gorgeous. Are they real? As in, do they actually exist?"

"They do. I assume they do, anyway. I don't research this stuff; I just write the code. I make the monkey look like a monkey, in other words."

The world on-screen was so vibrant and detailed. There were birdsongs and jaguars screeching, bugs clicking. The leaves and flowers moved in an imaginary breeze as Yoshi and Spike hopped and tumbled through the landscape, chatting in a nonsensical, adorable language. I couldn't even imagine how long it took to write code for every little ant, every movement, every color.

And that garden in the backyard . . .

Strange that Will's house was so stark by comparison. He could use a visit to Crate & Barrel, yes sir. Pier 1 Imports, even better. The house itself had character—an arched doorway into the living room, a built-in china cabinet in the corner of the kitchen, old wooden floors. It could be just as beautiful as the backyard with a little effort.

And here was an entire world of color, sound and movement on the screen. There was more to Will Harding than I had realized.

It was a very pleasant thought.

Yoshi and Spike were staring at a line of leaf-cutter ants. I steered the bugs away from a puddle and over to a little tree, then, cruelly, clicked on the anteater and dragged it over. "Circle of life, yo," I said as the anteater extended its hideous tongue.

"Excuse me?" Will asked.

"Nothing. I'm playing God in here. This game is amazing. Yikes! Where did that jaguar come from? Run, anteater, run!"

I wasn't sure, but I thought I heard Will laugh. Something squeezed in my stomach.

"Dinner's ready," he said, appearing in the doorway. "Want to eat?"

I put down the control. "Sure."

The table looked lovely. Candles, the flowers, my food on platters. His plates were white (and painfully boring), but at least they were china. I always pictured him eating out of the biodegradable cartons I used. The kind of guy who only had one fork, one spoon, one glass. That kind of thing.

The thought occurred to me that maybe he'd bought an extra plate, fork and spoon just for me.

We sat down, and he nudged the beef toward me. I helped myself to some of everything, then took a bite. "Oh, man, this is good," I said. I may have moaned a little. The beef was velvety and tender, the orange and ginger flavors rich without being overbearing, the little bite of pepper adding just the right balance. The snap peas had a clean, crisp freshness. "Oh, Madonna," I murmured.

"Do you always eat food like this?" Will asked.

"Like what?"

"Like a porn star."

I smiled slowly. "Yes. I'm Italian. I make love to food."

He looked at his plate, his cheeks reddening. It was kind of adorable.

I watched him eat. It wasn't porn, alas. And it wasn't with gusto. My mother would have checked him for a fever, he was so reserved. He even put down his fork between bites. Freaky.

"So why am I here, Will?" I asked when it became apparent that he again wasn't going to make conversation.

He set down his fork and knife, looked at me across the table and folded his hands together. "Right."

"Is this a date?"

"No."

Sigh.

He took another sip of wine—another glug, really— then set the glass down. "Today is a significant day in my life."

"Ah." He didn't elaborate. "Your birthday? I could've brought a cake."

"No. Do I have to tell you?"

"Yes."

It took him a minute to answer. "I lost some friends on this day. Two years ago."

Well, shit. "I'm really sorry, Will." Lost . . . probably not in the *can't find* sense of the word, or even in the *breakup* sense, since guys didn't really do that. "What happened?" I asked.

"I'd rather not go into it."

So they'd died, then. His grip on the wineglass was tightening. That stem was thin, and I feared for its safety. On the other hand, if Will got a cut, I could tend to him.

That thought didn't make a lot of sense.

"Okay," I said. "Well, we can talk about something else."

His grip relaxed. A car accident, maybe? Fire? Mud-slide? Golf-course lightning strike? All sorts of horrible deaths flashed through my mind. I was my mother's daughter, after all.

"How many friends?" I couldn't help asking.

"Three."

Three! Shit, that was a *lot*. If I lost Georgia, Louis and Dante, I'd probably walk off a cliff.

Suddenly, his solitary state made sense.

I lifted my glass and clinked it against his. "To your friends," I said, and my eyes filled with tears.

"Thank you," he said, and I wanted to hug him.

"Are you sure you don't want to talk about it?"

"Absolutely sure." He didn't meet my eyes.

Screw it. I got up, went around the table, sat on his lap and hugged him.

"Oh. Uh . . . okay," he said, his back stiffening.

"You need a hug, that's all," I said. One of my tears plopped onto his hair. "Don't read into it. Come on. Hug me back."

He put his arms around me and then, after a second, squeezed a little. His face was against my boobage. It had been a long time since someone's face was there, and I won't lie. It felt nice. His hair was straight and soft and sticking up in odd places, and I leaned my cheek against it, breathing in the smell of his shampoo, kind of minty and clean and . . . well, nice.

"Thank you," he said. "Can we be done?"

"You bet." I stood, tugged my skirt down and started back to my side of the table.

Will caught my hand and stopped me. "Thank you," he said again.

He stood up, still holding my hand.

He looked at me a long minute, and once again, I had the

unsettling, buzzing feeling that he was . . . seeing me. "You've lost someone, too," he said. It wasn't a question, and a chill snaked up my spine.

"Well, sure. Most people have. Everyone has, right?"

"That's why I asked you over."

"Why?"

"I figured you might understand. There's a sadness about you."

I blinked. "No, there's not. I'm the happiest person you ever met." I smiled to prove it.

He just looked at me, squinting slightly. "No. You're sad."

"I'm extremely happy, Will. Trust me."

"It's okay, you know. To be sad. And . . . stuck."

"Of course it's okay. Not that I am. Sad *or* stuck. Well, sometimes I am. But that's not the point."

He said nothing, and I felt my earlier softness toward him turn to stone. The point *was*, I worked happiness like it was my job. Because it was! It *was* my job! Cooking for people, bringing delicious, nutritious food to their homes; what could be a nicer, more cheering, more wonderful thing in the entire world, huh? Not to mention I was the world's best friend/sister/daughter! Even to people like Will Harding, I was so *massively* nice, so frickin' happy all the time, it would make your teeth hurt. I was here, wasn't I? On a Tuesday night when I could've been at Dante's soft-ball game, ogling firefighters, no less.

"Who was it?" he asked. "The person you lost?"

I dashed the tears out of my eyes—tears for his friends, because I was a kind, empathetic and *happy* person, mind you. "None of your business. It wasn't like you were falling over yourself to tell me your sad story."

"Okay. I'm sorry."

"My sister. My twin sister. We were four." So much for my wall of silence.

And then, horribly, my mouth was all weird and wriggling, and these awful sounds were coming out of me, and tears were spurting out of my eyes, and I had no idea what was happening.

Will put his arms around me. His hand cupped my head, and he pressed my scrunched-up face against his shoulder. My hands fisted in his shirt, feeling the slight stiffness from starch, and I cried, the sobs barking out of me.

Every time I told someone she had died, she felt a little more gone.

Will didn't say anything, just held me gently, one hand on my back, the other in my hair. He'd asked me here to comfort him, and here he was, comforting me instead.

It only took a minute. Okay, more like three, possibly five, but eventually I stepped away, and Will disentangled his fingers from my hair. I grabbed a napkin and wiped my eyes, leaving smears of black.

"Sorry," I said. The tears kept coming, though the sobs had stopped.

He refilled my wineglass, then led me into the living room again, that place of sterility and cold comfort.

But he put his arm around me. I kicked off my shoes, took my wine and sat there, blackish mascara tears leaking into his shirt.

I hadn't cried in a long time. Not for Frankie, because this was what happened. It took an age to patch the crack in the dam when the whole ocean pressed against the walls.

Will's hand kept going into my hair, poor naive hand that it was. But it felt nice, even if my curls wrapped around his fingers like a malevolent thornbush. I guess my clip had come out at some point, because my hair was loose now. Will turned on the TV to a show about naked survivalists in Africa that Georgia loved. We watched in silence as they argued and napped and ate lizards, their naughty bits blurred out.

"That's someone's job," Will said. "Pixelating out nudity."

"Dumb," I said. "It's just boobs and crotches."

He may have chuckled. His chest moved, but he was silent.

"I could survive everything except the bug bites," I said eventually.

"How about dysentery?"

"I'm not saying I'd love dysentery, but I'd tough it out. The itching, though . . . that would make me insane."

"Are you done crying now?"

"I seem to be." He smelled nice, like laundry detergent and starch. He may have ironed his shirt.

"Do you want to talk about your sister?" he asked.

"No. Want to make out instead?"

The question shocked me. But not really. Part of me wasn't surprised at all. After all, he was the man who'd let my ice bag leak all over his leg. The man who made a little paradise where once there was nothing, who'd asked me here on what had to be a horrible day for him, because he believed I'd understand.

Will was the person who saw I was sad, even when I hated admitting it to myself.

He pulled back a little and looked at me.

"Sorry about the mascara," I said. "I hope you like raccoons."

"A lot of people think they're just big rats."

"Are you one of them?"

"No. I think they're cute."

There was a little smile playing around his mouth and those downward-slanting true-blue eyes, and I found myself smiling back, just a little bit.

He kissed me then, a soft, gentle kiss. Then he stopped, looked at me again, and threaded his brave fingers into my hair and kissed me for real, leaning me back against the couch so I was almost lying down, and his mouth moved slowly, thoroughly.

Holy St. Francis, I would not have guessed that Will Harding could kiss like this. So that a thin gold wire seemed to wrap around my insides and tug in the most wonderful, electric pulse. My hands went into that soft, straight hair, and I traced a finger around his ear. I felt his tongue against mine, tasted wine and ginger, and melted a little deeper into the couch.

There was something exceedingly horny about making out on a couch, the TV on in the background, as if we were teenagers trying to fool the grown-ups. Will's arms were solid, his lips warm and firm and so good at what they were doing, moving down my jaw, onto my neck, and we fit together in a way that was unexpectedly perfect.

When I wrapped one leg around his and his hand was under my shirt, he stopped, resting his forehead against mine. "Want to go upstairs?" he asked.

"Do you?" I said.

His lashes were straight, and longer than I'd noticed before. "Yes."

"Then upstairs it is," I said, and he slid off me, stood up and held out his hand.

....

A very respectable amount of time later, I lay naked in Will's bed, flushed and a little sweaty and more than pleased with myself and him both.

Guess he didn't have a thing against fat girls after all.

Then again, shagging had never been the issue. Dating . . .

dating was harder. But he'd had me over for dinner (which I'd brought, granted), had wine (ditto), and, well . . . yes, I guess I'd initiated all this.

Shit. I hoped I hadn't pressured him into anything with the tears and all. The Sad Tale of the Lost Twin. Then again, he was lazily sliding one finger up and down my forearm in a way that left little tingles and bubbles of delight. He didn't seem in a hurry to have me leave.

The hall light was on; otherwise, it was dark in his room. His comforter was beige, tragically. I slid an arm under my head, feeling my snarled hair. I'd have dreads before the night was over. It would take half an hour to untangle this mess, and it would be totally worth it.

"You ever think about decorating your house?" I asked.

"No."

"Why not?"

"It's fine the way it is," he said, a hint of irritation in his voice.

"It's very sad and boring the way it is."

"It's a little early for you to start redecorating my place, don't you think?"

I squashed a smile. A little early . . . but not out of the question. That felt very relationshippy to me.

I rolled on my side to look at him and put my hand on his neck, feeling the pulse, strong and steady under my palm. "Will you tell me about your friends?"

His hair was spiky from sexy time, his cheeks ruddy. He took a deep, slow breath, nodded once. "It was a mass shooting. They were all . . . they worked together. Two other people were shot, but they lived."

My hand, which was still on his throat, squeezed involuntarily, choking him, and I yanked it back. "I'm so sorry. Oh, Will. I'm so, so sorry."

I'd seen the video—run, hide, fight. Even that, viewed on YouTube in the comfort of my living room, had scared the wits out of me.

Also, Sandy Hook Elementary was less than an hour from Cambry-on-Hudson. I couldn't drive down I-84 without crying every time I passed the exit.

"Were you really close?" I asked.

"I don't want to talk about it anymore, Marley. Please."

"Okay," I whispered, my throat tight. "I'm so sorry, though."

He nodded, still lying on his back and looking at the ceiling.

I could cut him some slack for being . . . himself. Losing three friends in such a senseless, violent way had to be gutting. I took his hand and squeezed it, but even so, I could feel the wall coming down between us. While he might have just slept with me, he wasn't about to engage in any real intimacy.

In another second, he'd get out of bed, thank me for coming, and this would be a onetime thing.

Please don't be like everyone else, Will. The fervor that came with the thought was a little surprising.

"If you want, you can tell me about your sister," he said, reaching out and taking a strand of hair between his fingers, and I felt limp with relief and gratitude.

"I don't talk about her too much," I said.

"You don't have to."

"We were fraternal twins. Are fraternal twins." I swallowed. "I was big and strong, she was little and fragile. She had some breathing issues, I guess. My family is thin on the details."

"What was her name?"

"Frankie. Short for Francesca." I cleared my throat. "I don't really remember her."

"Four is pretty young."

"Yeah. But we—my parents, that is—they have a shrine to her in the living room. Same house we've always lived in, although my parents, they just decided to move. So they're selling the house, and it's . . . I don't know. It's hitting me hard."

He nodded. Didn't ask anything else.

It was kind of nice.

"Do you want me to go home?" I asked. "Be honest."

"No."

"No, you won't be honest, or no, you don't want me to go home?"

"The latter."

"I'm always a little unclear on which one that is."

His mouth moved in a slow smile. "I don't want you to go home. But you can if you want to."

I thought of my cheerful blue bedroom, all the throw pillows and family photos, the cluster of mirrors on one wall, the fresh flowers from my garden on the night table, the fridge that practically bulged with good food, the Ben & Jerry's I'd been saving.

Will's bedroom was as sterile as the rest of his house.

But he was here.

"I'll stay," I said, and with that, I wrapped my arms around his neck and kissed him.

And thought maybe, just maybe, I had a boyfriend.

Emerson would've been proud.

CHAPTER 27

Georgia

Shop at a store for regular people. Again.
(Note to self: Never do this with Big Kitty. Ever.)

Admiral stared at Zeus and licked his chops.

"Don't you dare," I said. "Don't even think about it. I don't care about your past. You've turned over a new leaf."

Having a rabbit in a house where a former racing greyhound lived was probably not a good idea. But Zeus—who was adorable and tiny, a miniature black bunny about the size of a kitten—had been here since Monday, when Mason brought him over. His cage sat on the wide sill of my bay window. At the moment, he was huddled in the farthest corner, whiskers twitching, not daring to look away from Admiral, as if he knew what the dog was thinking.

"Stay away, Admiral," I said. He looked at me with a wounded expression, as if saying he'd never even think of murdering the poor bunny (at least, not while I was in the room).

Why did I have a rabbit in my house, you ask? A good question, and the answer filled me with horror.

Mason was performing in the school talent show tonight. Doing magic.

I know.

When he told me it fulfilled the public speaking requirement for both school and his list, I'd been stricken with sympathetic terror, which I tried to mask with great enthusiasm. "Magic! Wow! Yes! Who doesn't love magic! I love magic!"

That stupid, *stupid* list. Why had I thought it was a good idea?

I mean, bad enough to have to stand up in front of a thousand of your schoolmates and their parents in a fricking huge auditorium and do anything at all. But magic? *Magic?*

"Can I keep little Zeus here?" he'd asked. "My dad . . . he doesn't like animals. I'll come visit him every day, and then after . . . well, I'm hoping Dad will let me keep him. Maybe. If I build a hutch or something."

"Sure!" I said. "Absolutely." And of course, when my brother said no, I'd keep the bunny in my own backyard.

He kissed the rabbit on the head. "Isn't he the cutest thing you ever saw?"

"Yes," I said. At least now I wasn't lying. He looked like a handful of black fluff with ears.

But a magic trick? Mason told me how it was that the little bunny would be under the false bottom of the hat (like there was a person on earth who didn't know this trick), and how he'd reveal the bunny just like that. Ta-da! "Totally old school, but everyone loves it."

Did they, though? "How does your father feel about this?" I asked.

"Oh," Mason said. "Uh, I told him I was doing stand-up. You know, magic can be really funny, right?"

"Sure. Yes. Everyone loves magic and, um, laughing."

"My teacher said I was the only one doing a magic act."

Obviously. "What are the other kids doing?"

"Most people are singing. A couple dancers. One kid? He beatboxes."

"What's that?"

"It's really cool. He makes these beats with his mouth, like hip-hop rhythm and stuff. He'll probably win. Everybody likes him. Plus, he's a senior."

"Well, this is really brave of you."

He nodded. "You'll come, right, G?" He bit his tortured nail.

"Of course, honey. Nothing would keep me away."

The second he left, I'd texted Marley.

Magic??? she wrote back. Oh, God. I'm coming, of course. Yikes.

And yet, Mason was so excited. He even had—gulp—a cape. The name of his act? Mason the Magnificent.

He was going to be *crucified*. High school students were not renowned for their kindness. A cape, a wand, and a rabbit . . . oh, my poor little nephew!

But I hadn't tried to talk him out of it. He was lit up with excitement, had bought Zeus and stowed him here. Who was I to try to tell him his idea was social suicide? Or was that my duty as his aunt?

So now it was Friday morning, the day of the talent show. St. Luke's was closed for Cultural Heritage Day, one of the many obscure holidays Mr. Trombley inserted into the school calendar. I didn't mind sleeping in, since I was wicked tired these days. That fun run (which had been very little fun, FYI) had wiped me out; I hadn't been the same since. Exercise was clearly not good for everyone.

I thought of the trip to Glacier next summer. Marley was right. I had to get in shape. I'd ask my doctor about it today, since I was finally going for that checkup.

It was warm for early October, and I figured I'd take Ad down to the courtyard and away from Zeus, who was looking extremely stressed. Just as I picked up my book, my doorbell rang. When I opened the door, I was not pleasantly surprised.

Mother, clad in a low-cut white satin shirt, flowing black skirt with a slit up to her thigh and freakishly high black pumps with metal spikes on them. Her fake hair was done up in a bun at the nape of her neck. The overall look said sadomasochistic tango dancer.

"Hello," I said.

"I know you have the day off, so don't bother with excuses," she said.

"I do have plans," I said.

"Georgia, your clothes are ridiculous," she said, giving me the stink-eye.

Yes, I was clad in yoga pants that had never seen a yoga studio and a T-shirt covered in rabbit and dog hair. But I'd been *reading*. There was no reason to dress up for reading. Books didn't care. Books were just happy to be read.

"Would you like coffee?" I asked. In addition to her outfit, she had on full Kabuki makeup—smoky cat eye, eyelash extensions that looked a little freakish on a woman her age, and a deep red lipstick on her artificially swollen lips.

"No," she said. "Now that you're down to a reasonable size, you should flaunt your figure and find a man. Just because you married that Puerto Rican doesn't mean you've ruined your chances for life."

"He's not Puerto Rican. He's Spanish and Dominican. And American, let's not forget that. Born in the USA."

"Whatever. That nice Blaine Cummings is divorced again, you know. Cheated on the second wife, his mother told me. I gave her your number to pass along to him."

"Oh, a twice-divorced cheater! He sounds wonderful."

"You can't be so fussy, you know. You threw away your fertile years."

"I'm thirty-four. Weren't you older than that when I was born, Mom?"

"I was twenty-nine," she said.

"Birth certificates don't lie."

"Stop stalling. Let's go shopping. I'll pay." She sat down on my couch, moved a pink and red throw pillow with a frown, and stared at Admiral. He lay obediently at her feet, accepting her as his dark master. "That thing over there," she asked, jutting her chin at Zeus's cage. "Is that a rabbit?"

"Is it? I thought it was a grizzly bear. Be right back."

I went upstairs to change. The truth was, I did need some new clothes. And two hours spent with Big Kitty now would allow me to decline future invitations into the foreseeable future. To the Lawn Club, for example, a place I hated . . . or dinner at her house, when she and Hunter would criticize my life choices in front of Mason.

My doctor's appointment was just after lunch, so I had a great excuse to keep the shopping ordeal from lasting the whole day.

Twenty minutes later, my mother and I were in downtown Cambry-on-Hudson, walking toward Crave, the most expensive boutique in three towns. It was a rather ugly name for a store, putting me in mind of drug addicts, or my late-night food binges, or vampires. The store was on the same street as Bliss, the wedding dress boutique owned by Jenny Tate, my neighbor. She was changing the window display—a gorgeous, long-sleeved lace gown surrounded by gray wooden crates full of chrysanthemums. She saw me, gave a big smile and waved. I waved back.

"If," Mom said, "and I mean *if* you get busy and stop mooning over that Latino, you could get married again and we could get your dress here. She's very good, that girl."

"I'm not mooning," I said. "And yes, she's very talented, and also a woman."

"Have you been on even one date since he left you?"

"Yes, actually."

She stopped dead. "Anyone of high quality?"

"What do you mean by high quality? Caring, intelligent, kind? If so, yes." I thought so, anyway. I was still kind of hung up on the fact that I was pretending not to remember Evan Kennedy, and he *definitely* didn't remember me. We'd gone out for a drink a few days ago—our second date—and it had been more of the charming nothingness we seemed to excel at.

"I *meant*, Georgia, can he support himself and a wife and family?"

"I don't know. I haven't asked for his W-2 just yet."

"You laugh, but look at me. It's a good thing Joseph was rich so I could get a decent alimony. That trust fund of yours won't last forever."

It would, actually, if I didn't spend it all at places like Crave. I might not have enough to be in the one percent, but thanks to my grandparents and my father's careful management of my stocks, I'd never be homeless or hungry.

"You could always have gotten a job, Mom," I said. "You're a Bryn Mawr graduate. You're very smart and, um, fashion forward."

"Women from my generation didn't work, Georgia."

"No, no, of course not. Unless you're thinking of women like Helen Mirren and Toni Morrison and Ruth Bader Ginsburg and Jane Goodall and—"

"Are you done, Georgia? We're here." Mom threw open the door to Crave. "Eliza!" she cried. "My poor daughter is dressed like a hobo. Help her!"

"Big Kitty! Hello, hello!" Eliza said, dollar signs lighting her eyes. She was as tall and thin as a praying mantis—or was it preying? *Preying* was more accurate in this case. She reached out for me with her long arms and beamed. "Aren't you beautiful! She looks exactly like you, Big Kitty! Darling, everything in the *store* will look amazing on you. Get in that changing room and strip down, darling."

Oh, God.

"She's lost weight, Eliza. Finally. Last year at this time, she was enormous! There'd have been no way she could shop here," Mom said with a merry laugh.

I let my mother's cruelty go, as I usually did. "I have a doctor's appointment at twelve thirty," I said. "We have to be quick." Because two hours was nothing. My mother could spend a week in a shop like this one.

"Oh, dear," Mom said, sitting down and whipping out her phone. "I was hoping we could have lunch at the club. I wanted to show you off to my friends."

So we could look at our salads and dream about pasta, and she could pass me around to the middle-aged cheating males for inspection. Now that I wasn't fat, I was acceptable. She'd taken me to the club plenty of times, but never to show me off. Criticize, yes. Show off, no.

For the second time in a month, I stripped down to my underwear and tried not to hate it.

"You need some proper foundation garments," Eliza said. "We'll squish those rolls into oblivion!"

I didn't have rolls. I had . . . well, I had some loose skin. Not a lot, but it was there. My body wasn't exactly symmetrical or flat. That's the thing when you lose a lot of weight. You very rarely look like a person who was never fat.

But I *wasn't* fat. There was no way anyone could look at me and think the word *fat*.

My mother whipped back the curtain. "You can get surgery for that, you know. Some cold lipo or laser tightening would smooth things out perfectly. And if I were you, I'd go for implants. I'm thinking of getting mine a little bigger. And maybe getting the Brazilian butt. Why not, right?"

God.

In my guest bedroom, there was a photo of my parents on their wedding day. The truth was, my mom had been girl-next-door pretty, with a button nose and full cheeks. She'd had a perfect figure as far as I could tell.

Now she looked gaunt and sharp. Her cheekbones and nose had been altered, as well as her eyes and chin. Two face-lifts that I knew of. The iron breasts of the 1980s implants. A neck job. Countless injections and fillers. She didn't look young; she simply looked like someone who'd had a lot of plastic surgery.

I didn't recognize her in that old photo, where her smile was so wide, when happiness and not a surgeon's blade was the cause of her beauty. I had nothing against plastic surgery when it helped a person's self-image or corrected something that really bothered them. But the idea that there was always one more thing that could be enhanced . . . it got sad. My mom was almost seventy years old and was still obsessed with how she looked.

Why? What good would a bigger ass do her? If she wanted to attract men, well, she could. In fact, I'd always been a little shocked she hadn't remarried after Dad left, if only to show him she could find someone else, too.

If we'd had a different relationship, maybe we could've talked about those things.

Eliza returned with a few things. "Oh!" Mom said, snatching a sleeveless leopard-print dress with a black lace ruffle at the bottom. "I adore this. Georgia, you don't mind if I try this on, do you?"

"I was just thinking it would be perfect for you, Big Kitty," Eliza cooed. "The two of you could be sisters, you know."

I pulled the curtain closed to hide my eye roll and dutifully got started. The foundation thing was about as easy to pull on as trying to squeeze a bucking goat into a garden hose. Once I got into that, I rested a minute, then pulled on the skirts and dresses, showed them to Mom and Eliza, nodded and fake-smiled.

They were clothes. I looked fine. My criterion for work clothes was whether or not I could sit on the floor without flashing my little darlings, but I didn't tell that to Mom and Eliza. I could wear these jeans on a night out with Marley. This dress would be good for one of the St. Luke's fundraisers. I could wear this skirt and blouse when I went to court for my clients.

I tugged on the last outfit. I hated that something this shallow was making my mother happy to be with me. Then again, I made her happy in so few ways, I might as well throw her a bone.

"Georgia, wear that out of the store," Mom said. "No need to look like we don't care about ourselves when we're in public."

"Sure." The outfit *was* cute—flippy little black skirt to the knee, blouse printed with lemons and cats. My students would like this getup, at least. I donned black tights and stepped into the suede booties Mom had deemed *edible*.

When Emerson, Marley and I had written down this particular item—*Shop at a store for regular people*—I remembered our glee, our longing. The three of us pictured being Julia Roberts in *Pretty Woman*, swinging down the street in our adorable outfits, the envy of all who saw us. Life would be perfect if we could shop on Rodeo Drive and wear those tiny-sized dresses. Even if we had to be prostitutes to get there.

But now that the moment was here, I realized they were just clothes. Cute, some of them, but not exactly the golden ticket for a perfect life.

"This was fun, wasn't it, darling?" Mom said as Eliza handed us our bags. Mom had six to my two.

"It was," I lied. "Thank you so much, Mom. I'll walk to the doctor's, no need to drive me."

"Good! You could use the exercise. We'll have lunch another time." She tilted a cheek at me, and I dutifully air-kissed it.

"I'll see you tonight, right?" I said.

"What's tonight?"

"Mason's talent show."

She frowned. "Oh. Yes, Hunter mentioned it. What's he doing? Does he have talent at something?"

"At many things, Mom. I'm sure he'd love to see you there." I wasn't about to tell her what he had planned. She might tell Hunter, and Hunter would very likely forbid Mason from coming if he thought his son was going to do something less than cool.

"Well, we'll see. I'm off. Love you, darling," she said.

My mouth fell open, but she had already turned, fluttering her fingers as she left.

I couldn't remember my mother ever saying that before. No, really. Not *ever*.

There was the familiar burning in my stomach. It might've been rage this time. Was it possible that my mother *hadn't* loved me until now, when I was able to shop at fucking Crave? Was this the criterion for maternal love? I hoped she *didn't* come tonight, because right now, I wanted to slap her.

My phone cheeped, reminding me I had a doctor waiting, so I took a few deep breaths and kept walking, my mind blurry.

In the past few months, I'd gotten a big raise and a promotion. A good-looking guy had asked for a third date. I'd had a free undercarriage wash. Just yesterday, Debbie Lareau invited me to join a book club. She was one of the mean moms at St. Luke's, the type who always wore two-carat diamond studs with her Pomegranate & Plum workout gear and gossiped about everyone, including her closest friends. Despite my education, family money and whatever other credentials I might have, that group of moms had always treated me like the help (until I lost weight, that is). And now my mother had said she loved me. In public, no less.

Back when I was fat and something nice happened, I knew it was because of me. Not because of my size.

The secret world of the skinnies was real, just like Emerson had always said. But now that I was in it, I wasn't sure I liked it here. My throat tightened, and my stomach ached. I caught a glimpse of a woman in the reflection of a window, and it took a second to realize she was me.

Shit. I looked good. Horribly, it was *nice* here on the skinny side of the world. Yes. It was nice to shop without wanting to cry. Nice to date a good-looking guy. Nice to have a mother who sought you out and said she loved you. Nice to get a raise and a promotion and that stupid undercarriage wash.

It was just that I wanted those things because of who I was, not how I looked.

I nearly walked past the doctor's office. But as soon as I noticed where I was, I felt the automatic shame that accompanied these visits. Going to the doctor when you're fat is a string of humiliations. The second you walk in, you only have one problem. You could have a spear through your heart, and the doctor would say, *Eighteen hundred calories a day, lots of green leafy vegetables, and forty-five minutes of cardio every day, and that spear will be no problem!*

Not that I was in a mood or anything.

The nurse showed me in and led me to the scale.

"Oh! Someone's been working hard!" the nurse chortled, tapping my weight into her iPad. "Good for you, hon. Let's check that blood pressure." I waited as she pumped up the sleeve. "Nice and low! One hundred over sixty-two.

Pulse is one hundred, which is a little high. Did you have coffee today?"

"Yes."

"No worries, then." She drew blood, put a Band-Aid on my arm and tapped a few more things into the iPad, then beamed at me. "Just get changed into the johnny coat, and Dr. Lott will be right in."

I obeyed and changed. Sat on the exam table, considered reading a *Newsweek* from two years ago. Then the door opened, and Dr. Lott, my GP for the past few years, came in.

"Georgia! You look incredible!" Dr. Lott said. She was slim and beautiful, about my age, and not for the first time, I wondered why I hadn't chosen a doctor who looked like Morgan Freeman instead.

"Hi, Dr. Lott," I said.

"Call me Annie."

Another first. Another star on the Skinny Life chart.

She looked at the computer. "Look at all this weight you've lost! Good for you, Georgia! You must be feeling a lot better!"

So many exclamation points. "I've actually had this pain in my stomach."

She nodded. "How long has this been going on?"

"Um . . . eight months? It got worse after a . . . a family crisis in April."

"Sometimes, when the stomach shrinks, it can feel like actual pain."

"This *is* actual pain."

"Of course! How long have you been dieting?"

"Well, my friend is a chef, and she started bringing me meals about two years ago. So my diet definitely got better. But I'm a little worried about the pain. That's when most of the weight really started coming off."

"It's amazing, isn't it?" she said, smiling. "Your metabolism wakes up just like that. Portion size, good healthy food and poof! You're a new you."

"Except for stomach pain."

She palpated my stomach for about five seconds. "Any pain here?"

"No. It's more like a burning."

"Try some Tums. They're great for calcium, anyway. Listen. You might have a little stress from—what was it you said? A family crisis?"

I nodded.

"Right. And on top of that, your body is going through changes. But they're all good. You look fantastic."

"The stomach pain is pretty bad sometimes, Dr. Lott." I spoke slowly, so she could follow along.

She nodded kindly, and for the second time that day, I felt like slapping someone. "It's hard. Your body is having to relearn how to do everything—digest the good food, stop storing all that fat, metabolize. Try some good fat and a few carbs before you load up on the protein. It's probably just gas. But keep up the hard work! Your body will thank you."

She went through the rest of the exam at lightning speed—listened to my heart, lungs, squished my ovaries, did the Pap smear.

"Everything looks normal. We'll call you with your blood work and Pap results. Any other complaints?" she asked, peeling off her gloves.

"None that I haven't mentioned."

"You're doing great. I'm so proud of you!"

I didn't dignify that with an answer. Just changed back into my little clothes.

When I got home, disaster greeted me.

Zeus was lying on his side, looking like one of those fluffy keychain thingies.

His little rib cage didn't appear to be moving. "Shit!" I said, dropping my bags. "Zeus? Zeus? Honey?"

Nothing. Not even a twitch.

Eyes wide, I looked at Admiral, who wasn't making eye contact. "What did you do?" I demanded. He put his head on his paws.

Damn it! I should've put the rabbit in the bathroom and closed the door. Why hadn't I thought of that? What was I going to do now?

I took the rabbit out of the cage, and Admiral's ears pricked up. "Don't even!" I said. Could you do CPR to a rabbit? We were about to find out.

"Marley!" I yelled. "Can you come up here?" No answer. I stomped my foot to let her know it was urgent, but still nothing.

Then—horribly—I put tiny little Zeus on the coffee table. He was so fluffy and small. And maybe still warm? Or was that just his fur? "Marley! Help me!"

There was no noise from down below. Marley wasn't home, then. Shit!

Well, there was no one else except my dog, who'd swallow Zeus in one bite. I rolled the bunny on his back and leaned down. Oh, God. Weren't rabbits vermin? I blew at his face, which just made his whiskers quiver. Put my lips a little closer. What kind of diseases could I get from a rabbit? Was there rabbit-borne flu? Or was that just the plague in nicer terms?

I blew again.

The thing was dead. Dead on my watch. Mason was going to be heartbroken!

With my nephew on my mind and in my heart, I put my mouth over the bunny's nose and mouth and blew as if I were blowing out a match. Did it again. At least he *seemed* clean. Smelled kind of nice, actually.

Gah! My mouth was on a rabbit! A rabbit who pooped where he ate!

Another poof of breath, then, guessing where his heart was, I pressed. Oh, the ribs were so tiny!

Wait. Google was made for this exact moment. I stood up, started toward my computer, then grabbed Zeus in case Admiral was feeling frisky.

Typed in *Can you give CPR to a rabbit.* A lot of hits— great! A video, thank God.

Nope. It was some dad pretending to resuscitate his daughter's stuffed animal. Not funny, Google.

Okay, here was something. Actual instructions. *Lay rabbit gently on his back.* Done, though maybe I'd been clutching him a tad too hard. Then again, maybe that was good.

Say his name and see if he responds. "Zeus! Zeus, wake up!" Admiral barked. "Did you hear that, Zeus? Speak to us!" Shit. Now was not the time for giggles.

Is his chest rising and falling? Maybe? It was hard to tell. I looked more closely. Crap. It wasn't, not that I could see through all that fluffy fur, anyway. *Can you hear or feel his breathing?* I put my cheek close to his little tiny nose. Admiral joined me, panting his doggy breath. "Quiet, boy. Go away. Not you, Zeus. You stay here, and don't go into the light!"

Check his airway to see if it is obstructed. Okay. The rabbit's mouth was about the size of the head of a nail. I couldn't see anything except rather adorable teeth.

Start CPR immediately. NOTE: Attempting CPR on a conscious rabbit may cause him to become frantic and combative. Be sure your rabbit is up to date on his rabies shots.

"Great," I muttered. I had no idea what Zeus's status with rabies was. Maybe, in fact, he died from rabies. Wouldn't I have noticed, though? Should I risk it?

I should, for Mason's sake. Plus, I could get shots if the bunny was infected.

The idiotic things you do for love.

Tilt your rabbit's head back. Place a tissue over his mouth and nose to prevent disease transmission. "Sure, now you tell me," I muttered.

I followed the rest of the instructions, trying to see if Zeus's chest rose or fell, trying to get a pulse. Snorts of horrified laughter kept bursting out of me, making Admiral wag his tail.

This wasn't working. Zeus, though supposedly immortal, seemed to be quite dead.

My front door opened, and I leaped up, bunny in one hand, and put my arms behind my back.

"Hey," Marley said. "What's going on?"

"Thank God it's you. I thought you were Mason. I just killed his rabbit." I held out my hands, poor little Zeus looking so tragically adorable.

"No!" Marley said. "How will he do his magic trick?" Then, the traitor, she started to laugh. "Maybe the dead rabbit will be funnier than a live one?"

"I just gave him CPR. I breathed into his tiny snout."

She bent over, wheezing. "Stop, or I'll wet myself."

"Shut up. It's true. I may have rabies." Oh, we were damned. Both of us were laughing so hard we were staggering. I put the poor little corpse down on the coffee table, then snatched it back up when Admiral went for it. I moved the bunny to his cage on the mantel.

"I need to get another tiny black rabbit right now," I said. "Mason has cross-country until four thirty, and he doesn't want Hunter to see the rabbit before the show, so he's coming over at six thirty and then plans to walk over to the high school." With a dead rabbit, unless I could find a replacement. "You're still coming, right?"

"I wouldn't miss it for the world. Especially now."

"Can you cover for me if Mason comes by? Just say the bunny's sleeping, or you let it out and it's hiding or . . . uh, God, I don't know."

She glanced at her watch. "Sure. Just be back by four thirty when I have to feed the hungry. Don't worry. I'll cover."

"Do you have any Catholic saints I can pray to?" I asked, grabbing my bag and keys.

"Sure do. St. Francis for animals, St. Jude for lost causes." She snorted again.

I left, muttering prayers that the black rabbit population had been especially fertile last spring.

CHAPTER 28

Marley

Hold hands with a cute guy in public.
(For crying out loud. It's not like I'm asking for a Nobel Peace Prize.)

Georgia was taking her damn time finding a rabbit. Four pet stores had failed her, according to her increasingly frantic texts. And as much as I wanted to stay, I had to get moving. In twenty minutes, my twice-baked potatoes would be finished, and I'd have to go downstairs and get ready for the evening swing.

I glanced at the mantel. Poor little bunny. Not that I particularly liked rabbits—there was something furtive and creepy about them, those little claws, those wide-set eyes.

I couldn't stop snorting with laughter. The image of Georgia—Georgia Sloane, Princeton and Yale graduate!—doing bunny CPR . . . well, here I went again. "Sorry, bunny. No respect for the dead here."

Which of course made me think of Frankie. She would probably disapprove of me, laughing over an innocent like that. Then again, maybe she'd be laughing, too. I'd never get to find out what kind of person my twin would've been.

I lay down on the super-comfy microfiber couch and put a throw pillow under my head. Admiral came over and wagged. "Aren't you a beautiful boy," I said. He dipped his head in modest agreement. I did love dogs. Maybe I'd get one, too.

Rabbits, though . . . ick. They were basically rats with cuter ears. I shuddered. I wouldn't have tried to bring one back from the dead, no sirree.

Ad put his head on my chest, and I fondled his silky ears.

It had been a really nice week. Mom and I visited a medium who didn't seem like a quack and said the usual nice things about Frankie, but in a more sincere way. I'd called Eva and had more than a thirty-second conversation with her. Dante and Louis invited me and only me over and told me not to bring a thing, which made me feel pampered and special. Georgia and I were finalizing options with Emerson's estate and adding a few lesser-known charities. Georgia had legal hoops to jump through before we could evict Ruth, the thought of which filled me with pleasure every time it crossed my mind.

And I'd slept with Will again. After the first time, I Googled the date and the horrible words *mass shooting* and found an article. It was hard to read—three people killed, two injured, the shooter taking his own life. Small wonder Will was a little withdrawn.

But just last night, he'd texted me and asked if I would bump his usual five fifteen delivery to the last on my list and stay to eat with him. So I did, and we ate seared trout with a light cream and dill sauce over a hash made of potatoes, Brussels sprouts and carrots. Which we ate *after* sex, thank you very much, because Will had looked at me a second, his expression its usual blank self, then taken my face in his hands and kissed me.

Kissed me very well.

So . . . two nights of sex, two meals at his house. I was thinking it was time for a date. And what could be nicer than a high school talent show? Quite a lot, I realized, but still.

I picked up my phone and called him. "Hey," I said when he answered. "Would you like to go out tonight?"

"No."

"Great! There's a high school thing—wait. What?"

"No, thank you," he said.

"Are you busy?" I asked. I mean, he never was that I knew of. Five nights a week, he got his dinners from yours truly. And yes, I'd driven past his house once or twice back when I was trying to decide if he was a serial killer. He always seemed to be home. I wasn't even sure he had a car.

"No, I'm not busy. I'll be home. You can come over if you want."

Wasn't *that* the limpest invitation ever? "I have plans," I said, trying to sound haughty and frosty and terribly important.

"Okay. See you soon."

"I—yeah. Fine. Bye."

He was right. I'd be delivering his food within the hour.

Admiral sighed, putting his head on my stomach so I could resume stroking his ears. Pretty soon, I was going to have to go downstairs and flash sauté the veggies, put stuff into containers, the usual. I also had a menu to write for a potential catering job—a private party for a posh couple Jenny and Leo knew, who wanted all organic, fresh, locally sourced produce and a lamb that had skipped to its death wearing a crown of dandelions.

I didn't love those gigs, but if I earned enough in the next year, I was pretty sure I could afford to open a storefront downtown, expand my business with drop-ins and hire a delivery person. Eventually, I wanted my home to be just a home, not a business.

Preferably a home with a family in it.

And although I'd only slept with him twice, of *course* I'd already been wondering if Will was husband material. Come on. I was an Italian Catholic in my thirties. I'd already named our first three kids.

Will had hugged me so . . . so perfectly when I cried the other night. There had to be more there than the guy who seemed so empty. Then again, we women loved doing that, didn't we? Filling in the blanks with unicorns and rainbows, getting crushed when unicorns turned out to be imaginary (which they totally weren't, of course).

Okay. Back to the present. Where was Georgia? She hadn't answered my last text requesting an ETA.

I had to go. Looked like I'd have to take the dead rabbit with me and stash him at my place, because what if Mason's practice let out early? He had a key to Georgia's, and he couldn't just walk in and see his beloved fluffball dead. I lugged the cage down into my apartment and put it in the living room as far from the kitchen as possible, scrubbed up in the bathroom just in case any creepy vermin germs had gotten on me, braided my disobedient hair and started putting the final touches on my deliveries.

Food was so beautiful. The bright green of the pesto, the smell of basil and garlic, the sensual gleam of juicy meat . . . yeah, yeah, make fun of me. I loved feeding people, and I loved eating.

Just then, my e-mail chimed. It was from someone named Jonathan Kent.

Dear Ms. DeFelice:

Allow me to introduce myself. I'm the publisher of *Hudson Lifestyle* magazine. We've heard many good things about Salt & Pepper, enjoyed the information and pictures on your website, and wondered if you

would be interested in doing an interview and photo
shoot with us in the near future. I am envisioning this
as a cover story.

For more information, please feel free to contact me
during business hours. Thank you for your time.

Jonathan Kent
Publisher, *Hudson Lifestyle*

"Oh, my God! Holy crap!" Little squeaks of joy were
coming from my mouth. A cover story! About Salt & Pepper! And me! A photo shoot! A frickin' cover story in a
glossy magazine! My business would boom!

I typed back an enthusiastic note to Jonathan Kent, who
sounded like a very elderly, very proper Englishman, de-
leted a few exclamation points, left a few in, hit send and
within seconds got a satisfying reply.

Wonderful. My administrative assistant will be in touch
on Monday. Best wishes for a pleasant weekend.

I danced around a little more, wiped the happy tears
from my eyes and took a moment to look out the window at
the chrysanthemums, dahlias and zinnias, still in brilliant
bloom. I would be in a photo shoot, a real one this time, and
Mr. Jonathan Kent or his minions had already seen my
photo. And they'd liked what they saw. So doing my own
photo shoot was leading to this real one.

"Thanks, Emerson," I said. "I wish you were here."

Then, practically floating with joy, I got ready for my
deliveries, which went smoothly. It was only when I pulled
up in front of Will's house that I remembered I was irritated
with him. I went into his house as usual, walked past him

without a word (noting that he smelled like Ivory soap, which was a favorite of mine), put his dinner on the counter and folded my arms. Glared. I wanted a quick apology so I could tell him my happy news, get a kiss and be on my way.

"Thank you," he said. "Let me get your check."

Back to his serial killer android self.

"Will. Why are you blowing me off tonight? Come to the talent show with me."

"No, thank you."

"Why?"

"I can't make it."

"Come on. It'll be fun."

He cut me a cynical look.

I tried again. "Okay, how's this? Maybe it won't be fun, but my best friend's nephew, who as you might recall, is like my own nephew in my heart, is performing *magic* in front of his classmates, and he's going to need people in the audience who'll clap."

"I'm sorry. I can't."

I threw up my hands. "Do you have a reason for this, or are you just being a dick?"

"The former."

"A dick, then."

"No. I have a reason, and I don't want to go into it right now. Here's your check. Thank you. Good-bye."

"Fine. You're not getting laid tonight. Probably not to-morrow, either."

"Crowds make me . . . uncomfortable." He looked at me, then past me, out to his miraculous, beautiful garden, then back at me. "But I hope your friend does well."

It was clear he'd just told me something that hadn't come easily. "How uncomfortable?" I asked.

"Very."

"Did you always feel like that?"

"No."

Ah.

"Will, did you ever see a therapist after you lost your friends?" I asked, my tone a lot more gentle.

He sighed. Nodded once. Folded his arms in front of him, classic body language for *Can we please not talk?*

And I did have to get going.

I kissed him on the cheek. "Okay. You get a pass this time. I'll see you soon."

"Thank you." He paused. "If you wanted to come over later tonight or tomorrow, that would be . . . nice. You could bring your nephew. Your friend's nephew, I mean. You said he likes computers. I know a lot about them."

I smiled. "Thank you for the offer. I'll call you tomorrow."

I left in a significantly better mood. Will had let me see something about him. Not very much—uncomfortable in crowds—but something. That was a step in the right direction.

I finished my rounds, which were unfortunately heavy, it being Friday. When I got home, I took a shower, breathing in the smell of my latest shower gel, on sale at Marshalls for only $4.99, and got dressed. Too bad Will wasn't coming, because by the time I was dressed and ready to go, I looked kind of gorgeous, thank you very much.

All of a sudden, I jumped. Someone was pounding on my door. Will? Had he had a change of heart?

"Marley! Open up!" It was Georgia. She was wild-eyed, and I yanked open the door. She was holding a live rabbit in both hands. "What did you do? I just got a text from Mason."

"I don't know," I answered. "What did I do?"

"He has the rabbit!" Georgia screeched.

I looked at her hands. "What rabbit?"

"The *dead* rabbit! He thinks it's asleep!"

"Oh, shit." I glanced over to the cage at the far end of the living room—yep, it was empty. Grabbing my phone, I saw that I'd missed two texts. Damn that habit I had of accidentally silencing my phone.

The first one was from Georgia.

Found another rabbit, thank God! Be home asap.

The second one, just two minutes later, was from Mason. I read it aloud. "'Marley, thanks for keeping Zeus. You sure tired him out. He's zonked. See you later I hope!'"

I had left my door unlocked. I usually did. My trusting nature and all that.

Georgia and I looked at each other, agape in horror. "My nephew cannot pull a dead rabbit out of a hat in front of six hundred of his peers," she said.

"No. No. That would be bad. Um . . . what do we do?"

She bit her nail. "We . . . we find him and take the dead rabbit and switch it with this one."

"Can't we just call him and tell him that Zeus One is dead?" I asked.

"No! He loves Zeus One!"

"He's fourteen, Georgia. Rainbow Bridge and all that? No?"

She swallowed. "He's sensitive. If we tell him, he might . . . I don't know. Cry during the act or something. Or not go on, and he actually gets school credit for this. If he doesn't go on, Hunter will lecture him, and it will be bad enough, because Hunter thinks he's doing stand-up comedy. If he knew about the magic ahead of time, he'd torture Mason, and now—"

"Okay, stop talking. We'll switch rabbits. How do we do that?"

"I don't *know*! The show starts in half an hour."

"Let's go, then. I'll drive. Don't make me hold the rabbit. They creep me out."

We ran to my car, which still smelled like pesto and meat and reminded me that I was starving. Flew over to the high school. The parking lot was mobbed, and well-dressed parents and children streamed inside. "Text him, text him, text him," I chanted as we pulled into a space, cutting off a sleek Mercedes.

"I can't! I'm holding the bunny."

"Okay, fine. I will." I dictated a text into my phone. "Dear Mason, hi, honey, good luck, can we see you beforehand? So excited! Really want to see you before you go on, okay?"

We got into the auditorium, which was crowded with people. "Hide the rabbit," I whispered.

"Right." She looked down. "I don't have my purse."

"Pocket?"

She shook her head, eyes wide.

"Fine," I ground out. "Put it in mine." My jacket had wide, deep pockets. If the rabbit peed or pooped in there, I would have to kill myself. I cringed a little as she transferred the wee beastie and it settled against me, one of its back feet thumping against my hip. "Ew. Make this happen fast."

"Hello, neighbors!" It was Leo and Jenny, who wore a black turtleneck that stopped about an inch above the waistband of her very expensive-looking jeans. Skinny women. They had no idea. The rabbit thumped again, and I twitched.

"Hey, guys," Jenny said. "What are you doing here?"

Georgia didn't answer.

"Her nephew is performing tonight," I said. "And you?"

"I have a student or four playing," Leo said. "Jenny insisted on coming because she adores me."

"That's mostly true," she agreed. "Georgia, what's your nephew doing?"

"Magic," Georgia said.

Leo winced, then fixed his face.

"It's okay," I said. "We all feel that way."

"Well. See you guys in there," Jenny said. "Good luck to your nephew." Hand in hand (sigh), they made their way through the crowd into the auditorium. Georgia stood there, jabbing her phone.

"Hey," I hissed. "I have a live rabbit in my pocket that's maybe about to chew through the fabric of my coat and start eating my liver. Can we transfer the goods, please?"

"I'm trying!" Georgia whispered back. "He's not answering his phone."

"Georgia. Marley. How are you both tonight?"

Oh, God. If there was one thing to guarantee Georgia freezing up, it was the molten, dark chocolate voice of Rafael Santiago.

My bestie made a squeaking sound, like a mouse dying.

"Mason asked me to come," Rafe said. "I hope you do not mind." He only had eyes for Georgia, and man, if some guy looked at me the way he looked at her, we would be doing it on the floor, crowds or no crowds, children or no children, rabbit or no rabbit.

"Uncle Rafe!" came a voice, and it was Mason's. Thank *God*. "I'm so happy you made it! Hey, Marley! Hi, G!"

"Son." Crap. Mason's tight-ass father who always pretended not to know me walked up to what was now turning into our pretty big group.

Mason's face fell a notch. "Hey, Dad."

"Hello, Hunter," Rafe said.

Hunter ignored him, instead focusing on Mason. "What are you wearing? Is that a *cape*? You're not wearing that onstage, are you?"

"Magicians generally wear capes," Georgia said.

I jerked as the rabbit thumped again. Did that mean it was scared? Sick? Murderous? Did death await me with nasty, big, pointy teeth?

"You said you were doing stand-up," Hunter said.

"Well, it's a little of both," he said. His eyes darted to Georgia's.

"I'm really excited," she said. "I got a preview, and he's fantastic." She stepped on my foot and tilted her head at Mason's hand.

Mason did not have the hat. He was holding a wand, but no hat.

"Where's your hat?" I asked, ever subtle.

"Backstage."

"I have to go to the bathroom!" I blurted. "Good luck, honey. I mean, break a leg!"

I dodged and twisted through the crowd, going into the auditorium, up the stairs onto the stage. The rabbit was freaking out in my pocket. Soon, I would start screaming.

"Hi!" I said to a pretty girl. "Do you know where Mason Sloane's stuff is?"

"Um, no?" she said.

"The magician?"

"Oh, him." She rolled her eyes. "Over there, maybe?" She pointed, and yes! There was a top hat.

Damn it. The lights were going down. I ran to the hat, jerked out the false bottom and pushed Zeus the Second in, my skin crawling in a massive wave of heebie-jeebies as his little claws scritched my palm, and braced myself to grab Dead Zeus.

"Marley?"

Mason again! I closed the false bottom of the hat and straightened up. "Honey! Just . . . I got lost!"

The dead rabbit was still in the hat. Did rabbits cannibalize each other? Would Zeus Two die of terror, being in a dark place with a corpse?

"Go sit down," Mason said. "They're in the ninth row." He picked up the hat.

"Mason—" I began.

"You can't be back here," said an adult. "Please find your seat."

"See you after," Mason said. His eyes were worried as he looked around at all the other kids, the girls dressed in dance gear or gorgeous dresses, the guys dressed not in capes.

"Good luck, honey," I said. What else could I do? I prayed, that's what. St. Francis, St. Jude, St. Nick, St. Anyone. "Help him out, Frankie," I whispered as I made my way to the ninth row.

Georgia jumped up. "Did you do it?"

"Sort of," I whispered.

"What does that mean?"

"The alive one is in there. But the dead one is, too."

"Oh, my God." She clasped her head with both hands.

"Please, take my seat," Rafael said. This put me in between Georgia and Hunter, with Rafe on Georgia's other side. "I don't think my former brother-in-law is pleased to see me," he added in a lower voice. "You are doing us both a favor."

Great. So now it went Rafael, Georgia, me and Hunter. Why did I have to sit next to the evil brother? Hadn't I already had a vermin in my pocket this night? Did I have to sit next to one, too?

"Is there any way we can fix this?" Georgia whispered.

Rafe looked at us, tilting his head. "Is there a problem, ladies?" he asked.

"No!" I said merrily. "We're great." To Georgia, I whispered, "I'm sorry. I did my best. He came up right when I was—"

"Can you be quiet already?" Hunter said. He didn't make eye contact, just stared at the stage, jaw locked, arms folded tight.

"Hello, Hunter, nice to see you again," I lied.

"Do we know each other?"

"Marley DeFelice. I've been your sister's best friend for almost twenty years, and I'm a big fan of your son." I forced a smile.

"No wonder he has no friends, hanging around middle-aged women all the time."

"Shut up, Hunter," Georgia said, her voice tight.

"Just stating a fact," he said.

"And he does have friends," Georgia said. Rafe touched her shoulder, and she jumped.

Maybe he has no friends because his father's an asshole, I thought. Another possibility. "He's a wonderful kid," I said.

Hunter scanned me, snorted and looked away. I knew that look. *You're fat. You don't matter.*

"Oh, I made it! Thank goodness!" Georgia's mother squeezed into our row. "Hunter, let me sit next to you, darling."

"Yes, by all means, Mrs. Sloane," I said. We all stood up and shuffled to let her past so she could sit on the other side of her son.

I caught a glimpse of some familiar faces a few rows behind us. Georgia's father and stepmother and the two little girls. Because this night was cursed, we were stuck sitting with Hunter and Big Kitty, instead of the nice branch of the family.

I touched Georgia's hand, nodding at her dad. Her face lit up, and she gave a small wave.

Their family was complicated, that was for sure.

For the next forty-five minutes, I sat sweating with nerves. Georgia, too, was dying a slow death, shifting her legs, her arms, rubbing her forehead, biting her nails. Not only had she somehow killed a rabbit today, she was sitting next to her ex-husband. And she might have rabies.

I wished Will was here. I hoped he wasn't too lonely. I hoped he was sitting in his garden, drinking wine and reading a good book, not hunched in front of his computer, working.

The kids were way too talented. Of course, Cambry-on-Hudson was the type of place where the children took violin lessons in the womb, which was painful for the mother but paid off at these sort of events. There were gymnasts and singers and dancers, three violinists (see?), a cellist, Leo's four piano students, and a girl who did the soliloquy from Hamlet.

And then, finally . . .

"Okay, folks," said the principal, who was acting as master of ceremonies, "we're changing it up a little. Mason the Magnificent, performing some magic tricks for your pleasure!"

"Jesus," Hunter muttered. "A magic act."

I wanted to kick him.

Georgia leaned forward. "Shut up and be supportive," she hissed.

"Stop fighting, children." Big Kitty sighed. I could smell the alcohol fumes on her breath and hoped she hadn't driven herself.

Mason came onstage, his shoulders hunched. "Hi, everyone," he said, and his poor little voice was shaking. "Um . . . you guys know Penn and Teller, right? They're like a married couple? Because only one of them gets to talk."

I bit my lip. The poor child! "Haha! Hahaha!" I fake-laughed. "Good one. Totally like my parents." No one else in our group spoke.

"What do you call a magician on a plane?" Mason said. "A flying sorcerer!"

Crickets.

"Hey there, Kendra." Mason forged ahead. "Looks like

you survived Avada Kedavra, because you're drop-dead gorgeous!"

Nothing. A few groans.

"Ha!" I said. "Harry Potter! Good one!"

I looked over at Georgia. Tears were welling in her eyes. Before I could reach over to squeeze her hand, Rafe put his arm around the back of her seat. Murmured something to her. She nodded.

"Can I have a lovely assistant from the audience?" Mason asked. The sweat glistened on his face, which was blotchy with terror. How he wasn't peeing himself or running offstage was beyond me. "Adele! How about you?" His voice shook. "Come on up here and have some fun."

"That's the girl he likes," Georgia whispered.

"He is very brave," Rafe murmured.

The audience waited, shifting irritably as, after too long a pause, a very pretty girl—one of the violinists—came up onstage.

"Whoa, what's this? I think you need to wash your ears better, Adele, because look what I found!" Mason pulled a quarter from behind her ear, then dropped it on the stage, where it rolled away.

This time, there were a few chuckles. Not the nice kind.

It was agonizing. Whenever I saw Mason, he was so damn sweet and funny, smart and geeky in the best possible way. Here, when it mattered so much, all of that seemed gone.

"Adele," he said, his voice cracking, "can you look in my hat and see that there's nothing there, right?"

The girl looked and smiled gamely. "It's empty," she said.

"Right! It totally is." He tipped it upside down to demonstrate. Put his hand inside and waved it around, showing the audience.

"Okay, Adele, if you don't mind, uh, holding my wand?"

"Dude!" a male voice shouted. "She's way outta your league!"

Mason turned scarlet. "Oh, I didn't mean . . . I mean, not that way, but . . . Can you hold the hat, then?"

"Next!" someone shouted.

"Hang on one second," Mason pleaded. "This is the best part."

"Oh, God," Georgia whispered.

Adele took the hat.

"Abracadabra!" Mason said, reached in the hat—*Please, Frankie*—and pulled out a clump of black fur. I braced myself.

The clump was moving.

Fast.

In fact, the clump was . . . uh . . . well, there were two rabbits, all right, and they were both quite alive.

Oh, yes. Alive and mating.

Mason, mouth open, held the rabbits up. There was a stunned silence . . . then a roar of laughter.

The bunnies were humping as fast as bunnies do, and somehow, the top one was gripping the bottom one, who was just sort of dangling there (best not to think about the physics involved).

I looked over at Georgia. Her eyes were wide, her mouth open.

"You're really good at CPR," I said to my friend, and she looked at me, then started laughing and crying both.

Onstage, Mason put the rabbits down. The top Zeus jumped off and hopped away.

"You can't just leave her like that," Mason said, getting another belly laugh from the audience. Then, sure enough, Top Zeus came hopping back and mounted Bottom Zeus for another round.

The audience went crazy. People were wiping tears from their eyes, rocking back and forth. And yeah, mating rabbits is a pretty funny sight, especially when they look like children's stuffed animals.

When Top Zeus hopped off again, Mason said, "Adele, help me out, okay? We've had enough rabbit porn tonight."

They picked up the rabbits, Adele smiling warmly at Mason. The lad had the grace to simply lean into the microphone and say, "Thanks, everyone."

He got a standing ovation.

CHAPTER 29

Georgia

*Get closure with your ex after your marriage
breaks up because you were fat.
(Why am I making this so hard?
Can't I just tuck in a shirt and call it a day?)*

The night belonged to Mason.

When the crowd stood up, cheering, I had to choke back tears of joy.

Just six months ago, my beautiful nephew had overdosed on Tylenol. Now he was being clapped on the back by fellow students, parents reaching out to pat his shoulder and tell him how funny he was.

Dad and Cherish and the girls came over, ignoring the death stare from Hunter, the hiss from Big Kitty. Dad wiped his eyes, still laughing. "Fantastic," he managed.

"It was so cute how those bunnies were giving each other piggyback rides," Paris said innocently.

Rafe looked at me, smiling, and my heart swelled. He'd come here for Mason, and . . . well, that was everything.

The man of the hour finally made it to us, the bunnies alive and well in his hat, sexy time over for the night, apparently. He hugged me. "I was so scared," he whispered.

"You were incredible," I said, sneaking in a kiss to his cheek.

He went on to shake Rafe's hand, hug Marley, Dad, Cherish, my mom . . . even Hunter clapped him briskly on the back and said, "I had my worries. Good thing those rabbits were fucking."

I closed my eyes. That was my brother—swearing in front of our half sisters (whom he never acknowledged). God forbid he just say, *Great job, son.*

"I should be on my way," Rafe said to me.

"Oh," I said. "Rafe . . . you were so good to come. Thank you."

"I love Mason," he said simply, and the stone in my stomach grew white-hot.

"Can we talk?" I blurted. "Do you have a little time?"

He glanced down. "Not at the moment, I'm afraid."

My heart sank. "Right. I understand. It's Friday, I'm sure your restaurant is mobbed, and—" And he had a girl-friend who might not want him talking to his ex-wife. Rafe himself might not want to talk to his ex-wife.

"Tomorrow?" he said. "Perhaps you could come to the city?"

I let out a breath I didn't know I was holding. "I could. Thank you."

"Very well. Meet me in front of Pamplona at four o'clock."

"Okay. Thank you."

Tomorrow, that was good. That way I'd have time to think of something to say.

. . . .

I couldn't think of anything to say.

Marley and I were sitting in her living room Saturday afternoon, and I had a notepad and my laptop. I had Googled *how to get closure with your ex* and come up with 192,731 articles about why closure was impossible.

"So I'm guessing this falls under 'tell off the people who judged us when we were fat,'" she said. She had the list memorized.

"Well . . . sort of? Have you done that, by the way?"

"No," she admitted. "I have to. Camden, I guess. No one else leaps to mind. I told Will off, but now I'm not sure he needed it." At my questioning look, she said, "I thought he was fat-prejudiced, and I basically reamed him another orifice. But he's not. It's weird. He told me I was fat."

"What?" I sputtered.

"And I am."

"He can't just say that, though! It's so rude! 'Fat' is a four-letter word."

"He's kind of . . . odd. His point was that I am, which is true, even if he shouldn't have said it so bluntly. But also that it didn't matter to him at all. I mean, he definitely finds me attractive, since we're sleeping together, right? He told me I was luscious the other night."

"Luscious. I like that."

She smiled. "Yeah, I'm definitely hoping he's different. And yet we haven't gone out together in public, so maybe he's not." She paused. "Did Rafe have a problem with your weight?"

"I was pretty skinny when we were together," I said. "So no." That wasn't fair. "I was the one who had a problem with it," I admitted. "He didn't understand my food . . . issues. He thought if he found me attractive, it should out-weigh everything else. Forgive the pun."

"He's so evil." She smiled, and I did, too, a little.

"Hardly. Just kind of . . . obtuse? I only knew him a year before we got married. He couldn't undo the twenty-six years that happened before he met me."

"My mother still fights with my aunt over who was my grandfather's favorite. They say things like, 'Well, you think you're better because you're the oldest,' or, 'Don't think I've forgotten that you made eyes at Danny Kazinski when you knew I liked him.'" She fondled Admiral's silky ears, earning a doggy groan of happiness. "Maybe we never get over what happened when we were little."

"Are you talking about Frankie?"

She shrugged. "I was a twin, and now I'm not a twin anymore. I carry that with me every day. Maybe that's why I'm overweight. I was eating for two."

There was a scary honesty to what she had just said . . . Marley had told me how tiny Frankie had been, and I'd seen the pictures. Maybe Marley's weight issues all stemmed from that—her little girl self had eaten what the smaller twin could not. Though it went against my WASPy nature, I got up and hugged her. "I'm sorry," I said.

She wiped her eyes, the eternal weeper. "Well. Like I said, the stuff that happened back then is tough to shake. So what will you say to Rafe?"

I sat back down. "I don't know. I shouldn't have asked him to talk. I just wanted to . . . I don't know. Explain. Apologize."

"The whole marriage implosion wasn't just your fault, Georgia. It takes two to tango."

"Not really. He was . . ." My throat tightened. "He was wonderful. Is wonderful. He came to that talent show for Mason."

Marley pulled a face. "Well, he's not perfect. He divorced you, after all. Plus, he's very ugly, and that accent." She mock-shuddered. "Couldn't cook for shit, either."

"You're very kind." I paused and took a sip of coffee, bracing as it hit the sore spot in my gut. "So. Any clue what I should say tonight?"

"I still love you, you're wonderful, I'm sorry?" she suggested.

My heart rolled at the thought. "Yeah. I can't. It wouldn't be fair. It's been five years, and he has someone else. Heather."

"Well, you have someone else, too. The Kennedy who doesn't remember you."

I closed my eyes. Evan. Ironically, I barely remembered *him*, now that we were sort of dating. It was a mutually forgetful relationship. He was in Los Angeles for a few days (weeks?), doing whatever it was he did. I was still playing a game of mental chicken, waiting to see which of us broke first—either he'd remember me, or I'd admit I remembered him. Otherwise, there wasn't a lot there.

Rafe, on the other hand . . . The thought of being alone with him made adrenaline flow through my joints, making my legs wobbly and weak. I hadn't been able to eat a thing today, and I sure hadn't slept last night.

But hey. I looked great. The doctor even said so.

I flopped back against the couch. "I wish we were lesbians. We're perfect together. It would be so much easier than dealing with men."

Marley laughed and leaned forward for a fist bump. "I'm in. Look how well my mother took Dante being gay. She already loves you, besides." She sat back. "Don't worry about what to say to Rafe. The words will come."

Turned out, they wouldn't. At least, not when I needed them to.

CHAPTER 30

Georgia

Tuck in a shirt.
(God. This is so shallow, but I get it. I do.)

At three thirty, I got to Pamplona, which Google had informed me was on Leonard Street in Tribeca. My eyes welled up at the sight of it—everything he'd once talked about wanting was here.

The restaurant was on the ground floor of a beautiful sandstone building from the turn of the twentieth century, ornate without being ridiculous. Through the windows, I could see the walls were painted a deep blue, bright paintings on the walls.

Because I didn't want him to know I was early, I walked down Church Street, then up Greenwich. I was cold, probably from nerves. It was a cloudy October day, and the wind seemed to blow right into my bones as it stripped yellow leaves from the trees. Then again, I'd worn one of the outfits my mom had bought me yesterday—God, was it just yesterday? Seemed like eons ago. I'd put on makeup, skinny jeans, and yes, I'd tucked in my shirt, which was white silk. I wore the black suede booties and a strand of my grandmother's pearls. I looked . . . good.

I felt horrible.

My heart was racing. My brain kept skittering away from the looming confrontation. I wasn't even sure why I was here.

That last fight we had . . . the one that finally ended our brief, unhappy marriage . . . ugly things had been said. By me. Just remembering them now, those unkind, untrue things that were branded on my heart, made me close my eyes in a dizzy wave of self-loathing.

You're so smug. You think you're perfect. I have no space to breathe. You call it love, but you're suffocating me . . . And the last, the one that broke him and made him cry.

This entire marriage has been a waste of time.

Tossed off as if Rafael Santiago hadn't been the best thing that ever happened to me.

My half hour was up. I turned back onto Leonard Street and saw him standing in front of the restaurant, dressed in his chef uniform, and my heart tried to break through my ribs.

"Hello, Georgia," he said. He wasn't smiling today.

"Thank you for meeting me."

"Of course." He gave an old-world nod. "I thought it would be more private if we were not in my place of business. There is a quiet café just down the block here." He gestured for me to go first.

We went into a little bar—I'd forgotten that Rafe called all bars cafés—and sat down. It was mostly empty.

I was out of breath, and now a cold sweat had broken out on my forehead. My pulse had to be in the danger zone.

"Hi, guys. Oh, Rafael! It's you! Hi!" The server, a middle-aged woman with gray hair, bent down to give him a kiss on each cheek.

"Georgia, this is Elizabeth, my friend. Elizabeth, this is my former wife, Georgia Sloane."

Her expression flickered with disapproval. "What would you like, Rafe?" The snub was noted.

"An espresso for me. Georgia? Would you like a glass of wine, perhaps?"

"Sure. A Malbec, please?"

"Coming up."

She went to the bar, and I could feel her eyes on me.

"Your restaurant is beautiful, Rafe," I said. "I caught a glimpse through the windows."

"Please come for dinner sometime."

"I . . . I will." We both knew I wouldn't. "Cherish loved it."

Elizabeth brought the drinks, patted Rafe on the shoulder and went back to the bar.

"So about what would you like to speak, Georgia?" Rafe asked. There was that perfect grammar. Never underestimate its power.

I'm sorry. I'm sorry. I'm sorry.

The words were echoing in the beating of my heart. *Just say it, stupid,* a distant part of my brain urged, but my vision was getting kind of fuzzy and, and . . .

There was something wrong with me. The clammy sweat was spreading, and the music was too loud and echoing. I could see Rafe's mouth moving, his eyebrows coming together, those big brown eyes so beautiful. That was all I could see, just his face, nothing else, and I seemed to be floating and—

"I'm sorry," I said, and felt myself falling, slowly, so slowly, until the floor was under my cheek.

. . . .

Note: The emergency rooms of big-city hospitals are not romantic places.

At the moment, I was lying on a gurney in the hallway, having been delivered here by two overly cheerful FDNY paramedics. Where Rafe was, I didn't know. They didn't let him ride in the ambulance with me. I think. That part was fuzzy.

Now sitting across from me was a man with a bloody towel around his foot and what appeared to be at least several toes in a plastic cup. "You think they can reattach these?" he asked me.

"Um . . . I think so," I said. Because really, what else do you say?

"My name's Earl," he said, extending a bloody hand.

"Georgia," I said, recoiling. "I better not shake your hand. I might, um, have a cold."

Someone down the hall was yelling, over and over, "My kids aren't gonna get nothin'! Nothin'! Nothin'! My kids aren't gonna get nothin', because they're all little shits." She yelled this rhythmically, and I was considering making it into a song. At the same time, a toddler was screaming in one of the curtained-off areas, and from the sound of it, they were skinning her. An old woman sitting next to Toe-less Earl lifted up the neck of her johnny coat. "Are these mine?" she asked me, pointing at her sagging breasts.

"I'm thinking yes," I said. I should probably leave. I felt better now. Probably just needed to eat.

Then I heard footsteps and saw Rafe running toward me.

"Slow down," I said. "Don't want you to miss the sights."

He grabbed my hand in both of his. "All you all right?" he asked.

"I'm fine. Just embarrassed."

"You're not fine," he said. "You fainted, Georgia. And you look terrible."

So much for the new clothes and makeup. His hand felt so

good, though. "I should've eaten more, that's all. I skipped lunch." And breakfast, and dinner the night before. Stupid.

"Nothin'! Nothin'! My kids aren't gonna get nothin'!"

"Have you been sick?" Rafe asked.

"No. I went to the doctor yesterday."

"Well, you look awful."

"But the ambulance ride was fun."

To my surprise, his eyes filled with tears. "Do not make jokes," he said harshly.

"I'm sorry." A lump in my throat swelled. "You don't have to stay."

"And also do not be ridiculous, or I will call your mother, and *she* can sit with you."

I smiled a little at that. The truth was, I should call my dad or Cherish; they'd be here in a flash. But despite the fact that the old lady had decided to strip off the johnny coat, I couldn't bring myself to send Rafe away.

A second later, an orderly wheeled me into a curtained-off exam area. "Doc'll be right with you," he lied, sailing out.

"Please tell them to hurry," Rafe called after him. "She looks terrible."

"Stop saying that."

"It's true. Why have you lost so much weight? Your face is white as the moon. You don't look healthy, Georgia."

"I told you, I didn't eat much today. I was nervous."

"Why? To see me?"

"Yes." I looked away.

"Nothin'! Nothin'! My kids aren't gonna get nothin'!" Yep. Gonna make that into a rap song.

Rafe pulled up a chair and sat, taking my hand again. "I'm worried about you."

Damn it. My eyes flooded with tears. "I'm really sorry about this."

"Stop apologizing. You are not well. Is that why you wanted to see me? To tell me something about your health?"

"No. It was something different." I took a shaky breath, and he handed me a tissue. I wiped my eyes.

It wasn't on the list, not exactly, but it needed to be done. Now.

"I . . . I wanted to apologize."

He looked at me, an ocean of feeling in those bottomless eyes. Then he looked down.

"I didn't know how to be with you," I whispered. "You were wonderful, and I was scared and insecure and afraid, so I wrecked things."

He looked back up at me, and my heart twisted again. "Why were you afraid?"

"Because I was faking. I wasn't how I seemed. I wanted you to like me, and love me, so I . . . I tried to be somebody better."

"We all do that, sweetheart," called someone outside my curtain. Earl, I thought. "By the way, nurse, the toes in this cup? They used to be on my feet." Yes. Definitely Earl. "Think you can get a doctor to see me?"

Rafe smiled slightly. "The gentleman is right. We all do those things."

I nodded, pinching a fold of blanket. "I took it a little far."

"How so?"

That, of course, was the moment the nurse came in. "Hello!" she said. "Time to take some vitals." She strapped on the blood pressure cuff and pumped away, then released the valve. "Uh-oh. Ninety over fifty-four. That's a little low for us. Did you drink anything today?"

"Some water."

"She has lost weight and is very pale," Rafe said.

"How much weight?" the nurse asked.

I glanced at Rafe. "I don't really know." It was true. I didn't own a scale. "I went to the doctor yesterday. I'm sure I'm fine."

"Bloody stool?"

What every woman wants to be asked in front of her ex-husband. "No."

"Vomiting, diarrhea, stomach pain?"

"Stomach pain."

She tapped a few keys. "Did you have blood drawn yesterday?" she asked. "It might be in our mainframe."

"Yes."

She tapped away, then frowned. "Well, Jesus, didn't your doctor call you? Your hemoglobin is pretty low. I'm guessing you have a bleeding ulcer. The doctor will be in real soon."

Real soon apparently meant something different in a hospital, which was reassuring. If a team had raced in, I might've panicked. The minutes ticked past. I texted Marley, asked her to feed Admiral and let him out, and got an enthusiastic response back.

Hope this means what I think it means!

Sorry, pal. It definitely didn't.

"So you have been unwell for some time," Rafe said, his voice tight and angry.

"I . . . it appears so."

We didn't resume our conversation. He sat by my bed and scowled at me from time to time. Every time I tried to say something, I lost my nerve. Eventually, unable to take those hot Spanish looks anymore, I closed my eyes. Dozed off a little.

"Hello there." A resident—Dr. Argawal, according to her coat—came in. She was beautiful and not troublingly young. "Tell me what's going on."

And so I did, explaining the chronic stomach pain, loss

in appetite. Answered more horrific questions—was my stool ever bloody? Tarry? Black? Did I ever puke up anything that looked bloody? Like coffee grounds?

"Maybe you could wait in the hall?" I asked Rafe.

"Absolutely not," he answered, giving me another scowl.

"Let's take a look," Dr. Argawal said. She slid a tube up my nose, flooded my stomach with fluid (yes, it was gross) and tested it for blood. Then she numbed my throat and slid a tiny camera down the hatch.

"Thar she blows," she said. "It's not terrible, but yes, my dear, you have an ulcer. I don't think we need to transfuse you; I'm guessing you fainted because you didn't eat, silly girl, not because of blood loss, and you were really dehydrated. But that ulcer has been bleeding, and we don't mess around with that. I want you to follow up with a GI doc on Monday. And off the record, I'd recommend you ditch your current GP. This was a no-brainer."

I was given an injection of ulcer medication, told to eat bland food for the next two weeks, and handed three prescriptions.

"Just out of curiosity, have you been under a lot of stress lately?" she asked.

"Uh . . . yes. My nephew . . . had some trouble." Rafe's eyebrows drew together. "Also, a friend died."

"Who?" Rafe demanded.

"Emerson." My throat tightened.

His eyes widened. "Oh, no. Georgia, I am so sorry." He leaned forward and squeezed my hand; his eyes were worried.

"How's the nephew doing now?" Dr. Argawal asked.

"Better."

Rafe was looking at me, as ever seeing more than I wanted to show. I couldn't tell him about Mason . . . not now, not without permission.

"Good," said the doctor. "Now, you need to take better care of yourself, okay? Don't miss any meds—they work wonders. And don't skip meals. Make sure you drink enough fluids. No aspirin, Motrin or Tylenol until your GI doc clears you. And do not put off that appointment, you hear?"

I nodded, chastised, and the doctor looked at Rafe. "Check on her a couple times tonight. If there's any blood in her poop"—I winced; there truly was no dignity in the emergency room—"or if she vomits, you call 911."

"Thank you, doctor," Rafe said. "I will."

The doctor shook hands with both of us, then left.

"I'll take you to your home," Rafe said, not looking at me.

"I'll go to my father's."

"Your father has two young children who are probably asleep right now and will be all too excited to see you in the morning. You need to rest, and you need to be watched."

"I'll text Marley."

"I am staying with you." I opened my mouth to protest. "Do not bother arguing," he said. "I am staying with you."

Then he did look at me, and I felt it like a punch in the heart. My eyes filled.

"Georgia," he said, his voice low. "How could you ignore these problems and neglect yourself this way?"

I didn't have a great answer for that.

It was after midnight when we left the hospital, taking a cab up the West Side Highway. The Empire State Building was lit up in blue—the Yankees had just clinched the Pennant, according to the radio. Even this late, the city seemed to glitter with magic.

Once upon a time, I'd lived here with the man sitting beside me.

Maybe he was having those thoughts, too, because as we went over the Henry Hudson Bridge, leaving Manhattan, Rafe took my hand. But he still didn't say anything.

I directed the cabbie to my house. Rafe glared at me as I fumbled for my wallet, so I let him pay. Then, feeling shy and exhausted and nervous all at once, we went up the steps. Marley's was dark, but she'd left a note on the door saying she'd fed Admiral and let him out around nine.

Rafe had never been to my house before. I unlocked the door. "Welcome," I said. "This is my doggy, Admiral."

"Hello, Admiral," Rafe said, kneeling down to pet him.

My dog loved him. I loved him. Everyone loved him. That wasn't exactly news, but seeing Rafael Santiago's face being licked by my stately dog . . . well, it wasn't really fair, was it?

"Are you hungry?" Rafe asked, standing up.

"Starving."

"Does your stomach hurt?"

"Not at the moment."

He smiled just a little. "Show me to your kitchen, then, please."

I did, turning on lights as we went. "Have at it," I said. "I'm going to take a shower, okay?"

"Yes. Of course." He put his hands on his hips, then looked at me. "I am very glad you're not worse."

Then he hugged me, and I slid my arms around his waist and tried not to think about how I smelled like hospital and he smelled like cilantro. Just rested my head against his shoulder and closed my eyes.

"Call if you need me," he said, letting go, and I felt so empty without him.

"Come on, Ad," I said, and my dog followed me upstairs.

Twenty minutes later, I smelled like Icelandic moonflower, according to my shower gel, and felt a lot better. Toweled my hair dry and looked in the mirror.

There were dark circles under my eyes. Then again,

Rafe had seen me with a tube up my nose, so this was definitely a better look.

I got into my favorite Target pajamas—blue with little pink and yellow campers on them—and went downstairs.

"Ah, perfect timing," Rafe said. "Pasta with olive oil and Parmesan cheese, no garlic, no pepper, no salt, no spice, I'm afraid. The lady needs a bland diet, and the lady will have one."

He'd set the table for two, and so we ate dinner together for the first time since . . . well. Since a long time ago. Even this dinner was delicious, but I filled up after just a few bites.

"Your home is very welcoming and cheerful," Rafe said.

"Thanks. I really love it. I never had a place of my own."

His gaze flickered to his plate and back. "Yes."

"Where do you live now?" I asked. The lump in my throat threatened, but I mentally shoved it away.

"I live in SoHo in what was a former factory."

"Do you live with your girlfriend?"

"I do not."

The memory of her standing next to Rafe, so confident in her status as his girlfriend, flashed through my head.

"Her name is Heather?" I asked. As if it hadn't been seared on my soul that day in the park.

"Yes."

"And she . . . appreciates you?"

He didn't answer right away, then said, "Yes. I believe she does."

"What does she do for work?"

"She is a graphic designer and works in advertising. She is thirty-two years old, has one sister and grew up in California. Is there anything else you would like to know about her?"

It took me a few seconds to ask. "Do you love her?" The stone in my stomach burned.

Rafe let my question hang there, and with each second, I regretted asking it more. "I think we have talked about her enough," he finally said. His eyes were steady on mine, his gaze firm. "You, on the other hand, I would like to discuss very much. Shall we continue our conversation from the emergency room?"

"Right. That." I took a breath. "I . . . I guess I wanted to say . . ." *I never stopped loving you.* But what would that do? He'd moved on, and I didn't blame him. "I wanted to apologize for, um . . . not being a better wife. Better at being married. The truth is, I . . . I thought you were pretty perfect."

"And yet you cut me out of your heart within months of marrying me."

The words gutted me. "No, Rafe. You've always been . . . in my heart." That sounded like a cheesy song from the '90s. "I did love you." *Still do.*

"You loved me, but you did not wish to be married to me, to make love, even to talk to me. That does not feel like love, Georgia." His voice was tight.

I nodded. Told myself I would absolutely not cry because he was 100 percent right.

Rafe looked at his plate, idly twirling the pasta. "You said in the hospital you did not know how to be married. What does that mean?"

The clock over the pantry door ticked. Admiral curled up in his bed near the back door, and everything else was quiet.

"I always thought that if I told you the truth about me, you'd . . . stop."

"Stop what?"

"Stop loving me. I know that sounds very adolescent and stupid, but, Rafe, you were the first man who ever . . . the only man who ever . . ."

"Ever what, *corazón*?"

God, that name. I wished he wouldn't use it, and yet, I was so, so glad he had, even if it was just rote. Maybe he called Heather the same thing.

I swallowed hard. "You were the only man who ever looked at me that way. Ever held my hand. You were the first guy who ever kissed me, who ever called, who ever wanted anything to do with me. And I just didn't trust it. I thought if you knew . . ."

So much for the not-crying. I blotted my eyes on my napkin.

"If I ever knew what?"

"Knew . . . everything. That my own father, who loved me more than anyone else, still didn't love me enough to want custody. That my mother was embarrassed by me and my brother hated me and I had all of, I don't know, four friends in the world and only two I could really talk to. If I told you all that, I was afraid you'd see me differently, so I just . . ."

"You walled yourself off."

My stomach stone burned. Admiral, hating his mommy's tears, came over and put his head in my lap. "Yes. I'm sorry, Rafe. I loved you, and I never meant to hurt you. I just didn't know how to . . . how to *be*."

He threw down his fork, the clatter making me jump. "Did it ever occur to you that I am not a stupid man, Georgia? That perhaps I knew *exactly* who you were and loved you just the same? You are so much more than your mother's daughter and Hunter's sister. Do you think I am an idiot, that I did not know what you were hiding? I loved you with all my heart. You were my home."

Once again, his words sliced through me. My stomach pain was nothing compared to this.

He looked down at his plate. "You say you didn't mean

to hurt me, but for months, you chiseled away at our happiness, locked yourself away from me and made me wonder why you had ever wanted to be with me in the first place. How is that not deliberately hurtful?"

I pressed my lips together hard. "You're right. I was terrible. But Rafe, you just don't know what it's like, hating the body you're in. All my life, I've tried to hide my physical self, and there was nothing you could do to change that."

"I think you have a very distorted view of that physical self, Georgia. Yes, perhaps you gained some weight, but you were never . . ." He paused, maybe starting to realize how hard it was to talk about this stuff. "I always thought you were beautiful."

"I know. And believe me, I was grateful. But once a fat girl, always a fat girl. I didn't want you to know about all that . . . that . . ." I was crying again. "All that self-hatred. All that anger, disgust, all that fear that you'd see me differently if you knew. So you're right. I walled myself off, and I'm so, so sorry."

He drew in a deep breath, then another, not looking at me. "No, I am the one who is sorry. You have been through enough tonight, and I should not have raised my voice."

"Do you hate me, Rafe?" My voice shook, but I needed the answer.

He didn't answer for a minute, and my whole heart seemed to shrink and go dark. Then he did speak. "For a while, I did, yes." His voice was gentle. "You broke my heart. But my heart is healed now, so no, I do not hate you, Georgia. Of course not." He stood up. "Come. Time for you to sleep."

I went upstairs, Admiral leading the way, Rafe behind me. He'd never seen my bedroom. Never seen any of my house.

You were my home.

I got under the covers, and he put a glass of water on the table. "I will be in the next room," he said. "Call me if you need anything. I will check on you in a few hours."

"Rafe . . ."

His eyes, which could show every human emotion and then some, were so sad. "Yes?"

"When I said what I did that last night, when we fought . . . I've never said anything less true."

He closed his eyes for a second.

This entire marriage has been a waste of time.

Those were the words I'd chosen when I should've been begging him to forgive me, to understand. When I should've opened my heart to him, instead of pretending I didn't have one.

I should have said, *I love you more than I ever knew I could. You're the best person I've ever met. You are the light of my life. You're everything to me, Rafael Santiago.*

I could say it now . . . but I didn't. It was nearly five years too late, and Rafe had someone else in his life. He was only here with me because he was kind, because he couldn't say no to anyone, even the ex-wife who broke his heart.

"Thank you," he said. He dropped a kiss on my forehead, paused, and then kissed me on the lips.

Just one gentle, brief, perfect kiss, reminding me of everything I'd lost.

Before I could kiss him back, or pull him closer, or beg him to stay, he stood up, his face shadowed, and, without another word, walked to the door and turned off the light, leaving me in the dark.

. . . .

When I woke up the next morning and came downstairs in my pajamas, Rafe stood by the stove, buttering toast. The smell of coffee was thick in the air, and a frying pan of scrambled eggs sat on the stove.

"This wasn't necessary," I said, though my stomach growled. Admiral pressed against me, warm and reassuring.

"How are you feeling?" Rafe asked.

"Good. Better. Thank you for everything. For staying here, and . . . well. For everything."

"I am very sorry for kissing you. It was inappropriate for many reasons."

It always took me by surprise, how other people could just say what was on their minds so easily, so gracefully.

"I didn't mind." And then there were people like me, who gave tepid, disingenuous answers.

"It was wrong."

For him, yes. There was Heather. "Please don't worry about it, Rafe. You've been wonderful."

He gave that courtly nod they must teach in Barcelona. "At any rate, put lots of milk in the coffee to take away the acidity, *si*? I suspect you should not have any, but I also know you are addicted."

"Yes, chef."

He gave me a little smile. Then his phone chimed with a text, and he looked down.

Heather, I guessed from the way his face changed.

"I have to go, I'm afraid. You will tell Marley if you need anything, yes?"

"Yes."

For a second, we just looked at each other, and there was a world and years between us, and all the words I couldn't and shouldn't say.

He looked away first. "Take care of yourself, Georgia."

"I wish . . ." I began, then stopped.

I wished I could undo the past. I wished we could try

again. I had broken us, and in all the time since, I'd never once reached out until he'd been thrust back into my life.

"I wish you only the best, Rafe." My voice shook a little, but I willed my eyes to stay dry. "You deserve it."

"The same for you, *corazón*," he said, his voice achingly gentle and kind. "The same for you."

CHAPTER 31

Dear Other Emerson,

I see the way you look at me . . . at least, the way I think you must look at me. It's what everyone whispers, posts, says to my face. <u>Why did you DO that to yourself? How could you let yourself become so HUGE? Wasn't 250 pounds big enough? 300? 400? 450? Why didn't you stop? Why didn't you lose it while there was still a chance at being normal? Why didn't you get gastric bypass before you became so MONSTROUS? How the HELL does someone get so out of control???</u>

Well, I'll tell you.

First, get molested by your grandfather every summer from the ages of four through eight. I mentioned this, didn't I, Other Emerson? He tells you how <u>pretty</u> and <u>little</u> you are. You have those tickle fights. He likes when you sit on his lap. Then he starts coming into your bed at night. You hate what he does, but he's Grampy and you love him—sort of—and he says Mama would be upset with you if she knew. He's a grown-up. He would know about these things. Grandma died before you were born, and Grampy's important and rich—something to do with own-ing stores on the waterfront.

You eat to make yourself feel better . . . and, on some level, maybe you want to be _not_ little. Your weight makes you feel stronger. When you're nine and weigh more than a hundred pounds, he doesn't try anything. You _are_ stronger. You're not walking around on spindly little legs anymore. You have heft and presence. The world tells you you're not so pretty anymore, and it's a relief you can't articulate.

Then, your parents get divorced when you're eleven. You eat your emotions, Other Emerson, to fill the hole where your dad's love used to be. You go from chubby or (my personal favor-ite) _husky_ to fat. Because your mother is depressed, you cook for her.

Soul food. Comfort food. There's nothing food can't cure. Food in the mouth goes a long way to ease the ache in the heart.

Besides, it makes your mom happy to have you playing in the kitchen, melting butter, frying onions, adding sour cream. "My little chef," she says fondly, though you are a long way from little. You both love to eat. Of course you do! Everyone does! That's just normal. Your portion sizes, your junk food intake . . . not so normal.

You spend all your free time hanging around with your lovely, wonderful, sad, generous mother. She has clinical depres-sion, your therapist will tell you later (the same therapist who later dumps you as a client because, in her words, you refuse to help yourself). Your mother loves you so much, and you make her so happy. Everything the two of you do involves eating. You go out for ice cream. Make a fast-food run. Eat popcorn and Milk Duds at the movies. Mac & Cheese Fridays. Pizza every Sunday night.

She's fat, you're fat, it's genetic (it's not), you're "big girls," you're _cuddly_. Your pediatrician tells you about how to eat right, and you and your mother nod and promise to do better, then go out for ice cream. For a few weeks, you try to eat a salad a day before giving that up.

Puberty comes early for you fat girls. You've been growing breasts since you were seven. By eighth grade, you're spilling out of a C-cup. Your thighs balloon. Your stomach is huge. Gym class is a study in shame.

But . . . at least money is not a problem, since Molesting Grampy is now dead and Mama inherited a couple mil. So you go to fat camp for a month every summer, lose fifteen or eighteen or twenty-two or thirty pounds, come back, regain it and then some. But at fat camp, you find that the people you like the most are . . . fat! Is being fat really such a sin? These are some very fine people, Other Emerson! How dare you not see that?

Then, even though you're terrified of leaving home, of leaving your mother, even though the idea that she might commit suicide without you drenches you in clammy fear, you go to college. Not far, but far enough that you live there. Mama pretends to be happy, but you're swamped with guilt. Which makes you eat more.

Oh, and there's food everywhere. Your freshman fifteen is actually fifty. No one seems to notice — you're fat, you're getting fatter. You do a lot of secret eating. You shower at three a.m. so no one will see you. At parties, you stand against the wall, near the door. You might have just one piece of pizza and half a beer before you go back to your single dorm room and call up Domino's, because they deliver to campus. You start going home twice a week for dinner to check on Mom . . . and to be somewhere you belong.

You move back home after college and get your first job, as a research writer for a PR firm that advises the governor. Your boss is a nice person who probably hired you to prove she doesn't discriminate against fatties. She tries so hard to pretend there are no issues, even though you need a sturdier chair, even though walking in from the parking lot means you're drenched in sweat when you get to your desk. Your boss is stick-thin, which makes you obsess about food even more.

In the meantime, your mother is inexplicably losing weight. She's so sad all the time. So what do you do? You take her out to eat. Eating is always fun, right? It's what you've always done, you and Mama. You're afraid that her melancholy is going to kill her. You try so hard, make a fine time of it, going to your old favorites—Klondike Kate's, Deer Park, Margherita's for pizza . . . and then, of course, Wendy's, KFC, Dairy Queen.

Your father visits you from California—he hasn't seen you for three years, because he has a new family—and is visibly shaken at how big you've become. He offers to pay for a gastric bypass. You tell him to fuck off (even though now you wish you'd taken him up on it). He's never seen you angry; you've always been such a <u>sweet</u> girl.

But even though you've gone from fat to obese, you keep eating. You know what? You're still pretty. You still have friends, kind of. You talk on the phone with Marley and Georgia; you even spend a weekend on the Jersey Shore with them, laughing, eating, gossiping, eating some more. Eating healthy food, even. You save the real crap for home. You have a couple friends from college, a couple of not-bad coworkers—Laura, your stick-insect boss, never mentions your weight but looks at you with kind, sad eyes. Erin, who really deserves a better boyfriend, and loves venting to you. Carlos, the superstar who's about to be poached by Delaware's senior senator, even flirts with you, though he has a girlfriend.

Then your father <u>dies</u>—a heart attack! He wasn't even fat! Yes, it can happen to skinny people, too, Other Emerson. You are swamped with grief—you loved your daddy, even if he couldn't really be bothered to see you more often. You also have to live with the fact that the last time you saw him, ugly things were said. That he was horrified by your appearance.

That he wanted you surgically altered. That you loved him, but he didn't love you enough to bring you out west for his court-granted summertime custody. He leaves you a chunk of his life insurance. At least he remembered you enough to put you in his will.

So you eat more, Other Emerson. You start calling out sick, because let's face it—you <u>are</u> sick. You eat to the point of vomiting, you have stomach pains all night, you're constipated and have gallbladder attacks and still you eat fried seafood with french fries. You're no longer "just" obese; you're morbidly obese. Such a nice phrase, isn't it? You use up all your sick time, and your boss's eyes aren't so kind anymore. Carlos has left for Washington and Erin married her loser boyfriend. (You went to the wedding, and it was hell.) She doesn't want to go out for drinks anymore, and your two college friends have moved away.

You get bigger and bigger and bigger.

And then your mom is diagnosed with pancreatic cancer—those back pains weren't muscle spasms after all, like her stupid doctor said. His advice had been to lose weight. That wouldn't cure CANCER, would it, Doc? Three months later, your mother, your favorite person on earth, the only one who truly understood you, is dead. You inherit all the rest of Grampy's money, which Mama had barely touched. Good. That evil Grampy owed you.

You quit your job. You grieve. You eat. You diet. You binge. You diet harder. You fall off the wagon. You climb back on. You <u>leap</u> off the wagon. You purge. You go on phentermine and lose a hundred pounds. You start to feel hopeful and happy. Your heart does tend to convulse and flutter, since phentermine is essentially speed. So what? You take those chances! But when you end up in the ER because of chest pain, your doctor takes you off the wonder drug.

You cry. You plead. You beg. You don't care that your father died of a heart attack—you want your drug! Your evil doctor doesn't give in. "You can do this," she says. "The drug was meant to be a boost, not a lifestyle." The stupid sow. She herself could lose a few pounds, so what the hell does she know?

On the drive home from that appointment, you stop at Chick-fil-A and order two Spicy Deluxe sandwiches (540 calories each) with extra Polynesian sauce (110 calories each x 4), waffle fries (360 calories), superfood side (broccoli, 190 calories . . . so healthy) and a vanilla shake (500 calories). It's two o'clock in the afternoon. YOU'VE ALREADY HAD LUNCH; but as you sit in the parking lot away from the other cars, stuffing your fat face full of fat-filled food, you feel calm for the first time in days. Weeks, maybe.

Food. Your old friend.

Within eight weeks, you've gained back the hundred pounds you lost. You gain some more. You diet. You purge. You take laxatives. You order online phentermine that doesn't work as well as the real stuff. You eat more. You eat less. No matter what, the weight is not coming off. A pound here or four pounds there means nothing when you can gain ten pounds in a week.

You get another job, one for which you are overqualified, but it's okay! This will help you lose weight: the schedule, the social interaction, the good eating modeled by some of the workers there. Well, a few of the workers. Has anyone noticed Americans don't eat that well?

Then you meet a guy who thinks you're beautiful. He loves nothing more than watching you eat. He feeds you. He brings you food. He loves your growing body.

You gain another forty pounds. You gain twenty more. He tells you that he loves you. It's _fine_ that you can't get around easily—a relative term, believe me—because he loves taking care of you. You gain fifty more pounds, and he still wants you. You don't mind quitting your job because, hey, you don't need the money. Your boyfriend comes over every day, bringing you food gifts—ice cream cakes and thirty dollars' worth of fast food and giant bags of chips from Costco, and everything is mm-mm-good.

Other Emerson, it took me a long time to realize that Mica was just as prejudiced as any fat-hater. That he wouldn't have dated me if I'd been a normal-sized woman. He didn't want me to lose weight. He didn't care about my physical pain so long as it made me need him more. He didn't want what was best for me.

I was his fetish.

By the time I found that out, I weighed 601 pounds. I was big enough to be on TV. I found a website that explained Mica was a "feeder," a person who got off on my size, on watching me eat, on having me dependent on him.

My nasty cousin Ruth, who had gone three years without a job, called and asked if she could "rent" a room from me. By that, she meant live for free. I said yes, if she'd "help around the house." By that, I meant do the things I could no longer do. Take the trash out. Get the mail. Do the laundry. Eventually, wash me. Help me wipe my ass.

It became a hostile dependency, but at least I felt a little in charge. Ruth cashed my checks. Oh, yes, she did. With Ruth as my paid help, I could hide some things from Mica. I could cling to my illusion that we were just an unconventional couple.

Still, I love him . . . or I did. These days, as he brings me pizza and Popeyes chicken and Big Macs, I have to wonder. I can't stay alive much longer if I keep eating this way.

I know that fact to be true. I am eating myself to death.

No. I can't think those thoughts, because they're just too dark and painful. I'm just having a bad day, Other Emerson. Don't mind what I said before about being a fetish. Mica feeds me because it makes me happy. His face lights up when he sees me. Sex has become a logistical impossibility, but we still kiss a lot. He tells me I'm beautiful; he says he loves me. I have to believe he does. He absolutely does. Why else would he be here?

I wanted to be loved, and here he is, feeding me, heart, soul, body. Especially body.

Here's a confession, Other Emerson. Even in this huge, grotesque version of myself, I still love eating. Food never lets me down, even though I know it's killing me. I love tasting and chewing, I love an enormous forkful of food filling my mouth, my stomach. I love swallowing and eating and eating and eating some more.

I know it's an addiction. I know it's a sickness. I know, and I don't want to be like this, but the power of food, of wanting, of trying to be full is too great for me to resist. Food is the shield against every hurt and heartache I've ever suffered. The self-hatred, the disgust, the physical pain of bearing all this weight, the longing to do things I once took for granted—walking, fitting into a car, taking a shower—the disgust people show me . . . nothing measures up against the need to eat.

So that.

That's how you get this way, Other Emerson.

Now leave me alone. I have to write a letter, and then it'll be time for my lunch. You never know. I might even eat you.

I hate you, you skinny bitch.

CHAPTER 32

Marley

Hold hands with a cute guy in public.
(Or private. Baby steps.)

If you defined dating as "I go to his house with food and sometimes stay to watch a movie and also, we're sleeping together," Will and I were definitely dating.

It was very strange.

In the little bubble of his house, he was turning into a very respectable boyfriend. While he wasn't a fantastic cook, he did cook for me, not wanting me to always be the one. One night he made a roast chicken, his mother's specialty, he said. Served it with new potatoes (simple and delightful) and green beans (rather lackluster beans, but heck). No man had ever cooked for me, not counting my brother and Louis. So in that sense, Will's were the best green beans ever.

He liked hearing stories about my family and childhood (though we steered clear of Frankie . . . I didn't have a lot to say on that topic, after all, other than the Phantom Twin thing). While he didn't come out and say, "I'd love to meet your family," he remembered their names and asked after them.

But because he stood by his statement that crowds made him uncomfortable, we had yet to go out. At all. One

Sunday morning after I'd stayed over, I said, "Let's run down to the Blessed Bean for breakfast, what do you say?"

He was toweling off his hair, making it spike most adorably. He paused, then resumed. "No, thank you. I have coffee downstairs."

"But do you have meltaways? Because the Blessed Bean does."

"I have cereal. I can make you eggs and toast."

"Come on," I said. "The Bean is great. You won't be sorry."

"No, thank you. But if you really want to go, by all means."

"No, Will! I want to go with *you*." I paused. "It won't be that crowded at this hour. It's still early."

He almost said something then. Rubbed his forehead. Whatever flush of relaxation he'd been sporting earlier, post-shag, was gone, and his jaw was starting to lock.

"It's okay," I said. "Coffee here is great."

He didn't like going to the movies, but he said that was unrelated to crowds—he had a whopping huge TV, every station known to mankind: Netflix, Hulu, HBO, STARZ, you name it. No need to go out, right?

I told him about my other clients—Rachel and her triplets, old Mrs. Ames of the Kit Kat addiction who ate like a horse and didn't weigh more than a hundred and twenty pounds, the sloppy Putneys and my compulsion to clean their kitchen every time I dropped off food. I told him about catering a super-posh dinner party in the city, and my hope to open a storefront downtown.

In return, he told me about gardening. About the games he was designing. He mentioned a nephew who was now eight and lived in Santa Fe with Will's sister and brother-in-law. He even smiled when he told me about the little guy. But anything deeply personal? No.

But he picked me some flowers from his garden—roses and chrysanthemums, and wrapped their stems in a wet paper towel so they'd survive the six-block journey to my house. He let me watch him dig a hole for a new tree in the garden one day, and when I told him it would be much more interesting if he took off his shirt, he laughed, pulled it off and then came over and gave me a sweaty hug, which turned into sweaty kisses, which graduated to sweaty sex.

Insert the sound of my purring.

And yet, he wasn't an easy person to get to know. Most everyone I knew was an open book. If someone was asked a question, that someone usually answered. Not so with Will Harding.

But he was a good listener. He was smart. He could be funny. He was extremely invested in me having a good time in bed. Extremely. That quality was greatly appreciated, let me tell you.

Otherwise, I was well aware that I was making excuses, cutting him slack. Georgia had asked when she'd meet him, and I hadn't been able to give her an answer.

The truth was, I was afraid to find out if he was the real deal. If *we* were. Because if not, then what? Back online, where my swipes rarely resulted in anything other than twenty-three-year-old guys wanting a quick bang? I wanted permanence. I wanted what my parents had, what Dante and Louis had. I wanted a guy who looked at me the way Rafael Santiago looked at Georgia.

Finally, I bit the bullet a few weeks into our thing. "Will," I said as we were lying in bed, flushed and happy and holding hands, "I'd like you to come to my house and meet Georgia. And Mason."

He didn't answer right away, and my heart started to sink. It wasn't a big request. If he couldn't grant it, then I had to seriously doubt that he wanted anything more than this.

"Okay," he said. He kissed my hand. "Sure."

"Really?" I said. "Yay! That was easy! How about dinner on Saturday?"

"Um, I have a phone call with a company on the West Coast that evening."

"On Saturday?"

"Yes." He took a deep breath. "How about just dessert?"

I looked at his unsmiling, somewhat tense face and got the impression that this little request was bigger than I knew. "Just dessert is great. Thank you, Will."

"It'll be fun," he said, the lie so obvious I had to laugh.

"My house is very adorable. You might not hate it."

He smiled then. "I'll bring some design programs for Mason."

"I'm sure he'll love that."

On Saturday night, Georgia and Mason and Admiral all sat in my kitchen, the air rich with the smell of apple pie (whole-wheat crust made with coconut oil, apples, honey, all very nutritious and low cal and easy on the stomach for Georgia's sake).

"He should be here any minute," I said ten minutes after seven.

"We're in no hurry," Georgia said.

"Except I have to be back by eight thirty," Mason said. "My father said I need more rest if I want to up my times in running."

"I thought you hurt your Achilles," Georgia said.

"I did. But still. Rest is good." He bit a nail, poor thing.

At 7:23, my phone rang. "Well, shit," I said, looking at the screen. "Mason, make sure you never do this." I clicked to answer. "Hello, Will, we're all here and there's pie."

"I can't make it. I'm sorry. My call is going on longer than I thought. Maybe you can come here instead?"

"Uh . . . sure."

"Great. Sorry. Thank you." He sounded sincere, anyway.

We walked over. It was a cool night, the smell of autumn leaves sharp and lovely, mingling with the smell of the still-warm pie.

"Here we are," I said as we approached Will's house. Funny how the front yard was so bland when the back was Eden. We trooped up onto his little front porch, and before I could knock, he opened the door and kissed me. On the lips and everything. I felt my cheeks flare—he was kissing me! Almost in public! His shirt was damp with sweat, which was odd, because it was such a cool night.

When he pulled back, he looked at me and took a deep breath. Maybe his call hadn't gone well. But we were here now, so let the good times roll.

"Will," I said, "meet two of my favorite people. Georgia and Mason Sloane."

"Hello. Nice to meet you," he said. "Please come in."

"Thank you for having us over," Georgia said, her finishing school manners in fine show. "You have a lovely home."

I coughed.

He looked at her—*You call this lovely?*—and didn't answer, then turned to Mason. "Marley says you like computer games."

"Yeah, who doesn't?" Mason said. "Let me put this pie down. I almost ate it on the way over. So you make video games? Can I see any?"

"Sure," Will answered. "If you're interested in programming, I have some software you can have. Actually, a laptop, too. I get them for free."

"Really? Thank you! That's so nice of you," Mason said.

Before we lost the two of them in GeekLand, I asked if it was okay if I showed Georgia the garden.

"Of course." He looked at me, nodded once and went

into the living room with Mason. It was kind of sweet, actually. He was nervous meeting my friends.

"Come through the so-called lovely house and see the best part," I said to Georgia, leading her through the beige kitchen with its beige granite countertops and beige cupboards, through the beige den that contained nothing other than a desk and computer, and into the mudroom, which had exactly two pairs of boots (winter and rain) on the shelf and two jackets hanging on the hooks.

"Yeah, he needs to come shopping with us," Georgia said. "I don't see one picture on the wall. Is it possible this poor man doesn't have even one dog statue?"

"You can see why I thought he was a serial killer."

She laughed. Then she drew in a sharp breath at the sight of the garden. "Wow! This is amazing!"

Will had pulled out the stops. All the little Japanese lanterns were lit, and the Tibetan prayer flags fluttered in the breeze. There were subtle spotlights placed under the trees, along the fence and in the koi pond Will had just put in last week.

"Come on," I said. "Walk through the garden. It's kind of a Buddhist-monk-meets-HGTV experience."

We went down the winding little path, and as Georgia commented in amazement, I felt a rush of pride for Will. He might be a little clenched and difficult, but someone who could make this out of nothing . . . the list of his flaws was balanced by these other things. He was hardworking. Dedicated. Nurturing. Patient. So what if he didn't watch *Downton Abbey*?

As we came back onto the patio, I noticed there was an addition since I'd last been here—one of those stainless steel gas heaters you see in outdoor restaurants, giving off a nice glow. The patio table had been set with dessert plates, forks and cloth napkins. A bottle of wine cooled in a bucket of ice. Candles were on the table, and there was a little jar of rosebuds in the center.

And yet he'd been running late on that phone call.

Or not.

"This is so beautiful," Georgia said.

The rest of the meet and greet was perfectly pleasant. Georgia asked easy, pleasant questions: Did Will like to read, where did he go to school, what were his favorite meals from Salt & Pepper? He, in turn, asked her a few, not quite as gracefully. He kept wiping his palms on his pants, and his shoulders were tense.

"Well, I have to get Mason back," Georgia said once we'd finished dessert.

"Mason, can I come to a meet sometime?" I asked.

"Yeah! Absolutely." He turned to Will. "I run cross-country. I've been injured, but I should be running again soon."

"Great," he said. "That's a really good sport, from what I hear."

"Do you run?"

"Uh . . . I used to. A little bit."

"Cool. Well, thanks for the computer and stuff, Will. Really."

"My pleasure. They were just sitting on a shelf. Glad you can use them. Shoot me an e-mail if you get stuck."

Georgia beamed. "Lovely meeting you, Will."

"I think I'll walk home later," I said. "Hang out here a little longer." Then I hugged them good-bye, gathered the plates and glasses and went into the kitchen. Will escorted Georgia and Mason to the door, lifting his hand as they went down the walk.

As soon as the door was closed, I jammed my hands on my hips. "You didn't have a call to the coast, did you?"

"No," he said.

"Well, thanks for your honesty *now*! Why did you lie to me before? And why won't you come to my house? Why did you wait until almost seven thirty to let me know you weren't coming? We were just sitting there like lumps while you played Martha Stewart over here!"

"You don't need to yell."

"This is not yelling. You have not yet heard me yelling, Will Harding."

He ran a hand through his hair. "Okay. Come sit down," he said, gesturing to the world's most boring couch.

"No! I hate your living room. It's very brown. You need an accent wall and some decorations."

"Come back outside, then."

We went back out, and I took a few deep breaths of the cool fall air. It was getting colder, and I shivered. Will went inside and came back with a soft blanket and handed it to me. Humph. I wrapped it around my shoulders, not willing to let him off the hook just yet.

He sat down across from me and looked into my eyes. Didn't say anything.

Silence. I hated that. "Look, Will. It's one thing not to like crowds. I get it. You lost friends in a terrible, senseless act, and it was horrible, I'm sure, but you can't just manipulate and lie to me because—"

"I was there."

"What?"

"The day of the shooting. I was there."

The horror of that image punched me in the stomach. "Oh, shit. Oh, no. God, Will. I'm so sorry." My eyes filled with tears, and I covered his hand with mine. He squeezed back and looked away.

"Yeah. So it's a little more complicated. Technically, I have PTSD."

"Of course you do. Who wouldn't?"

"Going out, being away from home . . . it's tough. But I'm trying. I wanted to come tonight, but I don't . . . ah, shit."

"You don't what, honey?"

There was a pause, and then he smiled a little. Oh. I'd called him honey.

Then he rubbed his eyes. "I don't like to leave here. It's hard for me to feel safe away from home. Even having people here is nerve-wracking."

"I noticed you were a little sweaty."

A little huff of laughter escaped his lips. "Yes."

"You did great, you know. They really liked you."

"Good, good. I liked them, too."

We sat there in the beautiful garden, holding hands across the table. "Do you want to talk about it?" I asked, swallowing. It was not the type of thing a person longed to hear about. "The shooting?"

He pulled his hand away and fiddled with the tablecloth. "I guess I have to tell you, don't I?"

"Well . . . no. But maybe it would be better if you did."

He sighed, rubbed his forehead too hard, so that I wanted to pull his hand away. "It was at our office. Nenos Game Design in Houston. We had this guy, a new hire, a tools engineer, and he didn't work out. He was just kind of . . . odd. So he was let go."

He was quiet for a few beats. "And then he came back about a week later. I didn't know what the sounds were . . . I was in the back with Jane. She was the head programmer, the one who had fired him. We heard the noise, and she said, 'Is that . . . is that *gunfire*?' like hearing elephants would've made more sense."

His hands were shaking. "She was pregnant."

Oh, no. Please, no. Had a pregnant woman been one of the victims? I didn't remember reading that detail.

"There was another shot. I got up; I closed the door to

her office," Will said, his voice flat. "It was like a drill, almost, except for the . . . screaming. I turned off the lights, locked her door . . . it was just that little doorknob lock, nothing that would really keep anyone out, and told Jane to get under the desk. She begged me to stay with her, and I did." He looked at me, his eyes bleak. "I tried to keep her quiet, because she was . . . well, hysterical. Called 911, said there was a shooter and then we just . . . waited."

In halting sentences, Will told me the rest. He could've gone out. He wanted to. In those brief but endless minutes, he thought about taking the fire extinguisher, spraying the shooter in the face, or hitting him with it. And if he had, maybe the last victim wouldn't have been killed.

That last victim had been his best friend.

But Jane had been sobbing, pleading, saying, *Don't leave me, don't leave me, don't leave me.* So he stayed, crouched behind the desk, trying to keep her quiet, flinching at the sound of each bullet. He figured he could at least shield her with his body if the shooter came in.

Will wiped his face. His eyes were dry, but he was drenched in sweat, his leg jiggling under the table. "We . . . we, uh, heard him try the door, and we thought this was it. I . . . I had to cover Jane's mouth so she wouldn't scream. Then we heard the sirens, and there was another shot, the closest one yet."

"My God, Will," I said, wiping my eyes.

"That last shot . . . he'd killed himself. We didn't know that, though. We just stayed there under the desk until the SWAT team came in." He swallowed hard. "Then we had to . . . uh . . . walk past . . . everyone. That was it. We were safe then."

I jumped out of my seat, unable to have anything between us, and sat on his lap, hugging him. "I'm so sorry," I said, stroking his hair. "I'm so, so sorry."

"Thanks." His voice was hoarse, his arms dangling at his sides like dead things.

God. No wonder he was so tense all the time. No wonder.

"You have to know," I whispered, because my voice was rough with tears, "you probably saved that woman's life. And her baby's."

"I just hid, Marley."

"No," I said, my voice fierce. "You stayed with a pregnant woman who was going to be killed."

"Yeah." His tone told me he'd heard it before.

"Was she okay?"

"Yes. Had the baby two months later. Named him Will."

I smiled a little at that. "So clearly she thinks you saved her life, too."

He cleared his throat, and I got up, pulled my seat closer so I could see his face. "So you have PTSD . . . what is that, exactly? I mean, I know what it is, but how does it work?"

"Like this. Like an idiot who can't go to his girlfriend's house because he might get shot along the way. Or, if he does make it to her house, he might have a panic attack because a shooter could come in at any second. It's embarrassing and ridiculous, that's how it works."

"Honey. You survived hell. Give yourself a break."

He gave me a look. "I know. In my head, I know a lot. The problem is, a panic attack . . . You think you're dying, you can't talk, you can't move. Then I started to . . . obsess about what would happen if I had a panic attack when I was driving. What if I caused an accident and killed someone? What if people saw me collapse on the sidewalk?"

"They would probably help you," I said.

He scrubbed a hand through his hair. "Logically, I know that. But there's this horror of someone seeing me like that. I guess it's shame."

"You have *nothing* to be ashamed of," I said, my voice shaking. "You were a hero that day, Will."

"Right. Except I could've helped more, maybe. But I didn't, and this is my punishment. I moved back to New York because I wanted to be closer to my parents, and I thought it might get better, but it didn't. I started sitting in restaurants so I could face the door, and then I stopped going to restaurants. Then I couldn't handle the grocery store. Then it was everything."

He looked at me. "That's when I met you. You're the only person I've let into this house in a year and a half except for my parents."

"Are you seeing a counselor?"

He nodded. "We have Skype sessions. It helps. Not as much or as fast as I want it to. We're working on it. The backyard was the first phase. Next step, take out the trash, which I managed last week. A personal triumph."

"Stop knocking yourself down, bub."

He smiled again. "Next, I'll try to walk down the block." He sighed. "It sounds so stupid, working up to walking in my own neighborhood. That night you told me about your friend, and how she couldn't leave her house . . . I understood that. I know what that's like."

"It doesn't sound stupid," I said. "And you'll make progress, Will. You'll get there."

"Thank you. For listening."

A chunk of my heart broke away. "Oh, honey. You're welcome."

He picked up my hand and studied it a minute, then kissed it, and my heart melted a little more.

"Do you want me to stay over tonight?" I whispered.

"Yes," he said, looking up at me with those sad eyes. "I do. I really, really do."

CHAPTER 33

Georgia

Tell off the people who judged us when we were fat. *(Check.)*

Eat dessert in public. *(Also check.)*

Two weeks after my night in the ER, I had a date with Evan Kennedy. I should've been more excited about that. I mean, we were kind of dating. No. We *were* dating. We'd had that drink, that dinner, and a few days ago had gone to a movie during which we'd held hands and after which he'd kissed me, asked me if he could come over for a drink, and was perfectly pleasant when I told him I had parent-teacher conferences the next morning and needed my sleep.

Which brought us to today. The sexpectation date.

Marley and I were in a yoga class, my presence here signaling that the end of days was upon us, and the Four Horsemen of the Apocalypse would be cantering in any second now, snatching us out of downward dog and carrying us off into an agonizing afterlife that could well include more yoga. God! Who knew my hamstrings were this tight? Who knew I even had hamstrings?

The room was dark (at least there was that), candles flickering in the front, flute music not quite covering the sound of my grunting. Marley, who was freakishly limber, had yet to break a sweat. Me, I was soaked through.

There were some people I knew here—some of the yoga moms from St. Luke's, dressed in, yes, you guessed it, Pomegranate & Plum. Khaleesi's mom (who was named Ellen; how was that for disparity?), Cash's and Dash's moms, Hemp's dad. Every one of them said hello, and I didn't feel as out of place as I'd expected. Which was a surprise unto itself.

Maybe going to the gym wasn't the worst thing in the world after all. My opinion was skewed, being Hunter's sister and therefore deemed a failure at all things athletic.

"Step forward and into rag doll," the teacher intoned. "Uttanasana."

"And also with you," I murmured, getting a snort from Marley.

"So you looking forward to going out with Mr. Kennedy?" she whispered.

"Yeah, sure. He's nice. Clean. He smells good."

"Be still, my leaping ovaries," she said.

"Utkatasana," said the teacher. "Chair pose." I squatted, imitating the rest of the class, and immediately, my thighs began burning. "Now drop two inches," the teacher added. I obeyed, wincing. My breath came in little gasps.

"Do try to breathe," Marley said. "It will reflect poorly on me if my guest dies."

"You sure this is good for me?" I managed.

"Yes. So is this the date where you'll sleep together?"

I grimaced.

"Corpse pose," said the teacher.

"Thank God. This one I have nailed."

"What about Evan?" Marley asked. "Will you also have him nailed?"

I laughed, then tried to shush myself, as I was now a corpse. We lay on our backs and tried to belly breathe. "I don't know. Maybe. I'm sure it will be fine."

"Fine?" Marley whispered. "Fine? That's not a word we

use in describing sex, Georgia. Wall-banging, earth-moving, atheist-defying, wildly orgasmic, animalistic, but not *fine*."

"She's right," said Khaleesi's mother (grandmother of dragons?). "Don't settle."

"What she said," Dash's mother added. "You deserve someone great, Georgia."

"Aw," Marley said. "You hear that, G? Everyone knows. You're the bomb-diggety."

"Breathe in love, breathe out hate," the teacher said. "Breathe in positivity, breathe out your doubts. Savasana."

Yes, yoga was a little weird. But at the end of the class, I signed up for ten weeks of lessons.

Since I'd been put on the ulcer medication, I felt a lot better, but I hadn't gained back any weight yet. I didn't know if I'd ever have a normal relationship with food. I didn't even know what a normal relationship would look like.

But I was trying. I was eating three times a day with two healthy snacks, on a plan drawn up by my new doctor and Marley. Having the food mapped out kept me from skipping meals or panic eating. I was on the right path.

Later that night, as I was dressing to meet Evan, I took a good hard look at my reflection. The person in the mirror was attractive—the woman in the flowered dress, even though this dress was black. It stopped a few inches above my knee, and I wore sheer black panty hose (something I never bothered with when I was fat) and pretty fabulous black stilettos that were already making my feet cramp. A silver chain necklace gave the outfit an upscale, funky vibe, as did the fierce red leather bomber jacket Big Kitty had given me yesterday. "Just for no reason," she had said. "I thought it was your color." It was also one size too small— her message to me that I still had a way to go—but if I didn't zip it up, it looked smokin'.

"What do you think?" I asked my dog. He wagged his

tail. I knelt down and kissed his bony head, gazed into his eyes for a minute. "Thanks, Ad," I said. "Thanks for being my friend."

I grabbed my purse and keys and went down to the courtyard. Marley was sitting there, wrapped in a blanket, gazing at the sky.

"Ta-da," I said.

"Gorgeous. Go get him, tiger," Marley said.

Part of me wished I could stay home. I barely wanted to have dinner with Evan, let alone sleep with him.

And yet, two hours later, there I was, at a sleek restaurant overlooking the Tappan Zee Bridge, in a corner booth, sipping wine across from a good-looking guy, dinner in my belly, which didn't even hurt. No one had stared when I came into the restaurant. The maître d' complimented my jacket. The waitress didn't say how nice it was to see a brother and sister spending time together.

I guessed I was here. That place I'd yearned to be for so long.

Evan was telling a presumably amusing story about the plastic surgery practice he'd visited in LA. I nodded along, paying just enough attention to smile occasionally.

Did Emerson and the mysterious Mica ever go out to a snazzy restaurant and feel like they belonged? Would she recognize me now? Would my dating this handsome, successful guy make her happy?

That summer of her and Marley and me . . . that had been so wonderful. Ironically, every summer I'd gone to fat camp, I'd thought about being fat a lot less than I usually did. At Copperbrook, I wasn't an embarrassment; I was a valued client in the eyes of the staff, and just another person to the other girls.

One day, the three of us had been sitting under a tree, working on writing a play, one of the activities we were given, and out of the blue, Emerson said, "The nicest people I've ever met are all here."

None of us had wanted the summer to end.

Now the president of Camp Copperbrook wanted Marley and me to join the board. They ought to, after getting Emerson's endowment. Ten girls a year would be able to go to the camp, all expenses paid, and learn about taking care of themselves on every level—mind, body, spirit. If they were lucky, they might make lifelong friends, the way we three had.

It was a little shocking, sometimes, how much I missed Emerson. Knowing she was gone forever, that we'd never have any reunions, any weekends together, was like a kick in the head.

Worst, though, was knowing she'd never have any more chances. That's what the list was about. The chance to get it right. It wasn't about tucking in shirts and piggyback rides. It was about not letting your weight define you, and not letting it decide when you could be the person you wanted to be. She'd wanted us to stop waiting and start living, the way she never got to, not totally.

In the most innocent way, our eighteen-year-old selves had written a map to loving ourselves. The only thing wrong had been the title. It shouldn't have been "Things We'll Do When We're Skinny." It should've just been "Things We'll Do."

"Georgia?" Evan said. "Where'd you go?"

"Sorry," I said. "Just thinking about an old friend who died recently."

"No apologies needed," he said, though his tone held traces of irritation. "Do you want to talk about her? Or we could go back to your place and talk there. I drove up. There's a great place for brunch near here, too." He smiled in a self-deprecating way. *Hint, hint. I drove up so I could stay over. You could cry on my shoulder, and then we could have sex, and tomorrow, Belgian waffles.*

It wasn't the worst offer in the world. I could do it. After all, I hadn't gotten laid since I was married, and Evan was good-looking and fairly nice and liked me. Well, he liked the woman in the flowered dress. The woman who wore slutty shoes.

This is what I'd done with Rafe, too. That version of myself I thought he'd like best. Except Rafe had seen through that.

You were my home.

Rafael Esteban Jesús Santiago had always had a way with words.

Evan . . . not so much. He was kind of a shallow guy, this Kennedy. I mean, he was fine. He had good hair. He said all the right things, but . . . well, he was boring.

"Tomorrow is Sunday," he said, since I hadn't jumped on his hints just yet.

"Very good, Evan. I'm glad you have the days of the week memorized." I smiled to lessen the sting.

"And neither of us has to work."

"True."

"We could stay up late."

"And watch *Saturday Night Live*?"

"Or something," he said, raising an eyebrow.

"Would you like dessert?" the server asked.

"Yes, please," I answered immediately. I didn't want to leave just yet. "Do you have crème brûlée?"

"We sure do."

"I would love that, then. Thank you."

"You got it. Anything for you, sir?"

"Cappuccino," he said, not looking at her.

Off she went. Evan and I stared at each other. I stifled a yawn. The Tappan Zee Bridge winked over the Hudson, and the noise of the restaurant was low but lively, constellations of laughter flashing now and again.

"Are you really related to those Kennedys?" I asked.

He gave a demure chuckle. Really, there was no other way to describe it. "President and senators, you mean?"

"Is there another famous Kennedy clan you'd like to claim?"

"No. And yes. My great-grandfather was a third cousin of John F. Kennedy's grandfather."

I let that roll around in my head a minute. That was hardly American royalty, was it? I mean, if I spent enough time on Ancestry.com, wouldn't I also find that I was distantly linked to the Kennedys? Wouldn't everyone?

"Huh," I said. "I thought you were a little closer to the throne."

"Why would you think that?"

"At—" *Yale*, I almost said. *At Yale, everyone thought you were John and Caroline's cousin. And you never denied it. All those mentions of Hyannis Port . . .*

"Here you go," our server said, putting down a veritable lake of crème brûlée. "And your coffee, sir."

"Thank you," I said. I picked up the spoon and took a bite. Oh, it was perfect, the crunch of the caramelized sugar, the cool cream of the pudding beneath.

Eat dessert in public.

Holy crap. It was on the list, and I hadn't even thought of it.

"I love a woman who can eat," Evan said, giving me an indulgent smile.

Every hackle I had suddenly flared. "What does that mean?" I asked. "Does that mean I have your approval to eat my dessert?"

"No! No, not at all," he said. "I just . . . I don't know. I hate women who are always counting calories. I like a woman who enjoys food, that's all."

"Women would enjoy food more if men weren't always offering their opinions on how they ate and what size they are."

"Wow. I didn't mean to offend you. Eat your dessert if it makes you happy. Don't eat it if you're worried about getting fat. Your call. Jesus."

That was it. My jaw turned to iron. "Evan. We know each other."

"Uh, yeah, of course we do," he said, not all that nicely. "We're on a date."

"We went to Yale together."

His head jerked back. "What?"

"Yale Law. We were in the same class."

It was almost funny to see his mouth work, his eyebrows draw together. He *still* didn't remember me.

"I was fat," I said.

Evan closed his eyes. "Oh, God," he muttered. "So you've known all along?"

"Yes. I recognized you instantly."

"Well, you look *really* different."

"Not that different. My name is still the same. Same haircut. Same skin color, eye color, hair color."

"Look, calm down," he said, even though I was perfectly calm. Icy calm. "Can you blame me? I'm sorry I didn't recognize you, but it's been what, almost six years? And you've lost a lot of weight, obviously."

Had I? I mean, how heavy had I really been? Rafe had said something about how I saw myself and how I really was. I hadn't been that big in law school. Surely not unrecognizable. I took another spoonful of dessert, this time defiantly, my eyes narrowed on him.

I kind of hated Evan Kennedy, didn't I?

He leaned forward. "Georgia, I'm sorry I didn't know

who you were, but that's in the past, isn't it? I mean, now we have more in common."

"*What* do we have in common, Evan? Being thin?"

He paused. "Uh . . . well, we like kids. And scotch, right? Uh . . . I think you're great, and we have some chemistry, don't we?"

"But we sure didn't have chemistry when I was fat. You never asked if I liked kids or scotch when I was fat."

His eyes darted around the restaurant to see who was listening. Many people, that's who. I wasn't bothering to keep my voice down. "I guess not. No. I barely knew you."

"Because you didn't *want* to. Because I was fat. We barely spoke, even though I had a huge crush on you. I knew you were out of my league, physically speaking. Intellectually, I kicked your ass. I passed every single class with honors, and I know you barely scraped by." There was that photographic memory again.

I sat back in my chair. After all, a person didn't get to have these moments often in life. "We sat next to each other in Torts our first year. You wore a blue and black cashmere sweater a lot. One time, we walked back to the law school in the rain and we had a really nice talk, Evan. You were very polite."

He smiled. "Good."

"No!" I barked, slapping the spoon down on the table with a crack. "Not good, Evan! In four dates, you haven't had even a flicker of recognition about who I was. We spent three *years* in school together, but because I was fat, I didn't register! You only like me now because I match a certain image you have of what a woman should look like. What if I put on a few pounds? Would you like a woman who could eat then? Or would I become invisible again? So, sorry, not sorry, I'm breaking up with you."

The restaurant burst into applause.

"Yes!" said a woman at a table to my right. "Yes! You tell him, honey!"

"You're a real piece of scum, mister," someone else said.

Holy crap. My face burned. I hadn't meant to be *that* loud.

Then again, maybe being that loud was a long time coming.

A guy came over to my table. "You need anything, miss? Want me to get rid of this jerk for you?"

Evan's eyes were wide, his mouth slightly open. "I didn't do anything wrong," he said. "I . . . I'm totally confused here."

"You didn't do anything right, either," I said. I turned to my would-be defender. "Thanks for your concern. We're fine."

"If he can't love you when you're big and beautiful, baby, he can't love you period," said another female diner. Her male companion nodded sagely.

"Thank you," I said, giving a little wave.

Evan looked mortified. "I guess I owe you an apology," he said. "I genuinely didn't recognize you."

"I know," I said. "That's the whole problem. And I'm sorry I didn't tell you we knew each other right away. It was a test, and I think we both failed. Take care of yourself."

And with that, I got up, grabbed my jacket and purse and left, not even wobbling on those heels, to another smattering of applause.

I felt light. I felt like a balloon and sunshine rolled into one. Marley was going to go crazy when she heard this. Mason, too.

I couldn't wait. I group-texted them.

Eat dessert in public, check.

Tell off the people who judged us when we were fat. CHECK
AND THEN SOME!

Mason answered first. G, that's awesome!!! You're amazing!

Marley was a little less eloquent. Rocknroll, muthafuckah!
(sorry Mase!) Come see me the INSTANT you get home.

I slept like a baby that night, pretty sure I smiled the
entire eight hours.

In the morning, my good mood was slightly dimmed by
the knowledge that I had to have brunch with Big Kitty. I
opened my closet and looked at my clothes. Most of the stuff
that fit me had been purchased from Crave, and I wasn't
really in the mood to dress up. Instead, I chose a pair of leg-
gings and a long, shapeless sweater and added a pink scarf.
It was one of my favorite teaching outfits, since it was as
comfortable as pajamas and washed easily.

When I got to the Lawn Club, Mother was already seated
at a prime table near the window. The maître d' walked me
over, pulled out my chair and told me to enjoy brunch. A
glass of champagne was already waiting. Mom was drinking vodka with a wedge of lemon.

"What are you wearing?" she asked by way of a greeting.

"Clothing, I believe. How are you, Mother?"

"Why aren't you wearing something I bought you?"

"I wanted to wear this, Mom. I'm capable of picking out
my own clothes."

"Are you?" She squinted at me. "You've put on a little
weight. Don't backslide, Georgia."

I took a slow breath. Sipped the champagne. "Mom, I
don't think I mentioned I was in the ER two weeks ago."

"Why?"

"I have a bleeding ulcer. And . . . well, maybe a bit of an
eating disorder."

"An eating disorder?" she asked. "What does that mean?"

"I ate too much as a kid, remember? Then I'd hate myself for it, so I'd purge and diet. You know. You were there, obsessing over my weight with me. Obsessing over yours, too." I paused. "Did you ever wonder if you're anorexic, Mom?"

She huffed. "Please. You can never be too rich or too thin. I have *discipline*, Georgia, not anorexia. I'm *slim*. And you're practically there now. Was that the ulcer? Maybe it's not all bad."

Even though I'd had those thoughts myself, they sounded so much worse coming from my mother, who was supposed to love me. Protect me. Take care of me.

Then again, I shouldn't have expected a different answer. That was just naive.

"Do you ever get tired of it?" I heard myself ask. "Feeling like the best thing you have to offer is just a pretty face and a good figure?"

"Don't underestimate those, Georgia. Don't give up. You could be so much more than an almost-pretty girl."

"No, Mom," I snapped. "*You* could be so much more. Or you could've been. Instead, you're an aging coat hanger with a plastic surgery addiction. All my life, you've criticized me for one thing. I wasn't skinny. Imagine if you'd appreciated that I was smart and good-hearted. Imagine if you'd stuck up for me with Hunter, instead of letting that little monster terrorize me."

"There you go, exaggerating again." She sighed wearily, then wagged her fingers at someone. "Why can't you just take a compliment. You look good. Don't stop now."

"Mom. I fainted. There was a hole in my stomach that was bleeding. Maybe there are more important things than being thin. I'm smart, I'm nice, I'm a great teacher, but you never notice those things."

"You weren't happy being fat, though, were you?"

"No. But having a mother who constantly reminded me that I was overweight only made me want to eat more. Being miserable because my brother hated me only made me want to eat more."

"Oh, please." She sighed, taking a drink. "Must you keep score on everything, Georgia?"

I looked at her steadily. I knew she'd never admit fault with herself, never admit she was anything but a perfect mother. She would never, ever apologize.

But sometimes, you had to say things for yourself, even if you weren't heard. "No one in my life has ever made me feel as bad as you have, Mom. Not even Hunter."

"What about your father?" she said, sitting up abruptly. "I don't remember *him* being around much when Hunter was"—she made quote marks with her fingers—"torturing you. Maybe I could've used some help parenting you, instead of having an ex-husband who was out dating strippers while I was home raising you on my own."

"By raising me," I said, "you mean shopping and drinking and telling me I was fat? Turning a blind eye when Hunter was being such a shit? At least Dad didn't try to make me hate myself. And when he was around, he tried to rein Hunter in. Your son should probably be in therapy, by the way."

"Well, I guess you know everything. I'm a horrible mother. Maybe you shouldn't keep that red leather jacket, then. It cost two grand. Armani."

"Then by all means, I'll give it back. I know how things make you happy."

She huffed over her martini glass.

The waiter came over. "Are you ready to order, ladies?"

"I'll have a poached egg and one slice of whole-wheat toast, no butter," my mother said, giving me a pointed look.

I thought about getting up and leaving. Thought about throwing my water in her face.

I smiled up at the server. "Eggs Benedict for me, please," I said. "And a side of hash browns."

In a half hour, Big Kitty would forget everything I'd said and go back to criticizing me, lionizing Hunter and being the perpetual victim of her divorce. But for now, even if only for this tiny window of time, I'd said what I had to say.

I ate every bite of my breakfast.

It was delicious.

CHAPTER 34

Marley

Tell off the people who judged you when you were fat.
(If Georgia can do it, so can I.)

"There you are!" Mom yelled from the kitchen as Georgia and I came in. "I was starting to get worried. Dante, tell your nice police friends they're here safe and sound, even if my own daughter didn't call me to tell me she was running late."

"The tristate search has been called off," he said, giving me a hug.

"You didn't really call anyone, did you?"

"No." He grinned at Georgia. "Hey, you. You're looking awfully hot these days."

"Save it, gay guy," she said, but she blushed. Dante did have that effect on women.

Louis and Dad were cleaning gutters (code for avoiding the rest of us). I stuck my head out the back door, said hello, warned them against personal injury and crossed myself to ensure their safety.

"Georgia, sweetheart!" Mom said, emerging from the kitchen, taking off her apron. "Don't you look wonderful! A little skinny, but we can fix that. Are you hungry, dear?"

"Starving. It smells great in here, Mrs. D."

I'd brought Georgia with me because she loved my family, for one, and for two, I needed moral support. Seeing my parents' house being slowly packed up had my heart in a vise.

The family pictures that ran up the stairs were gone, the paint brighter where they'd hung. In the kitchen, the shelf made by Dante in eighth-grade shop class had been taken down, the decorative plates it held now packed (or thrown) away somewhere. All the little cracked crystal vases Mom had collected and lined up on the kitchen windowsills, gone.

But Frankie's shrine was still intact, the candles burning, Ebbers the Penguin staring out at us solemnly, as if daring my parents to lay a hand on him.

"Dante and I picked out some things for you," Mom said. "In your room, which we still haven't packed up because you refuse to come over. Go. And tell me if you want Great-Nonny's silver hairbrush and mirror set, because Eva wants it, too."

"Eva can have it," I said.

"Good," my sister said, appearing at the top of the stairs. "Because it's already sitting on the bureau in my guest room. Hey, Georgia."

"Hi, Eva," said Georgia. "How are you?"

She didn't get to hear an answer because Mom dragged her into the kitchen. But Eva didn't bother responding anyway, as social skills were not her forte. "Marley, get your ass up here." (See?)

I ran up the stairs.

"How do you do that?" Eva asked, giving me a confused look.

"Do what?"

"Run."

"I exercise."

She shuddered, headed down the denuded hall into my

room and flopped on my bed, which was still made up with the satiny lavender bedspread I'd bought after college. "Mom's mad at you," she said.

"Great. Why is that?"

"Because you haven't been over."

"We had lunch at the Eveready last week. And we saw another medium, who said Frankie is bathed in light and love and watches over us."

She groaned. "Why do you go to those things?"

"Why don't *you*? I'm not the only daughter, you know."

"Because I don't believe in that stuff. Also, I work."

"Don't start, Eva. I also work."

I looked at the stuff on my bookshelves and my old desk. Books, sure, I'd take the books, even if most of them were for kids. A high school cheerleading trophy for Most Positive Attitude; my diplomas from high school and college; a Mickey Mouse mug from a long-ago trip to Disney—oh, that Captain Cook's Tonga Toast! The Sand Pail Sundae! Forget the rides . . . it was always about the food.

"Speaking of your job, my doctor says I have to lose some weight," Eva said, picking up on the food vibe. "Got any tricks?"

"There are no tricks," I said, running my finger across the painted-on-velvet picture of a cat. "Eat better. Use Salt & Pepper. There could be a family discount if you're nice to me." I turned to her. "Seriously, Eva. I'd love to cook for you. Good stuff. You won't even know you're on a diet. It'll just be a lifestyle change."

"Fine. But don't give me a discount. Charge me extra, because I plan on whining a lot."

"I will." I paused. "Eva, does it bother you, being fat?" I asked.

She gave me a confused look. "No. Why? Does it bother you?"

"Yeah. Sometimes. We live in a skinny world."

"Really? Because I live in America, and we are not a skinny nation, hon. And from where I sit, you're one of the happiest people on the planet. You know. Aside from Frankie." She flopped back on the bed, staring at my ceiling. "I remember coming in here when you guys were little on Christmas morning. Dragging you out of your cribs so we could see what Santa brought."

"Really?" I'd never heard that story. "Tell me about it."

"I just did." She glanced at me and sighed. "You wore these fuzzy little sleeper things. You both had poopy diapers, but I didn't bother changing you, because I was, like, five."

I sat down next to her and scoured my memory banks. Nothing.

"I'm gonna miss this house," Eva said unexpectedly.

"You sure you're okay with the move?" I asked.

"What am I going to do? Throw myself on a pyre? Of course I'm okay. I'm glad, even. They've been stuck here for way too long."

"It's not a Siberian gulag, Eva. But why now? It seems so sudden."

"Let them fly, mama bird," she said. "The little fledglings have to leave the nest sometime."

"*I* haven't been keeping them here."

"Right."

"Spit it out, Eva, or shut it up."

She shifted her left boob to a more central position. "I want to say something," she said. "Don't interrupt, just let me get it out."

"I—"

"Shush! Just listen." She glanced at me, then back at the ceiling. "I'm sorry I wasn't a better sister. I'm still not a great sister, and I know it."

"Are you dying?"

"I don't think so."

I crossed myself. "Well, save the apology. You're fine."

"There's a reason you and Georgia glommed on to each other, isn't there?"

"I believe it's called friendship," I said.

"You two are more like sisters than we are." There was an unexpected hint of jealousy in her voice.

She was right. Eva was always around, more or less, but she never let me in. Georgia . . . I *knew* Georgia.

"The thing is," my sister said now, her voice a little rough, "when Frankie died, I hated seeing you without her. You were like an open wound."

My chest tightened with grief. "I don't have a lot of clear memories of her." No. Only that heavy, dark emptiness. The Frankie-shaped space.

"Yeah, well, you were fucking tragic."

"Thanks."

"Just trying to explain. One of the reasons I think Mom and Dad stayed here was because of you. They didn't want you to . . . I don't know. Lose something familiar, on top of losing her."

Thirty years, and we were finally talking about something real. I lay down next to her, both of us on our backs, side by side. "What do you remember about her?" I asked. "You were, what? Eight when she died?"

"Seven and a half." There was a long pause, and when she spoke, her voice was husky. "She was happy. She was so sweet and cuddly." My entire soul seemed to reach out for Eva's words, wanting to have something, anything of Frankie. "You, on the other hand," she went on, "were always running and breaking things, but Frankie . . . she was . . . ah, fuck it. She just sat there and smiled. At least that's how I remember her. But she was tired a lot. She was never healthy. All those food allergies, all that asthma. She caught every bug, every cold, every virus."

"Why did she die?" The words were a whisper.

Eva covered my hand with hers, a rare gesture of affection. "I don't think there was a big event. I think she just . . . wound down."

The lump in my throat was a boulder. A few tears slipped out of my eyes and into my hair.

"So let Mom and Dad move, Marley, and stop with the guilt-tripping, okay? Go shopping with Mom and buy some shit for the new place. You love that anyway, don't you?"

"I do," I said. "The guilt trips . . . they're not deliberate."

"I know. It's in our genetic makeup. Okay, if this is my last day of eating like an Italian, I'm gonna make the most of it. Ma! Is dinner ready?" With that, she lumbered off the bed and out of the room.

"Good talk," I called.

She was already thudding down the stairs.

I sat up and looked around. This would be the last time my room had furniture.

The lump in my throat came back with a vengeance.

Once, it had been our room, Frankie's and mine. Once, it had been painted pale blue; I didn't remember when it had been repainted yellow. The early photos showed two cribs, though I'd outgrown mine by age two. Frankie had never left hers. So tiny, and Mom was afraid she'd fall out of bed and break. All family legend, nothing I remembered.

"Marley! We're dying down here! Come and eat!" Mom bellowed.

I got up, and for a second, I stood where Frankie's crib had been.

Nothing. No memories.

I went downstairs and took my place at the loaded table, next to Georgia. Her presence (and Louis's) made today seem less morose, a little like a party, rather than the Last Supper. But it was weird—the picture of Pope Francis was gone (Dante and Louis had hung it in their kitchen), Nonny's silver tray brought from Italy (Eva), also gone. The good china was packed, and we were eating off the Pyrex.

It was good to see Georgia eating after her night in the ER. Tragically, that night had not gotten her and Rafe back together, despite my Insta-Rosary the second I saw him getting out of the cab.

But she told me she'd finally apologized to him, something she said was years in the making, and he'd been a prince. It wasn't "Tell off the people who judged us when we were fat," but it was something, anyway. An honest conversation about weight and its effects.

I couldn't help wishing they'd try again.

"So why are you guys moving after all these years?" Georgia asked, innocently.

"Oh, well, the winters," Mom said. "Mr. DeFelice and shoveling and the ice, you know. He could have a heart attack." We all made the sign of the cross, even Georgia, and Eva knocked dutifully on the table. "Just time for a change, I guess."

"It'll be beautiful down there," I said. Eva looked at me and smiled. "Mom, Dad," I added, "do you think I could have Ebbers?"

Mom jerked back. "No! That was Frankie's."

We were all quiet for a minute, until I said, "I know." Eva was scowling at me. But how was this a guilt trip? This was a reasonable request.

"Give it to her if she wants it," Dad said, topping off Georgia's wineglass.

"I will not!" Mom exclaimed. "We're taking Ebbers with *us*. He's like one of the family." She pulled her head back like an offended turtle.

"Okay," I said. "Fine. That's fine. It's just that Frankie was my twin, and I'd like to have something of hers."

"I'm aware she was your twin, Marlena Apollonia. Since you both grew in my womb."

"Can we not say 'womb' at the table?" Dante asked. "There are two gay men here who don't want to think about girl parts."

"You also grew in my *womb*, Dante Christopher, and were fed off my *placenta*. Fed very well, as a matter of fact. Ten pounds, two ounces, fourth-degree tearing."

Dante gave a dry heave while Louis laughed.

The subject of Ebbers seemed to be closed. I let it drop and scooped more spinach salad on my plate to offset the yearning for a second helping of lasagna.

"So guess what, Marles?" Dante said. "Camden and Amber? Camber, we were calling them? They broke up."

My chest squeezed. "Good," I said, just a hint of bitterness in my voice. "He didn't deserve her."

"Exactly what I said," Louis murmured. "The man has the IQ of a box of hair." He cocked an eyebrow at me, the look clearly saying, *You could do better.*

"I always thought he was nice," Mom said. "So handsome. I thought you and he would make a very nice couple, Marley."

Well, I slept with him a few times, Mom, but he didn't want to be seen with me in public.

"Camden's gross," Dante said. "A total whore. If Amber doesn't have an STD, it's a miracle."

Great.

"Don't talk like that at the table, son," Dad said.

"Dante, can't you find anyone for your sisters?" Mom asked.

I sighed. Loudly.

"Do *not* draw me into this conversation," Eva said. "I

love being a childless spinster. Pass the meatballs, Georgia." Georgia obeyed. Everyone obeyed Eva.

"Fine, fine. At least you'll take care of us in our senility," Mom said.

"As long as you're happy, Eva," Dad said.

"I'm great, Daddy."

"Well, I *hoped* to live to see my other daughter married," Mom continued. "Poor little Frankie didn't get a chance, Eva doesn't want any, but Marley, the clock is ticking, sweetheart. Can't you—"

"I'm seeing someone," I blurted. "Okay? I have a boyfriend."

There was a moment of stunned silence. Georgia raised her eyebrows, and yeah, yeah, I knew these were treacherous waters.

"Who? What? When?" Mom sputtered. "Why didn't you bring him?"

"I figured I'd let the dust settle over the move," I lied.

"What's his name?" Dad asked. "I can use the Google on him. Is he good enough for my little girl?"

"I think so. His name is Will. Will Harding," I said. I'd Googled him, too, and all that came up was his name on a list of children's video games. He was on LinkedIn. Not on Twitter, Snapchat, Facebook or Instagram, the freak.

"He can come to your birthday dinner!" Mom said. "So we can meet this mystery man you've been keeping a secret."

"Sure." It was the week after next, and the day before my parents moved to Maryland. "I'll tell him."

"You didn't mention him to me," Dante said in a voice that said, *And I* would *be told, being the perfect little brother, so the fact that you haven't told me is an indication that something's terribly wrong.*

"It's still new. He's shy. But sure, he'll come. Maybe not to the cemetery, though." Because of course we always visited the cemetery on my—and Frankie's—birthday. "Where are we eating again?"

"Roberto's," Mom said. "We'll come back here for cheesecake, of course." She glanced at the shrine, and her eyes filled with tears.

Our last birthday in this house. My heart wobbled dangerously.

Now all I had to do was convince Will to get out of his house.

....

Georgia and I decided to stop at Hudson's for a drink on our way home. She wanted to tell me what my mom had spilled while Eva and I were upstairs, and I wanted alcohol. She also said it was the kind of intel that needed a drink.

Hudson's was noisy and cheerful. Alice, the server, came right over, and we ordered a glass of wine apiece.

"Okay," Georgia said once the drinks had arrived. She settled back in the booth. "It's the fortieth anniversary of them moving in, the thirty-first of your sister dying, and your mom just can't deal with the big house anymore, according to your father. He wanted a change, thought it might do her good, and he's been working on getting your mom to move for the past five years. Before it's too late, he says, and they're senile and have hollow bones—his words—and will die falling down the stairs. Then . . . okay, now, don't freak out about this, promise?"

"Sure," I lied, my heart already thudding,

"He had a very minor heart thing in July."

"What?" I screeched. "He had what?"

"Inside voice," she said as heads whipped around to look at me. "It wasn't a heart attack. Just a little A-fib. Fast heart rate."

"And no one told me? My mother told you and not me?"

"Well, I'm a lawyer, hon. I have interrogation skills. And they didn't want to upset you. He's fine. It was just too much caffeine, they think, but it got them thinking."

"My father was in the ER, and neither parent said boo to their kids?"

Georgia tipped her head. "Eva knew. Not Dante, though."

"That damn Eva. Why her and not me?"

Georgia took a sip of her wine. "That, I can't answer. Maybe because she's terrifying and impressive."

I admitted that she was. "You know what she said to me upstairs? She apologized for being a crap sister."

"Is she?"

"No. But she's not the typical sister, either. I mean, she'd give me a kidney, but she wouldn't go to the movies with me."

"Speaking of, want to go see the Tom Hardy movie next week?"

"Hell's yes." I swallowed some wine, forcing myself to relax a little. "Thanks for coming with me, by the way."

"Better than dinner at Big Kitty's, that's for sure."

"Your mother does have great taste in vodka," I said.

"True. There is that."

We sat back in comfortable silence for a minute, looking around at the other diners. One of my clients, a Wall Street badass, saw me and waved, and I waved back. And speaking of clients . . .

"So I guess I have to make Will come out of his cave," I said. "Since I outed him as my honey."

She waited, her expression kind and patient. Some people had resting bitch face. Georgia had resting kind face.

"He's making me dinner this weekend."

"That's very thoughtful. Cooking for a chef." I nodded. "Do you guys talk?" she asked.

"We do. About my family, mostly. You. Emerson."

Georgia's face was a little too nice, bordering on sympathetic, and I didn't want to ask why.

"You're looking very spiffy these days," I said.

She grimaced. "Mother took me shopping."

"You know, she may be a cold bitch, but she has killer taste in clothes." I smiled. "Your color is better, and you seem more . . . relaxed."

"It was that yoga class."

I snorted. "It was one class, Georgia."

"Hey. I have my own membership now. And I feel better, too. The meds are doing their thing, and Mason seems solid, school's good . . . and I guess talking to Rafe . . . well. The wound is scabbing over."

"That's great." I leaned forward and clinked my glass against hers. "To us. You, and me, and Emerson. That list hasn't been all that bad. I'm closing in on the finish line, I think. Just have to get Will to hold my hand in public and take me home to his parents and all that good stuff."

"I think I may be finished, too." She hesitated. "One of my clients at the FFE? She's a therapist, and I filed some paperwork for her with the state. I asked her if she'd start seeing me. As a client."

"Really?"

She nodded. "I think I need to figure out how to be a little nicer to myself."

"Thank you, Jesus! Georgia! I'm proud of you!" I clinked my glass against hers again. "I think this will be great."

"Thanks. Oh, shit," Georgia murmured, her expression not changing. "Camden just came in. Don't turn around."

I whipped around. For a second, all that remembered love—or what I'd thought was love—flared in my heart . . . then withered, then turned to ash.

Camden saw me, his perfect face brightening, his blue

eyes glowing, and headed to our table. "Marley!" he said. "How are you? Man, it's good to see you!"

"Hi," I said with all the enthusiasm of dirt. Georgia gave him one of those icy WASP death stares I was convinced they taught at boarding school.

"Can I buy you gals a drink?"

"We're not gals," Georgia said. "We're women."

"Women, then? Bartender, another round, okay?"

"We're on our way out," I said.

"Oh, come on, stay," he begged, sitting down. "Hang out with me. I've missed you."

"I heard you broke up with Amber," I said.

He pulled a face. "Yeah. She dumped me." His hand was resting on the table very close to mine, and he reached out with one finger and touched my pinkie. "Guess she wasn't the one."

"Or you weren't," I said, pulling my hand away.

"You wanna hook up?" he asked, like Georgia wasn't even there.

"No, I do not," I said.

"Come on, Mar. Give a guy a break. You're not mad at me, are you? I missed you."

Tell off the people who judged us when we were fat.

Guess I wasn't quite finished with the list after all.

"No, Camden," I said calmly, "you used me. For five stupid years, I waited for you to date me, but you just had drunken sex with me once in a while and then treated me like . . . like . . . nothing."

"What are you talking about?" he said. "I texted you! Sometimes!"

"Aw, Marley!" Georgia said. "He texted you. Sometimes."

"I know. I'm getting choked up just thinking about it. Come on, G. Let's go home, where we won't be bothered by dopey men."

We stood up. "Bye, Cam," I said.

"Screw you, Marley," he said, standing as well. "You're lucky I ever slept with you!" To my utter shock, he gave me a little shove. "It was a pity fuck, and you should thank—"

And then Camden staggered back, crashed into a server and fell onto the floor.

I turned and saw Georgia shaking her hand. "Ouch! Ow!" she said.

"Did you *punch* him?" I squeaked.

"Of course I did!" she said. "I was defending your honor."

For some reason, that struck us as hilarious, and we were laughing, clutching each other's arms as Camden managed to get up, his pride in tatters.

"Out you go, asshole," said Matt, the owner.

"Me?" Camden said. "She's the one who hit me!"

"You deserved hitting," Georgia said calmly. "I found your manner hostile and aggressive and took measures to protect my friend. It's called use of physical force in defense of a person, New York Penal Law 35.15. 'A person may use physical force upon another person when and to the extent he or she reasonably believes such to be necessary to defend himself, herself or a third person from what he or she reasonably believes to be the use or imminent use of unlawful physical force by such other person.' Photographic memory, yo."

Alice, our server, high-fived her.

"Yale is so proud right now," I said.

Georgia dipped a napkin in her ice water and put it on her knuckles. "As they should be," she murmured. "As they should be."

CHAPTER 35

Georgia

Walk the walk. (*I mean, really. This is what the list is all about.*)

I'd been to two of Mason's cross-country meets earlier this season, but this one had me twisted in knots.

Hunter was coming today.

Mason's Achilles tendon had been strained since his second meet, so while he'd been trying to practice and stretch, he hadn't actually competed in a couple of weeks. He remained ever cheerful, admitting without envy or rancor that he was the slowest kid on the team.

That goal of his—to run the entire course without stopping to walk, as we'd done in the Central Park fun run—broke my heart and filled me with pride at the same time. Since I'd been dragged to many cross-country meets when Hunter was in school, I knew how great the difference could be between the first kids in and the last. They started in a mob, but almost immediately, the pack would string out into clumps, then into a ribbon, then the odd kid, then long stretches of nothing, then another stray kid, plodding or walking, drenched in sweat, red-faced and miserable, a completely different creature from the kids who ran as if the ground were air.

The course for high school kids was three miles long. Some kids could run that in sixteen minutes. Some in twenty. In Mason's case, thirty-three minutes and three seconds. As a normal human, I thought three miles in thirty-three minutes sounded quite accomplished. To runners, however, it was *wretched*.

Mason's coaches had only positive things to say—what a good work ethic he had, how he always smiled. Great potential, one coach said. A fantastic kid, said another. And the teammates seemed to like Mason. He wasn't excluded from anything and seemed at ease with the other boys. He'd reported that he'd started having lunch with Christian, the team captain and a senior no less, and Christian's friends. Mason wasn't quite one of the gang, being three years younger, he said, but at least he wasn't alone. Another thing to cross off his list.

The talent show fame had faded after a few days—only bad things seem to last in high school—but Mason was hanging in there. Doing better than hanging in there. He wasn't the pale, trembling kid who'd taken eleven Tylenol PMs. His smile was more genuine these days. His phone occasionally dinged with a text. He'd gone to the Eveready Diner with the team after the last meet; I knew, because I'd picked him up and seen the careful joy on his face at finally belonging.

But Hunter, whether he intended to or not, could change that in an instant. I knew that better than anyone. How many times had he slashed any pride I'd felt over the years? Win an academic award? *So what, you're fat.* Have a friend come visit? *She just pities you because you're a freak.*

Obviously, I was worried for my nephew.

Generally, the parents cheered on the kids; only a few were the horrible kind, screaming at their children to "work those arms" or "stay on pace." Most, though, had something kind to say to even the slowest.

Mason was the slowest. Not just among the kids on his team. Among all the kids.

In those two meets he'd run, Mason always forced a smile and a little wave, even if he was breathing hard, his face bright red, even when he'd been reduced to walking. Parents would call out encouragement, and he'd break into a painful trot, and my heart would nearly burst from worry and love and pride and fear.

Today I felt ill, because there was one parent who would *definitely* care about times and stride and form, who would be ashamed at seeing his son finish last, who might well humiliate him in front of his hard-won friends.

Hunter. It was a curse word in my mind. My brother was a runner, the kind who finished the 26.2-mile New York City Marathon in two and a half hours. Which meant he ran roughly three times faster than his son.

Marley had an extra-busy day, Dad was in DC, my little sisters had a mandatory dance practice before their recital, and Mom had had filler injections last night and was icing her face. So it was just me and my dog, set to go into battle if Mason needed us.

It was a sickening feeling.

I wished Rafe would magically appear, but I also had the feeling that after the night he'd had to babysit me, we wouldn't be running into each other so much. It had felt a lot like good-bye.

Admiral nudged me with his pointy nose, and I shook myself out of it. The kids were jumping around, warming up, stretching, doing little sprints. Mason saw me and trotted over.

"Hey, G! Thanks for coming!" He bent down and hugged Admiral, who wagged his tail and licked Mason's ear once.

"I wouldn't miss it, honey."

"Is my dad here yet?" He bit his thumbnail.

"I haven't seen him."

Some of the tension left his shoulders. "Okay, well, we're starting in about fifteen minutes."

"Good luck, honey. I'll be cheering for you. Does your Achilles feel okay?"

"Oh, yeah. I think so. I mean, we'll see, right?" He smiled a little, but it didn't fool either one of us. He started to walk away, shoulders tight.

"Mason! Mason! Hold up!"

Hunter. Mason froze.

My brother cut me a glance as he strode across the field, walking his designer bike—he'd bragged that it cost $10,000—geared up from his helmet to his toes. Yellow jersey with sponsor names, special sunglasses, mirror on the helmet, special gloves, special shorts, special socks, special shoes, lest anyone suspect he was a mere mortal.

"Son. Listen up. You pick the leader and you stay on his pace, you hear me?"

"Uh, Dad, Christian's times are way ahead of mine. I can't keep up—"

"Yeah, well, you can't pansy-ass this sport, can you? Make the decision to excel."

"Just do your best, Mason. That's all anyone can ask," I said loudly.

My brother turned on me, his face abruptly vicious. "Did anyone ask you? Don't you have a life of your own?" He turned back to his son. "It's all mental. Just make the decision to stay with the leader and don't pussy out."

"Okay. I'll try." Mason cut a glance at me, then quickly looked back at his father. "I . . . I have to go."

"Good luck, sweetheart," I called.

Mason trotted off, his shoulders drooping.

"Stop swinging your arms like a girl," Hunter yelled. "You can't be a great runner if you don't use every part of your body. Walk like a winner, run like a winner!"

"Jesus, Hunter, tone it down, okay? Just let him be. He'll give it his best."

"Said the fat girl who never did any sport of any kind."

"And yet somehow my life has been okay just the same."

"Has it? You're a lonely, divorced kindergarten teacher who lives with her gay best friend and had to buy a dog for company."

"For one, it's preschool. For two, Marley and I are both straight. For three, Admiral is a rescue. I didn't buy him. I adopted him."

"Who even cares, *George*? I'm gonna go watch from somewhere else," Hunter said, mounting his bike in a smooth motion. He glided off down the course, just enough to keep distance between him and me. God forbid people knew we were related.

The boys gathered at the starting line, the gun went off, and they pounded past.

By the end of just twenty or thirty yards, Mason was already falling behind. As he passed by, I yelled, "Looking great, Mason!"

My words were drowned out by Hunter, despite his distance from me. "Use your arms! Pick up those knees, Mason! Stay with the pack!"

We onlookers migrated to the next lookout spot; the course brought the kids in a figure eight, more or less. Hunter ignored me, ignored everyone, looking ridiculous in his Lance Armstrong outfit, sticking out like a neon lighthouse.

The fast kids were already charging up the hill from our second vantage point. There was Christian the Wonderful leading the pack by a ridiculous margin already, his parents cheering him on. "Go, Christian!" I said as he flew past.

"You're Mason's mother, aren't you?" Christian's mom asked. Out of the corner of my eye, I saw Hunter approach. That yellow was hard to miss.

"His aunt. Hi, I'm Georgia Sloane. Christian has been wonderful. Mason thinks the world of him."

"He's a sweet boy. Both of them are," she said, smiling.

"What camp do you send him to?" my brother asked without so much as an introduction. "Does he have a private coach?"

"No, just the school coaches."

"He could be great if you invested in real coaching."

Christian's mom stiffened. "He already is great."

"On many levels," I added.

"Thank you, Georgia. See you at the finish line." She didn't bat an eyelash at Hunter, just headed over to where she'd watch her son win, as he usually did.

More runners passed, some tall, some short, most skinny, but some not. Good for them, I thought. Good for the kids who carried some extra weight and didn't let that stop them.

The tension radiating off Hunter was rancid and thick, growing with every runner who was faster than his son. And that was every single runner.

"Where the fuck is he?" he muttered.

"He'll be along," I said.

"I wasn't asking you."

If only Hunter would get transferred to Outer Mongolia and give me Mason.

More runners passed, huffing along. The slow kids.

Maybe Mason had fallen. Maybe his Achilles tendon was hurting again. I almost hoped so, since it would explain his slowness and give him an out with his father, but then I felt guilty for the thought. Of course I didn't want Mason to be hurt.

Another runner came out of the woods. Still not Mason.

Hunter and I were the only adults left; all the others were at the finish line.

Once Mason came into view, he'd have a half mile to go to the end of the race. I didn't know how he could keep it up.

Then, finally, thank God, there he was. Hunter ran to the bottom of the hill to meet him. "Dig in, dig in, dig in!" he screamed. "You can do better than this! Work this hill, Mason! Get your ass moving!"

Mason's head went down.

Damn you, Hunter.

"Hang in there, Mase," I called as he climbed the hill, so slowly, but still technically running. "You're almost there."

"I haven't . . . stopped . . . yet . . ." he panted.

Oh, my God! He was doing it! Finishing the course without walking! "That's great!" I said. "Good for you, honey. You can do this." Then he was past me, disappearing into the woods for the final stretch. My legs burned just watching him.

Hunter had already stalked off to the finish line, his sinewy body tight with anger. I followed at a distance, Admiral trotting at my side, and joined the crowd. Almost all of the kids had finished.

There was Christian, barely even sweaty. "Great race, Christian," I said. "You came in first, I assume."

"I did," he said, grinning. "Thanks. How's Mason doing?" It touched me that he knew who I was.

"He's doing well," I said. "He said he hasn't had to walk yet."

"Good for him! He's working so hard." He flashed a smile and ran off (ran!) to his friends.

Time stood still. "Is everyone done?" one of the away-team coaches asked.

"One more runner out there," someone said.

Not many kids had the guts to run a race knowing they'd

be last. I was so proud of Mason, but I was also dying for him.

There he was, coming out of the woods, the finish line a couple hundred yards away. He was still running. His face was a mask of pain and concentration, and he looked . . . awful.

And then, something miraculous happened.

As Mason came onto the field, Christian and all the other boys—and the entire girls' team, too—gathered along the last leg.

"You got this, Mason!" Christian yelled, and as my skinny little nephew chugged along, Christian fell in next to him. The rest of the team followed behind, trotting slowly behind their captain, yelling encouragement. For Mason. No one cared how slow he was. They only cared how hard he was trying.

My nephew's face went from a mask of pain to wonderment. He picked up speed, his stride widening.

"That's the way, Mason!" one of the coaches yelled. The parents started yelling and clapping, and it didn't matter that he was the last kid, the slowest. Many of them called him by name. "That's right, Mason! Way to finish strong! Good job, kid!"

Mason started running faster, Christian keeping pace with him easily, talking the whole time. And then, with twenty yards to go, Christian fell back, letting Mason finish alone.

Mason's breath rasped in and out of his lungs, and his brows were drawn. Somehow, he was sprinting, the crowd was roaring, the coaches yelling, and Mason crossed the finish line with a time of 26:43.

The last one in.

His best time ever.

It was a hero's welcome. Christian hugged him, the

other kids high-fived him and Mason went to a trash can and threw up, as one apparently does.

I was trying not to sob.

"What a race he had!" Christian's mom said to me. "Congratulations!"

I gave a little wave, my throat too tight to answer, and she gave me a big smile and went off to her wonderful, wonderful son.

I stood alone, wanting to hug my nephew, kiss his cheek, tell him how proud I was, but he was having a moment with his peers. His aunt, no matter how beloved, didn't belong. I watched with love burning in my heart, so happy I felt like I could float away.

Oh, Leah. Are you seeing this? Look at your little boy!

"Am I the only one here who knows shit about running?" Hunter said. "That time was utter crap. And those kids having to run him home like he's some sort of . . . Jesus." He started to walk toward Mason.

Something snapped. I ran up behind my brother and grabbed his arm. Hard.

"You shut your ugly mouth, Hunter," I ground out. "Your son just set a personal record. He never stopped trying. He was amazing, and you're the only one here who doesn't see it."

"Are you kidding? He was ten minutes behind the winner on a three-mile course!"

"What's *wrong* with you?" I said. "Mason just ran his heart out, the entire team admires him for it and adores him for how hard he works, and all you care about is if he won. Don't you see what you're doing to him?"

"I'm making him *strong*, idiot," Hunter said. "What the hell do you know about raising kids, huh? From what I can see, you're a failure in everything. Divorced, fat, dead-end job, lonely—"

"This isn't about me, Hunter. You hate me, I get it,

message received a couple decades ago. This is about Mason. Your son. My nephew."

"Your *half* nephew," he said. "So drop the lecture."

My head jerked back. "What did you say?"

"Oh, my God. Mom still hasn't told you? Seriously?" His eyes were cold. "Daddy Dearest isn't your real father. I thought he would've said something, since the two of you are so close."

There was a sudden whooshing feeling in my stomach. My mouth opened, but no words came out.

That couldn't be true.

But all of a sudden, I knew it was.

And then, the words did come. This was not the time for me and my issues. This was about Mason.

"That boy isn't just *your* son, Hunter Sloane," I said, ignoring his bombshell. "He's Leah's, too. Remember her? How gentle and kind she was? How much she loved you? That's her boy over there, and while you're trying to make him over in your image, keep in mind that he's a lot like her."

His face flickered before the familiar bitterness dropped back into place. "Yeah, well, she's not around to help, is she?"

"And Mason almost killed himself. Remember that?"

"That was an *accident*," he spat. "A stupid accident."

"Or a boy so lost and miserable and sad he overdosed."

He stepped closer to me. "Don't tell me about my son. I know him best."

"No, you don't, Hunter! You have no idea who he is. Leah would rip you to shreds if she knew how you treat her son. She would hate the person you've become."

His head jerked back as my words hit their mark.

"Now, you go over there," I said, a fire raging in my chest—not my stomach. "You tell him how proud you are of him and how much you love him. You start counseling for your anger issues because you are bordering on emotional abuse. And if you cross that line, I will be up your ass so hard and fast I will shred your intestines, and I won't stop till I have custody."

People were giving us a wide berth. Good. I didn't care if they heard.

"I'm sorry Leah died," I said a little more quietly. "I loved her, too. She was a great person, and I'm sorry it's hard for you. But if you don't do better by my nephew and Leah's son, you will lose him. Do you understand me, you bitter little man? I will take your son away from you."

"He has to be strong," he repeated, but his voice was less certain.

"He already is, putting up with a father like you."

Hunter looked at me a long minute. Then he went to the mob of kids, found his son and hugged him. It was awkward, and Mason looked a little stunned, but it was, nevertheless, a hug.

....

A few hours later, my father and I sat in my living room across from each other. He'd come straight from LaGuardia after getting my text: Please come see me as soon as possible. I'm fine, but it's important.

We both had glasses of scotch. Big glasses.

"What was so important, sugarplum?" he asked.

"Right," I said, taking a deep breath. "Hunter mentioned something today about my parentage."

My father's face went white. Admiral, sensing a tremor in the Force, leaped up next to him on the couch.

"It doesn't matter, Daddy," I said. "I don't care."

His eyes filled with tears. "You are absolutely my daughter," he said, his voice shaking. "I don't care what Hunter said."

"But it's true, isn't it? We're not biologically related, are we?"

"It doesn't matter how you started out. You're mine. You're *my* daughter."

"Oh, Daddy," I said. "Of course I am. Of course I am."

"The second I saw you . . ." he said. "There in the delivery room, your face all red . . ." He wiped his eyes. "It was love at first sight."

I slid into his chair next to him, surprised that I fit. "Why didn't you ever tell me?"

"Why would I? In my heart, you're completely my child. Even more than Hunter." He leaned forward, drained half his drink, then settled back, his arm snug around me, even if it was shaking. "I didn't think Hunter knew."

"Well, he does. Told me at Mason's cross-country meet."

"Such a class act," Dad muttered.

"Is this why you couldn't take me when you got a divorce?" I asked.

His face crumpled. "I wanted full custody, or at least half. But your mother said she'd tell you, and I . . . well, I didn't want you to feel any worse than you already did. I guess I thought you'd be . . . unsettled if you knew. You weren't the happiest girl as it was."

"No. I wasn't."

"So I took what she gave me. I'm sorry, honey. I've wondered a million times if I should've risked calling her bluff."

I was quiet for a minute, trying to process everything. "So what happened? Did she have an affair?"

"You should ask her."

I took that as a yes. An affair, then. She cheated on my father.

She *cheated* on my *father*. Whatever small affection I had for my mother shriveled. "Does Cherish know?"

"Yes."

That made sense. She knew everything, really.

So I was a bastard. That almost had a cool ring to it, a pirate feel.

Somewhere out there was a man who looked like me, I imagined. Maybe he was fat. Maybe he had green eyes. Maybe I even crossed his mind sometimes. Maybe I had half siblings, even.

But who really cared?

The man sitting next to me, trying not to cry, was the man who'd looked under my bed for monsters, read me bedtime stories, told me I was his princess. The man who'd never once missed an appointed dinner or weekend with me, not once. The man who had a room for me in his apartment, fresh sheets always on the bed, wooden letters that spelled my name. He'd given me two sisters, and he'd given me a stepmother who loved me ten times more than my actual mother did.

He'd never said anything about my weight, either. Maybe he should have; maybe a loving conversation from him would've helped in a way that my mother's endless criticism never did. But maybe I needed at least one person who didn't seem to notice. At any rate, the past was the past. He wasn't perfect, but he was my dad.

"You're the best father in the world," I said. "I'm so proud to be your daughter."

Then my father did cry, and I did, too, but they were happy tears. The very best kind.

....

The next day, I went to Big Kitty's house and let myself in without knocking. I found her lying on the white couch, an ice pack over her eyes. "Is someone there?" she asked.

"It's your illegitimate daughter," I said.

She lurched up, the ice pack falling.

Ugh. She didn't look good, her eyes swollen and bruised—another eyelid lift, I guessed, in addition to her fillers. Her lips were comically inflated into an unnatural trout-pout.

"Did your father say something?" she asked.

"Which father? Daddy, or the sperm donor?" I had to admit, I was enjoying the look on her fairly immobile face. "Hunter told me," I said. "In his usual diplomatic way, at yesterday's track meet. I'm sure he was overheard." That would bug her. Let it.

"I need a drink," she said.

"Let's have you sober instead. It would be a nice change."

"Fine. Be cruel. I'm sure you're enjoying this."

I looked at her strange face and felt my hardened heart soften a little bit. *Knock it off,* I told it. *She's toxic. She's made you feel like shit your entire life.*

"I take it you had an affair, Mother."

She let out a huffy breath. "Fine. You're right. I had an affair. Your father was constantly working, I was bored, I met someone." Something flickered across her face.

"Did you love him?"

She cut me a look, her swollen eyes making her resemble an offended lizard. "I loved your *father*, Georgia. Joseph Sloane, that is. I loved him, he loved me, we got married, were happy, had Hunter, who was a handful, I admit. Your father was more critical of him. He thought Hunter needed therapy or some such nonsense."

"He does need therapy."

"Says Little Miss Judgment. Do you want to hear this story or not?" she asked.

"By all means."

Mother sat back against the couch. "Joseph loved me a great deal once, Georgia. When we were dating." She was quiet for a minute. "It's not easy, you know, to be in love with your husband and watch him slowly grow disappointed with who you actually are."

Her words hit me by surprise. Hadn't that been my exact fear with Rafe?

"And your father *was* disappointed in me," she continued. "It was painfully obvious. You know the saying: The honeymoon's over. Somehow, I wasn't enough for him. There I'd be, every day, waiting for him to come home, dinner ready, trying to be interesting, trying to be what I thought he wanted, and he got tired of me. I don't know what he expected."

"Did you have a job? Before Hunter?"

"No," she said defiantly. "I didn't need to work, Georgia. I had the house and . . ."

"And what?" Even someone as self-centered as my mother had to have something other than her reflection to fill her hours.

"I was on some committees," she said. "We had social obligations. Don't make that face. It was forty years ago." She pressed the ice pack to the side of her face and looked away. "Then we had Hunter, and he was everything to me."

"He gave you purpose."

Her head snapped back to me. "Yes. Exactly. Your father didn't love him the way I did. We starting fighting all the time. Your father worked ten hours a day in the city, traveled twice a month, and then he'd come home and criticize me for letting Hunter run wild. As if it was easy keeping that child happy. Joseph thought I was spoiling him."

"You were."

"It's easy to preach about how to raise children, Georgia, when you don't have any."

"Point taken."

"Oh, and listen to this. Your father even criticized how

I looked. You'll love this one, Georgia. He thought I should eat more."

"So you ate less."

She gave me an oddly triumphant look. "Yes. And then I met Don, and he was very different. He sympathized. He listened. He told me all the time how beautiful and delicate I was."

God. My poor mother. Her size and her beauty were the only attributes she cared about, and hearing that would've reassured her that she had value. "What did he look like, this Don person?"

"He was very handsome. A . . . a big man."

"Do you mean fat?"

"A big man." She cut me a look. "He was so confident. Also married, also had a son. That's how we met. At Hunter's school. We had an affair, I fell in love, and when I told him I was pregnant, I thought we'd both get divorces and be together. Instead, he offered to pay for the abortion."

Good God.

"I . . . I hadn't expected that," she said quietly. "I hadn't expected that at all. I thought he loved me. And, not to toot my own horn, but I *was* very beautiful, Georgia."

"I remember."

She gave me another lizard look—I guessed I was supposed to reassure her that she still was—but continued. "So I told your father. He and I hadn't slept together in months, so there was no pretending you were his."

"Did you think about getting an abortion?" It was a hard question to ask.

"Georgia. I would never do that. You were my . . ." Her voice shook a little. "My baby."

She touched a purple, swollen eyelid—was she crying?—then flinched at the pain it must've caused.

It dawned on me that my mother *hated* how she looked. That all these procedures and surgeries were a pathetic attempt to go back to the way she was the last time she'd been happy. That her obsessive thinness was a way to feel superior, because, in her heart of hearts, she felt the opposite.

I felt an unwelcome surge of pity.

No, no. Nope. She had cheated on my dad, had been the other woman, had placed no importance on the vows of marriage for either of them. She had gambled and lost big.

But she didn't abort me, either. She could have, and she didn't.

"What happened to your lover?" Had I ever met him at the Lawn Club? Playing tennis? At St. Luke's?

"They moved shortly after I told him I was keeping you," she said, and my shoulders dropped an inch or two. "Florida, I think. I don't know where they are now. I suppose you could look him up, but I never have. If you want his name, that is."

"I don't."

She paused. "You look like him."

"I gathered. It explains a lot." I took a slow, deep breath. "Why didn't you let Dad have joint custody when you guys got divorced?"

Her swollen eyes narrowed. "Isn't it obvious?" she said. "You loved him best. If I let you live with him, I'd barely exist as far as you were concerned."

There was a long pause. I let it sit there.

"Why did you get a divorce, anyway?" I finally asked.

Her puffy lips tightened. "Your father and I had no real relationship after I got pregnant with you. He said he'd stay and raise you as his own, but he wanted nothing to do with *me*. He also told me if I had another affair, that would be it." She sat back against the couch cushions and fiddled with her ring.

"Ah. So you had another affair."

"I thought it would get his attention, and I was wrong. I'm *sorry*, Georgia. Obviously, I'm not perfect."

Suddenly, my whole childhood needed some rethinking. "I'm going now," I said, getting up and heading for the door. "I'll see you around."

"Georgia." There was an accusatory note in her voice. "I did my best, you know."

I paused. Maybe she had. My mother was not a brave, big-hearted woman with surprising insights and gentle humor.

But I was.

I was.

"Take care of that face, Mom. I'll see you soon."

Then I left, feeling stronger and brighter than I had in a long, long time.

CHAPTER 36

Marley

Go home to meet his parents. *(Nope.)*

Be in a photo shoot. *(Check.)*

On Sunday afternoon, I went over to Will's a little early. Fine. An hour and a half early. I missed him, even though I'd seen him last night, and the feeling filled my chest with happiness.

As usual, his shades were pulled, and from the curb, his house looked utterly unremarkable, the plainest house on the block. I smiled a little. If people only knew about Eden in the back. Maybe in the spring, he'd start working on the front. Maybe I could help him, since I knew a thing or two about gardening myself. Or I could just watch him, and ask him to take his shirt off, and he'd laugh again, that low, unexpected, gravelly laugh.

I was making dinner here for the two of us, and the plan was to invite him to my birthday. It would be hard, yes, but he'd been making progress. A small family dinner . . . I mean, hey. My family was nothing if not accepting. He didn't even have to come to the restaurant (though I hoped he would). He could just show up at Mom and Dad's afterward for cake.

The truth was, I needed him there. My birthday—mine

and Frankie's—would be the last night I would ever be inside my parents' house, the place I'd lived almost my entire life. We'd had so many fantastic meals thère, so many laughs, so many tears, so many perfectly wonderful mundane days and nights that blurred together. There was an overlying sadness to our family, of course. But my God, we loved each other! Our house, where my twin had spent her short life, had held all that love in its humble rooms and tidy yard. Never again would I smell that unique perfume of home—tomato sauce and minestrone, Ivory soap and cellar must, Clorox Clean-Up and wax from Frankie's candles.

Georgia would come to my birthday dinner if I asked. But I never had; my family and I celebrated on our own, the ghost of Frankie a little too present on our birthday.

No, I wanted it to be Will, because I loved him. It had crept up in inches on me, that love, but now that it was here, I couldn't see it leaving anytime soon.

The other night, when I was cleaning up after dinner—a firm believer in They Who Cook Shall Not Do KP—Will had come up behind me at the sink, put his arms around me and rested his head on my shoulder. "You're beautiful," he said. Just that. But he stayed like that a long minute, then kissed my neck, making a tingling warmth spread down my side. I even felt him smile, just because he was glad I was there.

Wasn't that what love was? Happiness just because you were with your person? Not having to try to convince and fake it till you make it . . . all you had to do was be.

Well, well. Here I was, sitting in my car, getting all moony over a guy I'd once called a serial killer. I got out, went up to his door and was just about to knock when I heard voices. I froze, fist raised.

He had company. Now *that* was unexpected.

"It's been wonderful seeing you, baby," came a woman's

voice. Will always kept a few windows open an inch, so I could hear them easily. "You look wonderful."

"Thanks, Mom. Dad, it's fine. Leave it."

His parents! His *parents* were over. How nice! I knew they lived upstate, but he hadn't talked about them much. This was great.

Then again, maybe it wasn't that great . . . from where I stood, anyway, which was literally and figuratively outside. I hadn't been invited. Even if it was a spontaneous visit, I only lived six blocks away. He could've called me. And I really, really wanted him to introduce me to his parents.

Shit. It was on the list and everything.

"I hate to pry," said the mom, "but are you seeing anyone?"

I held my breath, waiting for the answer. I could just go in. That would answer the question, wouldn't it?

"Mom, I thought we agreed you wouldn't ask that anymore," Will said.

And that was all. I stood there, still poised to knock like a dope. *Then again, it wasn't exactly a no, either,* said the part of my brain that had spent five years waiting for Camden to date me.

"Leave him alone, Leslie," the dad said.

"I'd just like to know if my son has a special someone," she said.

"I don't."

The words hit me like an arrow to the chest.

"See? If he did, he'd tell you. Take care of yourself, son. We'll see you soon."

Oh, God, they were leaving. They'd see me, and that was the last thing I wanted at this moment.

I bolted down the steps and around the corner of the house, behind the rather ugly rhododendron bush, and watched

Will's parents leave. They looked perfectly nice. They held hands. They drove a Volvo.

And then they were gone.

He didn't want his parents to know about me. The feeling was horribly familiar.

Go home to meet his parents.

Yeah, right. Their son had just denied my existence.

I went up his steps. Knocked.

He answered almost right away, and frowned. "Hey," he said. "You're early."

"Is that a problem?"

He glanced down the street. "No, of course not. Come in."

I did. Sat on the brown couch in the unadorned living room. "Do you have any wine?"

"Yes. Since you seem to like it." He smiled.

I didn't smile back. "Of course I like it. I'm human."

He got me the wine. Water for himself.

"So what did you do today, Will?" I asked.

"Worked. Read *Game of Thrones*. You were right, it's addictive."

I waited. He said nothing more. I took a hearty swallow of wine, then another.

"You okay, Marley?"

"I'm great. How are your parents?"

He didn't look away, just took a slow, deep breath. "I gather you saw them leaving."

"Just a glimpse. You look like your father."

"A lot of people say that." He looked at his hands, perhaps aware that he was in deep, deep shit.

The clock ticked from the kitchen. I waited. Debated asking, *Why did you tell them you didn't have a special someone? Huh? Why didn't you mention me?*

But I knew the answer. He didn't want them to know.

"It's my birthday this week," I said. "Wednesday."

"Happy birthday."

"I'd like you to come for dinner that night," I said, my voice flat. "To Roberto's, about twenty minutes from here. I want you to meet my family."

His face was like a door shutting. "I'm not sure I can do that."

"Then come to my folks' house afterward for cake. It will just be us. The DeFelice family. Me, my parents, my sister, my brother, his husband."

"I . . . I don't think that's going to work."

"I think it will. I have a lot of faith in you. You were brave enough to save a woman's life during a mass shooting. You can meet my family."

"Marley—"

I set the wineglass down on the table so hard I was surprised it didn't break. "I know you have problems, Will, but so do I! My birthday is also my dead twin's birthday, in case you didn't do the math. My parents are moving out of the house they've lived in my whole life, and it will be the last time we're there. You have a hard time with crowds and leaving the house, and I know you've been making progress on that front. So make more progress, because I would really, really like to have you with me."

"I want to do it, Marley, but—"

"Do you? Because you didn't mention me to your parents ten minutes ago when your mother asked if you were seeing someone."

He closed his eyes and leaned his head against the couch. Busted. "That's not about you. And I'd go to your birthday if I could, but—"

"No. Don't tell me why you can't do it. Think about why I'm worth it. Me coming over here is not enough. I'd like to go places and do things and interact with other people, and I'd like you to do those things, too. I want more than a relationship that just has me coming here to eat, watch movies and have sex."

Granted, those three things were among my top five favorite things to do in life, but yeah. More than just that.

Will rubbed his forehead. "I'm sorry, I can't."

The words were like a slap. "Okay, then."

"Marley. It's not like I'm going clubbing or to Broadway shows or the Caribbean without you. I have some issues."

"I know you do," I said more gently. "It's time to move past them."

"I don't see why this"—he waved a hand between us—"is so terrible."

"This"—I waved my hand back—"is not terrible. It's just very limited."

He shrugged. "For now."

"When does *now* end, then? I mean, you haven't even been to my house. We can't even get coffee together."

"This is all I can do. For now."

"Well, I'm not going to be a secret booty call."

"You're more than that."

"Am I? Because it doesn't feel that way. Our entire relationship consists of me kind of being at your beck and call, always on your terms." The image of Camden and Amber at drinks that night flashed in front of me. "I can't do that anymore."

He rubbed his forehead and looked at the floor.

One more try. "Will," I said, my voice shaking, "there's a shrine to my sister in my parents' living room, and we're taking it down. Please come. Please be there for me. I think I deserve it."

Nothing.

Well, goddamn.

"Fine." I said. "Salt & Pepper is dropping you as a client, sorry to say. And this"—I waved my hand between us—"is done."

....

At noon on my thirty-fifth birthday, *Hudson Lifestyle* sent a photographer and a reporter over for my cover story. I'd cooked all morning to showcase various dishes, and the photographer, Kate, took pictures of me in the kitchen, me in the garden with a handful of the last parsley of the season. She took close-up shots of the cute, biodegradable Salt & Pepper boxes, food porn shots, and even one of me in regular clothes, eating fettuccine with pesto. The reporter asked questions, Kate put me at ease, and it was quite nice.

Be in a photo shoot. Emerson would've been so proud of me. Me, on the cover of a glossy magazine, celebrating the business I had created with my own two hands.

Afterward, I did my deliveries early, since I had dinner at Roberto's with the family at seven. I very nearly turned onto Redwood Street, where Will lived. Paused for a minute, feeling my chest tighten, then course-corrected and went to Rachel's.

As usual, the three girls swarmed my legs, professing their love of me, their hatred of broccoli, their desire to have me live with them. "Play with us! We want to play restaurant, Marley! Please! Please!"

"I'm afraid not, princesses," I said. "I have a family dinner tonight."

"Go play upstairs, girls," Rachel said, and off they went, a little flock of sisters. They were so lucky.

"I know you don't have time to play restaurant, but do you have time for a glass of wine?" Rachel asked, smiling.

I glanced at my watch. "One small glass of wine, if you don't mind me drinking and running."

"No, that's great. How was your day?"

"It was good," I said. "I had a photo shoot for *Hudson Lifestyle*, and when the issue drops, I think business is going to boom."

"Oh, good for you! You deserve it. Your food is amazing." She blushed a little. "If you ever need a part-time assistant, it'd be my dream job."

I paused. "You're hired," I said.

"Really? Thank you, Marley!"

"I mean, it'll be a lot around the holidays, and it won't be every day, but yeah! I could use the help. I imagine that with four-year-old triplets, you won't always know your availability, but we can work around that."

"Oh, this will be so much fun! By the way, they're five now," she said. "Just had their birthdays."

That stopped me in my tracks.

They weren't four anymore. They'd made it. "Thank God," I blurted. "Thank God." My eyes filled with tears, and all of a sudden, I found myself telling Rachel about Frankie.

She didn't freak out, didn't burst into tears. She just hugged me close and was absolutely lovely.

A little while later, after I'd dried my tears and hugged the girls, I drove down to the cemetery to meet my family and lay the white roses on Frankie's grave, as we did every year on this day.

We stood in a little knot, looking at her headstone.

Francesca Gabriella DeFelice, precious daughter and sister. Heaven's sweetest angel.

"I'll come every week, Mom," Dante said.

"I'll come at least once a month," Eva said. "Don't worry. Not one weed will dare show its face."

I didn't say anything. Truth was, I hated the cemetery, as

beautiful as it was. It would be good for Eva and Dante to step up. I didn't always have to be the one to do everything when it came to Frankie.

Dinner was excellent, as it always was at Roberto's. When Mom asked if my friend was coming, I simply said we'd had a miscommunication, and he got the date wrong. Didn't want to sully the evening by making people blue.

All through dinner, though, I pictured him coming through the door, running a hand through his perpetually disheveled hair, looking around till he saw us. He'd smile at me, and he'd be a little sweaty, and that would be just fine with me.

He didn't come.

And it was fine. We had a few laughs, Dante and Louis telling a story of a naked woman who didn't want to leave her apartment building, despite the flames and smoke, since the neighbors would see her "wobbly bits." Eva told us that she got to fire someone who'd been watching porn at work, and had followed him to the elevator, dinging the receptionist's desk bell and chanting, "Shame, shame, shame." My father toasted me and told me I was a wonderful daughter, and Mom kissed me seven times throughout dinner and hardly cried at all.

It was when we got home that things got tough.

The only furniture left in my parents' house was a folding table and six plastic chairs . . . and the shrine, all four candles burning, the pictures of Frankie, Ebbers the Penguin looking back at us from his shelf.

"Dinner was nice, wasn't it?" Mom asked. She was nervous, of course. She was leaving her children, moving to a different state, away from everyone she knew. She was more than nervous. She was terrified.

I was terrified, too. The idea that my parents were going

to be four and a half hours away made my knees feel sick and wobbly.

"Dinner was great," I said, realizing I hadn't spoken yet. "I love that place." Not a lie.

"Who wants wine?" Dad asked, holding up a bottle and a stack of plastic cups.

"I do," we all chorused.

What would Christmas be like this year? I'd never *not* spent a Christmas here, or an Easter, or a Fourth of July, for that matter.

"We want you to all come down for Thanksgiving," Mom said. "We have plenty of room. Two guest bedrooms and a nice sofa bed for you, Marley. Okay? Okay. Good. That's settled."

There was no way I could go. It was my busiest time of year.

Except maybe, with Rachel, I could. She'd be more than just an assistant, I already knew. She was going to be one of my best friends. Georgia would love her.

So even if Will didn't want a real relationship, I still had people. My life was full. I had a job I loved, my family, my friends, hobbies and ambition.

In a way, Emerson's list taught me something I hadn't anticipated. You didn't get everything in life. I'd always thought if you worked hard enough and tried to be your best self, the universe would listen. But it didn't always. As my grandfather used to say, God was not a grocer; you didn't hand him a list and have him go through it, checking off everything you'd asked for. You could be fulfilled just the same . . . and you were also allowed to be sad once in a while.

It wasn't my job to be always happy, always perky, always up for anything and always there for everyone. I got to have a little heartache, too, just like everyone else.

But if I thought too much about my parents leaving, I was going to start bawling, and I did want to save that for home. My parents didn't need to see my tears.

"Cake time!" Mom said, the fake cheer thick in her voice.

Ricotta cheesecake, my favorite, was sitting on the table, waiting for us. In raspberry glaze, she'd written, *Happy Birthday, Marley & Frankie*.

I wondered if ricotta cheesecake would've been my sister's favorite, too.

We held up our plastic cups. "To Frankie," my mother said. "Happy birthday, honey."

"To Frankie," we echoed. Dad's eyes were shiny.

"And to you, Marley," Mom said, tears streaming down her face. "Happy birthday, sweetheart. You're a wonderful daughter."

"To Marley," my family said.

My throat was killing me. "One more," I said, my voice tight with tears. "To you, Mom and Dad. Thank you for making this house a wonderful home for all of us. We hope you have many happy years in your beautiful new place. I think you're so brave for doing this, and I can't wait to come see you." My voice broke a little.

"Hear, hear," said Dante and Louis.

"Well said." Eva touched her cup to mine. "Good job, sis."

Mom went to cut the cake. She always started on the *F* in Frankie's name.

"Wait," I said. She did, turning back to me.

"Mom . . . Dad . . ." My voice was shaking. "Can you . . . can you tell me something about her? Something I don't know? Because I'm afraid I'll forget her. I—" Tears slid down my face. "All I have left is the Frankie-shaped space. The space where she used to be."

I was sobbing now, and my mother took me in her arms.

A second later, I felt my father's arms, too, and he rested his head against mine. "I don't remember her," I whispered. "I'm sorry. I want to, but there's nothing there."

"Oh, my baby," Mom said, crying, too. "My little Marley, don't cry. Don't cry, angel. You were the best sister in the world. You loved her so much, and she . . . she just adored you."

"She did," Dad said. "She lit up every time you came in the room. You used to make her laugh so hard."

There was a strange sound, and I looked up. It was Eva, and she was crying, too. "Shit," she said. "It's true. She loved you so much, Marles."

Then we were all group-hugging, a big knot of family, laughing and sobbing and holding each other tight.

"I don't want to leave her behind," I whispered.

"You can't leave her," Dante said, wiping his eyes on Louis's shirtsleeve. "She's not in this house, Marles. She's with us. Especially you."

That was true. Not an hour of my life passed where I didn't think of her, yearn for her, miss her, love her. I didn't know how *not* to love her.

Dad disentangled from the pack and went over to the shrine, and we all separated, sniffing, blowing noses on birthday napkins. He came back, holding Ebbers the Penguin.

"Here, honey," he said. "You keep this now. You should've had it all along."

With hands that shook, I took my sister's beloved cuddle friend and looked at his flat black eyes. Then I hugged him and buried my face against him.

I remembered that smell. Thirty-one years, and he still smelled like Ebbers, musty and with a hint of sweet little girl sweat.

All of a sudden, memories slammed into me, into my

heart, into my head, into my bone marrow, a stream of them, fast and clear and pure.

Me, climbing into Frankie's crib, the squeak of the springs, her delighted laugh.

Frankie's face against mine, so close I could smell her breath, her skin so pale, her hand against my cheek.

The two of us in the tub, playing with a tiny blue sponge shaped like a dog, floating him on the soap dish, Frankie's eyelashes starred from the water.

Frankie's little body pressed against my left side, warm and soft, her thumb in her mouth, her head tipped against my shoulder, the two of us like puzzle pieces, my arm around her, tingling and asleep but knowing not to move because my sister needed me.

She was with me. She always had been. As long as I lived, so would a part of my sister.

I sucked in a breath, then another. "I remember," I said, laughing and crying at the same time and hugging Ebbers against my heart. "I remember you, Frankie."

. . . .

It was, we agreed, the most tear-soaked birthday in the history of birthdays.

It was good, like something had been set free in all of us. We ate some cake, and kept hugging each other at every opportunity, blotting our eyes, laughing, embarrassed, happy. So strange, and so right.

As I was cutting Dante a third (third!) piece of cheesecake, because he was the baby and incapable of doing it himself, the doorbell rang.

"Probably the McIntyres, coming to say good-bye," Mom said. "For the fourth time." She went to open the door.

It was Will.

I sat down abruptly on the plastic chair. My eyes flooded yet again.

"Hello there," my mother said. "Can we help you?"

He didn't answer. Instead, his eyes locked on mine, and he brushed past my mother and knelt in front of me. He had a bag in one hand, flowers in the other, and he set them on the floor, then took my hands.

He was here.

He'd come after all.

"Are you crying?" he asked, and his voice was so gentle.

I nodded, speechless, tears slipping down my face. His shirt was stuck to him with sweat.

"Are you okay?" he asked.

I nodded again.

"Who is this person?" my father asked.

"Pretty sure it's the boyfriend," Dante said.

"Huh. He's pretty cute," Eva said.

"I'm sorry I'm late," Will said, ignoring everyone else. "It . . . I had a little . . . trouble on the way, but I'm here now." His soft blue eyes were intent on me. "Am I too late?"

"Of course not! There's still cake," my mother said.

"I don't think he's talking about that," Louis whispered.

"It's not too late," I managed. "Are *you* okay?" Even his hair was sweaty, like he'd run down from Cambry-on-Hudson, and his hands were shaking.

"I'm horrible. Never better. Can I kiss you?" he asked.

"Oh, boy. Who needs more wine?" Eva said, ever the romantic.

I didn't answer. Instead, I wrapped my arms around his neck and kissed him. Kissed him with a full heart, an overflowing heart, because he'd come, and God only knew what that had taken, given his current state. But he was here, because he'd decided in the end that I was worth it.

"What's in the bag?" my mother asked.

"Oh, right," he said. "Um, a clean shirt, for one." My family, my wonderful, warm, welcoming family, laughed. "And this."

He put a little blue box into my hand. Tiffany blue. My mouth opened a little, and a strangled noise came out. "You went to Tiffany?" I asked.

"Their website, to be honest. They overnighted it." He shrugged. "Coming here was hard enough."

"Wait a second, young man," said my father. "If you're proposing, it's tradition that you ask the father first. Or at least tell him your name."

"Will Harding," he said, not looking away from me.

He was smiling.

This wasn't the most romantic place—my parents' empty living room, me in a plastic chair holding Ebbers, my family waiting.

Frankie looked on from her pictures. And, I thought, looked on from my heart. Smiling, I imagined.

"Marley . . . when I first hired you," Will began, "I hated having you come in, I admit that. You were so—big. Not that way," he amended hastily. "Not size. Your smile, your laugh, the way you talked about food, the way you were so full of life. I couldn't wait to get rid of you."

I laughed a little at the honesty. My eyes were still leaking. Louis smiled into his cup.

"Then," Will said, "I started trying to get you to stay a little longer. I'd make you wait for your check so you'd stay a few more minutes. Then I'd find myself looking at the clock all day, waiting for you to come. You've been the bright spot in my day. In the entire past year, you've been . . . everything."

"That's beautiful," my mom said, sniffling.

It was. My heart felt too big for my chest, too full and so *happy*.

"I know I've asked a lot of you, and I'm sorry. And I'll make it up to you if you let me. I love you. Marry me."

I sucked in a shaky breath. "You sure it's not just about the food?"

"Marley," he said, a smile starting in the corner of his mouth, "it was never about the food."

"Then I guess I have to say yes," I said, and my family burst into tears once more, and Will kissed me.

"Thank you," he whispered against my mouth. "Thank you."

CHAPTER 37

Georgia

Tell off the person who judged me when I was fat.
(It's not who you think.)

My best friend was engaged. Engaged, I tell you! I mean, what the even heck?

I was summoned down to Marley's the day after her birthday, where Will and she stood in her kitchen. "You remember Will," she said, then held up her left hand.

"Oh, my God! My God! Marley!" I immediately burst into tears, hugged her, hugged Will, hugged Marley again. "Hold on, I have champagne." I ran up to grab some—I just happened to have some Bollinger's lying around, thankyou-veddymuch; my dear old dad had pressed it on me the other night when I'd had dinner with him, Cherish and the girls. Came back down, Admiral beating me, and uncorked the bottle, pouring the golden liquid into Marley's adorable, pink-tinged champagne glasses. "To the happy couple," I said, my voice husky.

She looked *so* happy. Every clichéd word you could think of for a happy bride applied—beautiful, radiant, glowing, blissful, blushing.

The ring was frickin' gorgeous, too.

And the groom . . . well, I'd only met Will the one time,

but his eyes followed her with a gentle, rather smitten expression. I liked that in a man.

We went into her sweet little living room, and Admiral curled into his yogic ball at my feet, wagging his tail occasionally. "Tell me the story."

They did, taking turns, passing the story between them. Will seemed a little shy, but it was endearing.

He was holding Marley's hand. *Hold hands with a cute guy in public.* Well, we weren't in public, but this was an excellent start.

"When I first came in, I was slightly concerned her brother and his husband would beat me up," Will was saying.

"Wait," I said. "You proposed in front of her entire family? Everyone was there?"

"Yes." He raised an eyebrow, and I liked him even more.

"I think I'm crushing on you myself, Will."

"Go right ahead," Marley said. "I'm extremely secure."

"What did they say? Did her father take out his gun? Did her mother hit you with a lasagna pan?"

"Luckily, their stuff was all packed," Will said. He looked at Marley. "They were pretty incredible, actually."

"They are. They're like that," I said. "So . . . have you thought about when? I mean, it's been twenty-four hours. I'm assuming I beat Eva out for maid of honor." They laughed, and Marley assured me I had.

"It won't be too soon," Marley said. "We've only been dating a little while. We have some things to work on."

"I'm pretty badly agoraphobic and have PTSD," he said.

"Oh! Well! That's very . . . forthright of you, Will."

"I thought Marley would've told you."

"She didn't. She's very loyal with people's secrets." I took a sip of champagne. "You seeing a therapist? I know a good one."

"Way ahead of you," he said.

"Good. Well. Maybe you can make a list of goals," I said, and Marley and I started giggling.

"That's a good idea," he said, and we laughed harder.

"To Emerson," Marley said. "I wish she could be here." Her beautiful brown eyes filled with tears.

"Me too," I said. "She'd be so happy. She'd love you, Will," I added, to be generous. But I thought it was true. Emerson had been the least judgmental person I'd ever met. If Will loved Marley, and she loved him back, that was all the criteria a person would need.

"Speaking of Emerson, when will the paperwork be done on her house?" Marley said.

"I have to go down and file for transfer of ownership."

"I'll come, too. I can't wait to kick out that horrible cousin. And give the house to that family." We were planning to furnish the house for them, all new stuff for a fresh start. It was going to be a huge surprise.

"Won't the cousin have squatter's rights?" Will asked.

"Georgia graduated from Yale Law, babe. She loves nothing more than a good fight."

"Hear, hear," I said. "But we can talk about that later. Will, did you love Marley from the very second you laid eyes on her?" I asked, settling back against the throw pillows.

"I did," he said.

"You did not!" she exclaimed. "You said I made you nervous."

"You did. You got under my skin—"

"Like one of those spiders that lays its eggs," I said, making Marley snort her champagne.

"Exactly," he agreed, smiling at me. "And you know how it is. Once you meet her . . ."

"You just can't give her up," I said, laughing. "Will, you and I have a lot in common."

I pictured us from the outside, from the courtyard, three people and a dog, all of us laughing, love shimmering around us, the love of this new couple, the love of old friends. The pretty little town house on the pretty little street, a hint of winter in the air, the warm lights of Marley's apartment glowing.

In that moment, there was no place I'd rather be, no *one* I'd rather be, and no friend I'd rather have in the entire world.

I left about an hour later, buoyed by their happiness. Gave Admiral his bedtime snack, affirmed that he was the best dog in the entire world, changed into my jammies and brushed my teeth.

The house felt a little empty after the festivities below. A little quiet.

My reflection in the mirror showed a person looking a little rabid from toothpaste foam. But her eyes were bright and happy, and while her hair could use a trim, she looked . . .

She looked . . .

Fuck it. Who cared how she looked?

Before I knew what I was doing, I grabbed my keys. "See you later, Ad!" I said. I got into my car and headed south. To the city.

To Tribeca.

I wasn't going to stop and think and rehearse. I knew where I had to be, and that was enough.

The traffic gods were with me, because I made it in less than an hour. (Also, I may have been speeding just a little.)

I double-parked in front of Pamplona, and it was only as I walked through the doors that I realized I was wearing my sock monkey pajamas.

Welp, it didn't matter. I was here.

"Can I . . . um, can I help you?" asked a very beautiful young woman at the front desk.

"I'd like to see Rafael Santiago," I said. My voice was

calm. *I* was calm, freakishly. Then again, this had been a long time coming.

"He's really busy," she said, eyeing my pj's.

"I'm his ex-wife."

Her eyes widened. "I'll be right back."

She went to alert him (or security), and I stood there. God, the restaurant was beautiful. It made my entire soul happy to see it. Every table seemed to be filled, and Spanish guitar music played softly over the sound system. Candles flickered, and the food smelled divine.

Oh, and everyone was looking at me. I gave a little wave.

I wasn't drunk. I wasn't even tipsy. I'd had half a glass of champagne at Marley's. No, I was just here, in the moment, as they said at yoga class. I was finally here.

Rafe and the beautiful maître d' came up to the front. "Georgia," he said, and then my whole heart rolled over in my chest. He took me by the arms. "Is everything all right? Your family? Mason?"

God, those eyes. Those beautiful, honest eyes.

"Everyone is fine," I told him, my voice husky.

So yes, it was getting quiet in here. I had mentioned the sock monkey pj's, right?

"Are you all right, Georgia?" he asked. "You are wearing your . . . ah . . ."

"Right. I kind of rushed over." I smiled a little. "I needed to tell you something." I glanced around. This was his restaurant, his work of art, and I had already made a scene. "Um . . . do you have an office?"

"No." He glanced at his patrons, gave them a nod. "Come with me."

He murmured something to the maître d' and led me down the hall, past the restrooms, to the coatroom. Not the most scenic of places. In the movies, it would be in front of the whole restaurant. In real life, this would have to do.

"Are you sure you're all right?" he asked. "This is very unexpected. You could have called."

I swallowed. "I know I look, um, unbalanced. But I'm not. I'm . . ."

It was suddenly important that not another minute pass before I said what I had to say.

I took his hands, his beautiful hands, in mine and looked into those dark, dark eyes. My heart was pumping so hard that I could feel the pulse in my throat, my wrists, my knees.

"Rafe," I said, my voice shaking, "Rafael. You were the best thing that ever happened to me. When we were together, I didn't know how to love you, or let you love me, because I hated who I was. Our divorce was completely my fault."

"No, Georgia," he said, "that is not the case."

"Let me say this. I was the problem. I didn't talk to you, I didn't try to fix all the things that had made me miserable in the past, and I was obsessed with how much I weighed and what that said about me. Instead of paying attention to what really mattered—you, us—I just thought about myself. If someone had ever obsessed over my weight and judged me as harshly as I judged myself, I would've hated them. And I did. I hated myself because of one thing. It was stupid and shallow and destructive, and I ruined us."

His eyes were growing wet. "I should have listened more. I didn't know how . . . difficult this was for you."

"I wouldn't let you." I squeezed his hands hard. "So now, I wanted to tell you—I *need* to tell you now, before another day passes, that I love you, Rafe. I've always loved you. I always will. You're the love of my life. I know you have someone else now, but . . . well . . . I still needed to tell you. You're the best person I've ever met, and for the rest of my life, I'll be lucky because I knew you."

"Corazón," he said. "I—I do not . . . I cannot at this

time . . ." He sighed. "You know I love you still. You know that. It has never been in question. Never."

My heart surged, and I put my hand against his heart. No, it never was. From almost the moment we met, I knew Rafael Esteban Jesús Santiago was, first and foremost, the most honorable, decent man I'd ever met. I should've trusted him when he said he loved me. I should've heard *that* instead of the ugly echoes from my past.

"But you are right, Georgia," he said softly. "There is someone else. I cannot just walk out of here with you. She does not deserve that."

Right. That put a damper on things. I let my hand fall. "No," I whispered. "I'm sure she doesn't. I just needed to tell you."

We looked at each other a long minute. My eyes were wet, too, and my heart . . . well, it was finally being sincere.

"Thank you," he whispered. "But you should probably go home."

I smiled, sort of, though my mouth was wobbling. Then I hugged him, hard and fast, and left, passing the diners, wishing they could've had some Hollywood scene where Rafe and I'd be kissing right now, where champagne would be uncorked and everyone would be smiling.

Instead, I walked outside, alone, as the first snowflakes of the season drifted down onto my sock monkey jammies.

My car had already been ticketed.

It was okay, I told myself as I took the orange paper off my windshield. I'd be okay. Even if I felt like I'd been punched in the heart, at least I'd said what needed saying.

It didn't stop me from crying, even so.

CHAPTER 38

Dear Other Emerson,

I think this might be the last time I write to you. I'm not doing too well. My leg hurts, my chest hurts, and I'm so tired, but I had to write to you one more time. I'm sorry I said I hated you. I don't.

I think I might be dying, OE. I think this is it. Pretty soon, I'll ask Ruth to call an ambulance, and make her call Georgia and Marley, because I want to see them one more time. I don't know where Mica is. He hasn't been coming around this past month as much. That's maybe another sign that I'm on my way out.

I didn't make it, Other Emerson. I never became you.

I want you to have a good life. Stop working so much, even though you have a great thing going there. Marry Idris. He loves you so. Have beautiful children with Cockney accents and love them with all your heart.

I keep thinking of Camp Copperbrook. Me and Marley and Georgia. I was looking through my old journals the other day, and I found that list we made. I'll give it to them.

I wish I hadn't shut them out. I wish I'd been honest with them about how lonely I was, how scared of myself. I wish I'd said yes to that weekend the last time Marley asked. I wish I hadn't been so afraid of what people think. I wish we hadn't thought of ourselves as ugly ducklings when we were swans all along.

I can't waste time right now, though. I can't think of all the things I didn't do, or all the things I wished for. I don't have a lot of time. It's okay. It's fine now.

I dozed off there for a while, Other Emerson. I feel foggy now, and weak. I think I'm letting go.

There was a day that summer, when we were all eighteen... the sky was so blue, and the pine needles smelled like heaven. The day we lost the oars, our last full day of camp. Our last day together, when we were just floating in the lake, and the sun was warm and strong, and we were so, so happy.

I feel that way now, Other Emerson. Isn't that funny? I feel happy. Georgia and Marley will be here soon. I'll get to say good-bye.

It feels like I'm back in the lake, because I'm floating, sort of. I'm so <u>light</u>. I remember the sound of the three of us laughing. I love them so much, and I can feel how much they love me.

I can just about hear my mother calling me. My mama! I've missed her so much! I can't wait to see her.

It'll be okay, Other Emerson. Don't cry. I've been so tired for so long. I want to go home. I'll be so happy when I finally get home.

CHAPTER 39

Georgia

Let go.

In mid-December, about six weeks after Will and Marley had gotten engaged and I'd poured out my heart to Rafe, Mason and I took our usual walk to the park.

My nephew was doing so well. I didn't know if my brother (half brother) had changed that much—do people ever?—but Mason was doing great. Since that meet, he hadn't mentioned Hunter so much, and his nails weren't chewed to the quick anymore. He was running indoor track, and last weekend, he'd seen the latest Marvel Comics flick with some of his friends.

It was cold enough that we could see our breath, and Admiral wore a little sweater, because he was skinny and spoiled. His ears pricked up at the sight of the baseball field, and Mason let him off the leash. Round and round he went, a gray blur of athletic doggy perfection.

"I asked my dad if I could take piano lessons. Said it would be a nice Christmas present," Mason said.

"What did he say?"

"He said we didn't have a piano, and I told him you did,

and you lived down the street from a piano teacher. So he said he'd think about it."

"Good for you, honey." I looked at him, this favorite person of mine. His face was changing, losing its boyish softness, his jaw becoming more defined. There was even a little stubble on his chin. "Mason," I said carefully, "I have to ask you something."

"Go for it."

"Did you try to kill yourself last April? Because I know you didn't just have a bad headache."

He looked at me with his mother's clear, kind gray eyes. Then he scratched his head and turned back to watch Admiral. "I didn't have a headache," he admitted, his voice calm, and deeper. "I just wanted to go to sleep for a while. A long while. I didn't want to die, but I was just so tired of being, like, miserable and lonely all the time. I thought if I could sleep for a weekend or so, I'd feel better. I didn't know about the liver stuff. But no, G. I didn't try to commit suicide."

"You're happier now, right?"

"Totally."

"And you'll never hurt yourself?"

"We're not talking sprains, right? Because I can't make those promises. But if we're talking about, you know . . . suicide, yeah. I promise. Don't worry, G. I won't leave you."

The words brought a lump to my throat. He *would* leave me, of course. Even now, he was leaning on me less, doing things with his friends, bonding with teachers. In three and a half years, he'd go off to college, out into the world, and the memory of these years when his aunt was his favorite person would be just that—a memory.

He'd leave, but in the right way, and I'd let him go.

I squeezed his arm. "I love you like you were my own son, you know."

He snorted. "Kind of gross, since you're my father's

sister, but thanks." He looked at me a long minute. "I love you, too, G. You're the best."

....

That weekend, Marley and I drove down to Delaware to kick out the evil cousin and turn the keys over to the new owners.

We'd had painters come in and give it a nice fresh coat (which had made Ruth complain about the fumes), sand the floors (ditto) and get rid of most of the furniture. We were keeping some things in the house—the cute little enamel-topped kitchen table, the Fiestaware. The TV. We'd ordered furniture from our favorite stores and had a truck meeting us there.

It was with great satisfaction that we pulled up in front of Emerson's house to find Ruth standing there, looking like she'd just eaten the rotting testicles of a dead hippo. The furniture store truck was already there, and one of the movers gave us a wave.

"Well, I guess this is it, Ruth," Marley said. "See you never."

"I'm sure you're very proud of yourselves," she said, "kicking an old woman out of her home."

"I know I am," I said. "And you're forty-eight, Ruth. Only your heart is shriveled and dead." I handed Ruth an envelope. "Your eviction notice."

"I'm not poor," she said. "You can laugh over how that fat pig screwed me out of an inheritance, but I saved. I won't exactly be living on the streets." She went to her car, pulled out a box and dropped it unceremoniously on the curb. "Here. Even though you've been very unkind to me, I thought you'd like to have these."

"Also, that pesky law," I said. "We own everything in the house, so if you didn't give it back, it'd be larceny."

She humphed and got into her car.

"Good riddance," Marley muttered, giving her the finger, though Ruth was already pulling away.

I went over to the box and drew in a sharp breath.

Emerson's journals.

"Marley," I said. She came over.

"Oh. Oh, jeesh." Her eyes filled. "Should we read them? I mean, they were her diaries."

"I don't know," I said. "We'll take them back. We can decide some other time." But I cracked one, and the sight of her pretty handwriting made my eyes well.

"No crying," Marley said.

"Hypocrite."

"Come on. We have work to do. We'll cry later. For now, let the good times roll," Marley said, and I loved that about her, her ability to pivot, to keep moving forward.

We unlocked the front door and stood back as the movers brought in our purchases. A lovely blue velvet couch, a polka-dotted recliner. A coffee table, end tables, some lamps, beds for all four bedrooms, including a California king for the mom. Pots and pans, a mixer, a blender, a coffee maker. A rug for the living room. New glasses, new dish towels, a bright yellow kettle. A few dog statues, because we couldn't resist. But mostly we just supplied the big-ticket items. The Williams family could do the rest. It would be their home, after all.

We'd also left them gift cards to Pier 1, HomeGoods and Ikea. Had to be true to our design aesthetic, after all.

It didn't take as long as I'd expected. Just a few hours after we got there, Emerson's house was a far cry from the first time we'd seen it just four months ago.

Then we went in the backyard and stood in front of the window that had been Emerson's glimpse of the outside the last year of her life.

I took the list out of my pocket. Marley had the matches. She struck one, sheltering the flame with her hand, and I held the paper to it. In silence, we watched as it caught. Then I dropped it to the ground.

In just under a minute, it was blackened ash.

"To Emerson," I said, hugging Marley tight.

"To Emerson," she said, her shoulders shaking with sobs.

When we pulled apart, we looked at each other, both of us teary-eyed. "We did it," I said, my voice shaking.

"We are awesome." She handed me a tissue, and I wiped my eyes and blew my nose.

"Okay, let's go," Marley said. "Let's do some good in this world."

I grabbed my bag, which held the envelope that contained the deed, and we walked around the block.

Emerson's lawyer had ascertained that the Williams family still rented the house on Emerson's block, and it wasn't hard to spot their place, the sore thumb of the otherwise charming neighborhood. We'd learned that Natasha Williams had been widowed seven years ago, when her littlest was just a baby. She had two other girls—an eleven-year-old and a fourteen-year-old. Natasha worked as a licensed practical nurse, and her mom had come to live with them this past year, the lawyer said.

Three generations of girl power under one roof would've made Emerson happy. After all, she and her mother had been so close. The memory of the house as her prison would be erased by the family, we hoped.

We knocked on the door. "I'm nervous," Marley whispered. "My heart is pounding."

"Mine too." I grabbed her hand for luck.

A woman opened the door, and I immediately remembered her. The lady with the casserole. She'd come to Emerson's wake with her girls.

"Natasha Williams?" I said.

"Yes. You're . . . you're Emerson's friends, aren't you?"

Marley squeezed my hand, and I looked at her. "Do you want to tell her?" I asked.

"No, you do it."

I looked back at Mrs. Williams. "You're right, we're Emerson's friends, and we have some happy news for you." I paused. "Emerson left you her house in her will."

She frowned. "I don't understand."

"She wanted you to have her house. She said you were very kind."

"Is this a joke?"

"Not at all. Can we come in? I have the deed right here."

Looking very suspicious, she let us in, and as we sat in her tiny, worn kitchen, I explained the details, how a trust would pay the taxes, how there'd be some money put aside each year for home repairs. The sight of her name on the deed was what made her start to cry. "I barely knew her," she whispered.

"Well," Marley said, covering her hand with her own, "you made a big impression."

"This feels like a dream," she said. "I can't believe it. Are you sure you have the right person?"

"She was very specific," I said.

"I helped her once. When she fell. Otherwise, I'd just wave if I saw her. My girls shoveled her walk when it snowed."

"Sometimes you never know how much those little things matter," I said.

"Want to come see it?" Marley asked. "It's furnished. You could sleep there tonight if you wanted."

"Are you sure? This is really happening, right?"

"It's really happening," Marley said.

Natasha wiped her eyes. "Girls!" she called over her

shoulder. "Mom! We just got some news. Some amazing news."

A few minutes later, the five of them stood on Emerson's front porch. You know those shows where a family gets a house . . . They opened the door. There was squealing, a lot of crying, a lot of exclamations. The grandma blessed us over and over.

Marley was crying. I was, too. Happy, happy tears.

Emerson would've been so glad.

The ride home was so different from the last time we'd left Delaware. Instead of grief and shock over our friend, we felt only love. We talked about Camp Copperbrook, the time we'd met in Philly for a weekend, the other time on the Jersey Shore.

My ulcer was gone, according to my GI doctor, and I was eating more. I'd gained a little weight back, but I liked it. I wasn't skinny, I wasn't fat. I was just me. I was pretty sure I was almost normal in terms of size and eating. I'd never get that perfect body, and there'd be times when I ate Oreos for lunch, and times when I skipped lunch altogether, but that wasn't the end of the world. Mostly, I was just happy to be myself. My body worked. It was getting stronger every month, thanks to the gym. I was alive.

"How's Will?" I asked.

"Getting there," Marley said. "He went grocery shopping Sunday and came back completely soaked in sweat, but he did it." The pride in her voice was obvious. "And . . . guess what? He's taking me to his parents' house the day after Christmas. Meet the parents! Ta-freakin'-da, Emerson! The last thing on my list!"

"Whoo-hoo!" I said, beeping the horn. "Emerson! Did you hear that?"

We talked and laughed and sat in silence the way old friends can, and in what seemed like no time, we were crossing the beautiful Tappan Zee Bridge. It had started to snow, lush, lazy flakes drifting slowly from the sky.

"My mother wants to know if you'll come to Eva's on Christmas Eve," Marley said as we took the exit for Cambry-on-Hudson. "Have you ever had the Feast of the Seven Fishes, G? My mother makes Mario Batali look like a microwaving hack."

"Thanks, but I'm staying over at my dad's on Christmas Eve," I said. "I love seeing the girls on Christmas morning."

"And how does Big Kitty feel about that?"

I shrugged. "Fine, I guess. I'm going to her house Christmas afternoon for exactly forty-five minutes and one glass of wine, and then Admiral and I have plans to snuggle and watch movies for the rest of the weekend."

"Or," Marley said, looking out the window as we approached our house, "you might have plans with that guy there."

I glanced where she pointed, and then lurched to an awkward stop, my front wheel scraping the curb, nearly hitting a tree.

Rafael Esteban Jesús Santiago was sitting on the front steps of my town house, talking to Mason, petting Admiral. Rafe wore a blue-and-green plaid scarf, and snow was falling gently, dotting his dark hair. At the sight of my car, he looked at me, and smiled.

He *smiled*.

I just sat there, strangling the steering wheel with both hands.

"Get out of the car," Marley said.

"Right." I obeyed, my arms tingling with nervousness. My legs wobbled, too.

"Hiya, G! Look who I found sitting here."

Rafe stood, brushing the snow off his hair. "Hello, Georgia," he said. "Marley."

"Come with me, Mason," Marley said. "We have very important things to discuss. You too, Admiral."

She gave me a huge smile, took my nephew by the arm and towed him away, Admiral following.

"Hi," I said. My mouth was dry.

"How have you been?"

"Good. Great. And you?"

"Very well. Your family is good, yes?"

"Yes. As good as we get. You know."

"Mason seems wonderful."

"Yep. Yes. He is." I swallowed.

"Corazón," he began, and suddenly tears swamped my eyes, and I looked down. A sob hitched out of me. "Ah, Georgia, please wait to cry until I have finished my speech," he said, and I could hear the smile in his voice.

Please, I thought. *Please.*

"Look at me, Georgia," he said, folding his arms.

I did, even though it was hard.

He didn't speak for a long minute. "I have to admit, after you came to the restaurant, I was angry with you. It has taken you five years to say what I hoped always to hear."

I nodded, dropping my gaze to his scarf.

"And there was Heather. She was also angry with you."

"Right," I said.

Then he tipped my chin up so he could see my face. "However, there is the fact that I have never stopped loving you, either, Georgia Sloane. You said I was the love of your life. You are the love of mine. So. Let us try again, shall we? We will do better this time."

Then he smiled with his eyes, his mouth, his whole beautiful face, and I kissed him with all the love I'd ever had for him, and not just love. The gratitude, the joy, the *wonder* you feel when you finally surrender to love, to trust, to your true self.

Life was kind and full of chances. Sometimes we didn't take them. Sometimes we hid our truth and acted out of fear. Sometimes we turned away and closed the door.

But sometimes there were moments like this, when I was kissing the only man I had ever loved, and the snow fell gently around us, like a blessing.

Good luck, I imagined the universe saying kindly, infusing the phrase with gentleness and faith. *Good luck with everything.*

GOOD LUCK
WITH *THAT*

KRISTAN
HIGGINS

DISCUSSION QUESTIONS

1. The author chose not to reveal the exact weights and sizes of Georgia and Marley, leaving you to draw your own conclusions. Did that bother you, or did you appreciate that choice? How did *you* picture Marley and Georgia? What size do you consider overweight? How do you think body image affects women who aren't overweight? Do you think not knowing their weight affected your understanding of them as people? Does someone's weight influence how you judge them?

2. Do you think Marley and Georgia each had an accurate view of her own size? How do you think a bad self-image follows you, no matter what the scale says? Is it true what Georgia says: "Once a fat girl, always a fat girl"?

3. Why do you think Marley has a more positive self-image than Emerson or Georgia? She comes from a family that loves to eat, where everyone except her brother is overweight. When you grow up in a family that overindulges regularly, do you think you can ever get past those habits and the emotional components involved with food?

4. Marley is a twin without a twin and feels the need to fill that void through friendships and romantic relationships. How do you think the ghost of Frankie has helped and hurt her through the years? What about her family's treatment of Frankie? How much do you think the loss of Frankie affected Marley's physical self?

5. Marley is someone who embraces the idea of "healthy at any weight." She eats well most of the time, loves to exercise and has a pretty positive self-image. In one scene, she takes a hard look at her body and decides she will not only accept it in its current size but appreciate it. Do you think it's possible to overcome negative stereotypes you hold about yourself?

6. Georgia feels that her food issues destroyed her marriage. Was she naive in thinking she could be married to a chef? What might she have done differently to protect against her negative self-image coming back to haunt her once she'd fallen in love?

7. Georgia's brother, Hunter, is negative, intolerant and often cruel. Have you ever met someone like him? How do you think his treatment of Georgia as a child sabotaged her in her adult life? Do you think it's possible for someone like Hunter to be a good parent? Do you know anyone like Georgia and Hunter's mother, who treats each of her children in a vastly different manner?

8. Emerson's weight and eating issues are not romanticized—the difficulty of her day-to-day life, her isolation, the lies she tells others and herself, the constant obsession with food. Do you know anyone like her, and if so, do you ever discuss food issues with them? How has that been?

9. Rafe, Will, Hunter, Georgia's father, Camden, Evan . . . Are the men in the book bothered by the weight of the women? Which ones are, or aren't, and why? Do you think fat prejudice comes more from women than from men?

10. Emerson, Georgia and Marley are not the only female characters with weight issues in this book. Who are some of the other characters who have weight problems, and what are the issues they represent in the story?

11. Marley, Georgia and Emerson have a very deep bond. Although Georgia and Marley saw each other more often, both women still felt very connected to Emerson over the years. How can friends stay close without spending time together? Do you have any long-distance friends who are especially close to you? Why do you think Marley and Georgia remained so close?

12. Do you think our culture has impossible beauty standards? Are these changing at all?

CHAPTER 1

Emma

"You don't have a brain tumor," said my best friend, who, conveniently, was also a neurologist.

"Are you sure?" I asked.

"Yes, Emma. Don't look so disappointed."

"I'm not! I just . . . you know, my vision was wonky last night. Then I spaced out driving into the city today." Granted, last night I'd accidentally turned on the superbright flashlight while it was aimed right at my face, but still . . . the retinal afterimage had taken some time to subside. As for spacing out, I drove into Chicago a few times a week, so it was normal that I didn't take note of every detail on the forty-five-minute drive. Still, I couldn't help asking, "Are you sure it's not parahypnagogia?"

"Stop looking up medical terms," Calista said. "You're

healthy. You're not dying. Riley will not grow up mother-less, and besides, she's sixteen, and if you did die, I would adopt her and raise her as my own. Screw her baby daddy."

"I did screw him. Hence our child. But I'll make sure you get custody. She does like you better."

Calista smiled. "Of course she does. Are we still on for drinks Thursday?"

"We are. Thanks for checking me out."

"Stop staring into flashlights."

"You put it that way, it sounds so stupid," I said.

"It *is* stupid, hon. Now go. I have actual sick patients."

I kissed her on the cheek and walked out of her office. Yes, I was a hypochondriac. But I was also a single mother, so my death did figure prominently into my daily musings. As a therapist, I knew that was a normal fear—leaving my daughter, the upheaval it would cause her. She'd have to live with her father back in Connecticut, and he had two other kids (and a wife). And what would happen to my grand-father, who'd taken me in when I was a knocked-up teen-ager? We still lived with him, and I didn't want him to be alone. I'd lost my own mom at a young age . . . Would Riley be as screwed up as I'd been?

Calista was right. I had to get over this. I knew I was healthy, but diagnosing myself with all sorts of horrible diseases was kind of a hobby. After all, the Internet was invented for a reason.

But I trusted Calista, who was brilliant *and* my friend. Feeling considerably cheered, I walked out onto Michigan Avenue, blinking in the spring sunshine. The Magnificent Mile glittered, washed clean by two days of bone-chilling rain earlier this week, but in typical midwestern fashion, we suddenly seemed to be in the middle of summer, even if it was only May.

No brain tumor. Hooray. Also, drinks with Calista,

which still sounded cool and adult, despite our being thirty-five. Unlike me, Calista was single with no kids and had her act completely together, whereas I still felt like I was faking the adult thing.

Except where Riley was concerned. I was a good mother, that I knew. Even if she was struggling a bit these days, I was on it. I was there. I stalked her social media accounts and read her texts (don't judge me . . . she was still a minor child, after all). Tonight was Nacho Night at our house, and even if Riley had been a little sullen these days, nachos would surely cheer her up.

The twisting skyline of the City of Big Shoulders glittered in the fresh air. I loved being in Chicago proper. Today, before my brain tumor check, I'd seen a client in the shared office suite I leased with a group of therapists. I was still new to the profession and grateful to have access to the posh space. Most of the time, I worked from home, doing online counseling for people who didn't want to be seen walking into a therapist's office. TheraTalk, the secure Skype-like software that let me see patients online, was less than ideal, but that was okay. I found I counseled the really troubled people better with a little distance.

Pain was always hard to see up close. If I teared up online, or wanted to smack a client, it was easier to hide.

But the office made me feel like a proper therapist, and my client today, Blaine, was an easy case. She had adjustment disorder, which was the general diagnosis that allowed me to get paid by her insurance. Blaine had never *adjusted* to her in-laws and liked venting about them. I'd suggest ways to answer that didn't involve curse words or the throwing of wine bottles, which was Blaine's fantasy, and she'd nod and agree and come back next month with a new story. Easy-peasy and actually kind of fun to hear the tales. Her real issue was feeling confident enough to contradict her mother-in-law and not backing down, but we were getting there.

Maybe I'd swing by the Ghirardelli shop and get some ice cream. Then again, we had ice cream at home, if Pop hadn't eaten it all, and I couldn't justify spending six bucks on a cone.

I walked past an empty storefront, then jerked to a halt. Turned around and looked. My hands and feet tingled before my brain caught up.

Yep. That was a harbinger of doom, all right.

To the untrained eye, it looked like a pink leather handbag, adorably retro but with a sassy blue tassel sexing it up a bit. Nevertheless, I knew what it was. A pink purse of doom.

Shit, shit, shit.

For a second, I forgot where I was, transported instantly to my childhood, when I always felt like an outcast, like a stupid, unwanted kid, like I'd done something wrong just by breathing.

GENEVIEVE LONDON DESIGNS, *Coming Soon*

ACCESSORIES, FASHION & HOME GOODS
FOR THE DISCERNING CONSUMER

My reflection in the glass showed me for what I was—not a discerning consumer, not a fashionable woman, just an ordinary-looking person with her dark blond hair pinned up in a graceless bun, wearing dark pants and a dark shirt, both polyester. This morning, I thought I looked nice. Crisp. Professional.

Right now, I looked droopy, hot and . . . scared.

This was not how Genevieve would've crafted me.

For years, I'd done a bang-up job of forgetting that

Genevieve London was my grandmother and had raised me from the age of eight to eighteen. It was easy, considering we hadn't spoken for seventeen years.

Riley would see this, of course. She knew her great-grandmother was *that* Genevieve London, though they'd never met. Some of her friends had Genevieve London purses and shoes. The arrival of one of her shops in Chicago would not be good news. Riley, being sixteen, was bound to have strong feelings about this one way or another. Bad feelings, probably, given the black rain cloud she'd been living under for the past few months.

Coming soon.

At least I'd had this warning. God! Imagine walking past this store's grand opening and seeing the Gorgon after all these years. I could use the drive home today to figure out what to say to Riley and how to head off any expectations she might have . . . like the idea that Genevieve might want to see us.

Riley's friends hung out on Michigan Avenue all the time, now that they were sixteen, and someone was bound to see the store and tell her . . . and Riley was sure to tell them she was Genevieve's great-granddaughter. Would her friends even believe her? Genevieve London was an international brand. Riley and Pop and I . . . we were just regular folks.

I hurried up, walking briskly to my car, sweat streaming down my back. I'd dressed up today to look the part, but I regretted it now. My left heel was rubbing in the unfamiliar pump.

All these years without a Genevieve London boutique in Chicago. Sure, Genevieve's stuff was in all the high-end department stores, but a dedicated store . . . ugh. I'd been naive enough to imagine she'd stayed out of Chicago because she knew we were here. But no. Her empire was expanding still.

I didn't want to assume this would bother Riley . . . and I didn't want to assume that it wouldn't. I didn't want her to think I was upset. I didn't want her to feel rejected, and I didn't want her to get her hopes up, and I didn't want her to sublimate any of those feelings if she had them, and I didn't want her to feel she couldn't tell me about them if she had them, and I didn't want her to feel that she *had* to tell me about them if she didn't want to.

Being a single mother *and* a therapist was very complicated.

A few years ago, I'd told Riley the facts: Genevieve London of the adorable purses was my grandmother, and I'd lived with her for ten years after my mother died because my father couldn't take care of me. I explained that Genevieve wasn't the nicest person, so we didn't talk anymore. Since my father never came to visit, it was easy not to say anything more about the London side of the family.

I only told Riley because my grandfather (on my mother's side, clearly) had recommended it, and Pop was seldom wrong. Can't hide the truth forever, he said. I'd answered that I didn't want to hide it as much as ignore it, which he said was the same thing.

To the best of my knowledge, Riley didn't tell her friends about her link to Genevieve; the girls never mentioned it or asked me questions when they came over, the same three girls Riley had been friends with for ages.

But sixteen was the age when you tried to impress your friends, after all, and how many girls had great-grandmothers who designed handbags owned by Adele, the First Lady and Oprah, or had a two-page ad spread in the spring edition of *Vogue*? I pictured Riley and her friends going into the store, a snooty manager giving my precious daughter a cool once-over before cutting her down with a razor-sharp comment. Because if I knew my grandmother, she'd have instructed her manager to do just that. She would've written it herself and told her staff to practice it. "Ms. London doesn't *have* a great-granddaughter," the manager might say. "Is there something I can show you?"

My grandmother had eviscerated me; I didn't want her near my child.

Traffic on 290 West made the trip home longer, and the midwestern heat pulsed down through the windshield, daring my Honda's AC to keep up. By the time I pulled up to Pop's humble house in Downers Grove, my skin felt hot and tight, and the rearview mirror showed my blond hair flattened by heat, a clenched jaw, red cheeks, and worry making my brown eyes look too wide. Overall, a little on the crazy side.

I took a deep breath. "Hi, honey," I said, practicing. Smiled. "Hey, baby. No, not 'baby.' Hey, sweetheart, how are you? Did you have a good day?"

My grandfather wasn't home; though he'd retired last year from his job as an elevator mechanic, he still did electrical work on the side. My other grandmother—the nice one—had died when I was seventeen, just a year and change before I came out to live with Pop.

Riley's shoes, the kelly-green Converse high-tops, were in the middle of the living room, and there was a glass next to the sink that hadn't been there this morning when I left for the city. "Hi, honey!" I called. "I'm home!"

No answer. I listened and heard nothing but quiet.

I went upstairs, trying hard not to run, wondering if I *should* run, and if I had run that day so long ago, if everything would have been different.

I knocked once, harder than I meant to, and threw open Riley's door.

My daughter lay on her bed, earbuds in, looking at her laptop, and the relief made my knees wobble. You never realize it until you're pregnant, or holding your baby in your arms, but your heart, soul and peace of mind will never be yours again. The tiny hijackers take over before they draw their first breaths, and you would do anything to keep them safe. Anything.

"What?" she said, taking out one earbud.

"Hi! How was your day?" My voice was too loud, too bright.

"Fine." Her tone indicated otherwise.

It was okay. She was here, and she was safe and alive, even if it was one of *those* days, then. The dark days. Normal teenage behavior, hormones, etc. She was due to get her period in about three days (yes, I kept track), so it was probably just that.

She was so beautiful, my girl—blazing red hair down to her shoulders, thick and curly, milk-white skin with freckles, and her eyes. Her blue, blue eyes, clear as a September sky.

Telling her about the Genevieve London store right now didn't seem like a good idea (or I was a coward, or both). I sat on the edge of Riley's bed and put my hand on her shin, unable to resist touching her. "How was lunch today?" I asked.

"Gross." She flicked her gaze at me, then resumed watching whatever was on her screen. "Hamburgers, not French toast sticks like they said. The meat was gray."

"That *is* gross. How about if I make French toast for supper?"

"You don't have to."

"Do you want me to?"

She shrugged.

"Are you going to Mikayla's tonight?"

Another shrug. That wasn't good.

"Okay. Well, French toast for supper, extra syrup for my

girl." I kissed her head, and she gave me a half smile, and I felt the painful rush of love I always did for my only child. *Thank you. Thank you for that smile, for still talking to me, for being my favorite person, my greatest love.*

Feeling fairly stupid, completely reactionary and tentatively happy, I went back downstairs.

My daughter was safe. She almost smiled. She wanted my French toast. I thought she was okay.

This uncertainty was new for me. Until this past year, Riley had been a sweet, happy person. As a tot, she'd played for hours in cardboard boxes, or pretended to be a waitress or a hairdresser. It wasn't so long ago she'd still been playing with Josefina, her American Girl doll. She loved books and babysitting. While the statistics said most of her peers were having sex and trying out drugs and alcohol, Riley still read the warrior cats series and slept with Blue Bunny, her first stuffed animal. I was grateful . . . no tweeny fuming, not for my girl. Jason, her father, had been a happy teenager. Me, not so much, but I liked to think my daughter's sunniness was at least in part due to my good parenting.

Physically, she'd been a late bloomer—athletic like her dad, thin, getting her period just before she turned fifteen, only recently needing a bra. At first, it had been okay; a little weepiness every twenty-nine days, cured by a girls' night with just the two of us watching obscure shows on the National Geographic channel, eating brie and apricot jam on crackers.

When I myself was sixteen, I'd been so aware of my odd status in Stoningham—the ward of an important, wealthy woman but abandoned by my parents, desperate to be normal, whatever that was. Riley had always seemed better, more confident, happier than I'd ever been, thank God. She'd been content to avoid romantic drama, had the same friends since she was eight, wanted to put off learning to drive till she was older. Her social life, such as it was, consisted of sleepovers with her longtime friends. She was a happy, happy kid.

And then came winter, and everything seemed to change.

The brie and shows about life in Alaska weren't enough. The long-suppressed terror buried deep in my gut showed its teeth, even as I used every tool and resource I had to convince myself over and over that Riley was . . . well . . . normal. *Not* clinically depressed. That the gods of genetics had *not* cursed her with the same thing that had haunted my mother.

Somehow, the things that had always seemed so good and wholesome took on a darker cast after this past winter. Why *didn't* she want to go to a dance? All her friends were going, weren't they? Was she clinging to her childhood in an unhealthy way, and if so, why? Was she afraid of growing up? Had something happened to her . . . rape, or bullying, or drugs? Was I missing something? Was it boy troubles? Girl troubles? Both? Was she gender fluid, or gay, or trans? None of those would change my love for her, but maybe she wanted to tell me. Should I just ask? Or would that be intrusive?

I analyzed her moods, trying to slip her some therapist questions without making her suspicious. Her pediatrician had pronounced her "completely normal with a side of awesome" at her annual physical, but still. When you know depression can be genetic, and when your own mother committed suicide, you watch like a hawk.

Genevieve London's overpriced, elitist store might throw my daughter in any number of unpredictable ways. And after seventeen years of feeling free from my grandmother, seeing the new store was just too much Genevieve London for one day.

A tremor of danger hummed in my gut, warning me there was more to come.

I ate one of the oatmeal cookies I'd baked the day before. I had an online appointment—this client liked messaging rather than videoconference, and that was fine with me. His problems were chunky—PTSD from a wretched childhood—and it was easier to be wise if I had time to think.

Then the landline blared, and I jumped, because who ever used landlines? The harsh ring of Pop's 1970s phone was horribly loud, and I snatched it up immediately. Probably a telemarketer. Since it was a phone from the days of yore, we had no caller ID or even an answering machine.

"Hello?"

There was a pause, and just as I was about to hang up, someone spoke.

"Is that you, Emma?"

Her voice punched me in the stomach, the unmistakable, blue-blooded tone of the Gorgon Genevieve herself, immediately recognizable even after seventeen years.

I hung up.

Almost immediately, the phone rang again. I let it, and the sound brayed through the quiet house. Two times. Three. Four.

"Mom? You gonna answer that?" Riley called from upstairs.

"Sure thing, honey!" I said, snatching it up again.

"Don't be childish, Emma," Genevieve said. That voice, so elegant and frosty, always with that tinge of disappointment.

The store. She was probably calling to tell me about the store. "What do you want?"

"I see we've lost all social graces," she said.

"Why would I waste them on you?"

She sighed. "Very well, I'll get right to it. I have cancer.

I'm dying, so you have to come home and do your familial duty. Bring your child."

My mouth opened and closed noiselessly. A) Cancer wouldn't kill her, because she was just too mean. B) I wouldn't go "home" if I had a gun to the back of my head. And C) she'd kicked me out seventeen years ago. Her final words hadn't exactly been a blessing.

"Funny," I said, "you talking now about family and duty. Oh, gosh, look at the time. I have to run. Have a nice death!"

"Don't hang up, Emma, for heaven's sake. It's so like you to fly into hysterics."

I clenched my teeth. "I'm not hysterical, and I'm not coming home. I *am* home, as a matter of fact."

"Fine. Come back to Connecticut, Emma, and say good-bye to me as I live out the last of my days."

"You haven't called me since I left, Genevieve. Why would I care about the last of your days?"

There was a pause. "We've had our differences, it's true."

"You kicked me out when I needed you most. Why should I care if you need me now?"

The frost of her voice turned to sleet. "You were irresponsible."

"And pregnant, and eighteen."

"As I said, irresponsible. At any rate, it's just for a couple of months."

I snorted.

"Must you make that unladylike noise?"

"Genevieve, I'm sorry. I don't care enough about you to uproot my child—it's a girl, by the way—so I can change your diapers in your dotage."

"Nor am I asking you to, Emma. I'm simply asking you to come home so I can see my granddaughter and great-granddaughter before I die."

"You blew your chance on us a long time ago. Besides,

don't you have a son? Ask him." Not that my father had ever taken care of *anyone* very well.

"This is not work for a man," Genevieve said.

"It's not work for me, either."

"Emma, it's not my fault that you were a floozy who couldn't keep her legs crossed and threw away her future."

"Sweet talk will get you nowhere, Gigi," I said, using the only nickname she'd allowed back then. God forbid I'd just called her *Gram*. "Besides, do you really want a floozy taking care of you?"

"I'll pay for your travel expenses and give you some money in the meantime."

"No, thanks. Hanging up now."

"Jason is separated from his wife, you know. Oh, but I forgot, you and he are still so close. Of course he's already told you."

My stomach dropped. The Gorgon had me there. Jason had *not* told me. And given that he was the father of my child, my one experience with being in love and my closest male friend, that stung.

Then again, Genevieve was the master of stinging. She was a wasp in every sense of the word.

I curled the cord around my finger. "The answer is still no. Please don't call again."

"Very well," she said. "Would you accept a bribe? Come home, and I'll make your child my heir." There was a pause. "My only heir. Even if she doesn't have a real name."

Riley was my grandfather's last name, my mother's maiden name. Another sting from the queen of wasps. "What about Hope?" I asked. "You're cutting her out of the will?" Hope was my much younger half sister, the child of my father's brief second marriage, and she lived not too far from Genevieve at a home for children whose medical needs were too complex for their families to handle alone.

"Hope has a trust fund for her care that will last all her life."

"Good. Make me her guardian. Otherwise, we have nothing to talk about. Bye, Genevieve," I said.

"Think about it. We'll speak soon."

"No, we won't." But she had already hung up.

I went to the kitchen table and sat down, my mind both racing and empty at the same moment.

Genevieve was dying. I waited for some emotion—rage, satisfaction, grief—to hit me. Nothing did. My stomach growled, so I ate another cookie.

Once, I had loved my grandmother and wanted desperately for her to love me. That hadn't happened. Try getting someone to love you for ten years and failing . . . It leaves a mark.

So she was dying. I told myself I didn't care. What about Hope? Would my sister care? Would she miss Genevieve, who, from what the staff at her facility told me, visited at least several times a month? It was hard to tell; my sister was nonverbal. She was a sweet girl, full of smiles and snuggles when her seizures weren't stealing away her days, or her rages weren't taking over. She had a severe case of tuberous sclerosis, and every complication that went with it.

At least Genevieve had done right by my sister.

An image of my grandmother and her housekeeper/ companion Donelle on the terrace in the summer flashed through my head. Cocktail hour observed religiously, their laughter, the breeze coming off Long Island Sound. My room, painted the faintest blush pink, my giant bed and fluffy white comforter, the tasteful throw pillows, the window seat that overlooked the wide expanse of grass, the rock walls that bordered the yard, the giant maple tree. The bathtub I could fill so deep I could float in it.

I also remembered how I wasn't allowed to have posters in my room, or funny signs, or the tie-dyed pillow I made with Beth, my best friend in high school, or the goldfish I won at the Ledyard Fair. I wasn't allowed anything Genevieve deemed "tacky." I wasn't allowed a bulletin board on which to pin mementos or souvenirs. I had to make my bed and replace the pillows exactly as Genevieve wanted, and the second I took off my shoes, they had to go into the closet. It wasn't a prison by any means, but it wasn't really my room, either . . . it was a catalog page from Genevieve London Home Designs, and my personality was not welcome.

I remembered Genevieve's rage when I told her I was pregnant. How she'd told me to abort my baby or give her up for adoption. Five minutes ago, she'd offered to leave that same child millions.

Like that could undo everything. I'd made a life with my baby, got through college an inch at a time, working nights at a grocery store, leaving Riley with Pop, fighting to stay awake in class.

Money wouldn't undo the past.

And yet . . . Riley was almost done with her junior year, since she'd started kindergarten a year early, being a smarty-pants. We'd already looked at some colleges online and visited the University of Chicago in April. I didn't have a lot saved for her college, but I had some. A little bit of every single paycheck had gone into a savings account since before she was even born . . . but when I say *little*, I mean it. A drop in the bucket. I was hoping Jason would help—counting on it, really—though, legally, he wasn't obliged to pay anything. He had another family back east, and while he'd never missed a child support payment, he'd never given any extra, either. He worked in construction; his wife did tech part-time.

Genevieve, however, was frickin' loaded. Her company

was traded on the New York Stock Exchange. Sheerwater, her house in Stoningham, Connecticut, had to be worth at least $15 million alone.

It didn't matter. Riley would be fine; I'd take out more loans even though my own were still choking me and would be for a long time; she'd take out loans, too. Maybe she'd get one of those full scholarships at the Ivy League colleges for incredibly bright kids. Maybe do a couple of years at a community college. Maybe Jason would take care of everything.

I wasn't going to sell my soul, not even for my daughter. It wasn't worth it. We couldn't go. We *shouldn't* go.

We weren't going to go.

CHAPTER 2

Genevieve

Here are some facts about getting older.

You hate young people because their manners, clothes and speech, as well as their taste in books, music, film and television, are all inferior.

You leak when you laugh, cough, hiccup, sneeze.

Putting on a bra becomes nearly impossible. Your arms don't bend that way anymore. Nylons are even worse, because you can lose your balance and fall.

You go through a second puberty, sprouting hair from your ears and nose while your eyebrows and lashes thin and your upper lip grows hairs as thick and sharp as wire.

You wait all day to have a drink.

You nap when you don't want to and can't sleep when you do.

You have regrets. Once you dismissed them as a waste of time, but as you get older, they creep back.

....

I was always an attractive woman. A great beauty, to tell the truth. Grace Kelly and I could've been sisters, people used to say. It was true. My parents had been quite attractive . . . I always thought like marries like in most cases. Of course, you see the aberrant couple—Beyoncé and her rather homely husband (yes, of course I know who Beyoncé is, I do live on this planet). But more or less, beautiful people marry beautiful people. And if one is extremely wealthy but also homely or plain . . . Prince William, for example . . . one can marry a great beauty like Kate Middleton and create attractive children.

I was beautiful *and* wealthy *and* went to a fine school. I took care with my appearance and wardrobe, watched how I spoke and was well aware that I projected an image. Garrison said he knew the first moment he saw me that I would be his wife, and that was exactly what I'd hoped for—that the best-looking young man from the best family with the best prospects and, of course, the best heart would see me and know in an instant I was the one.

I didn't let him down.

After he died, I most certainly did not fall apart and start leaving the house in a bathrobe or letting my hair get long and stringy. Did Jacqueline Kennedy? Did Coretta Scott King? Joan Didion? I think not.

Not only did I keep up appearances, I exceeded them. I became a style icon and an industry leader. Well into my forties, heads still turned when I walked down Madison Avenue. I was sleek, chic, tall and slender, and I wore three-inch heels every day. Though I didn't date publicly, I eventually had a few gentlemen friends . . . lovers, if you must know. My financial adviser. An art appraiser from Christie's. I would never marry again, nor did I want to, but I enjoyed the occasional dinner in the city, a night in a suite at the Mandarin Oriental or the Baccarat (never the Plaza . . . their rooms were so tacky).

And then, abruptly, I became invisible.

That was the first inkling I had that I was aging out.

Ready to find
your next great read?

Let us help.

Visit prh.com/nextread

Penguin
Random
House